What people are saying about ...

REBEL

"There's nothing more romantic and enchanting than a novel set in sixth-century Scotland and penned by author Linda Windsor. Kella and Alyn's tale in *Rebel* is no exception. Loaded with romance, adventure, treachery, and the mystical, this was my kind of read!"

Elizabeth Goddard, award-winning
author of *Oregon Outback*

"Linda Windsor delights me every time I read one of her books, whether it be romantic contemporary or impeccably correct historical. In *Rebel*, Linda takes the reader to sixth-century Scotland, a place filled with intrigue, peril, and romance. I came away in awe of a master storyteller and inspired by the integrity, nobility, and courage displayed by the characters. Don't miss this third and final book of the Brides of Alba series."

Donita K. Paul, best-selling author
of The DragonKeeper Chronicles
and The Chiril Chronicles

"In a land filled with superstition and pagan beliefs, one man risks all to take a courageous stand for the one true God. A story of faith, truth, and unconditional love, *Rebel* will leave you cheering. This is Linda Windsor at her best."

Vickie McDonough, award-winning author
of the Texas Boardinghouse Brides series
and coauthor of The Texas Trails series

"*Rebel* is another wonderful story wonderfully told. I love the strength of the characters and the wonderful feel of the period. I'm sorry to see this series end."

DeAnna Julie Dodson, author of *In Honor Bound*

"Linda Windsor has crafted another beautifully moving tale, painting it with unforgettable characters, breathtaking landscapes, inspiring faith, and enduring love. *Rebel* is an immensely satisfying conclusion to the Brides of Alba series."

Tamara Leigh, author of *Restless
in Carolina* and *Dreamspell*

REBEL

OTHER BOOKS
BY LINDA WINDSOR

HISTORICAL FICTION
Fires of Gleannmara Trilogy
Maire

Riona

Deirdre

The Brides of Alba Trilogy
Healer

Thief

Rebel

CONTEMPORARY ROMANCE
Piper Cove Chronicles
Wedding Bell Blues

For Pete's Sake

Moonstruck Series
Paper Moon

Fiesta Moon

Blue Moon

Along Came Jones

It Had to Be You

Not Exactly Eden

Hi Honey, I'm Home

NOVELLAS
Brides of the Emerald Isle

(with Vickie McDonough, Pamela Griffin,

and Tamela Hancock Murray)

Unlikely Angels

(with Annie Jones, Diane Noble, and Barbara Hicks)

THE BRIDES OF ALBA

REBEL

LINDA WINDSOR

David C Cook®
transforming lives together

REBEL
Published by David C Cook
4050 Lee Vance View
Colorado Springs, CO 80918 U.S.A.

David C Cook Distribution Canada
55 Woodslee Avenue, Paris, Ontario, Canada N3L 3E5

David C Cook U.K., Kingsway Communications
Eastbourne, East Sussex BN23 6NT, England

David C Cook and the graphic circle C logo
are registered trademarks of Cook Communications Ministries.

The website addresses recommended throughout this book are offered as a
resource to you. These websites are not intended in any way to be or imply an
endorsement on the part of David C Cook, nor do we vouch for their content.

This story is a work of fiction. All characters and events are the product of the author's
imagination. Any resemblance to any person, living or dead, is coincidental.

Scripture quotations are taken from the King James
Version of the Bible. (Public Domain.)

LCCN 2012935340
ISBN 978-1-4347-6476-8
eISBN 978-0-7814-0868-4

© 2012 Linda Windsor
Published in association with the literary agency of Alive Communications,
Inc., 7680 Goddard St., Suite 200, Colorado Springs, CO 80920

The Team: Don Pape, Ramona Tucker, Amy Konyndyk, Caitlyn York, Karen Athen
Cover Design: DogEared Design, Kirk DouPonce

Printed in the United States of America
First Edition 2012

1 2 3 4 5 6 7 8 9 10 11 12

032912

To my mom and children,
for their continued support and sacrifices to allow
me time to research and write this novel.

My son Jeff's by-the-Good-Book faith helped keep me grounded,
while my daughter, Kelly, challenged me to find ways to *fish* for men
who discount Scripture from the other side of the boat.

To David C Cook,
for all their efforts to make this project the best it can be.

And finally, to my heavenly Father,
the Great Creator who continues to show me how to fish in places
I never would have looked. Thank You, Jesus, for Your love and grace.

Dear Reader,

A magazine article explaining what happened to the Davidic line after the nation of Israel scattered (1 and 2 Kings) started me on a research journey that resulted in this Brides of Alba series. Throughout the series, we learn of the Grail Church, formed specifically to preserve not just the Grail treasures, but two blessed bloodlines—the Davidic bloodline, preserved by the sixth-century BC marriage of Zedekiah's daughter to the Milesian High King of Ireland, and the apostolic bloodline established in first-century Britain by Joseph of Arimathea and Jesus's close circle of family and friends. Tradition holds that the lines exist through Britain's modern royals. At the most, it's plausible, given the numerous sources (some are listed in the Bibliography), and at the least, 'tis great fuel for fiction. I leave the rest to the reader to discern. (For more information on the Grail Church and the sacred bloodlines in Albion's history, see *Arthurian Characters* on p. 361 and *The Grail Palace* on p. 365).

 In *Healer*, Book One, I introduced the O'Byrne brothers— Ronan, Caden, and Alyn. Their clan's twenty-year feud, a result of the Grail Church's arranged matches gone awry, is ended when a wounded, bitter heart and a lonely, forgiving one come together to heal the breach, proving all things are possible with God's healing love.

In the second book, *Thief*, I found a delightful old Scottish proverb that became the middle brother Caden's theme: "*Love of our neighbor is the only door out of the dungeon of self.*" After being the villain in Book One, Caden needed a door out of his prison of exile and shame. But don't we all have a prison of some kind? Mine is occasional dips in chemical depression. Sometimes I have to force myself out of my "cell" when I don't feel like it. The reward is relief from my own troubles and the joy of helping someone else. In *Thief*, escaping his prison sets Caden free to live and love again. Even if his heart—and purse—are stolen by his match in mischief and in love.

Now in Book Three, *Rebel*, Alyn O'Byrne doubts his calling into the priesthood after an alchemical accident in the East leaves the scholar riddled with guilt. He returns home, wounded and running from his destiny—and lands in the midst of court intrigue, church politics, and a marriage to a woman carrying another man's child. While Lady Kella gets a hard-earned lesson in the difference between love stolen in shame and the wonder and forgiveness of God's unconditional love, Alyn becomes an example of how God does not call the able but enables His called. So, like us, both are flawed, both have doubts, but a flicker of faith is enough for God to use them for His glory and good.

Behind their stories is a setting filled with little-known traditions of Britain's early history and church that shed light on the Arthurian legends buried in the mists of time. This setting is the late sixth-century Scotland of Arthur, prince of Dalraida, the only historically documented Arthur.

Most scholarly sources point to Arthur, Merlin, and even Guinevere/Gwenhyfar as titles, so it's easy to see why the Age of Arthur lasted over one hundred years. The Dark Ages become even darker when you consider that there was no standard for dating and even the records that exist are written in at least four different languages. Neither names, dates, place names, nor translations are completely reliable. So I quote eighth-century historian Nennius: "I have made a heap of all I could find."

I read and reread Scripture as I worked on this project and endeavored to show how nature magic or early science, medicine, and astrology were studied and practiced by Christian priests, druids, and nonbelieving druids. It is their fruit—good or evil—and to whom they gave the glory for their knowledge and success that separates the wheat from the chaff. Imagine the fine line a priest and scholar such as Alyn walked. It's no wonder he found himself in doubt at times.

> *Beloved, believe not every spirit, but try the spirits whether they are of God: because many false prophets are gone out into the world.*
>
> *Hereby know ye the Spirit of God: Every spirit that confesseth that Jesus Christ is come in the flesh is of God:*
>
> *And every spirit that confesseth not that Jesus Christ is come in the flesh is not of God: and this is that spirit of antichrist, whereof ye have heard that it should come; and even now already is it in the world.*
> *(1 John 4:1–3)*

Bear in mind that *druid* in that time was a word for any professional—doctors, judges, poets, teachers, and protoscientists, as well as priests. *Druid* meant "teacher, rabbi, magi, or master," not the dark, hooded stereotype assumed by many today. Alyn, though an ordained Christian priest, also qualified as a druid in this context. He saw beyond the parables, which he cherished and taught as a priest.

> *And he said, Unto you it is given to know the mysteries*
> *of the kingdom of God: but to others in parables; that*
> *seeing they might not see, and hearing they might not*
> *understand. (Luke 8:10)*

> *I am the vine, ye are the branches: He that abideth in*
> *me, and I in him, the same bringeth forth much fruit:*
> *for without me ye can do nothing. (John 15:5)*

In Matthew 10, verses 1–5, Christ equips the disciples with power over disease and demons. *But* He goes on to tell them not to use these gifts to amass fortune and recognition for themselves. They are instructed to go in poverty and depend on the generosity of those they help for their basic needs. Instead of glory and praise, they are to expect hostility sometimes.

This series endeavors to show the Christian perspective of the mysteries of God—the science that was often considered by the uneducated as magic and its use for good and glorifying God, versus its use for self-edification and glorifying the unbelieving druidic scholars. It demonstrates that the more man understands of creation, the more reverence he should have for the Creator. Woven through all of the above is the emphasis on worshipping the Creator, not the creation.

And since the church is made up of humans with all their flaws, the story begs the reader not to throw out the sinless Christ with the dirty church water. I once had done that myself as a college student, after seeing hypocrisy in the church and learning of the church's many dastardly historical deeds. Praise God, I came full circle.

My hope is to demonstrate the differences between Christianity, or Creator worship, and New Age thinking, which is really the Dark Age creation worship revisited. The reader will learn how much we have in common with nonbelievers and where we differ, so that we might build on our commonality a bridge to Jesus Christ. Maybe it will keep another from leaving the faith of their childhood or enable the reader to witness more effectively for Christ to those obsessed with man's knowledge and creation.

I mentioned in my last book how my daughter had been stalked and assaulted in college, blamed God and turned against Him, and became involved in Wicca, or white witchcraft. It was through research of the Dark Ages that I learned, by God's grace, to witness to her effectively when she would not hear anything from the Word. I continue to include this type of faith-affirming information in *Rebel*.

Everyone knows the story of how the disciples fished all night to no avail. Then Jesus told them to try the other side of the vessel. They did and netted a boatload. My child would not listen to Scripture, but Celtophile that she was and is, she was all ears about the history and oral traditions of that era and culture, which evolved into many of today's New Age beliefs. These historical and oral traditions underscored or clarified what Scripture revealed and separated the sheep from the goats.

The results of my *fishing* for my daughter were not as instant as the results the disciples saw. Our journey took many years before my daughter was ready to jump into the boat. But the net had been cast and repeatedly *mended* each time I found something new to share—some common ground to draw her to Christ. Both mother and daughter have emerged stronger from that storm—stronger in faith, friendship, and love. We still love the Celtic music, history, and lore of our heritage but know now what a vital part God played in it. I share this story because maybe someone out there needs to know how to approach a beloved nonbeliever who will not hear Scripture or traditional witness but must be reached from the other side of the boat.

This is my calling. To reach out and enable others to reach out effectively to those who are swimming on the other side of the boat from the written Word—using a net that will bring them to Christ, the Living Word.

Linda Windsor

CHARACTER LIST

Indicates a historical character/place

** These Arthurian characters have been so mythicized that some scholars would say they never existed, while others would place them in different time periods. The references used in Rebel put them in the late sixth century and list them as historical. Arthur of Dalraida is known to have existed as evidenced in historical records of the time.*

*GODODDIN

Angus—a name and a title of Queen Gwenhyfar's protector king of Strighlagh (Stirling); capital of Gododdin

*Arthur—High King or warrior leader of the Cymri kings (brotherhood of the Welsh and Britons); historic prince of Dalraida; no kingdom of his own except Gododdin through marriage to its queen, Gwenhyfar

**Elyan—prince of Gododdin; Gwenhyfar's brother

**Gwenhyfar—queen of Gododdin; Arthur's second or third wife; high priestess of the Grail Church; a Pictish princess born in Meikle

O'BYRNE Clan of Glenarden
(colors are red, black, and silver/gray)

Aeda—Tarlach's late royal Pictish wife; mother to Ronan, Caden, and Alyn

Alyn—Tarlach and Aeda's third son

Brenna—Ronan's wife; lady of Glenarden; a gifted healer; formerly of the Gowrys subclan

Caden—see *Trebold*

Conall—Brenna and Ronan's son; older brother to Joanna

Daniel of Gowrys—prince of Gowrys; friend of Alyn; cousin of Brenna

Egan O'Toole—Glenarden's champion

Ervan—son of Vychan and Glenarden's new steward

Fatin—an African monkey; gift to Alyn from Prince Hassan at the Baghdad School of Wisdom

Joanna—Ronan and Brenna's daughter; named after Brenna's late mother

Kella O'Toole—daughter of Egan O'Toole and the late Wynn of Erin; foster sister to Ronan, Caden, and Alyn; scribe to Queen Gwenhyfar

Rhianon—Caden's deceased wife from Gwynedd of North

Wales; daughter of Idwal and Enda; mistress of Tunwulf in Din Guardi; practiced witchcraft

Ronan—Tarlach and Aeda's eldest son; the Glenarden king/chieftain

Tarlach—Alyn's late father and former clan chief/king also known as "the Glenarden"; of royal Irish descent (Davidic bloodline)

Teilo—Welsh bard; children's tutor at Glenarden

Vychan—Glenarden's late steward

Wynn of Erin—Kella's mother; died in childbirth

TREBOLD

Aelwyn—Sorcha and Caden's daughter; named after Sorcha's late adopted mother, tavern owner and singer/scop who was a former gleeman with her best friend, Gemma

Caden—Tarlach and Aeda of Glenarden's second son; brother to Alyn and Ronan

Eadric—Sorcha's cousin; a master bard

Ebyn—adopted son of Sorcha and Caden; rescued by Sorcha when his parents sold him

Gemma—female dwarf; like a second mother to Sorcha

Lachlan and Rory—Caden and Sorcha's twin sons

Sorcha—Caden's bardic wife; foster mother of Ebyn, and mother to Aelwyn and twin boys Rory and Lachlan; Myrna's daughter; Aelwyn's foster daughter

PERTH

Beathan—Fortingall's druidic adviser

*Bridei (Brude)—Overking of the whole Pictish nation

Brisen—healing woman

Drust—chief king of the southern Picts; cousin to Brude/Bridei (High King of all Picts)

Elkmar—Prince Lorne's captain

Garnait—a prince; chief of the Miathi of Dumyat

Goll—shoemaker in Crief

Heilyn—Fortingal's Christian queen

Idwyr—druid/wizard of the Miathi

Lorne of Errol—a prince of Perth; Kella's betrothed

Mairead—Grail high priestess of Mons Seion near Fortingall

*Miathi—rebellious border tribe with stronghold at Dumyat

KINGDOM OF LOTHIAN

*Aethelfrith—Modred's ambitious Saxon ally who overtook the Northumbrian throne after Hussa's death, exiling his cousin, the rightful prince, Hering

**Modred—king of Lothian; priest of the Celtic Church; Arthur's cousin; son of Morgause and the late Cennalath of the Orkneys

**Morgause—mother of Modred; aunt to Arthur; queen of the Orkneys; abbess of the Celtic Church

RHEGED

*Llywarch Hen—king of South Rheged

*Merlin Emrys—Arthur of Dalraida's late merlin adviser from Powys in Wales

**Morgein—wife to Urien of Rheged; sister to Arthur; daughter to Aedan of Dalraida

Ninian—Merlin Emrys's protégé; abbess of the Grail Church

*Taliesen—Rheged's historical bard; author of *The Book of Taliesen*

*Urien of Rheged—historical king of North Rheged; successor to Arthur as warrior-king leader of the kings of the north; immortalized in Aneirin's *Y Gododdin*

PRIESTS

Aunt Beda—abbess in Ireland; Kella's maternal aunt

Bishop Martin—former hermit priest of Glenarden who mentored the O'Byrne brothers and their brides and performed their marriage ceremonies

Cassian—archbishop of the Roman Church who returned as chief counselor to Arthur after the High King's pilgrimage to the Holy Land; Merlin Emrys's successor

BAGHDAD

Abdul-Alim ibn Shamoon—Alyn's late teacher (servant of the Omniscient of Simon)

Hassan ibn Yūsuf ibn Matar—Alyn's best friend in the East; a prince of the Ghassānid (foederati of Christian Arabs who protected Byzantium)

ADDITIONAL PLACES

Baghdad School of Wisdom—historic place of learning for scholars from the entire known world

Bardsley Island—burial place for great kings, druids, and saints

Dumyat—capital of the Miathi Picts in the Ochill Hills of Perth

Eboracorum—today's York

Fortingall—stronghold of the southern Picts

Glenarden—a lesser kingdom in the Pictish kingdom of Gododdin

Lockwoodie—village in Strathclyde

Mons Seion (Mount Zion)—mountain to the north of Fortingall; known as *Schiehallion*

Perth—Pictish kingdom north of Lothian and Gododdin

Trebold Law—Sorcha and Caden's home; a hillfort and inn on the Lader in Lothian

Note: See also Glossary on p. 355.

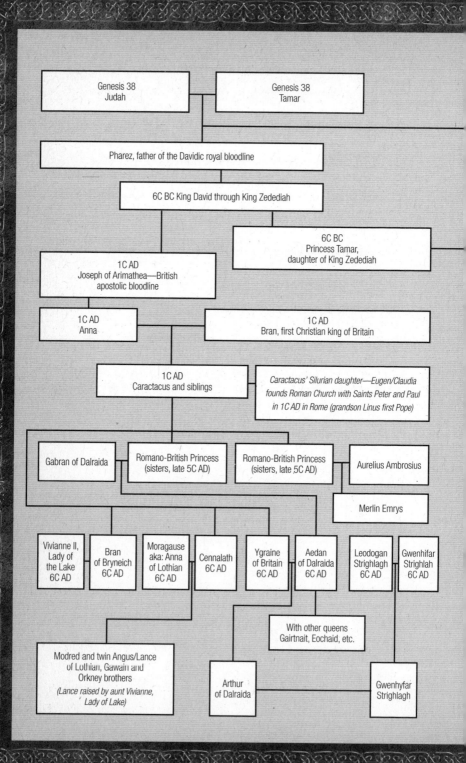

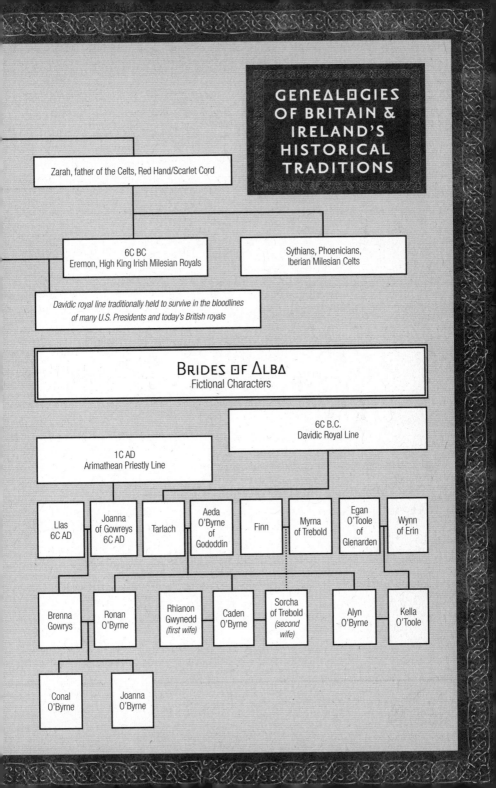

GENEΔⵔGIES OF BRITAIN & IRELAND'S HISTORICAL TRADITIONS

Zarah, father of the Celts, Red Hand/Scarlet Cord

6C BC
Eremon, High King Irish Milesian Royals

Sythians, Phoenicians,
Iberian Milesian Celts

*Davidic royal line traditionally held to survive in the bloodlines
of many U.S. Presidents and today's British royals*

BRIDES ⵔF ΔLBΔ
Fictional Characters

6C B.C.
Davidic Royal Line

1C AD
Arimathean Priestly Line

Llas
6C AD

Joanna
of Gowreys
6C AD

Tarlach

Aeda
O'Byrne
of
Gododdin

Finn

Myrna
of Trebold

Egan
O'Toole
of
Glenarden

Wynn
of Erin

Brenna
Gowrys

Ronan
O'Byrne

Rhianon
Gwynedd
(first wife)

Caden
O'Byrne

Sorcha
of Trebold
*(second
wife)*

Alyn
O'Byrne

Kella
O'Toole

Conal
O'Byrne

Joanna
O'Byrne

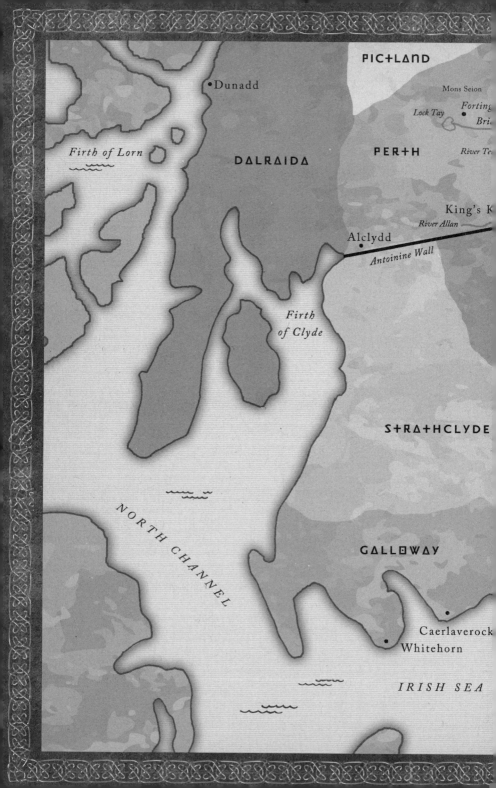

Scone
Forteviot
River Tay
FIFE
Firth of Forth
Glenarden
trighlagh
Battle of
CAMLAN
Ft. Cambioganna
River Carron
Falkirk
Fort Camlan
MANAU
Gododdin
Din Edyn
LOTHIAN
Traprain
Law
Trebold
Lader Water
River Tweed
Aberwick
NORTH SEA
Lindisfarne
Din Guardi
BRYNEICH
BERNICIA
GWENDOLEU
Hadrian's Wall
Carmelide
Solway
Firth
RHEGED
ELMET

LATE 6TH
CENTURY
ALBA

PROLOGUE

Carmelide

Late sixth century AD

Leafbud

Merlin was dead. The nightmare had begun for the Cymri—every Briton, Welshman, Scot, and Pict—be they Christian or still clinging to the old ways.

Kella O'Toole bent over her desk in the queen's scriptorium, well aware that her countrymen's freedom to worship a god of choice in his or her manner was at stake, not to mention that the threat of civil war loomed. This small room adjoining Gwenhyfar's personal quarters was the only place the official palace scribes and priests would not know what Kella was about.

Her heart beat with each scratch of her quill as she hurried to finish the last page of the copy of one of the most precious books in all Albion. She'd hoped to work with the original Hebrew scripts, those recorded by the hand of Joseph of Arimathea or one of Christ's apostolic family, to practice her translation of the language. But Merlin Emrys and Queen Gwenhyfar had hidden them away.

Kella's pen smoothly glided over the artificially aged vellum: *Arthur, Prince of Dalraida.* Only untold hours of practice as the queen's scribe and translator kept her hand from shaking. This copy had to be flawless. Kella had been working on it for the last year under Merlin Emrys's orders. She'd known he'd been ill, yet the news of his death that morning had still come as a shock. It didn't seem real that the man of so many faces—abbot, adviser to the king, teacher, astrologer, and man of science—had gone to the Other Side.

Only a week ago, he'd retired to his cave with none but his devoted abbess Ninian to take his final confession and give him his last rites. Now that Merlin Emrys's last breath had expired, Ninian prepared his body to be sealed in the farthest reach of his cave for a year. Once the flesh fell away, leaving clean bones, the Grail priestess would return to transport them to Bardsley Island to rest in one of its holy caves with the bones of Albion's greatest holy men and kings. Gwenhyfar would transport Arthur's similarly one day.

A wave of nausea swept through Kella's stomach. Her pen froze. *Please, Lord, no. Not now.* She put the quill down and relied more on a sip of now-cold tea laced with mint and elderberry than prayer for relief. God was so distant, she often wondered if He was real. Not that she'd ever mention her doubts aloud. She took another drink of the tea and flexed her stiff fingers.

In the opposite wall a peat fire in the hearth offset the damp chill of early Leafbud in the chamber. This was no time for illness, nor anything else to distract her from her duties. The heritage of Albion's faith rested on her being able to finish this before Archbishop Cassian took total control of the church and its documents. The Davidic lineage passed on through the Milesian Irish royal families was well documented and kept in Erin, but Kella's project protected the foundation of the British church laid by Jesus's family and followers. Tradition had it that they'd come to Britain in the first century after the Sadducees set them adrift on an unforgiving sea, in a boat with no supplies, oars, or sails. Yet God waived the death sentence so that Joseph of Arimathea, his niece Mary—the mother of Jesus—and their company made it to the safety of Iberia, Gaul, and on to the Northern Isles, from there to spread the gospel throughout the Western world.

And here Kella was, a humble warrior's daughter with no such holy or royal connection—at least not within the relevant last nine generations of her family—taking part in such a vital task. Kella would write for the queen until her fingers fell off.

Father, help me, Kella prayed, taking another swallow. *Even if I am unworthy, fallen in Your eyes, I'm trying to help Your cause.*

Nothing. Kella felt no relief from the threat of her stomach—only more frightened and alone than ever. Maybe she was the only one God didn't listen to.

Father, I know I have sinned and am unworthy, but I beg You, help me.

Kella started from her introspection as Queen Gwenhyfar, garbed in hunter-green robes with embroidered trim, entered the rooms. A band of beautifully worked gold crowned her long, braided raven hair. Her sleek, dark beauty was a contrast to Kella's untamable honey-kissed curls, pale complexion, and robust build. While it pleased Kella to hear her father say how like her fair-haired mother she'd become since she'd matured to womanhood, how she longed to be one of those light, willowy girls instead of small but well-rounded.

"I'm nearly done, milady. Only Arthur's late sons to add." She paused. "And King Modred."

Wryness twisted the skillfully painted heart-line of Gwenhyfar's lips. "Leave room for Urien of Rheged." At the surprised arch of Kella's brow, the queen added, "Cassian may yet have his way."

"Aye, milady." The Roman archbishop just might, but Kella didn't have to like it. The stern, richly robed priest had joined Arthur in Rome on the High King's return from a pilgrimage to the Holy Land. Nothing had been the same since. Cassian's presence dampened the gaiety of the court, as if it were a sin to enjoy life. As for Arthur—

"Rome has found a new way to conquer," Gwenhyfar told Kella. "Christ didn't come to dictate, but Cassian has."

Rumor was that he'd even convinced the High King to renounce his cousin Modred as his successor in favor of Urien of Rheged. Considering that Arthur's queen and the territory he fought most to protect were Pictish, choosing a Briton would not be a wise move.

"Be sure Modred's name is written in first," Gwenhyfar warned her. "We want Cassian, should he get his hands on this, to believe he has the original. 'Twould be as good as he would want to destroy any record of the British church having been established with equal authority to Rome's."

"Why is the king so blind to this man's purpose?" Kella asked. Nausea rolled over her again. She fought the urge to put her hand on her stomach, instead embracing the tea with both hands.

"Arthur has not been himself since returning from the Holy Land," the queen lamented. "He'd hoped to reconcile his grief over losing his sons. But his spells of melancholy, outbursts of rage are worse … though he's always had a fierce temper. A man with his responsibilities must be fierce or die." Gwenhyfar narrowed her gaze at Kella. "Are you not well?" She leaned over and wiped a smudge of ink from Kella's forehead. A hazard of a scribe's work.

Kella winced a smile. "Something I ate this morning does not agree with me. A piece of cold meat and bread on my way here."

"You must take better care of yourself. Take your meal at the board, not on your way to anywhere. No wonder your stomach protests."

The queen mustn't suspect. Kella herself didn't *want* to suspect the reason for her missed courses. Two, unless she commenced this week.

"I will tomorrow," she said. "Porridge, honey, and fresh cream."

The very thought of her favorite breakfast made Kella shudder inwardly. She breathed in relief as the queen walked over to the pages Kella had finished. They were all neatly rolled and stored in a wooden rack designed for that purpose, exactly where the originals had been. Gwenhyfar pulled one out, examining the yellowed vellum. "Emrys's genius will be sorely missed. I can't tell these from the originals."

"It bewilders this feeble mind how he made them look so old without destroying them," Kella marveled. She'd once been to the merlin's cave, which was hardly the average hole in the side of a hill. It had many chambers, and each one was a wonder.

One room was the shop of an alchemist; another an office lined with books and scrolls. Another's roof was a funnel that opened to the sky, with a great glass disc said to bring the stars and planets down to earth for Merlin's examination. Now his body lay in a far innermost chamber, his spirit already departed to be with his Savior.

"Never say your mind is feeble, Kella," the queen chided, drawing Kella back to the window alcove where her desk was situated to make the most of the sunlight. "Few men can boast the mastery of five languages and a fair hand to match. My cousin Aeda would be most proud of you."

At the mention of the foster mother who'd raised Kella after her own mother died in childbirth, Kella smiled weakly. "Aye, I hope she would."

Her foster brothers, Ronan, Caden, and Alyn, used to mercilessly tease Kella at Glenarden, where her father, Egan O'Toole, was champion. They'd called her "Babel-Lips," because she talked endlessly and could pick up on any language or accent she overheard. During Kella's schooling in Ireland, where her maternal aunt was an abbess, both her aunt and the queen had agreed that the ease with which Kella learned new languages was as much the result of a gift as it was of study.

"You carry a Pentecostal fire in that brain of yours," Aunt Beda would tell her when no one else was about to witness the abbess's pride and affection for Kella.

But if that was so, why couldn't Kella feel God's presence, especially now when she needed it so much? She shuddered to think of what Mam Aeda or Aunt Beda would think of her now. Her aunt had warned her time and again that a moment's folly could ruin a maiden's life forever. God would forgive the maid, but she and the child conceived would have to face the consequences.

"And I would have been lost without you," the queen continued, caught up in the church's concern, "especially since Cassian returned from Rome with Arthur."

The new archbishop had eyes everywhere—on the queen and Merlin Emrys in particular. He considered the Grail Church even more suspect than the Irish Celtic Church, about which he had little good to say. Gwenhyfar had ceased to use the royal scribes for her communication, which led Cassian to scowl at Kella whenever they met by chance in the palace. The only things he held more in contempt than the British church were women in the church or court, except as lowly servants or brood sows.

"What sway has the man over the king that you and Merlin Emrys do not?" Kella pressed.

Emrys had long been Arthur's adviser, although the last year or so he'd kept to his cave, where he studied the stars and his *sciencia*.

"Better to ask what the Roman Church offers Arthur that the Celtic Church does not." Gwenhyfar's slanted green eyes narrowed. At least they appeared slanted. Everything about the Pictish queen was exotic—from her accent to the perfumes she wore.

"I've never really understood the workings of the church," Kella admitted truthfully. Although she knew enough to be certain she would be condemned for her mistake—for allowing love to lead her down temptation's sweet path.

"Back when Prince Arthur was but a wet-eared youth with great contempt for our faith, Abbot Columba predicted that the prince would not survive to inherit his father Aedan's kingdom of Dalraida,"

Gwenhyfar explained. "And we all have heard of the accuracy of the abbot of Iona's prophecies."

Yes, Kella had heard of the curse. But now in his early forties, Arthur had changed, repented of his indifference to God.

"So now the king hopes to counter the earlier curse of Columba's church with the blessing of Rome in his later years." Kella frowned. "You were … *are* a priestess of the Grail Church, even if it has been removed from Albion." With the increasing advance of the Saxons, the Angus of Strighlagh's son—a saintly warrior if ever there was one—had returned the Grail treasures to the Holy Land two years prior. "Is that how God works? Allowing one arm of His church to vex the other?"

Or maybe God had left with the relics. He didn't seem to be answering Albion's prayers for victory over the Saxons. The enemy spread like a plague.

"Nay, child. That is how *mankind* works." The queen's green gaze glazed over. With her palm she covered the jeweled silver cross she wore, and she turned to peer out the slit of the window in the alcove. "How we must grieve the heavenly Father."

Kella joined the queen, guilt clawing at her chest as she stared at the misty spray of the gray-green sea hurling itself against the rocks below the tower. When she dared not look at the tumult any longer, Kella spun away to take another sip of the tea.

Surely she had grieved God as well. And if she *was* with child, the consequences remained to be seen. For her, and for her beloved Lorne, who, along with Kella's father, Egan, protected the borders of Strighlagh against an uprising of Miathi north of the Clyde.

My father! Kella groaned in silence. Egan O'Toole would take off her lover's head if he suspected. No matter that her handsome Lorne had pledged his troth to her that night as she lay in his arms. He'd sworn his life was meaningless without her.

Oh, Lorne, hurry home to me! For all our sakes.

CHAPTER ONE

Carmelide
Late sixth century AD

Leafbud

One could become lost in the crowds gathering to honor the passing of Merlin Emrys of Powys. But lost was a familiar feeling for Alyn O'Byrne, no matter where he was. He'd hoped that coming home to Alba from his six-year sojourn in the East might help him find the man he'd once been and the calling he'd once embraced so fervently. But Merlin Emrys had been a vital part of that hope, encouraging Alyn to pursue his education beyond Scripture to the *sciencia* of the East.

"Everything mankind needs to know is in the Word," the sage had told Alyn, "but not everything there to know is written. To discern the gifts of creation, the properties of the seen and the unseen all around us, is to grow closer to the Creator of it all."

Those words had fired Alyn's natural curiosity and his soul's longing to learn the workings of creation and to grow closer to God.

"But some knowledge is dangerous, Merlin," Alyn protested beneath his breath as he was swept along with the crowd from the Solway waterfront to Arthur's Stone Castle, where the memorial service was to take place. "It drives us away from God as sure as sampling Eden's forbidden fruit."

"*One cannot escape from God.*"

That was what Hassan ibn Yūsuf ibn Matar—a prince of the Ghassānid, the Christian Arabs sworn to protect Byzantium—had told Alyn when Alyn announced he was leaving the Baghdad School of Wisdom and the ministry after the fiery accident that had killed their teacher. It was Hassan who had pulled an unconscious Alyn from the burning workshop. Hassan who had stayed by his bedside while Alyn recovered from the terrible explosion. Only Hassan knew of the demons haunting Alyn's soul … the voices that had driven away God's peace and presence.

Hassan and Alyn had become fast friends during their first week at the school, when Alyn had saved the womanizer from the vengeance of the local sultan. For that, Hassan pledged his everlasting friendship and loyalty. Like the sleeping monkey—a parting gift from his friend—curled in a sling beneath Alyn's cloak, sometimes Hassan's friendship was a blessing and, at others, a misadventure waiting to happen.

After much jostling, herding, and persuasion, Alyn stood with his back to one of the elaborately carved columns inside Arthur's great hall with the honored guests. Smoke from a central hearth curled toward the vaulted ceiling. Snatches of conversation regarding the great Merlin Emrys circulated through the crowd. Such a man as Merlin was thought to be beyond death's claws. Had they not seen his magic?

Grimacing, Alyn gazed at the colorful tapestries adorning the walls. Merlin was no more a magician than Alyn was. He was a man of science and a master of illusion. Some might say it was Merlin's spirit that brought to life tapestries hanging along the walls, but 'twas only the flickering of light from the torches mounted along the walls and in candelabras overhead. That and an occasional draft.

One tapestry in particular caught Alyn's eye. A new one. When he was last here, the queen's ladies had completed only its frame of Pictish art with mythological creatures and knotted lines. Now two figures rode on horseback in the center: a lady and a warrior wearing crowns—no doubt Arthur and his third wife, the raven-haired Gwenhyfar. Alyn had observed that the queen, his maternal cousin, was as able with the needle as she was at weaponry and diplomacy. He smiled, proud of his mother's Pict heritage and his father's Irish-Scot one.

The real Gwenhyfar, who sat next to her golden-maned husband on a dais at the head of the hall, stared straight ahead, as beautiful and still as the stitched one. Though her body was present, her thoughts seemed elsewhere, far from the drone of the priest presiding over the service.

Alyn's purpose in rushing to the event, besides to pay his respects, was to hear the inimitable eloquence of Rheged's bard, Taliesen, praising Emrys's royal and priestly Romano-British lineage, his genius in the arts and sciences, and his statesmanship to and stewardship of the British church. But instead, a cardinal-clad Roman bishop chirped repetitive lines in Latin. The message about the holiness of the Virgin and the suffering of her Son was hopelessly lost on most of the crowd.

Were he here, Emrys himself would draw his cloak of invisibility about his shoulders and walk out. Not that the man had such a cloak, but he could fade into a crowd as though he were invisible.

"This birdsong is best heard in a church, not in Arthur's great hall," someone called out.

"Aye, give us Taliesen," cried another.

A pang of guilt struck Alyn as he nodded in agreement with the rabble-rousers. The musical chant of Latin aimed to draw a soul close to its spiritual home and God's love, but what Alyn craved most now was the familiarity of his clan lands and family.

Let the rafters ring with how Merlin Emrys of Powys served the Son *and* Albion. His example spoke so much louder than this clanging liturgy.

Alyn searched the bejeweled and elegant guests of honor gathered on the dais for any sign of Merlin Emrys's old friend Taliesen. The bard's wife, Vivianne, Lady of the Lake, did not sit with her sisters— Arthur's widowed aunt Morgause and his mother, the church-robed Ygerna. Had Rheged's master bard gone to the Other Side as well in the years Alyn had spent in the East?

Perhaps when Alyn received an audience with the queen, he would find out more about the state of Cymri affairs and of his family in Gododdin. Correspondence between Alyn and his family had been scant at best. Even his native Cymric felt awkward to Alyn's tongue after his years of studying and speaking Arabic at the prestigious House of Wisdom. But 'twas welcome to his ears.

"Not a soul will be left awake by the time the bishop ceases trying to save this motley lot," a deep voice said nearby. Too close for comfort.

Alyn jerked away but broke into a grin upon seeing Daniel of Gowrys at his side. Before Alyn could reply, Daniel clapped him on the back, knocking his reply into silence. "Well, *you* don't look like much of a priest," his friend observed upon letting Alyn go.

"And you still look much the same … you fey highlander," Alyn managed.

Faith, those tattooed forearms were nigh as thick as some men's thighs. Daniel's long hair was unbound and tangled, save the fraying braids bracketing his square-jawed face. Mud stained the red, green, and yellow of his plaid cloak, which was fastened with a silver brooch shaped like a roaring lion.

Alyn leaned in with an exaggerated sniff and wrinkled his nose. "And you certainly smell like one."

After living in the East for so long with its baths and exotic oils and scents, Alyn found that it was taking time for him to reacclimate to Western hygiene. Or lack thereof.

Daniel brandished a sheepish grin. "Me 'n' the lads arrived just this morning. Roads are naught but mire, but the Angus was determined to be here. Won't let the queen and her people down, like some." He cast a dubious glance at the royal dais where one bench was conspicuously empty. Modred of Lothian's.

"Are any others here from Glenarden?"

The Gowrys were a subclan of the O'Byrnes, and his friend was the only one Alyn had recognized. Not that Daniel wasn't qualified to speak for Glenarden. Despite his untamed highland demeanor, he'd had a princely education at chieftain Ronan O'Byrne's insistence. Still, Daniel had been pained by the years spent at the university at Llantwit as much as Alyn had been thrilled by his own time there. Above all, Daniel was trusted by the Glenarden.

"Times are fiercer on the border than ever," Daniel told Alyn. "Note none of the Miathi Picts have come. And the rest of the border tribes present have sent no more than a token to represent them, much as Emrys was esteemed. They need every weapon-bearing man on hand. Truth b'told, I'd rather be one of them than here listening to all this holy gum-flapping."

"How did you find me in this crowd?" Alyn asked, though he knew Daniel's gaze was sharp as an eagle's, formed by a life spent mostly in the wild.

"I spied you coming in, though I scarce believed my eyes at first. I'm used to seeing you in something more colorful than this drab gray." Daniel picked at the wool of Alyn's traveling cloak. "When *did* you return? Surely Ronan and Brenna weren't expecting you when I left Glenarden."

'Twas Alyn's eldest sibling, Ronan of Glenarden, and Daniel's cousin Brenna of Gowrys who, thanks be to God's grace, had finally brought peace to their troubled clan lands by their loving union.

"Are they here?" Alyn glanced past Daniel, hoping to catch sight of his brother or more of the Glenarden folk.

"Nay," Daniel told him. "Ronan asked me to speak for Glenarden."

Disappointment clouded Alyn's heart. "My ship made anchor this morning. I came here when I heard the news of Emrys's death. Would that I'd come home sooner." *Or that Merlin's death is another of his tricks.* Alyn still could not believe the man was gone, especially when Alyn needed his genius most.

"The main thing is that you're here, though why you're still wearing your cloak wrapped so tightly about yourself makes me wonder if you didn't leave your mind back in the East." Daniel wiped perspiration from his brow and tucked his thumbs into his kilted wrap. "Are you hiding something in the folds?"

"I am." With a smug grin, Alyn tugged a fold of the wool away to reveal a creature curled like a sleeping baby against his tunic. "A gift from a friend."

"Faith, that's the ugliest babe I've ever seen! Sired by a bear, was it?"

"Fatin is an African monkey," Alyn whispered, closing the gap in hopes that the animal would continue his nap. "Who is the new archbishop?"

Daniel cast a disdainful glance in that direction. "Cassian, he calls himself. And Arthur's made him the new *merlin*."

"Adviser to the king?" Alyn cut his gaze toward the dais in disbelief. What would a Roman bishop know of Alba and its people?

Yet Arthur listened solemnly to every utterance from Cassian's lips while kings and princes from the pagan and Christian noble houses of the Cymri—the Briton and Welsh brotherhood—and even the Scot and Pict nations stood proud, if not interested, behind their shields in places of honor.

When at last Cassian stopped talking and motioned for his fellow priests to help him close the service with the Eucharist, some of the warrior kings waited dutifully for the sacrament. Others grumbled and shifted from foot to foot but stayed in tolerance for an end to the ceremony. But a few, devoted to their own gods of war and bounty, simply walked out of the hall in disrespect.

"'Tis a fragile peace the Dux Bellorum is weaving here," Daniel observed. "I'd like to think all in attendance will stand by Arthur when the need arises. Most of the great houses of Alba and Albion are here."

If not for Alyn's ring—onyx inlaid with a pearl-white dove symbolizing his connection to his cousin Queen Gwenhyfar—and some smooth talk, he surely would not have been admitted among even the lesser ambassadors and scholars of such an esteemed group. While a prince himself, Alyn's status of being third in line for chieftain carried little weight in state affairs.

A small but surprisingly strong tug on his cloak drew his attention to where Fatin peeked out with large dark eyes, cautiously taking in the crowded hall.

"Time for me to leave," Alyn announced to Daniel. "You have no idea how much trouble he can get into, especially in this crowd."

Daniel chuckled. "Nay, but I'd give good silver to see it. His jacket's fine as most noblemen's here." He poked gently at the monkey's belly. "Fatin, is it?" he crooned to the animal.

Ordinarily Fatin did not take right away to strangers, but this was no ordinary stranger. Daniel of Gowrys was more at home with animals than people. The monkey gave him a toothy smile.

Daniel couldn't help but match it. "I've heard of monkeys but never seen one close up."

Fatin, now wide awake, squirmed in the constraints of his sling.

Alyn hadn't had the heart to leave him in his cage at the docks with the other goods to be delivered to a nearby inn. He tightened Fatin's leash and looked for the fastest way out. Except perhaps in a circus, few Cymri had ever seen a monkey, much less one dressed in princely garb. Alyn could hear the cry "Demon!" ringing in his ears just at the thought of Fatin scampering across the sea of heads and shoulders.

Although Emrys would have enjoyed such a distraction, Alyn knew.

Smothering a pained smile, Alyn asked silent forgiveness for avoiding the Holy Communion. "Follow me," he said to Daniel, pressing his hand against the fidgeting Fatin.

Exasperation fanning his footsteps, Alyn took the closest exit from the hall. The door led to a columned Roman portico that connected the plain lime-washed stone of the Queen's Tower and Arthur's Hall.

The moment Alyn released the leash, Fatin wrestled free from his grasp and took to the vine-covered passage as naturally as his ancestors had their jungle trees. In no time at all, the small monkey found the right spot and relieved himself, chattering in bliss.

Daniel laughed out loud. "I'm sure the queen's garden needed water."

"All he does is eat, chatter, and—"

A splash announced Fatin's dive into a fishpond.

"Play in water," Alyn finished wryly as the black animal emerged with a shriek of horror at the icy temperature so different from his native waters. "He's yet to learn the chill of Alba's waters."

Daniel laughed out loud as the wet monkey shook himself and gave them an earful of his opinion. Alyn took off his cloak and held it out to the shivering creature, but Fatin eyed him warily. Like a babe, he'd had his nap and was ready for a romp.

"Come on, you furry excuse for breath," Alyn ground out, shaking his cloak. He didn't have the patience Hassan had with the creature. Not for the first time, he wondered why he'd even accepted the gift. "I didn't have the heart to tell my friend Hassan to keep the little beast after he'd purchased it for me to remember him by," he told Daniel. "But right now …"

Fatin scampered up a large arched trellis, swinging down under one side and up on the other, using his long, thin limbs and versatile tail.

"The East must produce some strange friends," Daniel observed, "if you remember him like that." The highlander reached up to the trellis and mimicked Fatin's chatter, all the while coaxing him to the edge.

The thick door from which they'd just emerged opened without warning. Startled, Fatin fled straight into Daniel's arms, soaking his tunic in the process. So as not to call attention to their presence in the garden, which was usually reserved for the leisure of the court ladies, Alyn and Daniel hastily stepped into the cover of the thick-vined arbor. Alyn had spent hours in this very spot, talking with his late mother's cousin, and he was certain Gwenhyfar would be delighted to hear he'd returned from the East—but it was awkward to be found here without invitation.

A woman rushed out of the hall, her hair a wild tumble of curls the color of summer wheat. Head down, the lower half of her face covered with her hand as if to conceal her identity, she marched straight for the arbor and smack into Alyn's chest. .

"Easy, milady—"

Her shriek withered behind the press of her palm against her mouth.

Alyn placed his own hand over hers to make certain it stayed there. "You've nothing to fear. We're only two guests who sought relief from the closeness of the assembly in the fresh air of the queen's garden."

Recognition rippled across the hazel eyes that possessed a chameleonlike quality to favor blue, green, or amber, depending on her humor and the color she wore. Today they were rimmed in blue. "Alyn O'Byrne!" Kella O'Toole gasped as he released her. "B-but when? How?"

Alyn thought he'd have known his younger foster sister anywhere. He'd watched her grow into womanhood. But when Kella backed away to collect herself, he was no longer certain. When he'd last seen her, she was pretty and ripe of figure, but today she was so stunning that his tongue turned upon itself, leaving him utterly speechless.

As if she distrusted her own eyes, Kella reached up and touched his natural hairline, where once he'd shaved it in the druidic and priestly tonsure of his station. But that seemed a lifetime ago. Now he wore his long, straight hair pulled tightly off his face with a leather thong, the rest falling down his back to his shoulders.

"You've got hair," she marveled. Her lips formed the perfect rosy O he remembered.

Alyn strove to analyze what exactly was different, but the scent of her perfume assailing his nostrils dulled his thought processes, enhancing his senses and leaving them hungry for more. How could senses make no sense?

"Welcome home!" Kella threw both arms about his neck and pressed a heavenly sculpted body against his with a more familiar childlike gusto.

Her lips were intended for his fresh-shaven cheek, Alyn's for her rosy one, but somehow his claimed hers as if following some primal order given and executed faster than his brain could process. Heat flushed through his body with an urgency he hadn't known existed until a moment ago.

"I, too, have hair, my lady," Daniel of Gowrys drawled. His wryness penetrated the heady cloud cover of Alyn's brain.

Reluctant, Alyn released the delicious Kella from his embrace. *Delicious*? Bards used such words to describe women, as if the human species could be compared to food. Emotions were mercurial things, not to be trusted. They made great literature for poets but left a man of *sciencia* unimpressed with their instability.

"I … I gave up the tonsure," Alyn stammered.

If Kella required more detail, he'd stand as if upon his tongue. Right now, *she* was enough reason for his doubts regarding his calling to the priesthood.

Her face as red as Alyn's felt, Kella opened her mouth to speak, but the *whatever-was-that-about?* in her eyes thankfully did not find voice. Instead, she turned her attention to Daniel, who puckered his lips in sheer devilment.

She stepped back, gathering a proper huff of indignation. "Daniel of Gowrys, the High King's dogs would think twice before kissing that bristly face." A tug at the corner of her lips betrayed her humor. "Though it is good to see you as well," she admitted.

"You always favored him," Daniel chided, "over me."

"I've known him—" Her gaze fell from Daniel's face to the wet Fatin. "What is *that*?" she exclaimed in horror. "Are rats mated with humans to produce such creatures?"

"*That*," Daniel announced, dislodging Fatin from his shirt and handing him over to Alyn, "is Alyn's new pet monkey."

"It's wearing clothes." She looked to Alyn for some kind of explanation.

Sure, her eyes could not be more round or filled with confusion. Perhaps Alyn was not the only one taken aback by the unexpected reaction resulting from their meeting.

"Fatin is a prince," he explained. The jab of Daniel's elbow brought home the foolishness of his reply. "That is, Fatin is a gift from an Arab prince," Alyn added hastily. "He has a royal wardrobe."

"He dresses better than most people I know," Daniel put in.

Kella cut him a sidewise glance. "You might learn from the little mite."

Alyn chuckled, relieved that his inexplicable behavior had been dismissed and the interaction of this threesome had returned to normal. "I see you two still love each other."

"Forever and always." Kella gave Daniel a wicked grin. "But I'd have him bathe before I greet him with a proper hug."

Kella had always been drawn to the glamour and customs of court life—to the point that it used to irritate Alyn no end. He'd done his best to warn her that glitter did not mean gold, nor perfume cleanliness of the body or soul.

Though she shone like the purest gold right now. And her cheeks were the first of this year's roses to bloom in the queen's gar—

Alyn reined in his rambling thoughts, heat scorching his cheeks. First, he'd regressed to a behavior more suited to Fatin's ancestors. Now 'twas as if Hassan's poetic brain had overtaken his.

It wasn't as if he'd given Kella much thought beyond that of a concerned older brother since he'd set off for the East to further his education. He'd left behind a sweet but sometimes shallow maiden who had an ear for languages and dreams of making a noble marriage.

As Kella peered at the monkey, now balled into the folds of Alyn's cloak, Alyn grasped for words. "His name means 'clever,' but I fear my friend Hassan gave it with too high a hope. The monkey just leapt into a barely thawed goldfish pond."

Kella cautiously touched the pet. Fatin hesitantly wrapped his tiny fingers about hers. "Does he bite?" she whispered, caught between alarm and the little monkey's charm.

"Not often," Alyn teased.

"I've only heard of one death resulting from monkey bites," Daniel chimed in.

Kella's eyes slashed them with disdain, but her even teeth worried her bottom lip as she stroked Fatin. "The poor thing is trembling with cold."

How could those lips taste like honeyed wine? Perhaps it lingered from the Eucharist. Alyn pulled his senses in line once again. Poetic fantasy, and annoying at that.

"Bring him into the Queen's Tower," Kella instructed them. "He can dry by the fire while I find out what brings home my wandering foster brother." She grinned at Daniel. "You can come too, if you wish."

Daniel declined. "If I'm to represent Glenarden in Arthur's court, I'd best return." He cut a glance at Alyn. "That is, if you two think you can control your joy at seeing each other again."

Kella gently withdrew her finger from Fatin's grasp. "We both turned our heads at the same time, silly," she explained, avoiding eye contact with Alyn. "'Twas a *mis-kiss*, nothing more," she added with a careless wave of her hand.

"Precisely," Alyn chimed in. Heaven knew, he'd not intended such a reunion.

Pivoting on beaded silk slippers, Kella gathered up the blue brocade of her skirts and led the way toward the Queen's Tower entrance. Her unmistakable air of authority was reinforced when the guard at the door immediately opened it and stood aside with a respectful "G'day, milady."

It was Kella, and yet it wasn't. Until Alyn could fathom the difference, distance was the best course of action.

CHAPTER TWO

Kella's heart beat like a captive bird's as she led the way into the Queen's Tower. She'd leapt at the chance to escape the oppressive crush of people at the ceremony, to finish preparations for receiving the ladies in the Queen's Tower during the interim between the memorial mass and the feast. While the men attended affairs of state, the ladies would enjoy rest and refreshment and catch up on news from throughout the kingdom. The fresh air that met Kella on the steps to the courtyard soothed the protests of her stomach caused by the concentrated bouquet of humanity.

And then there was Alyn, tall, dark, and unyielding as a stone wall. Alyn, come from the past like a dark god of passion and taking what remained of her present breath by seizing her lips and setting every female sensibility she possessed asimmer. What on earth had he been thinking?

"You certainly have moved up in station since I last saw you," Alyn remarked as if he greeted every woman he met as such.

Where was the somber young man she'd seen off to study in the East?

"I am impressed," he continued.

Impressed? The scholar hadn't completely vanished after all. Indignation nipped at Kella's humor as she led him past lavish tapestries that added color and warmth to the high stone walls, toward a stairwell that led to Gwenhyfar's private chambers above. Alyn might wait there with Fatin without disturbing the ladies.

How dare he simply appear after six years and—

Kella wiped her mouth with the back of her hand, but even as she did, she knew she would never forget such a kiss as long as she lived. Alyn was, for all intent and purpose, her brother! The one who had lived to vex her since she first drew breath in This World.

She didn't even love him in a romantic sense. Not anymore. The heart she'd foolishly saved just for him when she was a mere child had matured. It belonged to another, more deserving, man. One far more gallant and less maddening. One who appreciated Kella for her wit and opinions as well as her fairness. A man who wanted a wife and family, not a stone cell filled with amphorae and musty manuscripts. Lorne made *her* the center of his world. Study and prayer were Alyn's world, and he had never bothered with her except to annoy.

And she was certainly annoyed. Stepping inside the queen's parlor, Kella pivoted on slippered feet and lashed out at an unsuspecting Alyn with her hand. "How dare you!"

The slap cracked like thunder in the empty room and stung her palm like a thousand bees. With a gasp, Kella clasped her burning hand to her waist and stomped backward, glaring. "You're more devil than priest. I don't care how long you've studied," she ranted, "or if you studied with the Christos Himself. That kiss was most ill-gotten!"

'Twould have served him right had she lost her breakfast down the front of that fine-fitting tunic. Travel and time had bulked Alyn's boyishly slender, gawky frame, and his tailor knew exactly how to accent the manly taper of his torso to perfection. She tore her gaze away from the wall of muscle to her foster brother's face.

He tested the flaming red mark of her palm on his cheek with tentative fingers, meeting her gaze with his own midnight appraisal. Instead of his classic aloofness or mischief, his expression hinted of surprise and cooled to an unsettling study of her, as if she were some specimen to be examined upon a board.

Just when Kella concluded that he was utterly without remorse, he reached for her hand. "You are right, Kella. I am more sinner than priest." He lifted her fingers to his lips, brushing the knuckles gently. "And I was wrong. I do not know you that well."

"Indeed not." So why *had* he kissed her so … so thoroughly? She sniffed, all the more disconcerted. Who was this pretender posing as her foster brother? "Never *that* well."

Unsettled by the tension, Fatin began to chatter and dig into Alyn's shirt. Wincing, Alyn broke the clutch and unfastened the gold embroidered jacket as tenderly as though the animal were a babe.

"It won't happen again," he promised as he removed the garment and tossed it near the fire to dry. Ever so gently, he rubbed the little monkey's fur with his cloak. The way a father might …

Kella's skin ignited again. Still, she couldn't stop watching him, although he didn't seem to notice. It was a relief when he changed the subject.

"I am disheartened to hear of Merlin Emrys's passing." Alyn fastened Fatin's leash to a chair near the fire and knelt to stir the coals. "I'd hoped to consult with him. Alba has suffered a huge loss."

"Arthur even more," Kella put in, "although I wonder if he has the wit to realize it. For every alliance the Dux Bellorum makes, another falls apart."

The monkey climbed on Alyn's shoulder as he rose. "No, you don't, mischief." He put the creature back on the chair. "Have you any fruit? He loves to eat. I fear food and mischief sums up his purpose on This Side."

Kella hastily retrieved an apple from the bowl on a nearby table and handed it to Alyn. He withdrew a dagger from his belt and cut the fruit into pieces.

"How did you come by him?" she asked.

"An Arab friend gave me the little beast as a parting gift to remember him by. Prince Hassan ibn Yūsuf ibn Matar of the Byzantium Ghassānid." At the surprised hike of Kella's brow, Alyn explained, "They are the Christian-Arab foederati who defend Byzantium. A fierce and proud people."

"So you weren't confined to prayer and books alone?" she observed.

Alyn shook his head. "Nothing quite so boring after all, eh?"

"I never said books were boring," Kella pointed out. "It's the priestly life that I would find tedious. Those dark, cramped cells and all that praying day in and out."

"Perhaps it is to someone as full of life and beauty as yourself, though I've heard you've now mastered five languages. I'm impressed you could sit still that long."

Kella pulled a face at the halfhearted insult. "It comes easily to me. Of course, I was raised in three of them—the Irish or Scot, our Brito-Welsh Cymric, and your mam's Pict. And the classics in Latin and Greek are most entertaining."

"Aye, they are that." Alyn cradled Fatin and took the chair near the fire, where he spread out the tiny, ornate jacket to dry faster. "But tell me, is there any news of my brothers and their families?" he asked upon handing the remainder of the apple to Fatin. "The most recent missive I received from Caden said that he and Sorcha were finally expecting a child."

Kella's belly quivered. Or was it her imagination? What would Alyn say if he knew—

"Their daughter Aelwyn will be two this Easter," she replied. "Sorcha named her after Aelwyn's foster grandmother."

Astonishment claimed Alyn's face. "Two years," he said to no one in particular. "Time has flown on fast wing."

"Ronan and Brenna and their two offspring?"

"Most well," she assured him. He mustn't find out that she was expecting. Not until she and Lorne could make things right. The priestly Alyn would never approve.

"The southern Picti are proving worrisome again," she continued. "They'd rather fight the Scots and Cymri than Saxons. The queen expects rebellion if Arthur chooses a Cymri king to succeed him rather than his cousin Modred, but my betrothed is striving hard to bring the Pictish princes around to Arthur's way of thinking."

Alyn spun away from the fire. "Your *what*?"

Kella stopped herself from covering her belly. It was instinct to touch the product of their love whenever Lorne's name crossed her mind. Instead she brushed the front of her skirt of unseen lint. This talk of family and little ones had addled her brain. That and Alyn's kiss … his gentleness with that tiny creature.

That she still tingled from the kiss had to be the result of her condition. All that was feminine about her was at its most sensitive right now, resistant to reason.

Her heart ... her *child* ... belonged to someone else. Someone who appreciated her and shared her ambition to rise in Arthur's court. Someone unlike the present company, who shared no princely aspirations. "My *betrothed*," she replied smugly. "*Prince* Lorne of Errol."

Alyn's lips twitched as he held her in his gaze. "You always said you would marry a prince." He motioned about the room, the wry edge to his voice giving way to praise. "And clearly you are highly esteemed by the queen."

"But I am ahead of myself," she added hastily. "We haven't announced our engagement officially. Lorne only asked me at Yuletide before riding off to Strighlagh to join the Angus's forces on the borderland. He will speak to Father there."

"And then to Ronan and Caden and myself."

Faith, she couldn't remain perturbed with her foster brother. For all his worrisome ways, she appreciated this protective side of him.

Kella fingered a brooch, gold shaped into a taloned creature that was half bird with the head of a cat. Pict artisans favored mythological creatures. The inlay of jewels and glass made it burst with color. "He gave me this. Isn't it lovely?"

"He'll need more than a pretty pin to win Egan's approval," Alyn observed. "Is he any good with weapons, or is he likely to be food for the wolves and ravens after a good fight?"

Just the mention of the possibility that Lorne might lose his life on the battlefield ran Kella's heart through, even though Alyn merely exercised his role as an elder sibling and meant nothing by it.

"He is a force to be reckoned with among Arthur's companions and possesses the eloquence of a poet," Kella informed him with pride. "Which is why he is among the chosen to speak on Arthur's behalf to his fellow Pictish rulers."

"And how vast is the land that he rules?"

"It is his brother who is king of the clan lands—"

"Which is why Prince Lorne rides with Arthur, *hoping* to win land of his own," Alyn finished maddeningly.

"Like yourself," Kella shot back.

"Aye," Alyn conceded, "but a priest and scholar's needs are meager. His knowledge provides his wealth."

Why had she ever blurted out her secret about Lorne? Tears sprang from what seemed like an endless stream of emotion of late. Kella turned away rather than let Alyn see them. She had managed to rise to her position by using her wit rather than feminine wiles, but this pregnancy had reduced her to a mishmash of feelings prone to erupt at the most inconvenient times.

"I should have said nothing," she said aloud. "I thought I could trust *you*, of all people, to share my happiness." She put her hands to her temples, where invisible fingers knotted the muscles there. "I beg you. Please say nothing of this. The time isn't right. No one knows but you, not even the queen."

She heard Alyn's footfall, felt his hands come to rest on her shoulders. "You have my word of love as a brother and honor as a man, little sister. Your secret is safe with me. But I can't speak for Fatin," he added playfully.

The tension coiling Kella's nerves broke free with a chuckle. This was the way it used to be. She could turn angry with Alyn at the flip of a coin, and before her anger was spent, he could disarm her with that rakish charm of his.

Her world righted again, she turned into his arms and returned his embrace. "Welcome home, Alyn."

After the service ended, Gwenhyfar appeared delighted to discover Alyn upon retiring to her private chambers. Kella, on the other hand, was definitely not herself. Her gaze retreated like a startled deer whenever she caught Alyn watching her, which made Alyn all the more observant, in spite of himself. He could not blame curiosity alone. He couldn't seem to take his eyes off her. There was a glow that transcended her natural beauty. It reminded Alyn of depictions of the Holy Mother displayed in churches from Albion to the Holy Land.

Or perhaps this new obsession was the result of his need for grounding—finding the man he'd been before being caught up in the lofty spiritual and intellectual world in the East. Kella belonged to the old Alyn. A man whose soul, reason, and emotions had been of one accord, not at war with each other.

"I want you to be my eyes and ears, Alyn," Gwenhyfar told him, once the amenities were behind them. Given the indentations of fatigue beneath her eyes, she needed rest but insisted on spending her short span of free time with Alyn and Kella. "I cannot see everyone's reaction from the throne. I need as many sets of eyes as can be mustered to discern reactions to the proceedings. I must know who is our enemy—and who is not." Gwenhyfar twisted the wedding band on her left ring finger, her expression almost a grimace of pain. Before Alyn could fathom a meaning behind it, she continued. "Were Cassian to bend Arthur's ear any further, I'd have no say in the decisions affecting our nation."

"But you are High Queen, milady," Alyn protested. And not only a queen of the Picts, but a priestess of the Grail Church. She was groomed to be a High Queen of the peoples, regardless of tribe.

"Cassian thinks politics and faith are the realm of men, that we women have no place in them except as servants and child-bearers," Kella huffed.

Funny, but that was the future Kella had always claimed to want—a wealthy, handsome lord for her to serve as husband, and children for her to raise. The passing of six years, combined with the influence of Queen Gwenhyfar, had wrought many changes in his once-fanciful foster sister. This Kella was certainly more fascinating.

"It appears Cassian has much to learn about Alba and its women," Alyn observed wryly.

Many Celtic women, those of royalty in particular, were trained in business and warfare as well as household administration. In times of war—and when was there not war on these shores?—the responsibilities of their husbands fell upon their shoulders. At times, they fought shoulder to shoulder with their men. Not even the Pax Romana had eliminated that necessity for survival.

"I am watched by Cassian's men as if I would betray my own husband *and my Christ*," Gwenhyfar added, as if the latter smote her worse than the first.

Another festering between the Celtic and the Roman Churches, Alyn mused. Most of the former druidic priestesses, like their male counterparts, had accepted Christianity. They'd become sisters and abbesses, brides of Christ. The example of Mary had given women an acceptable role beyond the Martha-like one of wife and child-bearer. Gwenhyfar was a Mary, educated in secular and ecclesiastical knowledge to serve God and His people as queen.

"I fear Cassian will sway Arthur toward a fatal mistake for our peoples. My husband needs the Pictish support I have brought him through marriage, reinforced by following Merlin's advice in naming Modred as successor to the title of Dux Bellorum. But rumor has it that Cassian advises Arthur to change his mind and name Urien of Rheged, a Briton who is no friend of the Pictish nations."

"Surely not!" No wonder Gwenhyfar was so pale and wan, Alyn thought. The Picts would certainly feel betrayed and would never swear allegiance to a purely British king.

The queen squared her shoulders and offered her arm. "So … shall we join the High King and try to keep him from tearing the Cymri alliance into shreds to please Rome?"

Alyn glanced to where Fatin unstacked a pile of kindling within reach of his leash. "I wish I'd left him in his cage now," he lamented.

"Nonsense. I'll have Maeven, the steward's wife, bring a cage in for him. Will he be friendly to her?"

Alyn nodded. "He's a bit shy of men but seems to like women. Especially if they give him fruit or nuts."

Gwenhyfar turned to Kella. "See to it, if you will, milady. Arthur will not hold the proceedings for my arrival."

Kella dipped in a curtsy. "As you wish, my queen."

"Thank you, Kella … milady," Alyn amended hastily. He offered his arm to the queen. "Let us pray, cousin, that whatever Arthur's decisions be, they are pleasing to God."

Yet even as he spoke, Alyn had his doubts. Rome had never understood the importance of the ancient bloodlines to the tribes of Albion—that they were as important as they'd been to the Hebrew nations of the Old Testament. The records of the survival of the Davidic kings and apostolic priests in the British Isles were ingrained in every Celtic priest, Alyn among them. The bloodlines didn't give the Celtic Church authority over Rome. They simply made them brethren and, as such, equals in faith and God's eye.

But would Rome *ever* accept anything not Roman as equal?

Chapter Three

After escorting Gwenhyfar to her elaborately carved throne seat and being acknowledged by the High King, Alyn wove his way through the crowd, looking for Daniel and hopefully a vantage point from which he might see the key players in the rapidly unfolding drama.

The influence and power of the members of the assembly was impressive, even though Merlin Emrys's tribute solely accounted for many. A well-planned strike in this hall by a Saxon contingent could wipe out most of the kings of the North and many of the South and West. To Gwenhyfar's right sat the steward of her land of Gododdin, King Angus of Strighlagh. On the High King's left was the red-robed archbishop, his pointed chin jutting out with an air of arrogance. Or perhaps it was the close trim of his beard that gave that illusion.

Alyn wasn't ready to judge the man yet, if at all. It wasn't his place or what he'd come home for. Then again, neither was playing the queen's eyes.

Next to Archbishop Cassian was the empty chair usually occupied by King Modred of Lothian. Given Modred's position as an archbishop of the Celtic Church, some interesting conversations must have taken place between the two church fathers. Neither

Roman nor Celtic priests would give on their positions regarding the proper worship of the Christos. Alyn wondered if the time Easter was celebrated or the way a priest cut his hair was all that important to God. Short of the bloodletting done away with by Jesus's sacrifice, Alyn figured it was the heart behind the various ways of honoring and worshipping the Almighty that mattered most to Him.

"O'Byrne!"

Alyn spied Daniel of Gowrys motioning him over to the column where they'd previously met. By the time Alyn arrived at the spot, a blast of trumpets heralded the beginning of the session. Arthur, wearing the scarlet of his maternal Brito-Roman lineage, rose and waited for the verbal buzz in the hall to fade. Before the dais, forming an elongated semicircle to either side of it, stood the kings and princes of Britain, shields presented before them.

There were lions, bears, wolves, boars, stags, wildcats, and foxes—representatives of the animal kingdom adopted by the old ones to represent the tribes. Most Christian kingdoms had replaced the old symbols of creation with crosses, while some incorporated the cross into their ancestral theme. Regardless, each shield told something about the man who stood behind it.

Most brilliant of all was the image of the Virgin painted on the High King's shield, where once a red dragon had breathed fire. The way the torchlight glanced off the polished, lacquered surface, Christ's mother shone as if with divine light. Alyn wondered how many times she'd been beaten and battered in battle while protecting Arthur, then repainted and restored. The High King was first and foremost a warrior, a leader into the fight and an example for lesser kings.

A king of kings.

But was any man up to that task, save Christ Himself? Would even Jesus be able to please the whole of this assembly, so rife with rivalry and suspicion?

"We welcome each of you, free men of Britain," Arthur began. He glanced around the circle of shields, which was broken only by the dais and open at the opposite end so that the rest of the assembly might more easily view the key players. "We entreat the Lord God Almighty to reign over these proceedings, that they might glorify Him and His plan for all of Albion. My lord archbishop, will you pray?"

A significant groaning and shuffling of feet evidenced that not all the participants recognized God as sovereign, or perhaps the archbishop's authority. But tolerance was ingrained in the Celtic mind, if not acceptance.

While Arthur ignored the contention, Cassian scowled at the gathering, his eyes narrowed as he searched out the dissenters. After a moment, the scowl was schooled into a beatific face. Cassian's voice put Alyn to mind of a bees' nest, producing an inflectionless hum. Thankfully, having exhausted himself of words at Merlin Emrys's service, the priest merely repeated Arthur's request for God's sanction of the proceedings, exacting an audible sigh of relief from the onlookers as he returned to his seat.

Again the center of attention, Arthur stepped off the dais and walked the circle of knights before him sunwise, stopping to briefly meet the gaze of each and offer welcome. His reception was clearly more favorable in the northern contingent than in the southern.

In the southerner's eye, Arthur of Dalraida fell short of the first Brito-Romano *arthur*, the great warrior who had preceded him at the battle of Mount Badon and ended Saxon incursions in the south for nearly half a century. The Grail Church had tried again and again to reproduce such a hero from matchmaking the apostolic bloodlines and those of the Irish-Davidic heritage, but to no avail.

After the present *arthur* had made a full round of his guests, he returned to stand before his throne like a giant sun god adorned in gold from his crown to his fingertips. "I will make this brief," he boomed, "for our kitchens are bursting with food and our cellars with drink." After pausing for the murmur of unanimous approval to subside, he went on. "I planned to make this announcement at the May fair in Strighlagh, but since all of our northern allies are here, as well as most of the rest of Britain's rulers, it seems fitting—"

"Not *all* are here," someone interrupted from the masses beyond the circle of nobility.

"Aye, King Modred belongs in that empty chair," another chimed in.

Like a gathering storm, discontent rumbled to the rafters as various factions took sides. Christian kingdoms mostly against the still-pagan ones, Alyn noted. Politics were complicated enough without a contest of faith stirring them.

Arthur raised the famed Excalibur from its jeweled sheath and beat the sword on the wooden planking of the dais.

Alyn flinched as if the shining blade had broadsided his temple. Black splotches winged across his vision, and he viewed the king and his company as through a haze.

Father, no, not now, he prayed. 'Twas the foreshadowing of a pain that, since the day of the explosion, oft sent him to bed, his brain writhing in his skull. Alyn thought the headaches had gone away after he'd made the decision to return home. Not one had he suffered on the return journey. He'd taken it as a sign from God that he was doing the right thing.

He blinked away the blotches and second thoughts until only Arthur was in focus—but the pain was setting in.

"The fact that my cousin Modred is not here is all the more reason for me to question his qualifications as my successor," Arthur claimed. "A High King should hear *all* his people, whether he agrees with them or nay. Not avoid them when he differs in opinion. A High King thus informed must then rely on the advice of his round table and God."

"My son has heard your mind is already made up." Queen Morgause stepped forward into the elliptical space before her nephew, the king, her chin lifted haughtily in challenge. "Why waste a trip here when his own people need and want him more than you?"

Cassian bristled in his seat, his disdainful gaze taking in the Orkney queen's white and gold-embroidered church robes that indicated her rank as an abbess. Alyn couldn't blame the archbishop for questioning Morgause's trueness to the faith. She had been a druidic priestess prior to her conversion to Christianity. During this time of transition from the old ways to the new, the understanding of the Way sometimes became as blurred as separating *sciencia*, or the wonders of creation, from superstition.

Or misuse. Alyn smothered a flashback of brilliant fire and the black aftermath of roiling smoke. The school elders had demanded he recount what ingredients had caused the fierce explosion. But he couldn't recall exactly. And even if he did, dare he reveal a knowledge with such terrible prospects? That they'd nearly imprisoned him until he revealed it was proof enough that it should remain secret.

"He should have heard such news for himself," the High King replied, pulling Alyn back to the present. "I need every one of the Cymri and Pict kings if we are to stop the Saxon wolves at our doorstep, milady abbess … my cousin Modred included."

Morgause simmered beneath her serene demeanor with the same distrust that fueled the tension over the crowd. "Then make your announcement, nephew, and may God have more mercy on your soul than your pompous little redbird adviser has on any who disagree with him." She turned in a swirl of robes, addressing the room. "Rome conquered our people once with the sword. Now it uses the Savior's sacred cross to force Britain to kneel once again to its authority."

"*God* is my authority, Abbess Morgause." Cassian sprang to his feet, unable to contain his contempt any longer. "It is His counsel I bring the king."

Alyn could hardly see beyond the dark splotches. Like ravens to a carcass, they would not go away, no matter how Alyn tried to clear his vision. And oh, the agony their wings beat in his brain, though his hearing was acute and stabbed pain through his head with every sound.

Morgause laughed without humor. "God is the authority of the British church as well. You would forget that in the first century our Lord's family and close friends brought the Word to King Bran the Blessed, while Bran's daughter Claudia and her husband, Pudens, opened the doors of their villa for Paul and Peter to found Rome's first church. They followed the apostles into martyrdom, and their son Linus was *your* pope's first predecessor. *Britons*, my lord archbishop," she declared above the rising tide of support in the hall. She pivoted, facing off with Cassian. "*Britons* helped found even your church in Rome, yet Rome has the arrogance to claim authority over us?"

Authority. Alyn swayed unsteadily. *Lord God, who has authority over these visions that refuse to let me heal?*

He grabbed his temples, as though to squeeze out the scene playing before his open eyes....

A raven, bigger than usual and black as night, flew without flinching at an eagle. The clash scattered the other birds away. The eagle was the larger, but the raven more tenacious, especially when the other birds circled round and joined its attack....

The swirling flurry of feathers made Alyn's stomach churn. He swallowed hard and breathed deeply to quell the nausea. Then, out of the corner of his eye ... *a beautiful white dove strayed into the fray. Spying the easy prey, the eagle withdrew from the raven's territory, but not before snatching up the dove in its talons and flying off.*

A roar threatened to shatter Alyn's ears. The room spun—

"Easy, laddie!"

Alyn became aware of the iron brace of Daniel's arms as his friend helped him down to a bench built around one of the great columns. "Since when have you taken to swooning like a lovestruck maid?"

Alyn's head still hurt, but the vision was gone, and the hall shifted back into focus. He pulled his tunic and shirt away from where they clung to the clammy skin of his chest. "I ... I had a terrible accident in the East. It's left me with crippling headaches and the strangest of hallucinations. Animals, birds ..."

And the dragons, he thought. But Alyn could pinpoint a source for the dragon dream. Emrys had long ago prophesied the Saxon white dragon conquering the Briton red, though no Briton wanted to acknowledge it.

"What's happened?" Alyn asked abruptly.

"Morgause took the first fray with unanimous pagan and Christian support," Daniel whispered. "But Arthur ended any religious debate gathering in Cassian's skirts, insisting this was a political alliance he sought, not one of faith."

"Wisely done," Alyn mumbled. Rising, he was surprised his knees were still wobbly. He shored them with prayer and sheer will. At least the pain was bearable now, and the nausea had subsided.

Arthur's voice penetrated Alyn's personal struggle. "I hereby name Urien of Rheged as my successor."

Protests battled cheers as the lord of Rheged stepped forward from the circle and, shield before him, took possession of the empty chair once occupied by Modred. Had swords been allowed in the king's hall, undoubtedly violence would have broken out. Instead the men beat on their shields, and the thunder nearly put Alyn on the bench again.

Lord, I promised to watch for Gwenhyfar, he prayed. *Help me to help her.*

"Then glorify Me."

The noise wreaked havoc in Alyn's head, save that one thought. Yet it was all he could do to keep his eyes open or avoid heaving his breakfast. And who would listen to a failure from the East, returned to lick his wounds?

The disorder grew to such an extent that Arthur could only silence it by driving the gleaming Excalibur into the dais. One could have heard a babe's sigh as several contingents of men walked out of the hall, mostly of the border or Pict tribes, rather than pledge their swords to Arthur's British heir apparent. Daniel was clearly torn between allegiance to his brethren of Alba and the High King.

"I prayed for something different but am not surprised," Daniel mumbled under his breath. "Still, Glenarden gave its word that its sword belongs to Arthur."

Alyn didn't reply. His gaze fixed on the large black raven painted on Urien's shield. He could feel the blood draining from his face, leaving a tingle of disbelief on his scalp. The raven—Urien—smiled across Arthur's empty seat at Gwenhyfar, though the queen did not return the gesture. She looked away, staring off at nothing as if oblivion was to be her fate.

Alyn frowned. Urien was married to Arthur's sister Morgein, though he'd been promised Gwenhyfar before Arthur, on Emrys's advice, had swept in with his Scottish military and saved her lands from Saxon invasion. And Urien had to settle for Morgein, the paternal half sister of the High King, a disappointment for an ambitious soul like the lord of North Rheged.

"What is the matter with you? Are you sick again?" Daniel queried at Alyn's side. "You're white as death."

"I'm fine." But Alyn wasn't fine at all. If he'd just had a prophetic vision, he wanted no part of it. Better the result of a head damaged by the exploding concoction he and Abdul-Alim had been working on. A punishment for Alyn's carelessness.

Around the room, shield after shield was raised to Arthur and Urien. Strathclyde, Gwynedd, Byrneich, and Elmet led the tide of allegiance, followed by lesser kingdoms.

"Do you not raise your shield to me, Llywarch?" Arthur asked when all those who remained had spoken.

The South Rheged king was tall of stature like Alyn. Despite his slighter build and the grace of a poet, Llywarch was known for his prowess on the battlefront. "Aye, I'll raise my shield to whom my kinsman of North Rheged raises his. Mind you," he added, voice raised for all to hear, "but for Urien, I would not be here. Your war in the North is of no concern to me or mine."

"At least Arthur's choice of Urien is bringing on some of the southern armies," Daniel observed.

Alyn nodded, but the replaying vision refused to release his fascination. Raven, dove, and eagle. A red eagle on a black banner leapt to Alyn's mind. Lothian's banner. Surely Modred wouldn't abduct Gwenhyfar. He'd not dare.

"Tell that to your people if the Saxons spill past us and into your land," Arthur told Llywarch, pulling Alyn's focus to the present.

"Your wily father Aedan and his Irish Scots would seize British land as fast as the Saxon Aethelfrith," Llywarch claimed. "Surely you see reason for my concern. And your father's fathers did not support ours when our first Pendragon held back the Saxon wolves gnawing at our eastern territory. Why should we support you now?"

"Because if we fall, the wolves will turn upon you, Llywarch," the High King shot back, as undaunted on the dais as on the battlefield. "Just as they have fallen upon us for not helping the first *arthur*, as you say." Arthur lifted his shield for all to see the shining Virgin in blue. "I give you my word, by the Lady on my shield, that my father Aedan is allied with us. And I welcome you, even those of you with similar reservations, for I am confident there is no meat to them and you are a great benefit to our—"

The great twin doors of the hall swung open, cutting off the High King. Arthur seized Excalibur as his royal guards admitted a rider and his mud-covered horse into the hall. Warriors groped instinctively for the swords checked in before they were allowed into the hall. But the sight of the king's red dragon on the rider's tunic quelled the alarm.

"What is this?" the High King demanded.

"News, milord," came the messenger's breathless reply. "Grave news." The young man slid off the lathered animal. "The Miathi have invaded Manau."

The Angus, a thick-muscled bull among men, bolted to his feet. "What of Strighlagh?" he roared above the furor spreading through the room.

Alyn's breath caught. The whole of Alba was unraveling before his very eyes. Arthur's grandfather Gabran had driven the Miathi—those who would not accept their new Scot overlords through marriage or surrender—north of the River Clyde a generation before. The remainder had merged in peace with the Scots like Alyn's mother and Gwenhyfar.

"Strighlagh held, milord," the man said. "Though the fortress is fire-damaged."

Gwenhyfar paled. "What of *our* men?"

The messenger shoved his dark, sweat-soaked hair off a pain-wrenched face. "'Twas a ruse, milady. Our soldiers gave them chase beyond the Ochill Hills...." He hesitated, then forced himself to go on. "Only a handful of our men returned."

A loud groan drew Alyn's attention to where Kella had dropped to her knees among the queen's attendants near the dais. She looked pale, as if death itself had kicked her full in the stomach.

Only then did the full blow of the news strike him as well. Egan O'Toole and Kella's betrothed were part of Strighlagh's border guard.

Chapter Four

Kella was frantic for news of Lorne and her father. But Arthur, the queen, and their council withdrew from the hall to discuss the Miathi situation, and the minutes had turned into hours. Rumors of all-out war flowed through the hall as the remaining guests tried their best to enjoy platters upon platters of food and pitchers of wine and beer from the king's larders. Speculation danced to the lively strings and pipes of the musicians playing from a gallery above the crowd, though the people did not.

Nothing Alyn or Daniel said could lessen her anxiety. Not even the antics of the little monkey Fatin exacted more than a wan smile. Kella's thoughts were with her father and the father of her child. Did they live—or lie stone cold in a grave? Or worse, had the wolves and ravens fed on their corpses and spread them over the wilds of the hill country? Kella shuddered. Instinctively she covered her belly with her hand.

"*Lose yer weapon, lose yer head,*" Alyn said, mimicking her father's thick brogue as he and Daniel tried to distract her with fond tales of the past. "I was five the first time I wandered into the practice field, and he gave me no quarter. Slapped a wooden sword in my hand and had me hold it straight out. Said, '*You aren't worth the trainin' till ye can hold a sword long as it takes for good bread to rise proper.*' I can't tell you how many hours I spent in the kitchen, holding that wooden sword and watching the cook's dough."

Kella's fear-stiffened heart warmed at the recollection. "Aye, he told me the same."

"*You*, milady?" the steward's wife exclaimed in surprise. Since the news was announced, Maeven had hovered like a mother hen over Kella.

"I *am* a champion's daughter, Maeven," Kella said proudly.

"That I know," Maeven replied, "but I thought you'd never seen light outside a scriptorium, the way you love books and writing."

"Suffice it to say, I fared better with sword and quill than needle and a cookfire."

"Amen to that," Alyn said with a bit too much fervor.

Kella smacked him, reading his memory exactly. "That bread burned because a kitten was stuck in the apple tree and—"

"Pardon, milady," a servant interrupted. "The queen will see you now … in her chambers."

A chill cold as a northman's fjord set in Kella's bones. *God be with me. With them.*

Alyn leapt to his feet as she rose. "I'll go with you."

"Aye, sir. Gwenhyfar asked for you as well, if you be Father Alyn," the man said.

"I'm Alyn O'Byrne," Alyn replied, his guarded tone checking Kella's escalating anxiety for a moment.

So much had been happening that her foster brother had never explained why he'd given up the priestly tonsure. He'd been proud of it when he left for the Holy Land. Taken great delight in insisting she call him *Father.*

"I'll watch the imp," Daniel assured Alyn, taking up Fatin's leash. "And wait for the good news," he added brightly. He gave Kella a wink. "Egan's too ornery to die."

And Lorne's too sweet and gallant.

Kella clung to those sentiments as she made her way across the courtyard to the Queen's Tower and up the stairs to her private parlor. The worst wasn't possible. *If it were so, I'd know something was wrong,* she told herself as she preceded Alyn into the room where the queen stood before the low fire in the hearth. *Call it women's intuition. Call it—*

Gwenhyfar turned upon hearing Kella. Her heart-shaped face was ashen, a mirror of regret. But it was the bloodstained scarf she held in her hand that grabbed Kella's gaze and refused to let it go. It was the gift Kella had given Lorne the morning of his departure for Strighlagh. No sword was ever so sharp as the anguish that cut through Kella.

"No!" strangled in her throat. Kella doubled over, as though to protect her little one from the devastating news. But there was no saving the child from its fate as a bastard. Not now. Lorne would never have parted from that silken scarf while he drew breath. 'Twas his oath.

Somehow, under the guidance of Alyn's viselike grip, Kella stumbled to a lounging couch where Gwenhyfar often curled up against the raised arm to nap before the fire. Alyn sat beside her, pulling her into his strong arms.

"Hush, *anmchara,* hush," he cooed against her head.

Yet Kella wasn't crying. Her sobs couldn't get past the knot of rebellion forming in her chest. Lorne couldn't be dead. Wounded, *thought* dead obviously, but not dead.

"Prince Lorne's captain sent this for you," the queen said gently from somewhere just beyond the black sea trying to drown Kella. "Elkmar tried to save the prince but saw him cut down before his very eyes. Later, when our men collected the dead and wounded, the scarf was all the captain could find. Your Lorne is among the missing."

Kella seized on the word. "*Missing?*" she whispered hopefully. She clasped her hands in thanksgiving and relief. "Missing isn't dead, now, is it?" She *knew* it. Her heart would not lie.

"He'd been grievously wounded, Kella," the queen cautioned. She folded her hands over Kella's, but Kella would not have sympathy offered for no reason.

"I mean no disrespect, my queen, but the Miathi certainly wouldn't have taken his dead body with them." She wove hope into reason. Kella would not accept Lorne's death without the body. She would have a body to mourn, or she would not mourn.

"What of Egan O'Toole?" Alyn asked, so low that Kella felt the question more than heard it.

"Like Daniel said, Da's too ornery to—" Kella began.

"Missing as well," Gwenhyfar told them.

Lorne *and* Da? Kella shook her head side to side in denial, pulling out of Alyn's protective embrace. "Nay, I'll not have it!" She shot to her feet in hot defiance and paced away and back, arguing as much with her raw emotions as her companions. "Hostages, yes, but *not* dead. Not without bodies. Tribes take hostages. Arthur has hostages in his court. Many chieftains do. You were one yourself," she told Alyn. "Remember?"

Why did he look so forlornly at her? Surely it wasn't pity. There was no need for pity.

"I know they are alive," she declared, increasingly belligerent. "I know it as sure as you are sitting there, Alyn O'Byrne, so wipe that pity off your face."

She poked at him with her finger, as she had when he'd annoyed her as a child. But Kella was no longer a child. She was the daughter of a champion and betrothed to a prince, the father of her babe.

"Kella—" the queen started.

"Please, my queen." Kella faced the queen, noting her motherly countenance of concern. "Would *you* accept such a terrible loss without proof?" When Gwenhyfar hesitated, Kella continued. "I will leave with the king's entourage on the morrow for Strighlagh. I would wager we'll hear soon enough what the devils want in exchange for my father and Lorne's release." She held out her hand to Alyn. "Will you come with me?"

Alyn shot a dubious glance at Gwenhyfar, but when the queen didn't protest, he nodded. "I will go to the ends of the earth for you and Egan, Kella. Daniel will as well, I imagine."

Nothing would please Kella more, save there being no reason to go at all. 'Twould be better if she had word from her da and a note declaring Lorne's well-being and love for her. But in light of the present situation, going with her friends was more than she could hope—

"But," Alyn added, checking her excitement, "I ask that you remain safely here with the queen."

Kella stared at Alyn as if he'd lost his wits.

"I agree," Gwenhyfar said. "The men will be traveling hard for Strighlagh. Women would slow them down."

"I can ride as hard as any man, milady," Kella protested. "You know it well."

"We both can … for a while," Gwenhyfar pointed out. "And you know your way with weapons, but only in the practice yard. Anything might happen along the way. Arthur made some allies today, but he also made enemies. Besides …" The queen inhaled deeply as though she needed to fortify herself, "I need you here, Kella."

Kella reeled a step backward in disbelief. "My queen, with all due respect, you ask too much of me. Would *you* remain behind?"

Gwenhyfar lifted her head in a regal pose that some considered haughty, but her green eyes brimmed with pent-up emotion. "I *am* remaining behind, Kella. Even though my brother is also missing."

All the defiance and rage that had kept Kella afloat in the midst of this tragedy fled her. "Oh, milady, I am so sorry." She'd been so caught up in her own pain that she'd not given thought to the others. Elyan, prince of Manau, was one of Arthur's youngest captains. "But doesn't that add meat to my theory that our men might live as hostages?"

"That is why we will follow Arthur to Strighlagh," Gwenhyfar told her with a forgiving half smile. "But it is imperative that the High King get there as soon as horses will carry him."

"Who will command Carmelide in your absence?"

"Urien of Rheged."

"The Raven," Alyn murmured, drawing Kella's attention.

A scavenger who benefits from the death of others. Kella shivered.

"The Briton is ambitious," Gwenhyfar conceded, "but he is also an excellent warrior. He has the skill and troops to hold Carmelide. My greatest concern about Arthur's choice to replace Modred with Urien as his successor is the division it will cause among our Pictish allies. As a Briton *and* a Pict, Modred was the better choice to unite the kings of the north." The queen shrugged. "Alas, I am not the Dux Bellorum, and the choice is not mine to make. Nor is it my choice to remain behind while Arthur rides out on the morrow."

"Cousin, if I might be so bold?" Alyn spoke.

"Yes, you may, little cousin," Gwenhyfar added with a wisp of a smile. "Though you are not so little anymore."

Kella had to agree with the queen there. Alyn had certainly changed. There was something dark and mysterious beneath the manly facade that had replaced his former tedious nature.

"I do not have a good feeling about your leaving Carmelide," he said. "I fear for your safety as well as Kella's. The north is no place for our women until this Miathi matter is settled."

Kella watched the queen's face, hoping that the strength she admired in Gwenhyfar, the strength she'd encouraged in Kella, held. A queen and a champion's daughter were no ordinary women.

"And who shall rally the women of Gododdin? The women who have lost men the same as we?" Gwenhyfar challenged.

Alyn stiffened, then nodded, resigned. "I had not thought of that. I only sought to protect you and my foster sister. You are both dear to my heart."

"As you are dear to ours," Gwenhyfar said. "Which is why I have a request of you—one that must be carried out by someone I trust implicitly. A servant of the Grail."

Alyn's ready bow checked midpoint at the mention of the priesthood, yet he replied without hesitation, "Glenarden is at your command."

Before Kella could ponder his behavior, the queen grabbed her attention.

"Kella, have the trunk we recently packed brought here at once."

The Grail genealogies? Knocked dumb by this sudden barrage against sense and emotion, Kella dipped hastily in acknowledgment and left the room.

Always thinking, that Gwenhyfar. If Cassian suspected the forgery, 'twas hard to say what the archbishop might do. His little blackbirds were everywhere, watching her and the queen. Waiting for any sign that might suggest Gwenhyfar and Kella still clung to the old ways. And they did. But only to the traditions established by the first-century Messianic Jews, and those celebrations adapted from the old ways, which focused on thanksgiving and worship shifted from creation's gifts to the giving Creator.

Sending the books to her homeland for safekeeping by Arthur's own party was ingenious. With or without Gwenhyfar's permission, Kella fully intended to go with it—for her queen, her da, and the father of her child.

And sooner was better.

It was only Alyn and his cousin now in the queen's chamber. Kella had retreated to her own rooms, claiming the need of time to compose herself. Alyn would have gone with her but for Gwenhyfar's urgency. Besides, Kella didn't seem to want anyone's company now that her despair had turned to anger, both at the situation and not being allowed to leave with the High King.

The trunk the queen had ordered brought to her chambers contained three book boxes made of wood and covered with leather, tooled by masters long crossed over to the Other Side. The boxes now lay on a table before him. Though the records of the ancient bloodlines were sealed within the boxes, Alyn could imagine the flawless script filling each timeworn parchment. To view the genealogies would be to view art and history, evidence that God had kept His promise to David that his descendants would rule forever. Not merely until Jerusalem fell, but again once the years of Judah's rebellion against God were paid in penance.

Although, given Albion's perilous situation and perhaps even Erin's in the future, the years of penance were far from being satisfied. To be sure, Alyn would not see the end of it.

Alyn ran his finger a breath from touching the knotwork bordering the edges of the first case, which held hundred-year-old copies of Erin's originals. He'd heard of these scrolls but never dreamed he'd be in their presence, much less handed the responsibility for their safekeeping. Six centuries before the Christ, this treasure began with the marriage of Zedekiah's daughter Tamar Tephi and Eoghan, *heremon* or High King of the Milesian Celts beginning the Davidic-Irish lineage—Alyn's heritage through his father, Tarlach.

In the second case held the beginning of the apostolic bloodline of Britain, those descended from Jesus's family and followers who fled from the Holy Land to convert and marry into Albion's first-century royal families. The same bloodline that Queen Morgause

had touted to Cassian earlier in the day. Alyn's sister-by-law Brenna
was of this lineage, as were many of Britain's kings and saints.

These genealogies were continued in book three with its *arthurs*
and *merlins*. The Grail Church had made so many attempts to join
the two in the hope of producing messiah-like heirs to keep Christ's
light alive. It was oft by marriage and, where needed, by a sword such
as Arthur's.

"Your Highness …" Alyn's voice cracked beneath the burden
of emotions ranging from utter awe and joy to abject despair. The
reverent silence that filled the room caused his words, low as they
were, to reverberate. "I am not worthy. You know well that I did not
pass the Grail challenge. I could not survive even a single full circle
of the sun in the *purgatory*."

Just to say the word made Alyn shudder.

Three days was the challenge. Three days in a subterranean
funeral mound, surrounded by the long-dead turned to bone and
dust. Memory of the stench of death gripped his gorge. But it was
the close darkness that made Alyn's heart pound away the seconds
into hours. His breath haunted his ears with its roar. He could not
abide closed-in places … not since childhood, when he'd accidentally
locked himself in his mother's trunk.

The swirling whirlpool of nightmare and inadequacy threatened
to suck him under.

"Few candidates manage to spend three full days and nights in
the tomb and among the dead as Christ did," Gwenhyfar told him
gently. "Some are driven mad. As a priestess, I have ministered to
many of them, just as I did to you. And still, even those who do pass
the test fall short of our Lord's example at some time or another."

But Alyn had wanted to be the best of all priests then. A Grail-worthy priest. Triumph over such an ordeal would set him above the others as his performance at university had done. And he had failed.

"God does not give us all the same gifts, cousin," Gwenhyfar reminded him. "Yours lie in *sciencia*. It is through knowledge that you have grown closer to God."

Would that were so. A fresh wave of suffering washed over Alyn's sore heart. He had not confessed the carelessness that had led to his teacher's death. There'd been no one he trusted to hear his shame, except his friend Hassan, who'd pulled Alyn from the burning labo-ratorium. Alyn hoped he might bury the memory, if not its scar, on Alba's welcoming shore.

"I failed at *sciencia* as well," he blurted. He ran his fingers over the smooth black hair that covered his once-shorn tonsure. "And, because of that, I am no longer a priest."

If he expected his cousin, a high priestess in Albion's fading Grail Church, to recoil from him, Alyn was disappointed. Her regal demeanor softened with compassion. "We are *all* priests of God, cousin, whether we wear the tonsure and dress or nay. Unless you are telling me that God no longer is welcome in your heart, that you disown our Lord Jesus as your Savior." Her brow furrowed. "Tell me that isn't so, cousin, for I cannot believe otherwise."

Alyn shook his head. No. He could never deny the Three in One—God the Father, the Son, or the Spirit. He saw evidence of them everywhere, in everything, including the very breath he drew that moment. "It is myself that I deny. My worthiness to serve a perfect God."

Gwenhyfar floated down in cloud of silken skirts to the cushioned bench beside Alyn. She gathered his hand in hers and drew it to her lips, where she kissed it. "None of us is, dear one. Nor does God expect us to be perfect. All He expects of us is to try, and when we fail, repent and try again. It is only by trying again and again, like a warrior who practices his throw, that we better ourselves, hence moving closer to Christ's perfection."

How could a high priestess understand? Gwenhyfar had been tested and passed. She'd proved stronger than Grail warriors *and* priests. She lived a life of purity, given only to God and her husband. Alyn's ambition to gain prestige and study under a new Egyptian scholar, his rush to attend the man's lecture, had led him to be careless in storing the elements and compounds in Abdul-Alim's workshop.

Everything had a specific place and jar shape due to the master alchemist's failing eyesight. And Alyn had to have put the wrong element in the wrong container. The last thing he recalled was Abdul-Alim heating a concoction of ingredients from those containers. Then a thunderburst of flame had thrown Alyn, who was hurrying to the lecture, out of the room and into unconsciousness.

Alyn had prayed to die at first from the agony of his burns. Then from the guilt upon hearing his teacher had been killed. And the endless questions, the harshest from the man he'd hoped to study under, had riddled him with doubt about his true motivation for knowledge and excellence. A great discovery would not bring back Abdul-Alim. Had it been for God's glory or his own that Alyn had sought so fervently to succeed? The question had haunted him since.

The burn scar on his chest smoldered hot as an iron in a smithy's forge, and the sobs were razor-sharp even now as he finished purging the story from his tortured soul. His despair wracked him as the queen held him in her embrace.

Gwenhyfar murmured comforting words against his head as though he were a broken child, not a full-grown man. How oft had his brothers teased that he would never grow up? It appeared they were right in their estimation of him. *God, how can You place such responsibility on my shoulders when I've failed You and others so often? What if I fail again?*

"You are a good man, Alyn O'Byrne, born to the royal lineage that Jeremiah transplanted from Jerusalem to Erin so many years ago." Gwenhyfar placed her hand on the most ancient of the records of Davidic kings. "I have faith in you, and more in the God who sent you to me at this time of need." She rose and moved to trim the wick on a lamp, allowing him time to regain his dignity.

How could she say such a thing? It hadn't been his intention, but he'd told her everything. The venting of his grief and shame had gone well past the verge of his embarrassment.

"God uses broken vessels. You are but human," she reflected with regret. "Moses killed a man. David was a murderer and an adulterer. We are *none* perfect, save His Son."

Aye, he was all that—broken and human.

"But we *are* forgiven. And I have no doubt," she said with a gentle smile, "that you, like Jeremiah, who never thought himself up to the task at hand, will try, and that God will enable you and be with you as He was with Jeremiah, in triumph and in storm. Elsewise, we *all* might be lost."

Again, the queen seemed to drift away. Her almond-shaped eyes closed, and dark lashes fanned upon her pale cheeks. She faced the Enemy through prayer, Alyn knew. How long had it been since he had been able to do the same? Such a battle came harder when the enemy was himself.

CHAPTER FIVE

With the red dragon flying on white banners in the stiff breeze, Arthur led his mounted warband through the main gate of Stone Castle just as the sun peeked over the eastern hills, casting a golden glow on a landscape recently back to life after the Long Dark. Archbishop Cassian rode with the Dux Bellorum, a mark of the urgency, since the high priest usually traveled in the comfort of his coach. The rest of the entourage, their wagons laden with supplies, would follow in three days, escorted by the queen's troops.

About the somber column, the browns of winter gave way to a joyful myriad of greens while wildflowers burst forth in bright yellows and pastels of every shade. By the time the sun made its full claim to the sky, the riders were on the Roman road that ran north toward the old wall binding the neck of land between the Solway and the Clyde.

Riding between the front and rear guards, Alyn took note of cumulus skirts gathered tight about the feet of the ascending hills to the north. If they stayed there, the journey to Strighlagh would take a pleasant, if cool, three days. If not, the progress would be slow and cold. Wet misery would engulf king and commoner alike.

Thankfully, there would be stops along the way at night where the king might enjoy the warmth of a great hall, and his company at least the cover of stables.

With a shriek that startled Alyn from his observations, Fatin leapt from his shoulder across the space between two mounts—provided by the queen—to land in Daniel's lap.

"What do you want, mischief?" Daniel grumbled playfully. He reached in his food pouch for a pinch of bread. The monkey's dark eyes fixed on the highlander's hand until Daniel produced the treat. Grabbing it with both tiny fists, Fatin nibbled away as if it were the finest delicacy.

"You spoil him," Alyn chided. "He complained most of the night from so many treats." While Alyn spoke to the queen, Fatin, under Daniel's care, had become quite the fascination in Arthur's hall, especially among the ladies.

"Then he's too charming for his own good," Daniel observed. "Most animals have more sense than to overindulge." He touched his temple with a rueful grimace. "Unlike we humans."

Judging by the deep circles under his eyes, the highlander had clearly spent too long listening to the assembly of talented bards and partaking of the High King's heath fruit. Alyn, upon at last hearing the great Taliesen of Rheged give Merlin Emrys his due praise, had wisely taken Fatin and retired to their reserved nook, for the space in the upstairs dormer at a nearby inn could hardly be called a room. There exhaustion's balm silenced the doubts and prayers vying for his conscious thought.

Without warning, Fatin grabbed at the lead line of one of the two packhorses trailing behind Daniel and yanked, causing the horse to bob its head in annoyance. These were another courtesy of Gwenhyfar, to carry the gifts Alyn had brought from the East for his family. And the cargo even more precious hidden among them.

"Easy, laddie," Daniel warned, taking the rope from the precocious animal. Baring a toothy smile, the monkey leapt to Daniel's shoulder.

"You must admit, Fatin is more charming than that contrary badger you had back at Llantwit," Alyn said, referring to their days at the university. "No one would come into our lodge."

"Precisely," Daniel shot back. "Unlike *some*"—he cut a sidewise glance at Alyn—"who would while the night away waxing eloquent on the thoughts of men long dead, I like my sleep … and my privacy."

"You didn't seem to mind overindulging in hospitality last night."

"A good beer and rousing bardic verse make an enormous difference." Daniel snorted. "Truly, some of your colleagues could bore the dead stump of a tree."

"Not a scholarly bone in your body," Alyn teased.

"Hah! I've learned far more from nature than I did from those eye-blinding books and droning masters. And she has a far more beautiful voice." Daniel held out his arm, and Fatin bounded back to Alyn without hesitation. "I suspect your bairn needs a nap."

"Why *me?*" Alyn complained as the monkey wormed his way beneath Alyn's cloak. There Fatin squirmed and grunted until Alyn helped him settle into his sling. Alyn had never been one for pets as Hassan or Daniel were. "If it wouldn't have insulted my Arab friend, I'd never have accepted the little beast."

"So you've said. But everyone needs companionship. You're no exception," Daniel observed. "And he certainly needs a mam."

"I'm *not* his mam," Alyn protested. "Perhaps you'd like to add Fatin to your menagerie of animals."

"He's a heathen. A hearth-lover like yourself." Daniel narrowed his gaze at Alyn. "And whether you admit it or nay, you're attached to the strange little beastie."

"I'm *responsible* for him," Alyn emphasized, "but I'd gladly pass him along to a good home." Inside Alyn's cloak, the monkey heaved a huge sigh and snuggled against his chest as if to get closer than skin itself.

While Daniel fell into whistling a nondescript tune, Alyn's thoughts wandered back to his parting conversation with Gwenhyfar. The first sunlight brought out the raven-wing sheens of blue and purple in her unbound hair, but, like Daniel, her face had betrayed the weariness of a sleep-deprived night.

"Now stop trying to be so perfect," she advised, "and let God do the rest." She was right, but *she* hadn't been careless with her respon-sibilities. Not like Alyn. "Your doubts are naught but the pangs of a sore and grieving heart." ·

Alyn had not taken the trivialization of his feelings lightly. "Have *you* caused another's death by frivolous negligence?" he'd challenged.

Gwenhyfar pondered the question for so long that Alyn found himself wondering now what thoughts had so furrowed her smooth brow and stilled her tongue.

"Not yet," she'd answered at last, but more to herself than to Alyn. A pall of resignation fell over her. "Frivolity is denied one in my position. Now I wonder if it was worth it."

"It isn't," Alyn averred. He'd learned the hard way, though in his case, his sin was ambition. But wasn't all sin folly? To think, he'd wanted to be like the highly esteemed Eastern scholar, the same one who'd turned upon him, almost ready to torture Alyn for the secret to the explosion. "Death is preferable to the shame and regret paid for a moment's glory."

"Try, then repent, and try again," she snapped, her impatience equal to his. With a glance in the direction of the leather bags containing the books, hidden in the exotic bolts of fabric for his sisters-by-law, Brenna and Sorcha, she regained her composure. "God will be ever with you," she added with more calm, "but you must listen carefully."

Still, urgency infected his cousin's dark gaze as she passed along the last of his instructions. He was to deliver the packages to Mairead, a priestess who resided in the village above the base of Mount Seion near Fortingall.

It was rumored that the mountain had once been home to the ancient watermen, first-century Jewish Christians so called because of their practice of baptism. Merlin Emrys spoke in awe of the knowledge hidden within the bowels of the holy mountain, calling it Albion's Mount Moriah.

Alyn fingered the rope Gwenhyfar had given him, now tied about his waist. It was a belt, knotted in a pattern that spoke volumes to those with the ancient knowledge. The intricate knots not only vouched for the trustworthiness of the bearer but served as prayer reminders.

"This belonged to Merlin Emrys," she'd told him. "The abbess Ninian sent it to help you pass unharmed among the Picts. 'Twill take you farther than our kinship."

The frustration and intimidation that overwhelmed Alyn as he'd donned the precious token revisited him, prickling at skin and spirit. Merlin's belt!

God, You continue to heap labors upon these unworthy shoulders, when all I seek is rest and refuge.

"So go with Arthur," Gwenhyfar had instructed. "Stand for me, cousin, when I cannot." She kissed his cheek, a touch light as the brush of her heavy morning robes against his boots. "Godspeed."

Stand for me, cousin, when I cannot.

The queen's choice of words struck him odd, now that Alyn had time to think about it. She and her company would follow in just a few days, and she could speak for herself. He scowled, searching deeper into the morning's recollection. It was almost as if Gwen was preoccupied by something in the future. Something she feared she would regret.

But *what?*

When the sun peaked in the sky, the Dux Bellorum's party stopped long enough to water and rest the horses. Wildflowers and golden gorse spotted the slopes around them as though artfully planted to create a most pleasing effect. Daniel was right in saying that nature's free-growing garden was as lovely as Gwenhyfar's well-tended one.

While Alyn and Daniel took the midday meal with Arthur's companions in a sunbaked glen, grooms and squires tended their steeds in the shade along the edge of a stand of trees curbed by a babbling brook. The warriors speculated about what awaited them as they took advantage of the sun's warmth and enjoyed the brief repast.

"I'm thinkin' by the time we arrive at Strighlagh, the bulk of our missin' men'll be there to meet us," one of Arthur's warriors observed.

"Aye," agreed another. "I've known it to take weeks, even months, for a scattered army to regroup and find their way back to their home after a battle."

"'Twould be a blessing if all this fretting was worry over nothing," Archbishop Cassian pronounced solemnly. "Let us pray it is so." He lowered his head, the shaven circle on the crown of his head shining like a mirror, and crossed himself in prayer.

Alyn did as well. Old habits were hard to break. In doing so, he caught Cassian's eye. Before Alyn could extract himself from the group, the bishop made his way to where Alyn and Daniel sat.

"Greetings, good sirs," the archbishop exclaimed. "The Lord has given us a magnificent day for travel, has He not?"

"A bluebird day, sir," Daniel acknowledged politely. He rose with Alyn in respect. Fatin cautiously crawled up on the Gowrys' shoulder and returned the archbishop's curious study of him.

"I am told that you are the queen's cousin *and* a priest of the British church," Cassian said to Alyn. "Yet you do not wear the tonsure of such an educated man, nor the robes of one of God's servants."

"I do not think a certain cut of a man's hair or his clothing is necessary to distinguish a servant of our Lord," Alyn replied. "Better his example do so."

"Quite so, quite so," the archbishop agreed. "But to earn the right to wear them is a mark of honor."

"Mayhap, but I *have* relinquished that right and taken my leave of the church service. At least, for a while." He didn't know why, but Alyn felt compelled to explain himself. "Perhaps my calling in God's service lies elsewhere."

"Has the study in the East lured you away from the Truth?" Cassian asked.

Fatin moved behind Alyn's head to the opposite shoulder as though playing hide-and-seek.

"For what appears as truth may not be so," Cassian said. "Your pet appears close to a human babe, dressed as it is. Yet, for all its engaging manner, it is still a beast."

"But just as much trouble." Alyn brushed the monkey's hand aside as it reached for the wolf's-head brooch fastening his cloak in place. The glitter of the wolf's small ruby eyes was a continuous source of fascination for Fatin.

"All knowledge has its merit … but only in the hands that God has prepared to receive it," the archbishop stipulated. "Genesis is the prime example of gaining knowledge and losing God." A seemingly innocent glance from Cassian in the direction of Alyn's packhorses caused a wary prickle at the nape of Alyn's neck.

Were the books the knowledge Cassian alluded to, knowledge best left in the Roman Church's hands? Or did Alyn accept the conversation at face value?

Refusing to follow the archbishop's gaze, Alyn exclaimed, "I cannot agree with you more, Your Grace. But forgive my lack of manners. " He turned to Daniel. "I don't believe you have met my good friend Daniel of Gowrys."

"A subclan of your Glenarden, no?" the archbishop asked.

So the archbishop had made it his business to find out about Alyn and his company. Had his and the queen's parting been observed? Alyn wondered.

"Aye," Daniel affirmed. "And close enough to stand shoulder to shoulder with our O'Byrne brothers for God and Arthur."

"Then God and I are pleased." The archbishop extended his bejeweled hand for Daniel to kiss.

The only hand the highlander had ever kissed was that of a bonnie lassie. Disconcerted, Daniel cocked one brow at the archbishop, hesitating.

Fatin came to his rescue. The large glittering stones on Cassian's ring had proven far more tempting than those in Alyn's brooch. Before Alyn could choke up on the leash, Fatin abandoned his usual caution and leapt onto Cassian's arm, grabbing at the precious cluster of stones. Startled, the archbishop staggered back and shook the animal away.

"My deepest pardon, Your Worship." Alyn hauled the monkey away and folded the protesting creature into his cloak. "Not only is Fatin a beast but a sinner beyond redemption."

The ever-present flock of black-robed colleagues shadowing the archbishop rushed to his aid, but Cassian waved them away. "I am fine, I am fine." A hearty laugh softened his heretofore solemn countenance. "Perhaps the monkey needs more time in prayer and reflection."

Has Gwenhyfar misjudged this Roman? Alyn wondered, joining in the merriment.

"I shall do my best for him, Your Grace," he promised. "But as to your insinuation that *sciencia* has drawn me away from God, my answer is nay, never. I believe that the more one learns of creation, the closer one draws to the mind of the Creator."

Cassian nodded. "Well said, sir. But to learn too much, too fast … perhaps we should be certain that we are ready for such knowledge, lest it lead to harm rather than good." He quoted First Corinthians. *"For after that in the wisdom of God the world by wisdom knew not God."*

Alyn stiffened involuntarily, not at the quote, but the implication of wisdom leading to harm. Had word of Abdul-Alim's death reached the archbishop? A blinding flash and the smell of burning sulfur came to mind, still as real as it had been the day of the explosion. If Alyn had reached Carmelide from Baghdad, why not the tragic news that led to his departure?

"I thank you for your wise counsel," Alyn managed. Provided the archbishop did not equate man's wisdom with *sciencia*, for creation was a product of God's wisdom. "But for now, my only goal is to return to my homeland and reevaluate my calling."

Nearby, one of the warriors moved to the edge of the group to relieve himself. Nothing out of the ordinary, considering they were all men. But one of the groomsmen's helpers lingering nearby bolted away as if stung by one of the hornets seeking the new blossoms at the edge of the wood.

"We are few who have heard the call clearly and consistently since our first commitment," Cassian replied, drawing Alyn back to the subject at hand. "Better to deal with your doubts now than later. However, if you should wish to speak about them to me, my son, I am more than willing to hear them. I have great respect for men of *sciencia*, even though my interest lies more in the Word."

"Your offer is indeed an honor, sir. I will keep it foremost in mind." Alyn bowed his head toward the archbishop, though he watched the hasty retreat of the young groomsman from the corner of his eye until the laddie disappeared into the thick underbrush.

There was something odd about the way the lad walked. And the fact that he wore his hood drawn over his head despite the brilliance of the day.

"Did you see that young groomsman shoot into the woods like his breeches were on fire?" Daniel asked after the archbishop had taken his leave to join Arthur again. "Blue shirt, dark trousers. Had a fine leather sling tied to his belt."

"Aye. Left his food behind." Alyn searched at the spot where the lad had disappeared into the wood. "Could be sick."

"Could be a girl, the way he walked."

Alyn glanced at Daniel, startled. In no time, suspicion took root. Kella hadn't said good-bye that morning, though Alyn attributed her absence due to a night in tears causing her to oversleep. Now …

A deep chuckle rumbled from Daniel's chest.

"This is not the least bit humorous," Alyn warned. "She's clearly taken leave of her senses to directly disobey the queen."

"Have you ever known a woman to be reasonable when her mind is set on something?" Daniel asked.

And Kella was the most stubborn of the women Alyn had ever met. If her genteel sensibilities had been offended by a man relieving himself, it served her right. His lips quirked. "Yon villain was likely the first man she'd ever laid eyes upon. Still," he added, sobering, "best we find out for certain before she embarrasses—"

A shout from the commander of Arthur's guard interrupted Alyn, signaling the break was over. "With continuing weather, we'll reach Lockwoodie by nightfall," the commander informed the gathering.

Lockwoodie and a fine tavern, if Alyn recalled right. At the moment, he was more concerned with finding Kella. Hands fisted, he struck off for the trees where she had disappeared, Daniel at his heel.

By the time the men reached the edge of the wood, they were joined by a rush of riders who'd come to claim their horses. In the confusion, any hope of singling out Alyn's foster sister was lost. She, if it was Kella O'Toole, was one groom lost among dozens of others who now assisted the warriors.

"Look for someone with their hood drawn," he advised upon mounting his own steed. And if not for a drawn hood, a bound head of wheat-gold hair.

But most of the lads wore hats, and several of them had wisps of fair hair poking out from under them.

"You're here," Alyn murmured to the sea of activity surrounding him. "I know you are. And when I find you, dear *sister*, you will pay."

It wasn't the first time Kella had disregarded his wishes ... his *plea*. But this time the single-minded young woman had gone too far. Kella had disobeyed her queen.

chapter six

Men were a vulgar lot, whether common or noble born. Lips thinned in disgust, Kella walked away from the stables at Lockwoodie tavern, wondering how long it would take for her companions to settle in sleep. In the tavern or stable, warrior or groomsman, they bragged about their exploits with women in detestable detail. Kella had chewed her tongue bloody to keep from reminding them that their mothers and sisters would be mortified to hear their words.

And, without the slightest warning, not one of them, the Dux Bellorum included, had any compunction about exposing himself to his fellows for nature's call. There had been a contest, for heaven's sake! At least Cassian and his priests had shown some decorum in remaining apart from the worst, but Kella avoided their company—and Alyn's—for fear of being recognized.

Truth was, she was exhausted. And filthy. She smelled like the horses she'd rubbed down after Arthur and his warriors went into the tavern. Muscles she didn't know existed ached mercilessly. The queen had been right in pointing out that Kella was not accustomed to riding sunup to sundown.

But Kella had done it, the same as Maeve, a warrior queen of legend who not only rode with her army while with child but fought as well. Kella had ridden with the servants on shaggy ponies following the warhorses in their dust, although the resulting grit had nearly been jarred from her teeth at times. Claiming to be assigned to tend to the supply ponies attached to Cassian's flock, she had blended in with the lads who had been hastily assembled for that service.

Only two more days, she consoled herself, making her way around the rear of the tavern to the kitchen a short distance away. A concoction of oak bark tea would do wonders to relieve the aches plaguing her body. And, mayhap, she might get an idea if the revelry inside was winding down.

Father, please make the High King as weary and sore as I. Aside from the cook and a young, greasy-haired helper, there were two other women in the back. Likely the innkeeper's wife and daughter, if Kella judged rightly. This authoritative twosome continually ran platters of food from the smoky kitchen to the great room inside where Arthur and his battle companions dined. As fast as the women disappeared, they reappeared with empty dishes.

"Here now," the cook shouted when Kella knocked timidly at the open door. A stout and intimidating soul, she was almost as wide as she was tall. "We sent plenty food to the stables for the servants. Plenty."

Kella took in the filthy apron stretched across the cook's belly. Though the scent of roasting meat over a fire had almost tempted her, second thought demanded tea and only tea for her distress. Shelves of jars and boxes, as well as dried herbs hanging from the beams overhead, held promise. "Beggin' your pardon, mistress, but I've a copper piece for a cup of oak bark tea. If you have it, that is, mistress."

The cook's dark eyes gleamed over round, heat-ruddied cheeks. She snatched the coin from Kella's hand. "Yer head plaguin' ye, laddie?"

"Aye." *And every other part of me*, Kella thought. "I'd be much obliged to you."

The cook cut a sidewise glance at her soot-smeared helper and sniffed. "Seein's how 'e's such a mannerly laddie, see to it," she ordered. The copper piece she stuck down in her bosom.

"Looks like the king and his company know how to revel proper," Kella observed while the helper pulled an iron kettle of water, which hung from a swing-arm bracket mounted in the stone hearth, out from over the fire.

"The mistress says she's lookin' for an early night once't their bellies are filled," the cook replied.

Kella sank against the jamb in relief. A moment later the helper came with the water and tea. "Here ye go," the girl said, dropping a clump of tea leaves into Kella's tin cup. Once Kella wrapped the cup in the excess of her sleeves, the girl carefully filled it with the steaming water.

"Best ye take it and be off afore the mistress comes back," the cook told her.

Probably because the big woman didn't want her employer to know she was taking coin on the side.

Grateful, Kella hastened away with a whispered "Bless ye, mistress."

Oh, for a hot bath and a soft bed, she thought as she made her way toward a thicket near the still, sparkling loch. Perhaps there she might drink in peace and wait for the men to bed down. Steam from the cup carried the scent of the brewing tea, warming Kella's nostrils. She could almost feel the relief it promised. Settling with a clump of birch to her back, she closed her eyes and took a sip.

It was hot and bitter without honey to make it more palatable, but she hadn't thought to test her good fortune further and ask for sweetening. Determined, Kella alternately blew on its surface and sipped what was cooled.

Not for the first time that day, Kella thought about Gwenhyfar. Would the queen ever forgive her for directly disobeying her command? Kella had written a letter pouring out her heart to Gwenhyfar and left it on her bed in the predawn hours. It told how she couldn't bear the torture of three extra days not knowing if her father and the man she loved were truly gone or, as she felt in her heart, making their way home even as she rode to meet them. Whatever Gwenhyfar decided as punishment for disobedience, no fate was worse than this torture of waiting.

Father, I know well that I have not been faithful to Your commandments. I know I've doubted You and Your love. But I am begging You, if not for mine, for the bairn's sake, let Lorne live. And Da, she added with a pang of guilt for putting her father last.

A sob worked its way up in her chest, tearing at her conscience and her heart. She could not choose between the two with love for each so firmly entrenched. They were a part of her, as was Lorne's child. And just as Lorne had to live for the babe, so she had to be strong for it.

Kella knocked the tears away from her cheek with the back of her hand and resolutely downed the last sip of the tea. The bark grounds that had settled at the bottom of the cup hung in her throat, the bitterness gagging and racking her with an involuntary shudder. Strangling out an unladylike oath, Kella lurched forward on her knees toward the lake water to wash out her mouth.

The dead saints' toes she swore by never tasted so foul, though whether 'twas the bark or the water, Kella couldn't determined. She cupped water to her lips and spat it out again and again until the grounds were clear of her teeth and tongue. With a miserable groan, she sank back on her calves and wiped water from the front of her tunic. 'Twas hard to say which hurt most now—her head, her heart, or her body.

She pressed her temples between her fingers. Her hair, which had been tamed in a braid and concealed under her cap, had come unbound. Its wet ends dripped on her shirt. She grabbed at her head in alarm. The hat was gone.

No! Kella frantically dipped for it at the water's edge. Surely it had fallen when—

"Looking for this, *milady*?"

Bolting upright on her knees, Kella looked up at the owner of the deep, questioning voice. He stood tall, shoulders squared against the moonlight at his back, too solid to be a ghost and smelling of horse and leather. But she couldn't make out his face. Ever so easily, she slid her hand toward the dagger in her belt.

"What in that devilish mind of yours could you possibly be thinking, Kella?" The familiarity of the reprimand was all that saved Alyn O'Byrne from the sting of her blade as he reached down beneath her arms and scooped her to her feet.

Kella foundered from a wave of dizziness at rising too fast and shock at being found out so soon. She'd been so careful to keep to herself. However did he—

"What do I do with you?" he chided. "You're too grown to spank, and I was taught not to knock sense into a woman, no matter how much she needs it."

Although part of her was panicked, relief took the reins of her emotions. Relief that she was no longer alone in this world of swearing, spitting—and worse—ruffians. Yes, her body ached. Her head throbbed. Her heart had been rent in two. And she was now wet and trembling from cold. But she was no longer alone.

"H-hold me," she stammered, stepping into a tentative embrace. She wished away the tears that sprang from her eyes, running salty down her face, but if wishes worked, she would not feel so lost and hopeless. Pressing her face against Alyn's tunic, she soaked up the warmth and support she so desperately needed.

"I am undone," she cried, "and I've no one—"

"You have *me*, Kella." Alyn enveloped her in his woolen cloak. The hands that had bruised her arms as he dragged her impatiently to her feet now pressed her against him. She felt the brush of his lips across the top of her head.

"Hush, *ma chroi*."

My heart. Da used to call her that … and hold her just so when her world turned against her.

"As much as I want to shake you until your pretty eyes roll in that fey head of yours," he confessed, "I cannot bear to see you cry."

Kella tried to steel herself with a shaky breath against the fatigue and helplessness overwhelming her. Aye, she wanted Alyn's support, but not because of these dreadful tears. Da had warned her against becoming one of those women who used tears to manipulate men. "*Take yer stand and say what ye mean*," Egan had told her.

But her reinforcing breath emerged as another weak-kneed sob. She fisted Alyn's tunic in her hands as if that might stem this shameful display of emotion. The muster at resolve didn't help, but the way he stiffened did.

"Easy, lassie, I've wounds not yet healed."

Kella backed away in the loose cocoon of his arms. "W-what?" What was he talking about? "Wounds, you say?" As whole and handsome as her foster brother appeared, never once did it occur to Kella that he might be injured.

"An accident in the East," he explained. "Nothing to worry about." He brushed her hair away from her face with his fingers. "You, on the other hand, are more worry than ten thousand accidents. I shudder to think of the trouble you will face."

"But I—" And *now* she had the hiccups. "I'm n-not sorry."

"Hah!" Alyn laughed. "Now *that* doesn't come as a surprise. Clearly you intend to vex us all."

"You don't … *hic* … understand," Kella blurted. And she dared not tell him. "None of you do." How oft had he warned her that the frivolous life at court had led many a foolish maid to dire circumstance?

"Oh, I think I do," Alyn replied with a tinge of wryness. "Patience was never one of your virtues. You are Egan's daughter, through and through."

At the mention of her father, she almost smiled. "I take that as a compliment—" She hesitated. "S-sir."

She'd meant to say *brother*, but there was something different about Alyn. First, there was that unexpected kiss in the garden, and now the feeling kindled again—something that seemed to sever old ties, yet draw them together at the same time. Just as Kella was about to pull away, Alyn released her.

"Daniel and I had a devil of a time finding you," he scolded, not without a hint of admiration. "You blended in well with the servants."

Kella crossed her arms over her chest, where the absence of his warmth left her cold and exposed. "I thought I'd done well enough to make Da proud, though not at the moment." She sniffed. She wiped her eyes again. "I swear, I can't seem to help myself." She stomped her foot in frustration and stared ice-hard across the lake, determined to stay the weeping.

Alyn moved to her side, respecting the distance she'd placed between them. Now she could see his face. The boyishly handsome features that had women, young and old, fawning over him were marked with concern and were sharper now, more rugged. How the ladies had mourned his decision to take up the impoverished life of a priest.

"You fear having lost the two people who matter most in the world to you. The queen will take that into consideration, I'm sure," he speculated, handing her the missing cap. "Though the weather may not be so sympathetic," he added, cocking his head toward the darkness creeping along the northern skirts of the sky.

"And you?" she asked. "Do you forgive me?"

"Already done … *Babel-Lips.*"

Kella laughed at the nickname she'd borne since childhood.

"Who knew I'd be a master of languages when you and your brothers gave me that name?"

"Given your ceaseless chatter as a babe, we should have been able to guess that one language would not hold enough words for you." Alyn shrugged off his cloak and draped it over her shoulders.

"My *babbling* has served me well, I think," she shot back, drawing the warm black, gray, and red plaid about her. There was something beyond horse and leather in its scent.

Alyn gathered up her unraveled braid and tried restoring it. "Best you keep this tucked down your back," he advised. "Though I don't see your ribbon."

She caught another whiff of his scent. A woodsy spice, most likely in some exotic soap Alyn had brought back from the Holy Land. Manly, to be sure.

"What?" she asked, when he hefted his brow at her.

"Have you another ribbon?" he reminded her.

She grappled for the hat she'd stuffed in her belt, but the strip of leather she'd used to bind her hair wasn't there. She started to drop to her knees to search the ground, but Alyn caught her.

"Never mind. You can use this." He tugged the lacing from his shirt with one hand and bound the haphazardly woven braid before stuffing it down the neck of her tunic. "From now on," he grumbled, "you travel only with Daniel and me...."

"Thank you," Kella averred in relief. They at least were gentlemen.

"As our servant, of course."

Kella stiffened. "O-of course."

"You'll heed what we say, as a proper servant should?"

Kella nodded as Alyn put his hand to her back, urging her back toward the warm, inviting inn. *Within reason.*

"You'll sleep with the horses, naturally, but one of us will be there with you, guarding our belongings."

"Fine," she agreed in a flare of disappointment. The vision of sharing a pallet on the floor with her civilized friends, warmed by a hearth fire, vanished. Oh well. At least one of them would keep her company in the cool, damp stable. Someone she trusted. That made her better off than before.

The tavern showed signs of the royal party settling down for the night. The window had darkened with the dousing of most of its lights. Daniel stood with crossed arms beneath a lantern when Kella and Alyn reached the stables.

"I see you found our wayward waif," he drawled, his brow hiked with a smugness that made her feel like a recalcitrant child.

"Aye, *he*," Alyn emphasized for any ears that might lean their way, "wandered off to the lake instead of keeping watch on the horses like we paid him to." He gave Kella a shove, causing her to stumble, but not so hard that she couldn't catch herself. "Seems we'll have to take turns keeping an eye on *him* as much as on the goods and horses. You take tonight. I've had enough nose-wiping."

Nose-wiping! Kella cut her gaze at Alyn. Gone was the tender heart and in its place a taste for revenge.

"Weaned from his mam too soon, eh?" Daniel teased.

Playful revenge, but just as insulting.

"Seems so. But he's all yours now," Alyn announced. "I'm off to join the king's company for a *toasty* night's sleep near the hearth."

With a mischievous wink, Alyn wrapped his cloak around him

and headed toward the inn. *That* Alyn she knew well. "What goes around, comes around," she mumbled under her breath.

"Aye," Daniel agreed, "and your round's coming. You're lucky he didn't strangle ye, the way he fumed on the way here."

Daniel tossed a length of wool from off his shoulder at her. Upon catching it, Kella recognized her cloak. Alyn hadn't been the only one searching for her.

She gasped. "How did you know it was mine?"

He pointed to his nose. "Carried the scent of lavender water. And what other man among us would leave all their earthly belongings unattended, except one used to havin' his things guarded and picked up behind him?"

Which explained why Daniel remained close to Alyn's things while Alyn had looked for her. So much for her smugness over how well she'd played the part of a groomsman. Kella hadn't thought about the lavender scent her clothing was rinsed in, or her perfume. As for leaving her things behind, all she could think of was easing her aches and pains and finding a place away from her coarse traveling companions.

"Come along. I'll show you where your bed's made up." He led her to a spot in the darkness under the shed roof where their horses were tethered, though how he could see eluded her. In the dark, all the horses along that side of the barn looked the same. "I made us a fine mattress of fresh hay, so go on and settle yourself."

Us. Kella's conscience checked her step. This was entirely inappropriate, though now was hardly the time to start considering such things.

"Thank you, sir," she managed. Besides, though she'd only known Daniel for the last eight or so years, she was fond of the rough highlander … though he was more tolerable when he bothered to bathe.

"Meanwhile, I'll be havin' another mug before settlin' down for the evenin'." Daniel caught her arm as she started into the niche he'd made. "Stay close and keep your dagger handy," he warned, "in case someone gets nosy."

Disbelief strained Kella's eyes wide as she realized the import of his words. Surely Alyn hadn't left one of Alba's greatest treasures *in a barn*!

"But I'll be close, so don't be wandering off again," Daniel warned in a louder voice. "Next time, we'll not be as understandin'," he added as he strode purposefully toward the fire and a barrel of beer that had been put out for the servants.

Kella breathed a sigh of relief upon realizing Daniel only meant to fetch his mug there and not the tavern. Once her eyes adjusted to the dark, she could make out a cozy spot piled high with straw, nestled between the horses. Alyn's *goods* were stacked at its head against a plank bulkhead that ran the length of the structure, dividing the space in two. Daniel had also moved her smaller Galloway pony next to his and Alyn's.

Feeling safe for the first time since leaving Stone Castle, Kella curled up in the generous length of her plain brown traveling cloak and wriggled until the hay conformed to her body. It was dusty and prickly, but not as bad as she'd imagined … once she'd moved the sword Daniel had hidden beneath it.

Closing her eyes, Kella conjured the vision of Lorne's laughing face, those sparkling pale-blue eyes and his mane of white-blond hair. Sitting atop his prancing bay stallion, he'd blown her a kiss as he rode off for Strighlagh.

She clasped her hand to her constricting heart. *Oh, Lorne, you cannot be dead. Not while my heart still yearns so strongly for you.*

"I will do what it takes to find you, beloved." She clasped the fine brooch that Lorne had given her, now hidden beneath her tunic. "I promise."

CHAPTER SEVEN

Alyn awoke well before dawn, soaked in perspiration. Above the snoring of his fellow guests, the faint voices of the women preparing the morning breakfast met his thundering ears. A dream had stolen rest from his slumber. Kella had married in Strighlagh, but she'd been most reluctant. And he'd been equally unenthused to conduct the ceremony for the faceless groom.

Pure nonsense, he told himself as he carefully took Fatin from his cage. The morning fog nearly hid the barn from view as Alyn closed the inn door behind him and shivered in the cold mist surrounding him. Hoisting the monkey onto his shoulder, he strode past a huge stack of firewood and some storage sheds. Near the barn, the early mist thinned enough for Alyn to see a familiar figure in the red and green plaid of the Gowrys, sitting by an inviting fire.

The permanent stone ring about it had been laid for the servants in the barn to warm themselves upon rising. Already the rough-hewn board set near it contained platters of bread and cheese, while porridge warmed on a trammel over the coals.

When Daniel lifted his head and waved, Alyn nearly stumbled.

The highlander's black hair was combed and freshly braided. And he'd shaved the beard that had started upon his leaving Glenarden the week before.

Alyn sat down next to him, allowing Fatin to leap from his shoulder and scamper up a hazel sapling. The monkey was prone to mischief but not to venturing too far from familiar faces.

"Well now." Alyn leaned over and sniffed the neat folds of the highlander's dress cloak. "Aren't *we* looking and smelling lovely?"

Daniel grinned sheepishly. "Hard to say, given the deed was done in the dark last night."

"Looks more like a knife fight." Alyn eyed numerous nicks where the blade had come too close.

Self-conscious, Daniel rubbed his fingers over his jaw. "Aye, and it feels like the other man won. But I was beginnin' to offend myself, and my mam raised me better than to keep mixed company in such a state."

Alyn grimaced. "Too bad. Part of me wants to make this as uncomfortable as possible for the rebellious little twit." He glanced over toward the shelter where Kella still slept.

"She did have a bit of a scare," Daniel informed him. "One of the groomsmen had more drink than he could manage and wandered into our niche while I was shaving. Before I could even get there, he came out like he'd run into a wildcat, all three of his eyes bugged out of his skull."

"Three?" Alyn challenged.

Daniel shrugged. "Some kind of tattoo or dark patch on his forehead. I don't think he meant any harm, but Kella emerged with her dagger brandished and snarling in bad humor."

The image Daniel painted made Alyn laugh, though it didn't take the edge off his irritation over her reckless scheme to go with them. "Good. Maybe it'll scare some sense into her."

"She made a hasty decision, same as you or me would, if we were in her position." Daniel's defense of Kella set Alyn back on his heels. "In fact," the Gowrys prince reflected, "we *are* in a like situation. Woe to the man who'd try to keep us from Strighlagh. Egan's like a da to us both."

"*We* are not women riding without proper escort," Alyn reminded him. "*We* didn't disobey the queen."

"Aye, and we're not with child, either," Daniel added, the gravity of his remark thinning his lips.

Alyn shot a look of disbelief at his companion. "What did you say?" They'd been speaking lowly. Surely he'd misheard.

"She talks in her sleep," Daniel explained. "So either the lady is with child, or she dreamed about it. But the way she huddled up to me last night—"

Alyn put his hands over his ears. He didn't want to hear it or envision Kella in *any* man's arms. She was his little …

She was a woman he cared for … deeply. One he'd not see hurt for the world. If this Lorne of Errol had seduced Kella, much less gotten her with child—

"A dream." Alyn seized on the idea. "That must be it."

"Like as not." Daniel leaned back from the fire as the smoke shifted toward him. "And it *was* a cold night out here." He went on with his tongue-in-cheek tone. "Though she's more than bonnie to any man's eye …"

Daniel's probing struck a nerve.

"Like *yours?*" Alyn tried to shake the inexplicable prick of betrayal, but he couldn't. "You *did* bathe and shave, cold and dark as the night was." Alyn trusted Daniel, of all the men he knew, like a brother. "Faith, a plaintive roll of those hazel eyes, and you've turned a preening peacock."

Daniel's gaze steeled above the set of his smile. "I was being polite," he replied as crisply as the air misting his breath. "Kella's too full of high ideas to my liking. Like you, she'll be book-blind and quill-cramped before her youth runs out." Without warning, he heaved himself to his feet and stepped away. "I'd move, if I were you."

Alyn followed his friend's gaze to the limb overhead, where Fatin let loose with a stream of urine. "That cursed beast—" Alyn scrambled away in the nick of time, while the monkey babbled in delight at the resulting sizzle on the hot stones that had been at their feet.

Equally amused, Daniel clapped Alyn on the shoulder. "Seems Fatin has learned a trick or two since riding with the Dux Bellorum's warband. Methinks he needs a sword to complete his attire."

Alyn ignored him. "Get down here, you poor use of good breath!"

Well aware of what Alyn wanted, the incorrigible Fatin clapped his small hands over his ears and looked anywhere but at his master.

"You've a way with beasts." Alyn turned to Daniel. "Do me the kindness of taking him for a jaunt down by the river. He'll not come to me when I'm riled at him."

Perhaps the imp would take a dive into the spring runoff of snow-chilled waters.

"But leash him," Alyn added on guilt-ridden second thought. "He's liable to test the waters and freeze his tiny"—years of priestly training edited his thought—"*bottom.*"

"I've need enough for a private jaunt," Daniel agreed. He held up thick arms banded with tattooed knotwork, almost reaching the limb where the monkey eyed him suspiciously. "Come along, laddie. I'll show ye what a *real* man can do."

Intrigued by the leather-bound braids that hung to either side of the man's head, Fatin jumped into Daniel's waiting embrace, but his large dark eyes followed Alyn's hand as he gave Daniel the leash from his belt. In a heartbeat, Daniel had fastened it to Fatin's collar. Not the least disturbed, the monkey held a braid in one hand and pointed to the large tree limbs overhead, chattering away with Daniel mimicking him—perfecting yet another animal call.

His thoughts and feelings simmering like the porridge before him, Alyn squatted on a length of log placed near the fire for warmth. *With child.*

The notion refused to set right in his head. Granted, strapping warriors had turned Kella's head when she first returned from her aunt's convent in Erin. Alyn had warned her of such things time and again, much to her vexation. But Kella seemed much more mature now than then. Smart enough to become the queen's trusted scribe instead of marrying for muscle and money.

More likely, after a long, hard day, she'd been like Alyn, too weary to sleep. And when she had, bizarre dreams assailed her that made no more sense than his had. Alyn rubbed his head, sore from the tossing-and-turning thoughts. But if Kella O'Toole slept anywhere between here and Strighlagh, it would be within his sight from now on. He owed that much to Egan.

He shoved to his feet. Best he speak *now* with the High King about their uninvited guest. It wouldn't behoove either of them to make Arthur look the fool. His reputation for fierceness on the battlefield was exceeded only by that of his pride.

⌘

Movement inside the tavern was brisk now that its patrons had been stirred from their slumber by the smell of freshly baked breads and mulled cider. Arthur sat on benches with Angus of Strighlagh and the archbishop near the warming fire in the middle of the room. The rest of the men were gathered in private clusters about the few boards that had been set up along the walls, though they were not so loud as they'd been the night before.

Ever gracious to the O'Byrnes, Arthur motioned Alyn into their tight circle the minute it was clear that he wanted an audience. Besides Alyn's maternal relationship to the queen, his late father, Tarlach, had been one of Arthur's most decorated captains, while his brother, Caden O'Byrne, had saved the High King's life on the Byrneich and Bernician border.

With more and more men readying to leave, Alyn cut to the problem at hand. Arthur would know soon enough that a lady had traveled with his warband unbeknownst to him. He advised the High King now rather than allow him to be embarrassed later.

"She did not expect special treatment for fear of slowing the Dux Bellorum's progress," Alyn continued. "Which she has not."

"Or …," Cassian countered, "she did not want Arthur to leave her behind as he would have done."

And rightly so. That is exactly what Arthur would have done and why Kella chose her disguise.

"To allow her to proceed is to reward her deceit, Your Highness." The archbishop cocked his head to the side at Alyn as if in challenge.

"Or to show consideration of her immense distress at not knowing if her father and the man she hopes to marry are alive," Alyn countered. "Every man among us is anxious to find out if those who are reported missing have returned hence."

"She disobeyed your queen," Cassian insisted. "Had a *man* disobeyed, milord, you would have him punished."

"But she is not a man. She is a grief-stricken woman," Alyn argued.

"Yet she struts about Carmelide with the queen, both of the notion that they are the equals of men." Cassian's chest swelled with righteous indignation. "If she wants equal consideration, she should have equal punishment."

"Her grief-stricken decision was ill-made, milord, but it was not betrayal." Alyn wondered what women had done that had generated such anger in the archbishop. Was it all women? Or only Kella and Gwenhyfar?

"*Betrayal?*" Arthur bellowed. The sudden change in his humor silenced the room. "Were it betrayal, woman or man would suffer the worse." The attention he drew withered as his fiery gaze circled the room, wandering from face to face. "A terrible example would be made," he promised. "Do you hear me? Terrible!"

His vehemence robbed Alyn of speech. That one word had flushed the High King's battle-scarred visage with white rage. But surely Arthur didn't think Kella …

Modred.

Alyn let out his breath, relieved only slightly. Of course Modred's absence at court bore heavily on Arthur's mind, although Alyn prayed a brief bout with wounded pride was at the bottom of it and that it had naught to do with this same Arthur slaying Modred's father for treachery years before.

"I suggest no terrible example, my lord king," Cassian said warily, steering the king's attention back to the present matter. "Nor do we speak of betrayal."

Arthur's nostrils flared as he drew long breaths to cool the fire so inadvertently lit.

"I suggest simply a matter of justice suited to Lady Kella's small transgression. As your counselor," the archbishop said, encouraged by the effort, "I recommend you send a detail of your men back to Carmelide with her and allow your wife to punish her as she sees fit." The archbishop crossed his arms as if the matter were settled, but the tension on his face evidenced that he, too, had clearly been taken aback by Arthur's outburst.

"You know my cousin Gwenhyfar well, milord. She would understand Kella's heart, which she knows to be loyal and filled with love for her family, the queen among them." At least Alyn prayed for Kella's sake that Gwenhyfar would forgive. As for Arthur, at the moment Alyn didn't know what to think of the warlord's state of mind, except that it was severely tested.

"My lord," Alyn pleaded, "surely compassion is the only justice suited to a poor soul so overwhelmed with shock and grief that she is not thinking clearly. You recall that it was Christ Himself, a King of Kings, who said from the cross, '*Father, forgive them; for they know not what they do.*' Clearly, Kella does not know what she has done in her grief."

"If Christ had the armies of Albion to unite, He'd find Himself on a cross once again," Arthur grumbled to no one in particular. He closed sad eyes, shoulders sinking as if the weight of Albion rested upon them.

The irreverence—and the High King's temporary blindness—set off a rash of making the sign of the cross among the clergy. Alyn had no need, for the burn on his chest, branded by the crucifix he'd worn on the day of the accident, stirred of its own accord. It was an affirmation. He'd thought much the same during the confrontation at the court. Albion needed miracles.

"*Glorify Me.*"

As sure as Alyn drew breath, he knew that Arthur needed the Word to bring him back from wherever his worried soul had taken him.

Overwhelmed by the urge to seek that troubled soul, Alyn placed his hand on the king's brow and prayed, "As I ask for your compassion and understanding for the Lady Kella, milord ..." This was madness. Alyn was surrounded by holy men of greater rank than he. Men who were not failures. "I ask of our Lord Jesus the same in the days ahead for you, Arthur, Grail-chosen High King. '*For God hath not given us the spirit of fear; but of power, and of love*' ... love, my lord,*"* he reiterated, "'*and of a sound mind.*'"

Second Timothy hadn't been on Alyn's mind, but those were the words that rolled off his tongue.

Second thought bombarded him. Would the suggestion of fear enrage Arthur?

Had God put it Alyn's mind? Of late, *someone* had been inserting unbidden direction in there.

Or was he losing his mind because of the accident?

A disdainful harrumph from the archbishop suggested Alyn had overstepped his bounds. Arthur's eyelids fluttered, but he seemed still engaged elsewhere, in a battle of the mind. Alyn felt his brow crease and flinch with the blows suffered from within.

One particularly significant jerk of Arthur's sword arm sent a startled Archbishop Cassian almost hopping a distance away from the High King and Alyn.

As though they were equally possessed.

ChAPTER EIGHT

Perhaps Arthur *was* possessed. Men in the room drew away, yet were unable to keep from watching. Even the pagans fingered their talismans.

Alyn sensed the suffering Dux Bellorum was surrounded by enemies, at least in his mind. But he was also surrounded by priests of God.

Placing a hand on either side of Arthur's temple, though he was well aware the king's sword hung within easy reach, Alyn looked past the suffering man and mouthed the word *pray.* The gesture thawed the robed flock from their shock, but none drew near Arthur. Instead they fell to their knees at a distance, signing the cross.

"Father God …" Alyn's plea faltered. Were his feet not riveted to the spot, he might have run. Scriptural words of comfort he'd memorized stampeded his brain, but coherence eluded him.

Then a surge of warmth from the scar on his chest powered through his arms, so hot that he nearly withdrew his hands. "In the name of Jesus," he said, "I pray against the enemy who torments your mind and fills you with dread, Arthur of Dalraida, for you are not alone in this battle."

The Word came, short but powerful. *"For I am persuaded, that neither death, nor life, nor angels, nor principalities, nor powers, nor things present, nor things to come, nor height, nor depth, nor any other creature, shall be able to separate us from the love of God, which is in Christ Jesus our Lord."*

Alyn's "amen" cut off the spiritual tide like the tap on a wine barrel. His hands fell away from Arthur, and he stumbled backward as though released from a powerful magnetic force. About him, an intense tension—and fear—infected everyone in the room. In the silence, Alyn could hear his own pulse beating in his ears.

Arthur sat, eyes closed, as if an effigy of stone.

Having put forth every effort at his disposal, Alyn knelt before the High King and spoke his heart. "Give into my care the Lady Kella, as Jesus Christ in His hour of torment gave His grief-stricken mother to John. Kella will remain disguised as my servant so that her presence will cause no stir among the men...."

Arthur's eyes flew open so suddenly that one among the priests gasped. Crystal-blue and penetrating, his gaze dropped to Alyn's. "There are dark places in a man's mind," he said, so low that only those closest heard. "Places where even God does not go. Yet ..." Puzzlement grazed his golden brow. He reached forward and fingered Alyn's belt. "You did, Merlin."

Merlin?

Cassian's gasp affirmed the High King's delusion.

Alyn attempted to cover it. "Aye, milord, 'tis Merlin Emrys's belt, an honor given to me by your queen." He gently removed Arthur's hand. "But 'twas not me, nor Merlin, who comforted you, milord, but the Holy Spirit."

It had to be, else Alyn would have been as dumbstruck as the rest in the room. Yet what he had seen ... not with his eyes—

"Indeed, yes," Cassian spoke up. "For we *all* prayed God's intervention for the spell that assaulted you so vicious and sudden."

No wonder Arthur trembled. The eagle tangled with the red dragon over a sea of blood. Not even angels, if indeed that is what the white birds were, could separate them, much less keep them from plunging into the red tide.

Birds, wings, blood ... that is what Alyn saw as he'd prayed over the High King. He needed to get home to Glenarden, to Brenna. His sister-in-law could surely heal this madness.

"I thank you." Arthur clasped Alyn's arm with the strength needed to wield Excalibur. "I thank you, Father Alyn."

Rather than correct the High King, Alyn bowed and stepped away as Arthur rose to his considerable height on steady feet. With a wave of his arm to encompass the still-wary brethren, he announced, "Thanks be to *all* of you." He arched, stretching his shoulders and back, and rolled his head first to one side then the other before motioning Alyn closer.

"I admit to being as anxious as Lady Kella to find out the extent of damage to the fortress and those who defended it," he whispered as Alyn leaned in.

"I assure you, milord, that my companion and I will see to her safety and sequester her from the rest of your men as is only proper. With your permission, of course."

"Granted."

Ignoring Cassian's scowl of disapproval, Arthur glanced about at the gathering of men still watching him as if ready to break and run.

With a hearty laugh, he returned to himself and clapped his hands on his stomach. "By the Virgin," he bellowed, "I pray no one else ate the sweetmeats last eve, for they set my belly to conjuring nightmares."

"Musta come from a bullock taken before knowin' his first cow," one of the young warriors remarked, taking up the effort to restore the normal humor.

Another, more seasoned fellow whacked the youth across the back of the head. "Ye simpleton, sweetbreads is the beastie's innards, not his *outards*," he bawled with a bawdy cup of his hands and thrust of his hips.

Guffaws of amusement erupted around the room, and the disquiet over their leader's behavior vanished. Arthur rounded up his captains and led them outside, the others rapidly following, save Angus.

The king of Strighlagh pulled Alyn aside as the younger man gathered his belongings. "What make you of *that*?"

Alyn didn't have to guess what *that* was. He was still shaken by the unfolding of the strange occurrence. "I think Arthur is greatly troubled by Modred's seeming withdrawal of support. Coupled with too much hard riding and too little rest, and the mind plays tricks on itself. Even my night was unsettling," he admitted.

Angus considered for a moment. "Aye," he agreed, "I have only to account for my loyalty and that of my men. The Dux Bellorum must rely on the loyalty of a shifty lot, if there ever was one." He gave Alyn a clap on the back. "Good to have you home, Father."

Alyn winced within at the undeserved title but replied, "Thank you, sir. It is good to be home." The title *Father* would not abandon him, no matter how Alyn strove to disown it.

Suspicion toward Alyn seemed to seethe in Cassian's gaze as the archbishop waited by the door until the Angus left with his attendants. Then Cassian caught Alyn's arm as Alyn followed them outside.

"A brief word, *Father*."

The innuendo in his tone confirmed Alyn's intuition that Cassian now considered him an enemy, if not a fraud. But if the archbishop sought explanation, there was none save what he'd told Arthur. The Holy Spirit had used him … and all the other clergy there.

Cassian kept his voice low. "I will be watching you closely, young man. I have never seen the High King lapse into such a trance."

Nor had Alyn. But it certainly wasn't *his* doing. Cassian would have been welcome to take authority at any time, but he hadn't. Annoyed, Alyn brushed the bejeweled hand away from him.

"And I pray, Your Grace, that God is watching *all* of us."

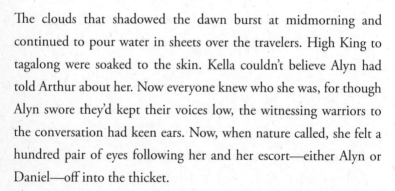

The clouds that shadowed the dawn burst at midmorning and continued to pour water in sheets over the travelers. High King to tagalong were soaked to the skin. Kella couldn't believe Alyn had told Arthur about her. Now everyone knew who she was, for though Alyn swore they'd kept their voices low, the witnessing warriors to the conversation had keen ears. Now, when nature called, she felt a hundred pair of eyes following her and her escort—either Alyn or Daniel—off into the thicket.

In spite of her isolation, talk wafted down the line of the spell Arthur suffered that morning and how Alyn had prayed him through it. She and Daniel longed to question Alyn about it, but he was as closemouthed as a clam bound for the pot.

Not for the first time since Alyn returned from the East, Kella wondered at the change in him and the accident that had turned his outgoing personality inward, where it simmered with mystery. Had he really summoned spirits in front of priests? And that kiss … When had her longtime friend acquired such a fierce passion?

What had not changed was his compassion. Last night, he'd offered it just when she needed it most.

Maybe God *had* answered her prayers for help. With a priest. A special one. Maybe God had forgiven her. The revelation caused a gurgle of hope in her throat. Uplifted for the first time since hearing the dreadful news from Strighlagh, Kella squeezed her eyes tight.

Father, thank You for sending Alyn home to help me find the man I love.

"Are you well?" Alyn cut his gaze sidewise, drawn from a long silence by her reaction. Rain ran off the hood of his oilcloth cloak and over his face.

"I was thanking God for being with us thus far. And for sending you and Daniel to help me find Lorne and Da." Kella couldn't tell if the half cock of Alyn's brow was surprise or disapproval. "Yes, I do pray," she informed him.

Alyn hadn't lost that way of making her feel as though she had to defend herself.

"Good. I'm pleased to hear it."

Kella exhaled heavily. She always fell short of Alyn's aspirations to godly perfection, even when she tried.

She'd not been born to any significant bloodlines. Her father, though a recognized champion among men, had won no lands to provide her a dowry worthy of a noble marriage. Her gift of penmanship and languages had been her sole deliverance to the noble life to which she aspired.

And now that she was so close to wedding a prince, here she was riding like a warrior into a battle where emotions and fear vied for dominance in heart, mind, and soul. Other women might shrink away in despair, but she was a champion's daughter with something to fight for—love and the child conceived in it.

Bedraggled from a night of deluge spent in an abandoned Roman fortress along the wall, Arthur's entourage approached Strighlagh. Neither Lorne nor her father was among the men who rode out to greet the High King and Angus. And the devastation! Kella hadn't been able to hold back her tears.

The village at the base of the rock hill was all but destroyed. Even the whitewashed walls of the fortress sitting regally above it had been smudged with smoke from the fires set at its base. Graves were still being dug as Arthur's party rode by, so the High King had stopped to pay homage to the lost.

The reception had been short of enthusiastic, but given the burden the people bore, no one could blame them, not even Arthur. He made no attempt to hide his tears as Archbishop Cassian prayed over the desolation for the lost and the survivors.

As soon as they arrived, Lady Elaine spirited Kella off to a bathhouse so she could relieve herself of the mud and warm her bones, which were chilled from the harsh travel. Two small ovens heated the structure, one at each end. Kella marveled at the luxury, although she'd been no less awed the night before when Daniel and Alyn not only erected a shelter beneath the decaying ramparts of the fortress, but brilliantly kindled a fire of wet wood. Having read rain forecasted in the sky, Daniel had collected tinder and kept it dry in his pack. Alyn then used some black salts and a clear liquid from this alchemy chest to light it when Daniel had misplaced or lost his steel.

Delighted as Kella was for the drying warmth, she couldn't help but notice Alyn's extreme caution with the ingredients for his tiny flame. He'd sweated profusely in spite of the chill and sworn them both to secrecy over it. Naturally, Kella asked outright if his accident was somehow connected to the powder and oil.

He shook his head. "These are used for skin afflictions, nothing more."

"But fire," Daniel pointed out.

"'Tis a use discovered inadvertently and best forgotten."

And that was that. As if Alyn were proud of it on the one hand and afraid of it on the other. More questions came to Kella's mind, but she decided to keep them to herself. For now.

Once bathed and dressed in a turquoise gown with a sleeveless black tunic of heavier weight, she felt like a woman once more. Her clean hair spilled in spirals from a beaded black headband as she accompanied Lady Elaine into the great hall later that evening. Remembering Gwenhyfar's comment about setting a brave example for Strighlagh's grieving women, Kella held her head high, though a raw sob burned in her chest.

"You show great courage and strength, milady," Elaine whispered as she led Kella to a U-shaped dais, behind which was a large mural of country life painted by none other than the Angus himself.

It was hard to believe the same hand that wielded weapons so skillfully had created such a vision of light and peace. On the king's platform, boards had also been laid on trestles in the same U formation and set with plates made of flat rounds of fresh bread. Each one was artfully decorated with colors made from assorted food dyes. Only Arthur, Cassian, Angus, and his lady had been given polished silver plates. A further mark of honor was the saltcellar set before the Dux Bellorum.

"How lovely," Kella complimented, admiring the variety of flowers, vines, and knots painted by the kitchen staff.

"Our cooks hoped to lend a bit of festive air, given the gravity of this homecoming," Elaine confided.

Most of the guests, seated to the left and right of the center where Arthur and Angus presided, already enjoyed the wine, meat pasties, and cheeses put out for their enjoyment. The lady of Strighlagh seated Kella, as the only other woman at the king's table, at an empty place at the far end of the left wing of the dais, which was headed by Cassian and reserved mostly for his brethren. Upon dipping her head in acknowledgment of the archbishop, Elaine took the end seat opposite him.

Acutely aware of the archbishop's disapproving scrutiny, Kella wondered to whom the empty stretch of bench between the lady and her belonged.

"Many of our women who have suffered similar losses as yours are sequestered in mourning," Elaine observed. "I can't help but wonder at the wisdom of you continuing into Pictish territory, given the uncertain state of affairs."

"With all due respect, milady, I cannot accept *my* losses until I have seen the bodies," Kella answered … she hoped not too sharply. She scanned the room for Da's wild thatch of red hair or Lorne's oiled white-gold mane as if she could will them there. "I am convinced that if bodies are missing, and the enemy has no use for dead ones, that they are hostages or refugees."

"It is plausible," Lady Elaine conceded. "Though Errol's captain's witness—"

"Is of a grave wounding," Kella reminded her. "A dead man cannot crawl away."

Elaine gave her a placating smile. "I pray you are right, Lady Kella. We've lost too many to those renegade Miathi. Would Arthur had kept Modred friend and together they rid themselves of the Miathi murderers, so that our full attention can be fixed upon the Saxon wolf Aethelfrith."

Modred was, at the least, indifferent to the Miathi problem. At the most, Arthur had made an enemy, and his enemy would become Modred's friend. Neither bode well for the effort to find her father and Lorne in the Pictish hills, even if the High King would give his blessing. Was that why the lady tried to dissuade her? Panic clutched Kella's chest. What if Arthur forbade her to leave, and Alyn and Daniel refused to disobey him?

"Miladies, to what do I owe the honor of being summoned to the High King's table, much less seated between two roses like the thorn that I am?"

Alyn. Kella knew it before she looked up to see him dressed in a splendid red tunic embroidered with black. A sterling torque of wolves' heads snarled nose to nose at its closure beneath his Adam's apple.

"*Father* Alyn?" Lady Elaine asked, though she knew Alyn of Glenarden well. "The Dux Bellorum requested your presence specifically, but I must say, you look more the prince than the priest."

The lady was right, Kella thought, nodding her permission for him to sit next to her at the questioning lift of his brow.

Alyn slid onto the bench, bunching the spread of Kella's skirts next to him. "Of late, I fear I'm not much of either," he replied to Elaine. "After my sojourn in the East, I'm torn between the study of *sciencia* and the formal service of God."

"Ah, a druid in our midst."

At the lady's mention of *druid*, Cassian stopped in mid-sip of the Gaulish wine he enjoyed. Clearly, with the disciplined silence of his flock, he had no trouble overhearing the conversation at the opposite end of the wing.

"Perhaps you might continue your work at Llantwit, where you were educated," Elaine continued thoughtfully. "There is always a need for good teachers at the university."

"Christian teachers in particular," Cassian spoke up.

Albion's universities had once been solely druidic, taught by masters with twenty to thirty years of study in natural philosophy, astronomy, mathematics, geometry, medicine, jurisprudence, poetry, oratory, and the languages of learning—Greek and Latin. But with the coming of Christianity, most of the druids had converted, and monasteries began taking over such places. Cassian objected to the few preexisting druidic schools like Llantwit, which still included nonbelieving masters in their staff.

"If you meant what you said about learning the mind of God through the study of His creation, that is," the archbishop said to Alyn.

Alyn met the subtle challenge, his voice as steely as the hard blue of his gaze. "I did, sir, and I do."

Cassian's skepticism faded with a smile that Kella recognized. He thought he was having his way.

"Then I shall be delighted to recommend you to the bishop there," he offered.

So, sending Alyn to Llantwit, away from Arthur, suited the archbishop's purpose. Kella sliced cheese from the wedge, enough for her and Alyn, though she kept Cassian clearly in the corner of her eye. After what Alyn had confided to Daniel and Kella last evening regarding the Arthur's strange behavior at the inn, perhaps the head priest considered Alyn's newfound favor with the High King a threat.

"I appreciate your offer, Your Grace," Alyn said. "But I am not yet ready to settle anywhere for a while. I am off to my home in Glenarden."

Another difficult homecoming … though Da might have made his way there after the battle.

"That is not what I hear," the archbishop replied, pulling Kella from her hopeful introspection. "But we shall discuss that later," he said as a young man carrying a lion-shaped pitcher of spiced and herbed water approached the table to fill the lavers for hand-washing.

The feast was ready to commence, and Kella's stomach, for all the anxiety she suffered, growled in anticipation.

CHAPTER NINE

Usually feasts were jovial and entertainment a must, but with the scent of burnt wood still lingering in the air, the urgency of impending war lay like a cloud over the atmosphere. The hosts and their guests were more focused on eating to the tunes of the harpers than merrymaking—Kella in particular. The travel seemed to have restored her characteristic hearty appetite as well as color to her cheeks.

When the servants placed honeyed puddings and fruits and nuts on the table, Alyn, more than glad to be done with the meal, allowed her to finish his portion in addition to her own. Though he wanted no part of it, his mind was on the business at hand. The business of impending war. Why he'd been summoned to Arthur's table vexed him as much as how Cassian knew that Glenarden would not be his ultimate destination.

Eyewitnesses to the attack and the later ambush came before Arthur's table to add their perspectives to what had already been reported. The village had taken the worst of the attack, but the marauders had set fire to the gates and wooden towers of Strighlagh's fortress as well, while those villagers who'd managed to take refuge behind its walls had watched, helpless, from the parapets as their homes and shops burned below ... some with their neighbors in them.

Elkmar of Errol told of the ambush. How the border guard leading Strighlagh had given chase along a pass, where they were showered on both sides with arrows and spears. Then the escapees turned upon their pursuers. Prince Lorne had tried to organize a retreat from the vulnerable spot, only to be outflanked by more of the enemy.

Or had he led the retreat? Alyn wondered. God forgive him, he wanted to think the best of Kella's beloved, but only the worst came to his mind.

"We were surrounded on all sides, milord," Elkmar told Arthur. "I saw my prince run clear through with a lance before I could get to him. Another of the—" He used a term unfit for a lady's ears and, remembering the ladies, cast an apologetic look their way. "Well," he murmured, "he cut off milord's head—"

With a tortured moan, Kella swayed against Alyn. He caught her from sliding off the bench, but she managed to come to herself. She leaned upon Alyn for support, clenching his leg so tightly with her fingers, he knew they'd leave their mark.

"But I made certain the blackguard fed the wolves that night, milady," Elkmar told Kella.

Alyn shot him a glowering look, incredulous that the oaf considered *that* comfort. "I think you should retire," Alyn advised Kella. Dislodging her death-like grip, he placed her hand, folded between his own, on the table.

Though unable to speak her objection, she shook her head fiercely, determined to bear up.

Lady Elaine handed her a glass of the strong red wine that had been watered down for the ladies. "I agree with Father Alyn. You've suffered enough—"

"I ..." Kella fortified herself with a breath. "I would hear of m-my father."

Although Prince Lorne's rear guard had cut a swath through the rear attack, the Glenarden men had led the sortie into the ambush.

"I never knew there were so many of the scoundrels in all of Alba," Elkmar declared to Arthur. "We were surrounded on all sides by three times as many as first attacked us. To be sure, there were more than Miathi having at us, though we recognized no one tribe apart from another."

That was not a good sign. Were the southern Picti allying against Gododdin? Increasingly troubled, Alyn listened to how the Strighlagh warriors returned in force the following morning to collect their dead, but Egan was nowhere to be found.

"I'm so sorry, Kella," Alyn whispered through his own despair. "So sorry."

The big Irishman was like a father to him and his brothers. Many of the slain Alyn had grown up with. So many friends. He held the silently weeping girl against him, fearing she might swoon again.

Across the top of her head, he met Cassian's narrowed gaze. It ignited Alyn's anger like drops to the powder. The devil take the man's disapproval. Kella needed Alyn, and he'd promised to be there for her. He needed to be there for her.

"'Twas as we surmised," Arthur declared above the growing furor in the hall. "Though I am loath to hear it."

He addressed the gathering. "People of Strighlagh," he announced, "you have seen it with your own eyes. Grieved it in your own hearts. Your brothers to the north have turned upon you like wolves on sheep. 'Twill break my queen's heart as it does yours and mine when she arrives a few days hence."

The mention of their beloved queen stirred the crowd even more, for Gwenhyfar was one of them.

Arthur, Pict only through his paternal grandmother, rose from the table. "But what will Gwenhyfar see when she rides into Strighlagh?" he challenged. "Will she see a beaten people licking their wounds?"

For a moment, Alyn thought that was exactly what the people believed she'd see.

But one man shouted from a nearby bench, "Nay, *never*!"

Then another … and another. Until the rafters in the hall shook with "Nay, never!"

Arthur drew his sword, its blade and jewels flashing light from the candelabras and torches in all directions, and held it over his head until the room quieted enough for his battle voice to be heard. "Or will she see brave men and women determined to rebuild and hold on to what is theirs?"

A roar of *ayes* overcame the room, waning only when Arthur waved Excalibur to get their attention. "And see our armies training to pluck the sting from our Miathi neighbors once and for all!"

It wasn't a question. It was a declaration. A promise, driven into the board with the High King's sword for all to see. Its thunderous reception continued even as Arthur signaled his captains to follow him into an adjoining room. Strighlagh … place of strife. So it had been since the first chieftains had constructed a wooden dun where the great stone fortress now stood, for it guarded the only pass into the highlands.

"I pray, sir," Lady Elaine told Alyn, "that you will persuade Lady Kella to remain at Glenarden while you and Daniel of Gowrys search for her poor father."

So that was how Cassian knew. Alyn gave Kella a stern look for having shared what he'd considered a confidence for the three of them alone, but she was so wretched, he checked the scold on the tip of his tongue. But with everyone who knew of their plans, the risk of the genealogies being stolen increased.

"I promise to do my best," Alyn answered Elaine, "but my foster sister is strong of will." An understatement if ever he'd made one.

He was helping Kella up to accompany the Lady Elaine to the ladies' tower, when Strighlagh's steward, Budoc, called him aside. "Pardon, Father, but my lord has asked that you join him and the Dux as soon as possible." The request of the steward—a graying man with a naturally loud voice, perhaps from his years of authority over the Angus's staff—sounded more like a demand wrapped in apology.

Alyn's thoughts churned as to why. He was no captain. He wasn't even a proper priest.

"As soon as I see to the ladies," he replied when no answer came to mind. He'd hoped for a good night's rest, though his dreams would likely be haunted by the descriptions of the bloodshed and destruction presented that eve.

"Budoc's wife will accompany us," Lady Elaine assured him, nodding to where a matronly woman with a crisp white apron hovered over the servants clearing the table.

"I'll be fine." Kella rose on tiptoe and planted a chaste kiss on his cheek. Hers were salt raw from the grief spilled upon them. "You go," she told him, forcing a brave front that he could see through. "You go and learn all you can. Anything that will help us find Da."

Unshed tears magnified the plea in her gaze just as her plaintive touch, the press of her hands against his chest, compounded it all the more. Alyn's weariness and reluctance fell away, replaced by a surge of determination. He would do anything to take the hurt away from Kella O'Toole.

Alyn watched and waited until the ladies disappeared through a side door before following the steward. The imprint of Kella's lips was branded on his cheek. When he entered the war room, he was prepared to go to the ends of the earth, or at least to Alba.

Alyn was stunned to find out that Arthur not only knew about his intent to search for Egan O'Toole but had summoned Daniel as well. More shocking was that the High King wanted the two of them to gather intelligence from the Pictish settlements along the way.

"You are asking us to *spy*?" Alyn cast an unsettled glance at the stoic Daniel of Gowrys to see if his friend had heard the same thing he had.

"Both of you have Pict mothers. And *he*," Angus of Strighlagh said, pointing to Daniel, "not only looks like one of them, but knows the highlands as well as any."

'Twas true. Daniel had hunted and healed his way from shore to shore in the north.

But this was beyond irony. Bad enough to be looking for Egan like a lost needle in a mountain range and deliver the genealogies to Mount Seion without Arthur's knowledge, but now—

"As a priest, Father Alyn, you will be well received, especially in Fortingall," Cassian chimed in. "Drust's queen, Heilyn, has requested a priest be sent there to found a church."

"Me found a *church?*" Alyn didn't mean to shout, but this was the last thing he wanted. He was barely responsible enough to discipline himself, much less others. "That requires taking along twelve brethren. We travel light."

At least that was the same dilemma Alyn's longtime friend and mentor Bishop Martin had faced years ago. The aging priest had sought seclusion in Glenarden's hills, but God had other plans for him.

"We ... the king and I," Cassian explained, "expect you to discuss the arrangements the Lady Heilyn is prepared to make with regard to her project, so that we might proceed from there."

"I see." Meaning Alyn was to find out how much money and land the lady intended to bequeath the church.

So was this God's plan or Cassian's?

"*Glorify Me.*"

Alyn felt ill. As if the birds and dragons were merely a thought away.

Have I no say in this, Lord?

Even as Alyn rebelled, he knew the answer. Daniel's resigned, grim expression confirmed Alyn's answer. He might say no to Cassian, Arthur, even to Kella, if for her good. But never to God.

Alyn merely hoped that it *was* God's voice he followed and not that of man.

CHAPTER TEN

The following day Alyn and his companions journeyed away from the Strighlagh curl of the River Clyde toward the north run of Teith. The sight of the highland hills rising before them, the mists hugging them, the heather and gorse clothing them in color, was enough to soothe Alyn's conflict-weary soul. Here and again it was possible to glimpse the sparkling silver expanse of the river as it wound close to the old Lindum road and gobbled up its golden carseland with spring's overflow. Between time, weather, and lack of maintenance, the passage was a mire of mud and sinkholes that brought traffic almost to a standstill.

Travelers on horseback or afoot fared far better than those with laden wagons, but the slow progress did allow more time to appreciate the surroundings. Where land had been cleared, farmers worked in their fields, clearing stones, tilling, and planting. Where the river wound close to the road, the occasional fishermen could be seen in the cobles, hauling in fat salmon in their nets. One might almost believe that the threat of war was no more than a dream.

Alyn purchased one of the big fish from an enterprising vendor at a crossroads village for supper later that evening. They set up camp

on the banks of the river where, years ago, Daniel's clan had saved
Alyn's eldest brother and his wife from a murderous ambush conceived by the middle O'Byrne brother, Caden, and his treacherous
wife, Rhianon.

Not that Alyn remembered the specifics. Rhianon had drugged
the wine, which, at the cocky age of sixteen and just having been
rescued as a hostage from their enemy, he'd drunk to excess. 'Twas
all over by the time Alyn came to his senses. His father, Tarlach, had
died a hero's death, saving Ronan's wife, Brenna. The witch Rhianon
had leapt into the river to her death—or so everyone thought. And
Caden was exiled, only to find a second chance with God and love
with his lovely bard Sorcha.

How fast the years had flown, Alyn mused, glancing sidewise at
Kella. Except for a sniffle now and then, she held her great grief in
uncharacteristic silence. Egan's loss was hard enough, but the brutal
slaying of her betrothed was surely doubly painful for her.

Especially if she carried his child.

Alyn tried to shove the afterthought aside, but it would not
leave. As intelligent as Kella was, she'd always been gullible, and
as such, a victim of the most outlandish pranks her foster brothers
could think of. And, as Daniel pointed out, she was a pretty flower
in the court ... and vulnerable.

The possibility that she'd fallen victim to moonlit kisses and sweet
words, even if they were of true love, tightened Alyn's grip on the reins
until his nails dug into his palms. Had Lorne of Errol any honor, he
would have controlled himself ... waited for the wedding bed.

Fatin, who'd taken quite happily to more travel, reached for
Kella to take him, whining until she noticed. When she patted her

lap, the monkey leapt from Daniel's shoulder into her waiting arms. He wound his small fingers into her hair as she cuddled him, exacting a halfhearted smile from her.

Alyn's indignation faded at the exchange. Lorne of Errol he could condemn without hesitation, but not Kella. Kella he wanted to protect.

God in heaven, Alyn prayed, *if this be so, wrap her in Your arms. She has broken Your law, but You are a God of second chances. A God of love.*

That evening Daniel proved himself a good cook as the three of them enjoyed the fresh, fire-baked salmon spiced with an assortment of herbs the highlander carried with him. Beneath that hardened exterior was the complex soul of a man who cherished all life, yet gave no second thought about killing for food; who wielded any weapon with warrior skill, yet possessed the knowledge and touch of a healer; and who lived his faith quietly, though it was solid as the oak under which they camped.

Kella ate her share and more of the fish and fresh loaves from Strighlagh's kitchen, though she gave her fruit to Fatin. When she was a child, her sweet tooth had rounded her figure more so than other girls her age, but maturity and height had stretched the cherubic figure into eye-catching curves.

Alyn checked to see if Daniel also noticed them when she stretched to grab another small piece of the fish, but the highlander was busy tossing a stone among others for the taut-bellied

Fatin to find. Unfailingly, the monkey always returned with the right one.

"He must have a good sense of smell," Daniel surmised aloud.

Alyn's attention shifted back to Kella, who stared at the two as though not really seeing. The glow of her cheeks came surely from the firelight and not from a recovery of the heart. Other than monosyllabic answers to questions, she was not his characteristic Babel-Lips.

No need to guess where her thoughts lay ... or with whom.

"I'll take the first watch," Alyn offered.

He scanned the site for the best view of the forest edge, which had been cleared away from the riverbanks to give travelers more warning of an ambush than Ronan and Brenna had had years before. If anyone had taken more than a curious interest in two men and a woman traveling on fine horses with a couple of packhorses loaded to capacity, he'd spy them in time to prepare for an attack.

From his belongings, Alyn withdrew a wooden staff, a fine piece of workmanship with Celtic and Christian symbols carved into its hard oak. To his astonishment, Cassian had presented it to him that morning.

"'Twas a gift from the bishop Columba," Cassian informed him, "but alas, I have no need for two croziers. It may be useful in those savage highlands."

That the bishop of Iona had blessed it was more than enough for Alyn to treasure it. He thanked the Roman archbishop sincerely. Of the two croziers, Alyn undoubtedly carried the better. Unlike the gold and jewel-inlaid staff Cassian carried, this cruder one was well balanced, fit for walking ... or as a weapon.

Kella shook herself from her self-imposed silence. "Let me stand watch."

"What?" Daniel had yet to learn Kella was her father's daughter in will and pluck.

"I can't sleep. If I do, I might dream," she explained. "And if I dream—" Her voice broke. "'Twill be of Lorne, and I cannot bear it."

Curse the man, Alyn swore to himself. Not that he'd think ill of the dead, but if Kella were in a family way …

"Troubled by dreams last night, were ye, lassie?" Daniel rose and brushed the dirt and leaves from his legs. "Well, I've somethin' in my pack that'll help ye sleep a dreamless sleep. A special blend of herbs and tea to soothe the soul."

Kella giggled at his courtly bow and bold wink. "That pack of yours must hold more than the Bible widow's cruse of oil."

That the mischievous Daniel made her laugh still irked Alyn later as he propped himself up against a tree to keep from nodding off. All Alyn had at his disposal to lift her spirits was a prayer and comfort from Scripture as she settled down by the fire.

"*God is with you. He will never leave nor forsake you. He will help you through this difficult time*," Alyn had said. But "*God is in control*" broke her grudging patience.

"If that is the case, then why did this happen?" Kella had snapped at him. "Why is Lorne dead and my father missing?"

Alyn couldn't bring himself to say 'twas the consequence of sin, not God's doing. If Kella were with child, he could not trouble her further. Besides, he'd questioned God himself. Why had Abdul-Alim suffered for Alyn's sin of carelessness? Where was the just God when that happened? Why hadn't Alyn perished?

"Why, God?" he whispered to the star-spangled sky. "I believe, but I don't understand."

Nothing. No voice, nor vision, nor a dagger of pain. Only his pulse, wrung from a bewildered heart, a lone beat against the utter silence.

'Twas *too* silent. The hair lifted on the back of Alyn's neck. The moonlit riverbank and forest edge were as still as Strighlagh's mural. But night creatures did not quiet without cause. He nudged Daniel's sleeping figure with his foot and, faking a yawn, turned back to the woods to put another log upon on the fire.

Daniel's eyes flew open as if he'd been awake all along. "Where?" he asked quietly.

"Trees," Alyn replied in kind.

Remaining still, Daniel narrowed his eyes, peering beyond Alyn. His hand crept toward the sword he slept with unsheathed and ready as Alyn tossed another log on the fire. A shower of lights shot upward, illuminating the area all the more.

As if it were a signal, the forest erupted in shrieks. Alyn's blood turned cold as four—nay, *five*—shadowlike men charged out of the wood toward the encampment.

"Somethin' tells me 'twill do nay good to declare yerself a man o' God to that lot," Daniel observed dryly as Alyn seized the oak staff.

"A priest might not use a sword," Alyn declared, far bolder than he felt, "but a staff is a worthy weapon." He hoped. For all Egan's training, Alyn had never had to fight for his life.

Kella bolted upright from a sound sleep and swung her head in confusion from Alyn and Daniel to the shrieking charge of the thieves. "Wha—"

"Get behind the tree and stay there," Alyn ordered. 'Twould at least protect her from flying lances or arrows. "And take Fatin with you."

Fatin was sleeping like a babe, curled up in his cage near Kella.

Daniel, blade in one hand and dagger in the other, let loose with a howl that would raise the hairs on a wolf's neck and charged head-long at the towering leader of the band.

They clashed like two bulls, but Alyn heard it for only a second before a thin, wiry sort with a long beard heaved a lance straight at him. Alyn dodged the shaft. Following Daniel's seasoned example, he threw himself at the brigand before he could turn his ax into the whir of blinding arcs and deadly angles it could become in practiced hands. A feigned thrust at his assailant's groin forced the man to swing wildly to protect himself. Then Alyn spun, catching his attacker broadside of the temple with the other end of his staff, just as Egan had taught him. The bone-crunching impact practically lifted the villain off his feet.

One!

Exhilaration rilled through Alyn as Long Beard's round and balding companion charged. Excess flesh quivering with each foot-fall, the man lumbered forward and swung the end of a gnarled staff at Alyn. Again, Alyn danced sideways, but the hard tip of the staff grazed him. Alyn clenched his teeth at the pain that ripped across his ribcage and hurled its outcry to his brain. The frustration and anger he'd suppressed since his arrival—his failures, his helplessness to comfort Kella—broke free, screaming in his mind louder than the panicked Fatin.

Lip curling, Alyn planted his staff in the ground before him as the heavy man struck it with all the might of his thick arms. The loud crack shot like a lightning bolt up Alyn's arms. But the earth cushioned the brunt of the impact. The thief's weapon rebounded off the oak, turning the man's considerable strength against him.

Still riddled with pinpricks, Alyn staggered toward the downed man with the intent of rendering him unconscious at the least, but the heavy man rolled to his feet with amazing speed for his size and bounded away in retreat.

Two.

Alyn sought the next. To his left, metal clanged against metal where Daniel engaged in a deadly dance of knife and sword with the equally matched leader, while the fourth coward circled the two with a spear, looking for an opening to catch him unaware. Alyn started for the coward when the man faltered several steps back, as though punched in the chest, and dropped his weapon.

The oaf still clutched his chest, looking about wildly for the source of the attack when a bloodcurdling yelp erupted behind Alyn. He pivoted to see the fifth thief speeding at him full tilt. With shoulders the width of an ox, he wielded a long sword over his thick-thatched head as if to split Alyn down the middle.

Alyn raised his staff with both hands to block the deadly downswing. Splinters from where previous blows had damaged the symbols dug into his hands as he steeled his grip.

The oak dulled the twang of the iron as it sank into its thickness, but not the blade's force. Alyn's knees buckled as if the sword now wedged dangerously close to one hand was a full-grown tree. The tattoo of an eye in the middle of his assailant's forehead made him appear a three-eyed monster as he struggled to free his weapon.

Taking advantage of the reprieve, Alyn hove the staff and sword upward with all the force his legs would afford. The momentum combined with Three-Eyes' own pulling effort sent the astounded man careening backward. Alyn atop him, he hit the ground with a crushing jolt that knocked the wind from them both.

A whoosh of fetid breath struck Alyn's face, but he found his knees for purchase and ground the staff against the man's throat until he ceased to resist. With a strangled gurgle that sent spittle dribbling down the side of his mouth, the man stared up, all wide and unstaring eyes.

Breath raw in his lungs, Alyn sat up, swaying in disbelief. But he hadn't cut off the brigand's breath long enough to kill him. He'd only meant to disable the cur.

Hadn't he? Doubt churned like storm clouds in Alyn's mind. He'd taken vows to save souls, not condemn them to eternal damnation. He swallowed a rise of bile in the back of his throat.

"Alyn!"

At Kella's shriek, Alyn glanced left to see her hefting a lance. She was a fine figure, even in a shirt and braccae. Like a Valkyrie princess, her wild mane glowing in the firelight as she loosed the missile … straight at him.

Instinct bowled him behind the cover of the dead thief. Just as Kella's lance whistled overhead, an iron-tipped spear plunged from behind Alyn into Three-Eyes' belly, where Alyn had sat only seconds before. He shifted over in time to see a spearman pitch back, the same one who'd been startled by Kella's stone. Now her lance was buried deep in his thigh. Scrambling, Alyn grabbed the end of the lance and twisted it. The spearman pulled away, screaming in agony.

When it broke off, Alyn flew at him with the ragged end, but the brigand limped off for the woods after the two who'd already disappeared, as if to outdistance death itself.

"Leave him be. Those three'll be too busy tendin' their own wounds to come for the dead tonight." Daniel leaned against the oak and wiped perspiration and blood spatter off his brow. More stained his green tunic and darkened the blade dangling from his hand. He grinned at Alyn. "He was a worthy opponent."

"I'll bet yon spearman wishes he'd taken off whilst my stone left him with two good legs," Kella spoke up, kneeling before the still-crying monkey to take it out of its cage. The sling she laid aside explained what Alyn had seen right before the hulk of a swordsman attacked. He hastily sought out the spot where he'd waylaid Long Beard, but the man had evidently regained his battered wits and slipped away into the night. Still …

Two deaths. Alyn made the sign of the cross. He wrestled to feel regret instead of relief as he stared at the spear buried in Three-Eyes' belly by his fellow thief. A spear intended for Alyn. The champion's daughter had saved his life with a lance. Perhaps Daniel's as well with her sling.

"Remind me never to object to your traveling company again," Alyn told her. Though somewhere in the back of his mind, he thought he'd fought to save hers.

"God's allowed the curs of this world to take two men I love," she declared with such vehemence that Fatin shrank away from the hand petting him. "So help me, I'd die before I'll let them take another."

Love? The choice of words cleared the field of clashing guilt and triumph in Alyn's mind. But then, she meant—

"Milady, we are beholden—" Daniel broke off with a gasp of pain. Reeling back against the tree, he inched down the bark, his face white as the archbishop's robes.

Only then did it dawn on Alyn that not all the blood staining Daniel's clothes belonged to the thieves.

CHAPTER ELEVEN

Kella had cried her last tear. Now she was angry. Angry that Lorne had suffered such a brutal end and that her father was missing. Angry that, after proving herself an able battle companion, she'd swooned into a dead faint at the sight of Daniel's gaping flesh wound. Thankfully, Alyn's priestly medical training served both men well. He stitched and then applied some of the black salts—those he'd used to start a fire—on the wound to avoid infection. Infection wouldn't prevent Daniel from guiding them to Fortingall. However, a fractured ankle yet to be set would.

Kella shuddered. 'Twas as if death stalked those she cared for. She petted Fatin's small black head. The monkey had finally settled in her lap, where he watched Alyn's every move, as if fearing his master would abandon him again. How he'd screamed in terror from the confines of his cage as the violence surrounded him.

Inadvertently, her gaze wandered to where the three-eyed thief still lay a distance away, impaled to the ground by his comrade's spear. Her throw had saved Alyn's life, though she'd struck the spearman's thigh instead of her mark on his chest. She needed to practice weaponry more. Had the lance gone lower, 'twould have given poor Alyn further cause for alarm as he dove behind Three-Eyes for cover.

Her heart warmed at the sight of Alyn tending Daniel's thigh. He was such a tender soul, yet earlier he'd fought like a demon with Cassian's staff. Her father would have been proud of him.

Will be, when he hears of it, Kella amended.

"The man with the eye tattoo," she said. "There couldn't be two marked alike. I'm certain he's the same one who stumbled into our stall at the tavern our first night out of Carmelide. Do you think Cassian might have hired the brigands to kill us and take the books?"

He might have discovered the forgeries, she mused. The priest served Rome, and Rome stopped at nothing to get what it wanted.

"Three-Eyes was after something, to be sure," Daniel managed through a tight grimace.

"Aye," Alyn agreed, "but the books may not have been the target. The goods I've brought from the East would bring a fine price at a spring fair." He cut off the thread next to Daniel's flesh with a pair of silver scissors that were not only functional but a work of art. "I've three pair of these for the O'Byrne brides, each fit for a queen."

"I count only *two*," Daniel pointed out. "*Brides*, that is. Unless you're keeping a secret from us."

Kella's breath caught. *Alyn* with a bride? A prick of dismay rendered her speechless.

"Our Kella was raised O'Byrne, even if not by blood," Alyn retorted as though his friend's observation were as absurd as Kella had thought.

Her breath escaped in relief. Though she could think of no reason her childhood friend shouldn't marry. Some priests had taken wives. Their titles were oft hereditary like the Levites of old. Another custom of which Rome did not approve.

"For me?" she marveled as Alyn handed them to her. "Why, they're *beautiful*."

"Though they'll never suffer overuse in *your* sewing box," Alyn teased.

"*I sew*," Kella objected. "When I have to," she added with a guilty twitch of her lips. A Middle Eastern artisan had fashioned the tool to look like an exotic silver bird, its long beaks overlapping for cutting. Even a finger curve had been worked into the natural shape of its body. "Thank you, Alyn. I shall cherish them."

"How about you tear some more bandages from this bolt of Egyptian linen?" Alyn suggested.

'Twas all they had save good shirts and a shift for binding Daniel's wounds.

"And I'm not even an O'Byrne bride," Daniel jested. Though his bravado faded as fast as the color on his face. "But I'll cherish this linen."

Alyn ignored him. "I'm off to find wood suitable for a splint," he told Kella.

Fatin dashed away from Kella and toward Alyn as he crawled to his feet, favoring bruised and slightly bloodied ribs. Kella had noticed the stains earlier, but he vowed they were not broken. "'Twas just a nasty swipe," he'd assured her.

With a halfhearted chuckle, Alyn scratched the monkey's head and held him for a moment's comfort. "All's well, mischief." But once Fatin sat contented on his shoulder, Alyn picked up the staff propped against the oak and ventured away from the campsite.

Kella watched the two until they disappeared in the darkness edging the trees. Despite his protests that he didn't want a pet, her friend had taken to Fatin like a father.

"He's a good man," Daniel told her as she unrolled an arm's length of the incredibly soft but strong linen.

"Aye, he is," she agreed.

"I'll not say he's better than your prince, but *I* find him to be more agreeable company."

Kella snipped the edge for ripping, brow arching at her companion. "You *knew* Lorne? Have you been to Errol?"

"I met Prince Lorne at Strighlagh."

"And …," she prompted.

"I'm thinkin' he considered himself prettier than the women he courted. And there were many with their sights set upon him."

Many. Kella ripped the strip away with a vengeance. But then a man as handsome and noble-born as Lorne certainly would have attracted many ladies. He'd admitted to a hopeless eye for a lovely woman but confessed that 'twas Kella's wit that set her apart from the other beauties and won his heart.

"Then I would suffer you as I have Alyn to remain silent at Glenarden about the betrothal," she asked. "We had not time to announce it or publish the banns."

Searching for her father was reason enough for their quest. At Daniel's solemn nod, Kella nipped another width of cloth, squeezing her eyes shut against tears. She might as well have cut her heart, the way it stung.

"Alyn suffers as well," Daniel observed quietly. "Not from a broken heart like yourself, but a wounded spirit. Perhaps the two of you might …" He struggled for a word, discomfited by a subject other than hunting, fighting, herbs, or animals, yet the set of his jaw showed his determination. "*Mend*," he said, as if that was the best he could do. He pointed to the scissors. "Like sewing … *together*."

"Sewing together?" Kella met Daniel's earnest gaze, grasping as hard as he.

In an effort to find relief, the highlander repositioned his injured foot and mumbled an oath of frustration when he failed. Whether at the pain from his wounds or fumbling words was hard to tell.

"I will do my best to help Alyn, though he has not confided in me as he has you," she guessed. "I have *always* cared deeply for him."

Concern dug in. Had she been so wrapped up in her own troubles that she hadn't given Alyn's torment from the accident sufficient thought? Was it worse than a poorly healed wound from an accident or doubts about a profession she'd always questioned?

At that instant, Fatin scampered into the firelight and presented Daniel with a stone. Perhaps the one Kella had fired from the sling hung from her belt.

"Will you look at that?" Daniel turned the stone in his hand. "It looks like the same one we tossed earlier."

"Maybe I used it in my sling." Kella wriggled her fingers for Fatin to come to her, but he waited for Daniel to play the game of fetch again.

Alyn returned to the site, carrying an armful of dried wood. "I've found a couple of straight boughs we can split for the splint, and more firewood." He dumped the wood near the fire and picked out the straightest. "These'll do just fine. Then"—his eyes followed the stone Daniel tossed for the monkey—"maybe the good Lord will let us pass the rest of the night in peace."

"Me and Fatin'll keep watch," Daniel offered. "Loose, he should make a fine watchdog. My eyes aren't broken and"—he pointed to his ankle, which seemed to swell by the hour—"like as not, this ankle will na' let me sleep."

"And once you're finished with Daniel's ankle," Kella put in, "I'll have a good look at those ribs."

Alyn shook his head. "I'll be fine."

"If I'm to be wrapped tighter than those mummies you told me about, then you will too," Daniel chimed in. He brandished a toothy grin. "Besides, she'll not give either of us a moment's rest till we humor her."

"Stand still, Alyn," Kella chastised.

Though stripped to his braccae and boots, Alyn might as well have been naked. He looked overhead, where the heavens promised a decent day's journey tomorrow, and tried to make out some of the constellations. But even though Kella's touch was chaste and tender, it worked upon him as if she had the practiced hand of a harlot. Sweat gathered on his brow, though the night was far from warm. His skin tightened beneath her fingers as though she scalded and froze it at the same time, instead of working in a muscle liniment.

"I'm not hurt on my chest," he declared sharply.

Daniel's snort from the fireside wasn't helping Alyn's humor.

Kella glanced up from her ministrations, catching the scathing look Alyn sent the highlander's way. "This raised scar says otherwise," she stated.

By all the saints, he could fall into those eyes and drown in the mist that formed there as she traced the scar with a fingertip. 'Twas battle madness, the blood frenzy still hammering his heart like a war drum. *And worse*, he thought as Kella stroked the raised outline of his scar.

"'Tis the scar from the large silver cross that melted during the accident. Months old," he grumbled in protest. "Faith, I should know where I hurt and where I do not." Alyn clenched his teeth, praying she'd not notice that he was on the verge of a man's worst embarrassment, and that she'd move no closer than she already was.

"Scarce healed, if you ask me," she shot back.

Kella turned away to get the binding she'd prepared for him. With a relieved swipe of his forearm, he wiped his brow. His side screamed in protest, breaking a fresh sweat.

Maybe one *was* broken. All he knew was that his misery had doubled, now that it received attention.

"At least *Daniel* appreciated the care you gave him," Kella said, sulking. She shook out the length of linen, enough that there would be none left for the ladies to make their delicate underdresses.

"That's because *I* knew what I was doing." Alyn dropped his head the moment he fired the words off. No taking them back.

A glance at Daniel found no help. The highlander sucked and chewed the inside of his cheeks as if to keep from laughing outright at Alyn's discomfiture.

Alyn tried not to notice Kella's eyes, which were narrowed as if in righteous indignation. "What I meant was," he backtracked, "that

I had the strength needed to bind his ankle tight, so the wrapping wouldn't give way, yet gently so as not to cause further pain."

Her head cocked in challenge. "You think *I* can't bind you tightly enough?"

Wet-hen mad as she was, Kella could bind the breath from his lungs. Alyn's muddled thoughts churned. "*Gently*," he corrected. "I feared you'd not be able to draw the bindings in with a firm but gentle hand. That is where strength comes in."

"Strength comes in to keep a full-grown man whimpering like a baby. That's where strength comes in," Kella fumed. "Now stand straight and raise your arms like a man."

Alyn had forgotten how infuriating Kella could be when she assumed herself to be in charge. Even as a wee lassie, she'd marched about commanding every animal at Glenarden, from ducks to kittens, imitating her father on the training field. Not that she had the means to back her authority.

But she had enough to arrest Alyn's breath as she looped her arms around him. Wisps of her hair tickled his chin as she leaned in close to smooth it against his back. Alyn closed his eyes, trying to block the sweet assault on his senses. But when she backed away and cinched for the first wrap, lances of agony displaced it—and the breath hissed through his teeth.

"Is that tight enough?"

If a rib had not been fractured, 'twas surely cracked now. "Just right," he managed. Though he wasn't sure there was room to breathe again, he held his tongue, lest she take out her festering rage at the enemy on him.

Adding insult to injury, Kella used the bright brooch her lover had given her as additional security, lest the strips she knotted should slip. "Damage it, and I'll damage you," she threatened.

The wrapping of his body seemed to have taken the sting from her peeve, for the warning was softened with a half smile. It was still on her lips when exhaustion claimed her not long after.

Between the discomfort of his ribcage and those lips, Alyn doubted he'd sleep at all.

CHAPTER TWELVE

Alyn rose before the break of dawn to bury the two thieves in shallow graves. 'Twas more an act of what was right in this world than of the heart. Plaguing his conscience further were the only words that came to him as he bowed his head in prayer over the mounds—Christ's warning in the garden. *"All they that take the sword shall perish with the sword."*

But it wasn't his first kill that had robbed him of sleep the night before or made Alyn wonder why he'd ever thought he could be a priest, as he and his companions made their way along the last leg of their journey to Glenarden. 'Twas the still-warm memory of Kella's touch upon his flesh. To be sure, 'twas but one torture traded for another.

Alyn had tried blaming the pump of excitement from the ambush while he watched wide-eyed as a moonstruck calf while she slept. Digging the graves with little more than a spear for a pick and a sturdy section of bark for a shovel had been a welcome distraction from repeatedly taking inventory of the lady's charms.

Alyn groaned as the litany started of its own accord again. The face of an angel, the spirit of a warrior, the mind of a scholar …

He stole a sideways look to where Kella fascinated even the monkey as she spoke in baby talk to him. Such babble *usually* sickened him and, he surmised, slowed a baby's speech progress. Not that Fatin would suffer.

Then there was her body, pure temptation itself in the belted tunic and braccae. Especially when he was close enough to inhale the scent of wildflowers and woman that was Kella's essence. She'd been that close last night, with no idea that the sweat of his brow came not from pain but from longing. An ache that plagued him every time Alyn allowed himself to dwell upon it.

'Twas more worrisome than a boil. Nothing took his mind away from Kella for long. Not the psalms he recited, the mental account of every vial and box so carefully stored in the alchemy case—

Or the possibility that Kella was with child … by a man she mourned deeply.

That by itself should have cooled Alyn's preoccupation with her, but nay. By high noon, a noble solution overran his desire-muddled brain. What if *he* married her?

That foolishness he blamed on an empty stomach. At midday, once they'd consumed the remains of the food packed by Strighlagh's cooks, Alyn's accustomed cool reason returned, as did the ache in his ribs. Both made the passage of time no less discomfiting.

The sun had completed better than half of its downward plunge on the green braes rising higher and higher to the west, when at long last the cliff where the O'Byrne dun presided came into view. Proud red banners with black wolf heads fluttered over the watchtowers to either side of the front gate. A well-drained road sloped from it, ambling through a checkered landscape of orchard, furrowed fields, and meadowland edged by forest.

From a thick stand of hazel and ash near the river below, two shaggy brown ponies with black manes and tails bounded at full gallop across the meadow. Leaning low over their backs, mite-sized riders ignored the indistinct warning shouts of their guardians, who brought up the rear at a more leisurely canter. Alyn recognized Ronan's dappled gray stallion as one of the horses. Or, considering the passage of six years, 'twas at the least Ballach's offspring.

"Uncle Daniel!"

Young Conall had changed far more than Alyn anticipated. His nephew still had his mother's eyes and that dimple that plagued the shaving blade of every O'Byrne man, but his baby-round face had begun to take on his father's angular profile.

Daniel broke the suffering-inflicted silence that had affected him most of the day to give the lad as low a formal bow as his wounded thigh would allow. It was swollen and pained him, but his eyes twinkled with affection. "I greet you a free man, Master Conall O'Byrne ... and *Lady* Joanna," he said to the second rider, a younger girl with a head full of dark curls that had escaped the straggling remains of two bows.

At eight, rosy-cheeked Joanna reminded Alyn of a buttercup. A bundle of yellow with flower-embroidered skirts hiked up to her knees, revealing the edge of the brown trousers she wore beneath. She stared at Kella, bemused by the men's clothing, but only for a moment. Rising in her stirrups, Joanna bellowed over her shoulder with glee in a voice that belied her delicate facade. "It's Aunt Kella, Mama! *Aunt Kella*! And she's dressed like a boy."

Alyn smothered a laugh at the sentry-worthy volume.

"Well, I'll be blessed!" Conall declared, at last recognizing Alyn. "'Tis our Uncle Alyn, Joanna … and with *all* his hair."

"Conall!" Lady Brenna of Glenarden finally caught up with her son's pony and gave the lad's wild locks a punitive tug. "Six years your uncle has been away, and *this* is how you make him welcome?"

"He only speaks the truth," Ronan told his wife. Time had treated them both well, brushing only a hint of gray at Ronan's temple. Brenna was as pretty in Glenarden's colors as the day she'd impressed Alyn by nearly winning the archery prize for the clan at the Strighlagh fair.

The eldest O'Byrne sidled his dappled gray against Alyn's mount and, before Alyn guessed what he was about, all but pulled him off the saddle and into a bearlike embrace. "This is indeed a grand—"

Alyn gasped, although how was a mystery since his big brother had crushed the air from his lungs. Thankfully Alyn's strangled reaction was warning enough for Ronan to let him go.

The questioning scowl he gave Alyn deepened when Ronan spied the splint on Daniel's leg. "What happened?"

Joanna preempted her father's inquiry with a squeal of wonder. "What's *that*?" She pointed to Fatin, who clung to Kella in the face of so many strangers. "Oh, Aunt Kella—" The little girl urged her pony next to Kella. "Where did you find such an *adorable*—" Joanna took care enunciating the big word—"creature? Is he yours? Did you bring him for me?"

"Brigands," Alyn mouthed to Ronan, hoping to discuss the ambush later rather than now in front of the children. "Actually, *Lady Joanna*," he addressed his niece, "the monkey is mine. A prince of the Ghassãnid gave him to me as a gift."

"*Mon … key*," she repeated carefully. "What a strange name for a strange creature."

"Who are the Ghassánid, and do they hunt monkeys in Baghdad?" Conall inquired. His bright-eyed expression suggested he liked the idea.

"This is an African monkey," Alyn explained. "And yes, sometimes monkeys are hunted for food."

"Oh no!" Horror washed over Joanna's cherubic countenance. "It's just a baby," she objected.

"But not often," Alyn assured her. Surely not even God would condemn a lie told to avoid the dismay welling in such beautiful brown eyes. "And the Ghassánid," he told Conall, "are a proud Christian Arabic people who defend Byzantium from its enemies. I'll tell you all about them later," Alyn added upon seeing more questions leap into the lad's eyes. He turned back to Joanna.

"Would you like Fatin to ride with you?" he asked.

Joanna's dark auburn curls bounced with her enthused "Yes!"

At Alyn's nod, Kella handed the monkey over to the little girl.

Fortunately, the pet's curiosity regarding Joanna was as keen as hers for him. Fatin went willingly onto the child's lap, focusing on her long hair.

"Now, he might pull your ribbons," Alyn warned her. "He loves bright ribbons and beads … but he also likes to be scratched between his ears, like so."

Alyn demonstrated, then let Joanna try. But it was the ribbons that won Fatin over … and made him the guest of honor for Glenarden, especially for the littlest lady of the keep.

Though the news of Kella's father missing in battle had already reached Glenarden, Ronan was anxious for all the additional details that she, Alyn, and Daniel could add. While the children cured Fatin's boredom after a day with his quiet companions, the eldest O'Byrne brother questioned the three travelers over a light repast served by Brenna herself and Ervan, Glenarden's new steward.

Kella wrung the hem of her tunic, fighting to keep her vow that she'd cried her last, as Ervan told of how his father, Vychan, passed peacefully in his sleep winter last. Though the old steward had run the keep with an eagle eye and iron fist, Vychan had been another *uncle* to Kella for as long as she could remember.

Too tired to eat, Kella nibbled on honeyed bread and savored one of Brenna's relaxing teas to the last drop. Thankfully, Alyn and Daniel had honored her plea not to speak of her betrothal. Nor were the plans to go into the north to find Egan mentioned … perhaps to postpone the objections that would surely come, especially about her accompanying them.

Unless Alyn had had second thoughts with Daniel's injury preventing his going. Too weary to face that possibility, she abandoned ladylike manners and leaned heavily with her elbows on the table, not even sure she had the energy to seek a bed.

When a handful of servants started setting up the hall for the evening meal, Brenna came to her rescue—Kella suspected Alyn's and Daniel's as well—by insisting they rest before supper. Alyn and Daniel were shown to Ronan's office, where two pallets were made up, while Kella occupied the guest bed in the adjoining room.

There she fell into a sleep as deep as that of the men Alyn had buried, a dreamless place where neither anxiety nor grief troubled her. How much time passed before the scent of food cooking and warming in the hall urged her senses awake, she had no idea. Struggle as she might to sink back into the sweet numbness of slumber, a growling stomach and the joyful screeches of Fatin and the children would not be ignored.

"Are they happy or dyin'?" Daniel grumbled, his voice traveling through the wattle-and-mud wall to where Kella lay.

"Either way, we'll not sleep through it" came Alyn's resigned reply.

In reluctant agreement, Kella rolled into an upright position on the plump pallet of her bed, feeling as if she'd just abandoned heaven itself. Cupping her belly with her hands, she whispered to the babe within, "Now I want you to think of how tired you are when *you're* the wee one making the loud noise."

Purple twilight painted the horizon a while later when Kella emerged from the guest chamber in her turquoise gown. Boards had been set up in the hall, and every rush light, torch, and candle had been lit. At the family table, Alyn and Daniel shared cups of beer with Ronan. Both Kella's companions had shaved and bathed and were now clad in clean clothing like herself.

Kella wondered if they felt as refreshed as they looked. No matter how hard she'd scrubbed her cheeks to bring out the rose in them, she could easily gobble a pinch of meat, a fist of bread, and head straight back to her oh-so-soft bed. How the nights of sleeping on the ground had deepened her appreciation of a well-stuffed pallet.

The boiled venison, poached salmon, wild field greens, and fresh breads served with Glenarden's own honeys and cheeses did honor to Brenna's intricate knowledge of herbs. Kella ate more than she'd thought possible and settled by the hearth to feed Fatin some fruit. The little monkey was so exhausted by all the attention from the children that he ate half an apple and, abandoning even Kella, sought the refuge of his cage for a much-needed nap.

While the tables and benches were cleared or broken down for the night, Alyn presented the few gifts he'd been able to pack on the horses. Queen Gwenhyfar promised to personally see the rest delivered to Glenarden, given his vow to deliver to Fortingall the precious books now stored in the chamber he shared with Daniel.

Lady Brenna was more thrilled with the teak box filled with exotic herbs and medicines Alyn presented her than the silver scissors and costly bolt of rose silk for a new gown. She marveled over the box's design. Much like Alyn's alchemy case, it had sealed separate compartments and folded into a light and portable case.

"It shall replace my old leather satchel," she said, referring to the medicine pouch the healer carried on her monthly rounds through Glenarden's hills and lowlands to see to the care and needs of its people. Her husband had even built a sick house apart from the keep for the hospitality and treatment of those who came from afar to seek her help.

Ronan would have built her a great hall for her patients, had she asked for it. Such love and devotion was rare in this world so filled with war and strife.

'Twas unfair that it be snatched from Kella's grasp ... with the slash of a sword blade.

'Twas *punishment*. All the day, she'd chased the word from her mind, but it would never drift far.

"Now *that*," Ronan said, upon learning Alyn had purchased cases of fine wine for both him and Caden, "is worth waiting for."

It was most likely on its way from Carmelide by now.

Fresh guilt hammered at Kella's mind. How dare she hope Queen Gwenhyfar would forgive her disobedience? She had not only broken God's law but the queen's orders. Being with child might be taken into account for Kella's rash disregard, but carrying one conceived out of wedlock begged disfavor, if not banishment from the court life Kella cherished.

Oh, what foolrede upon foolrede have I committed?

Not even Conall and Joanna's utter ecstasy over the toys that their cunning uncle had designed and made for them could lighten thoughts casting stone upon stone at Kella's conscience.

One toy was a pigeon carved by the hand of fellow scholar. Alyn took credit for the mechanical function only. The bird pecked the table, sprung up, and pecked again each time Joanna turned a small wheel. Fatin's former master Hassan had painted the creature so lifelike that even Daniel admired each distinctly carved and painted feather.

"My hand is steady for mixing and measuring, mayhap even surgery," Alyn explained, "not for carving or painting."

Conall's eyes grew and grew as his uncle unwrapped an extraordinary wooden sword. The hilt was embedded with sparkling red glass and its end carved into a Glenarden wolf's head. When Kella didn't think the lad could become more excited, his uncle removed a dagger of the same wood from its hidden sheath in the thick crossguard.

"I don't know which is the bigger child," Brenna laughed, pointing to Alyn as he grabbed a large wooden spoon from the table and challenged his nephew. Warmth and more kindled in the look she exchanged with her husband.

A blade of emotion wedged in Kella's throat. Her baby would never know such love and happiness. And because Kella was part of this family, she couldn't bring her shame here, even though she knew they'd take her and the child in.

"Ho, knave," Conall shouted.

Alyn, forgetting his sore ribs, leapt upon a bench to avoid the wooden sword's wild assault … where the pain promptly reminded him. "Hold, good sir," he gasped, grabbing at his side. "Your chase has sorely wounded me."

Conall's dark brow knitted with suspicion. "I haven't laid blade to you, you curmudgeon."

"Nay?" Alyn tugged up his tunic. "Then have a look at this."

At the sight of the bindings, Conall backed away, until his blue eyes steeled with second thought. "Those are *old* wounds."

Alyn held up his hands in surrender and stepped down. "Aye, but newly sore, nonetheless."

"What a lovely brooch you're wearing, brother." Ronan's badgering dripped with sarcasm.

Alyn caught Kella's eye. "'Tis Kella's—one of the gifts for her service at our cousin's court."

"It's as funny an animal as Fatin," Joanna observed from where she played with her bird.

Conall was less impressed. "You're wearing a *lady's* brooch?"

Undaunted, Alyn grinned. "You will too someday, Conall," he promised as he tossed aside his "weapon." "Especially if the lady is as pretty as Lady Kella." With an exaggerated sigh, he dropped down to the bench, changing the subject. "But 'tis love and compassion I need now," he announced. "If only I knew where to find it."

"*I* have love," Joanna volunteered. Leaving the pecking pigeon with Daniel, she raced at Alyn, slowing only when her mother reminded her of her uncle's injury. The little girl put her arms about Alyn's neck from one side while her brother, sword still in hand, embraced him from the other.

Alyn planted loud kisses, one on each flushed cheek. Grinning drunk from the attention, he sought out Kella at the hearth.

And drew her across the distance and into the warmth of their embrace.

"Now *this*"—he told her, reveling in the love surrounding him— "was worth coming home for."

Except it was *his* home that surrounded him with love and acceptance, not hers. And certainly not her fatherless baby's.

CHAPTER THIRTEEN

Alyn's grin faded as Kella leapt up from the hearth and ran through the group of servants clearing the floor to retire for the night. She'd been solemn all evening, her lips twitching a time or two at the children's antics, but he could practically feel the anguish that she must have suppressed. But when she fled the family gathering, it broke free, contorting the face she tried to hide behind her hands.

The abrupt retreat left all but Alyn and Daniel frozen in her wake.

Little Joanna pulled out of Alyn's embrace in alarm. "What's the matter with Aunt Kella?"

"Poor girl." Brenna rose from the table in concern. "How thoughtless of us to find such joy in Alyn's homecoming, when she must be in utter despair over Egan. One would think we'd forgotten his loss."

Daniel caught Alyn's eye, jerking his head toward the door, though Alyn needed no prodding.

"*I'll* see to her," Alyn insisted. He moved the children aside. "'Tis more amiss than Egan's loss," he explained.

To his surprise, the feisty healer backed down and cast her husband an *I-told-you-so* look.

What she'd told him, Alyn could only guess, for she not only had a healer's sharp eye, but the gift of second sight. He hoped to speak to Brenna about the visions later. Right now, Kella was utmost in his mind.

"Though, I … *we*," he added hastily for Daniel's sake, "are not at liberty to discuss it." Truth was, he wasn't sure how much he *could* tell his family. That decision would wait.

When Alyn stepped outside, the air was cool enough for a cloak. An instinctive glance at the quarter moon overhead promised favor to the dark clouds gathering in the north. Perhaps even rain. The pitch torches lighting the inner grounds made the shadows dance as Alyn made his way toward the training yard. Only a small number would continue to burn through the night, now that everyone was preparing for bed.

There was no need to guess where Kella had gone. Egan had a house of his own next to the weapons barn, a single room filled to the ceiling with weapons of all nature that the champion warrior had collected from Saxon, Pict, Welshman, and even his fellow Scots— any who'd dare stand up to him in battle or contest. Though little bigger than a horse stall with a circle of stone for heat, it was cozy.

When the fire was lit.

Tonight, when Alyn entered, it was cold, dark, and musty as a tomb from its prolonged abandonment. A hide covering over its only window blocked what precious little light the night afforded, so he found Kella more by sob than by sight. She sat on the bench board at the end of her father's bed box.

"I'm so sorry, Kella," Alyn commiserated, joining her. "We should not have celebrated so heartily. Your da deserves better than that from us."

"Aye." She sighed, but her head shook contrarily. "Though it's not my grief that tortures me," she protested. "'Tis my guilt—"

Alyn started as she pulled away from him and stumbled in haste out the door. He followed her but stopped short when she leaned upon the corner of the hut and retched. Again … and again.

Father God! Much as Alyn longed to comfort her, this was the one area where his best efforts to succeed failed him pitifully. A priest was expected to possess some medical abilities, but God had not given him the strong stomach of a healer. Would that he'd let Brenna come after all.

But Kella was so distraught, he battled the roil of his stomach and warily approached her. At the touch of his hand on her shoulder, she laid her warm cheek against it and leaned weakly against the outside wall. Her eyes were closed, but Alyn feared another outburst building with each rapid snatch of her breath.

"Hush, Kella. This cannot be good for you." He tried not to get too close, lest his senses trigger and turn upon him. "There is nothing you've done that can separate you from the love of God … or from mine."

Even unto retching, if he must.

"Real—*hic*—ly?" The hope in her small voice fortified him.

"*Ma chroi* …" *My heart.* A sweat broke cold in the wake of the blood leaving his face, but his determination grew. "Really."

The word seemed to lift the burden off her shoulders. She straightened and rolled against the building until she faced him. The warmth of her palms spread upon his chest reversed the blood flow from his face.

She looked into his eyes as though he alone held the key to her relief. "Then hear my confession."

Alyn's mind reeled as though mule-kicked. "Now?" He wasn't certain he wanted to hear anything about Lorne of Errol and his charms. Besides, Alyn wasn't a priest. He'd given up the tonsure and dress.

Gwenhyfar's words came back to haunt him. "*We are all priests of God, cousin, whether we wear the tonsure and dress or nay.*"

Kella sought out his hand, and his resistance crumbled. She led the way inside and patted the bench beside her for him to sit. Though Egan had fashioned the box extra wide and long, she huddled close to Alyn for his warmth, increasing his consternation by the breath.

He should have thought to bring a cloak. Better yet, let Brenna come. Alyn reached behind them, grappling for a blanket to answer the chill. At least one of them would be comfortable, he thought, wrapping it around her and making certain that it formed a wedge between them.

"I cannot bear this secret any longer. It preys upon my heart like a monster"—her words tumbled out—"ripping it to shreds again and again. And maybe …" With a heavy sigh, she laid her head against his arm.

"Maybe?" God be thanked his voice was calm, even though his mind and body did full battle—logic sorely outmaneuvered by the heart and senses. He knew Egan kept a jug of elderberry wine for when his stomach rebelled with too much merriment. "Go on," he said, digging around the foot of the pallet in the hope that it might still be there.

"Maybe God will stop punishing me," she told him.

Alyn latched onto the clay jug and produced it as if she could see it more in the light from the open door. "Here," he said, uncorking it. "Have some of your da's elderberry. 'Twill calm the stomach and the soul."

And wash away the sourness that even the thought of triggered a slight gag in Alyn's throat.

While Kella obliged him, he formed his answer carefully. "*God* doesn't punish us, Kella. If God dealt us what we deserved, we *all* would suffer worse than we do on This Side. Here, our trials are temporary. God's punishment will be eternal fire. What you and I face now are the consequences of ill-considered choices. Choices not simply to ignore His laws ... *but to ignore His love.*"

Alyn's last words stirred the shadows of his own guilt. Had he been so consumed with the past that he had ignored God's love and rejected His peace?

Kella nearly choked on the sweet wine. She bristled as she shoved the cork into the container and slammed it down. "How can you say that your *God* did not take Lorne from me as punishment? We did not wait for marriage to give our love and bodies to each other."

For the love of the saints, this was not for his ears.

"We'd every intent to marry, but *God*," she ranted, "didn't let that happen. How can you call it anything but punishment?"

These were the rants of a starstruck maiden. Lorne of Errol had taken Kella out of wedlock, without love enough to wait and honor her on the marriage bed. Alyn wanted to spit on the cur's grave. Worse, he wanted to take the man's life again.

"Perhaps …" Alyn's mind tripped over his anger. The more he heard, the more he needed forgiveness himself. "Perhaps you would feel more comfortable speaking to one of the priests at Bishop Martin's monastery."

"Humph."

"Kella, I've stopped my priestly duties. I struggle over my own folly leading to my teacher's death. Even if this were not the case, I know you too well." And to hear of her prince's love—or lack thereof—was unbearable. "It isn't proper for me—"

"Alyn!" Kella trapped his face between her hands and shook him. "I care not if you are priest, prince, or struggling sinner. There is no one I trust more than you, Alyn O'Byrne. None to whom I can say that I am with child without expecting condemnation."

With child.

Now it was Alyn who felt ill. Daniel was right. Alyn's worst fear for Kella was founded.

She sought one of Alyn's hands, holding it fast as she turned away. The yard lights silhouetted her head as she bowed like a broken doll, chin to chest. Her words were tortured. "Bless me, Father, for I have sinned in the eyes of God. I have lusted, though You know 'twas in love."

Alyn squeezed the fingers interlocked with his. *Father, forgive her rebelliousness, for she bears the pain of her own cross.*

"I pray for Your mercy upon me and my child in the name of Your Son, Jesus the Christ."

Help me to show her that the ways of mankind are not Your ways.

"Still, I accept the consequences as You see fit, but I beg You—" Kella moved Alyn's hand against her belly. "Spare this innocent, Father."

Touching a woman who was not his wife with such familiarity, much less one during confession, was unthinkable. "Kella, I am *not* God's hand. This is no proper confess—"

"You are a *priest*," she wept, "and I n-need God's touch." The fingers interlocked with his gripped him so that Alyn could not pull free for fear of harming her. "Tell me that God cannot t-touch me through you, H-his own priest," she charged brokenly. "I'm lost, Alyn. I and my ch-child are lost." She strangled with a sob. "Without hope."

"Glorify Me."

That voice again, the one Alyn had heard in Carmelide. Compassion rained as if the roof had opened from the crown of his head to the toes of his feet. Doubt and guilt washed away in the flood of living water.

Alyn dropped to his knees before the weeping woman, both his hands spread upon her belly. "Kella, hear me now, for I speak the Word of God. God's mercy endureth forever. There is nothing— *nothing*," he averred, a priest of God, robed and tonsured by the Holy Spirit, "that can separate you or your child from God's love.…"

Was it his imagination, or had he felt a winglike brush of life through the wool of Kella's gown? Joy quickened in a place where naught but reticence and doubt previously reigned.

"Or from mine." Alyn finished his vow a man. A man who knew without doubt that it was meant for him to care for and protect this woman and her child. Whether he imagined the babe reaching out to him or nay, whether he spoke as priest or man—none of those things mattered, not now. Not ever. This was God's will ... and his.

Alyn raised her hand to his lips, whispering against her fingers, "As you have confessed and repented of your sin before God, know now that you are forgiven, Kella O'Toole."

"You are forgiven, Alyn O'Byrne."

"God be thanked," Alyn mouthed as the guilt sloughed away. It had been an accident. He'd gladly have taken Abdul-Alim's place. But God had another plan. This one.

Hope floated Alyn to his feet. He gathered Kella up into his arms. "And I promise to love your child, Kella O'Toole, as much as I love"—he brushed her lips—"and *have* loved you, though I was slow to realize it."

"W-what?"

"Neither of you need suffer. No one need know." Alyn plunged heart first into the sweet tide overtaking him. "If we marry on the morrow."

"Oh!"

Kella laid her head against his chest, her silence long enough to give Alyn concern. Surely she had no choice. "I ... I haven't the right words of gratitude," she whispered at last, "or answer."

Kella's resolve and strength drained away with a lengthy sigh. Thinking her about to swoon, Alyn tightened his embrace.

But she gathered herself. "There is no other heart so generous and kind as that which beats beneath my ear." Kella backed far enough away to plant a kiss over the scar upon his chest. "I do not deserve such mercy." Her voice caught with emotion. "But I gratefully accept it ... for myself and this innocent child."

The betrothal and wedding plans were announced at once. Many of Glenarden's people had watched Alyn and Kella grow up together, so the news was received as if the couple were their own kin. Excitement buzzed throughout the hall, even though most of the servants and hearth companions were bedding down for the evening.

Once the women were settled, Alyn found himself in Egan's hut for the second time that night. This time with his grim-faced elder brother. It was the only private place ready to them. At least this time, Ronan had the forethought to gather a stick from one of the torches to light the bird-beak rush light sitting on a crude table beneath the window.

"Are you absolutely certain this is what you want to do?" Ronan asked once the door's latch fell into place.

Wrapped in his cloak of the same O'Byrne plaid as his brother, Alyn nodded from the very spot where an hour before he'd kissed Kella until he thought *he'd* swoon. The spirit that had carried him away still tingled within.

"This is the only thing I've been certain of in a long while."

He meant every word, even though Kella's response had been reticent. Given the circumstances, how could Alyn expect more? What was the proverb about time healing all wounds?

"Humph." The tight grimace of Ronan's lips told he was nowhere near satisfied with what Alyn and Kella had told the family about their decision to marry or the reason for their haste—that they had to deliver a package of immediate importance to the Fortingall.

"Is there anything more you want to tell me aside from the fact that you're taking your new bride into enemy territory for their honey-mead month at the request of the queen?" In that tone, 'twas no question, but a demand.

In truth, there was a lot Alyn wanted to share with Ronan.

"Does Gwenhyfar know that you and Kella are betrothed?"

If only his brother would stop firing questions at him. "No," Alyn replied with equal fire. "Just give me a moment to think where to begin."

Chapter Fourteen

Alyn joined his brother on the bed bench and began his story in the East. Unlike with Gwenhyfar, his voice was not belabored with anguish, for this very night he'd accepted the Word he preached to Kella. He'd accepted the forgiveness he'd had all along. He simply shared the account of the accident brought about by his carelessness, told Ronan of his guilt and doubts as to his worthiness to serve as a priest. But passion gained upon him as he finished with "until I met Kella again."

"But that was what … less than two weeks?"

Ronan's derision dug beneath Alyn's skin. It wasn't as if he was still a wet-eared pup. "'Tis hardly time to fall in love," Ronan told him. "When you left, you swore that Kella was too fickle for your liking. What," he challenged, "changed so drastically in such short a time?"

Brenna's *I-told-you-so* look came to Alyn's mind. Did she know Kella was with child? Was that what she'd *told* Ronan?

"In case you hadn't noticed, Kella has matured into a beautiful woman, intelligent as Brenna in her own way." Perhaps Alyn should remind Ronan of his readiness to kill their middle brother over Ronan's healing woman.

One thick brow shot up. Though his brother said not a word, it demanded volumes. Although Alyn could not call Kella his woman ... *yet*.

In a burst of frustration, Alyn threw up his hands, switching tactics. "What can I say, brother? No red-blooded O'Byrne male was meant to be celibate."

The second brow rose, Ronan's piercing gaze prodding Alyn from beneath it. But the eldest had not inherited all of their father's bullheadedness.

"The rest is between Kella and me," Alyn responded.

"Humph." As though he'd found his answer anyway, Ronan sat back and folded his arms across his chest. "How far along is she, laddie?"

Alyn's defiance crumbled. He should have realized that Brenna, with her healer's gift of foresight, would see through the plan, though he'd hoped for Kella's sake that no one would notice. That Kella might give birth elsewhere where curious minds would not count.

"Going on three months. Her *betrothed*"—Alyn made sure the word was understood for Kella's sake—"was beheaded in the same battle where Egan went missing."

"Oh!" A woman's gasp betrayed her presence outside and set off the last remnant of Alyn's tolerance.

With a far-from-priestly exclamation, he jumped to his feet and snatched open the door. Lady Brenna stood there, sheepish and shivering, in a fur-collared cape. But one look at her tear-widened gaze made the flare of Alyn's anger fizzle. He stepped back, motioning her inside and toward the seat next to Ronan.

"Milady."

But Brenna stopped, gathering Alyn's face between her hands, and planted a kiss on the middle of his brow. "You have the heart of a saint."

"And *you've* the ears of an eavesdropper," Ronan charged. "Did I not tell you that I would take care of this?"

Oblivious to his annoyance, Brenna sat beside him and wriggled beneath the shelter of his arm for warmth. "How she must suffer, *anmchara*," she told him.

If calling Ronan *soulmate* wasn't enough to dissolve his scowl, the glance she slanted his way was. "Just think," she lamented, "to fall in love like us and lose her lover to war before they could marry."

"'Tis tragic, to be sure," Ronan agreed, "but that means she doesn't love our Alyn. That my little brother, in an effort to prove himself noble of heart, is marrying a woman to save her honor."

"And to prevent an innocent child from growing up fatherless," Brenna finished. She beamed at Alyn. "Yours has always been a tender soul."

"A tender *head*, more like it," Ronan argued.

"*My* decision makes total sense. It benefits the both of us!" Alyn didn't mean to shout, but Ronan saw the world in shades of black and white, except when it came to Brenna. Yes, his eldest brother had had to grow up faster than Alyn and Caden. He'd taken over Glenarden as a youth when their father suffered an arm-paralyzing fit from which he never completely recovered. Ronan had been robbed of his carefree boyhood. But that didn't make him right in this case.

Nor did Alyn's words anger the beast that Ronan could be. If anything, he acted as if they'd won his argument. "Didn't I say it?" he gloated.

"'Tis a matter of sense *and* heart," the lady replied. "Did you not see it, the way he watched Kella all the evening?"

This was not a new debate, Alyn gathered. The back-and-forth continued, as though he were no more than the proverbial fly on the wall.

"And *she*," Ronan said, "looked as if she were dying herself."

"Why not? What with her father missing and the father of her babe dead?"

"'Twas hardly the look of a woman ready to marry for love."

"How could she not love a man who would save her *and* her child? And you know well, they've always been fond of each other."

"You heard what he said." Ronan did his best impression of Alyn, leaping to his feet as if ready for a fight, hands fisted at his side. "*My decision makes total sense. The laddie's treating this as if it were one of his experiments. Not a single word about love.*"

"Is that what this is all about then?" Alyn heard himself exclaim. "Well, all right then!" In a fit of fury, Alyn shoved Ronan so hard, he tumbled backward over the bench and onto the pallet behind. In another situation, the sight of Glenarden's chieftain, arms and legs aloft like a turtle on its back, would have made him howl with laughter. But his was not a humor of amusement.

"I love her," he bellowed. "Is that what you want to hear, brother?" Alyn ran his hands over his temples and paced away as far as the room would allow and pivoted on his heel. "I knew it the moment I first saw her and kissed her in Gwen's garden. *Soundly*, I might add."

Brenna *did* laugh at her upended husband. "Satisfied, my love?"

Ronan's stern veneer cracked with a grin. "Aye. But I wanted to hear him say it. None of this *logic*"—he spat out the word as if it were bitter—"that he's so fond of." Ronan rolled out of the box and to his feet. "You see, laddie, there's nothing logical about love." He seized Alyn's arm, shaking it. "But congratulations, anyway."

Alyn's response was guarded. These two had pulled his strings until he snapped. Part of him wanted to storm away, as Kella was prone to do. But their actions and words bespoke of naught but concern for him.

"I thank you, brother ... and sister," he replied, unable to totally suppress his sulk. "Though I pray you did not perform this same drama for Kella. She's been through enough as it is. Though I do hope that, in time, she'll come to feel as I do."

Brenna got up and gave him a hug. "You are her knight in faith-gilded armor. How can she not?"

Because her heart belongs to another man? Alyn wanted to ask Brenna that. Instead he stood and shoved open the door. There was more he needed from Ronan's gifted wife. As a healer, she might help him with the blinding headaches ... and the unsettling visions that accompanied them. At least, he prayed as much.

"But do tell me, milady," he inquired, "did you foresee all this in a *dream?*"

It only makes sense.

Kella groaned as she rolled over in her bed the following morning. Her wedding day.

But *why* did Alyn have to add *that* to his proposal?

Granted, it was true. If she married Alyn, few would know the baby was not his. Her honor would be saved. The baby would have a family and, no doubt in Kella's mind, a good father. She should be grateful for his offer. Even a little excited, for the kiss he sealed their agreement with had been as fervent as the one in the queen's garden. One that had almost made her forget she belonged to another.

Who was forever beyond her reach, she recalled as guilt assailed her.

And had she not once fancied Alyn, but for his maddening logic and preoccupation with his studies? His declaration of love would have put any woman's head in the clouds. While her heart still belonged to Lorne, Alyn's zeal left her staggered in its wake.

And then he followed it with, "*It only makes sense.*"

Stopping her midswoon.

Instead of answering in kind, Kella responded in cool agreement. 'Twas either that or smack him with the hand he held as they returned to the great hall to announce their betrothal. Once thawed from the shock, the O'Byrnes fawned congratulations upon them with breath-crushing hugs and handshakes. Though something told Kella that Daniel suspected the truth behind their facade of new-found love.

She could see it in his gaze as he beckoned her over to where he sat, leg propped on a bench, for a celebration kiss. Whether 'twas pity, concern, or both, she couldn't tell.

And Brenna knew, of course. No secrets could be kept from her keen intuition. And if Brenna knew, then Ronan did as well. Part of Kella was glad that her secret was out, at least among family. Yet how could their thoughts not be shadowed by her shame, even though they outwardly rejoiced over the wedding and surrounded her with love and acceptance?

Regardless, today she would become a priest's wife. It would even lend weight, as Alyn judiciously pointed out, to their reason for traveling north. A priest and his new wife would need a benefactress such as Queen Heilyn to help them establish a church and home. The practicality sapped what remained of bliss.

But what sort of home could Kella expect for herself and her child, once the books were safe? A cold stone cell in the middle of the highlands?

And would Alyn expect husbandly rights?

She shivered with uncertainty. She still loved Lorne in *that* way.

Although she had not forgotten the night that she'd rubbed the liniment in and around that horrid scar, how the muscles of Alyn's upper torso bunched with tension beneath her fingers. Somewhere in the midst of her genuine concern for his suffering, something more primitive had invaded her senses.

Kella tossed aside the woolen covers. How could God possibly forgive her, as Alyn insisted, when such thoughts plagued her?

Because Alyn would soon be her husband in His eyes. Because she would go as his wife and sin no more.

While her heart knew it betrayed another.

Despairing of peace, Kella closed her eyes in prayer.

Father God, help me. My thoughts spin in confusion, sometimes sinward, though I mean not to go that way. Keep me from temptation, for my fickle senses and rebellious heart have led me to naught but heartache and confusion. Help my heart to become of one accord with my mind in accepting Alyn as husband and father to my child. Show me the way You would have me go on this second chance You have, in Your mercy, given me.

A wondrous sense of renewal washed over Kella as she whispered, "Amen." She could almost feel ethereal arms wrapping tenderly around her and the babe in her womb. Tears trickled down her cheeks from what she'd thought, after last night's misery, was a dry well. Her beleaguered soul swelled with undeniable conviction.

And for the first time in a long time, she felt God had heard and would answer.

CHAPTER FIFTEEN

Alyn had *seen* his own wedding. Kella was the weeping bride he'd seen in the dream at Lockwoodie Tavern, and the priest and faceless groom had been himself rolled into one. It was surreal as the event unfolded that afternoon, just as he'd dreamt ... or almost.

Such dreams, Alyn had learned from his sister-in-law the previous eve, were frequently unclear. They were but shadows of possibility that the Holy Spirit brought into light when God saw fit. "Yet you are convicted in your soul," she explained, "that these are of God and not sleep's whimsy."

But Alyn had been too distracted for such conviction, although the notion of marrying Kella had taken root.

When Brenna heard how the headaches plagued him as much as the vision, she had invited him up to the second-floor room she shared with Ronan rather than venture into the night again for privacy. While Alyn sat on the end of their bed box, she placed her hands upon his head as she'd once done for his tormented father, Tarlach. Keeping her voice low so as not to wake the children sleeping beyond a privacy screen, she prayed for God to reveal the nature of Alyn's torment.

The scene of the explosion came alive in his mind, so real that Alyn felt the smoke scorching his lungs and the ram-like impact. He'd been on his way out the door when an invisible fist knocked him farther away, saving his life.

"Poor laddie," Brenna commiserated, her forehead pressed to his as though looking into his mind. "Such a great fire from such a small bundle."

But Alyn could see no bundle for the throbbing in his temples.

Nor could Brenna explain what she meant, when he questioned her. She didn't recall even saying it. "Just pray about it," she advised. "If it's important, God will make it clear."

Ronan fetched a soothing tea for Alyn, while his intuitive wife massaged the exact spots on Alyn's head that were about to burst with misery. "I've pondered why such pain oft comes with visions. Perhaps because that part of the mind isn't used as often," Brenna suggested. "Yet the pain and the frustrating lack of clarity must have their purpose. *God does nothing without purpose.*"

Brenna's observations echoed in Alyn's mind as he surveyed Glenarden's great hall, now draped with fresh garlands of flowers and vine for the wedding. The bundle Brenna mentioned was still a mystery, but truly God's purpose—and hand—was involved in bringing all this about.

He and Kella married in the orchard, accompanied by birdsong, surrounded by friends and family. The O'Byrnes' old friend Bishop Martin had come down from his cave retreat in the hills to officiate for the couple. The Gowrys clan, now dear friends but long-ago enemies who'd once held Alyn hostage, had showed up that morning after having received word yesterday that their prince, Daniel, had returned from Carmelide.

Ronan stood in for Egan. Not a dry eye was to be found when he presented Kella to Alyn, along with a handsome dowry her father had, unbeknownst to her, put away from his earnings on the battle-field and in contests. As a priest and youngest son, Alyn had the barest to offer in return, save his mother's gold ring and a deed to the same tract of land that his father had given Lady Aeda on their wedding day—enough to support the bride should she find herself a widow.

The servants who'd known Alyn and Kella since childhood played dual roles as guests and staff. When Alyn kissed his bride, their "huzzahs" were loud enough to be heard in Strighlagh. With no time for congratulations afterward, the servants dutifully retreated, an army under the steward Ervan's command, to the hall to put on the wedding feast.

All that was missing was Alyn's middle brother, Caden, and his family from Trebold in Lothian. Though had Caden delivered that bearlike clap-on-the-back congratulation he was famous for, Alyn would be seeing stars instead of his bride.

Bedecked in one of Brenna's gowns of ice-blue silk and with spring flowers woven into the braid crowning a cascade of long, shimmering spirals, Kella took Alyn's breath away. A maidenly blush bloomed on her cheeks, though her tear-reddened eyes betrayed exhaustion.

She'd wept through the wedding vows, babbling "I'm so sorry" at each pause. But given the recent loss of her father, none considered the bride's behavior unusual. Many cried with her, for Egan was as well thought of as his daughter. If Alyn could, he'd spare Kella further distress and take her directly to Egan's hut, which, at Kella's request, had been cleared of weapons and converted into a love nest for the two of them.

"Father will be honored," Kella told him when the plans had been made that morning.

Alyn had contained his doubt. All things *were* possible, but this was not probable.

"He always fancied you as my husband, you know."

Husband, Alyn thought, taking in the delicate curve of her jaw. And that small nose that could lift in such great defiance. Aye, he'd be at least that for Kella, if not quite in the way Glenarden's champion anticipated.

Kella turned suddenly now, catching him in his intent contemplation. "Have you second thoughts?" Her expression spoke more of worry than the humor she attempted.

Neither of them had gotten much sleep the night before. He couldn't but think that the food she'd barely touched on the silver charger they shared—a gift from Ronan and Brenna—was neglected due to fatigue.

Alyn raised her hand and kissed it where his late mother's ring sparkled on his bride's fourth finger. "None, wife. *Never*," he vowed. "Not about you *or* our babe."

Our babe. His certainty flinched at anxiety's prick. Alyn had not been around infants, not even when his nieces and nephews were born. He *had* witnessed childbirth in Baghdad's hospital but had been of no use.

It didn't matter. Having pledged heart and soul to the babe, as well as to its mother when he took his vows, Alyn would do what he had to do when the time came … which *should* be wait and pace while the women took care of the wife and bairn.

A happy squeal drew the couple's attention to where Ronan and little Joanna danced between two long rows of tables set up in front of Alyn and Kella's place of honor. Though it looked more like frolic, it was to music provided by a hastily assembled musical trio.

Glenarden's bard and tutor to the children, a Welshman by the name of Teilo, had plucked soothing tunes on the harp throughout the meal, but now his strings had turned lively. Lady Brenna revealed yet another gift as she joined him with a pipe. But most surprising of all was the bodhran player, ten-year-old Conall. He played the drum with a bone-shaped stick well enough to make his teacher proud.

"Why don't Uncle Alyn and Aunt Kella dance?" Joanna declared, once the tune wound down. "I thought a bride and broom had to dance at a wedding."

"That's *groom*," her father corrected. "And they are probably like the rest of us—weary from the wedding and the effort to make it a grand day to remember."

Taking up Ronan's cue, Alyn rose from the bench he shared with Kella. "Remember the long trip we took from Carmelide?" he asked Joanna.

The child held up pudgy fingers and counted. "Six days?"

"Aye," he said, "six days of hard riding, little sleeping, and fighting outlaws at night. It's enough to tire the High King's army, so you know your aunt Kella—"

"—would love to dance," Kella cut him off. She slipped her hand into Alyn's, whispering, "'Tis the least we owe them."

Her father's spirit would not allow Kella to mourn a moment longer. She remembered him sitting at the end of the family table, roaring with laughter, teasing the ladies, and watching, with a hawk's eye, the young men watching Kella. But when that sharp gaze fell upon Alyn, it lost its edge. How oft had Egan nudged her with a nod when Alyn sought to invite her into the hall merriment? That was why she thought it right to spend their first night together as man and wife under Da's roof. His blessing was here, even while—she was certain—he was away, using all his skills of survival to come home to her.

Once Kella took to the floor, the oppressive shadow her grief cast over the hall dissolved. Others joined in the clapping and stomping, swinging and skipping, twirling and laughter. She counted each person a blessing as she wove her way through the O'Byrne and Gowrys men, women, and children. Each hug renewed the spirit that had drained from her very soul these last days. Each congratulation whittled away at the stone in her breast.

Even Alyn seemed to gain a second wind. The darling of Glenarden's womenfolk from the day he was born overlooked not a one with his dancing and kisses. He even dragged Annie the cook and her girls from the kitchen for a reel. But then, Alyn had always loved the world, and it loved him. Tonight, his priestly and scholarly decorum was abandoned, and the lad of sixteen that Kella had adored was back.

"Gotcha!" Alyn grabbed Kella's hand at the end of the line and spun her into his arms.

As her husband.

He pressed his forehead to hers. "I'm done, my love. I've kissed every woman here, including toothless Annie, but now I'd have my wife."

His hand splayed at Kella's back, drawing her closer until the heat of his body drew the breath from hers. Or was it the heat closing in from the room? Even her clothing sought to smother her.

Alyn kissed her long but ever so tenderly.

Her body cried yes. Her heart, nay. Her senses drifted up as though trying to escape the contrary swirl of reactions. The room moved about Kella and her knees, but they had abandoned her—

Alyn swept her up into his strong arms, concern etching his flushed features. "To bed with you, milady."

His hoarse command shattered her thought into icy slivers, one falling upon another.

Would she?

Could she?

Celebrating a marriage was one thing. Consummating it—

'Twould be an insult to her child's father, hardly cold in his grave.

And an insult to Alyn for all his sacrifice if she refused him.

Kella could barely hear the tumbling thoughts over the chorus of cheers that gained and gained in volume as the guests realized she and Alyn were about to leave. But for Daniel's ear-piercing whistle to silence them, none would have heard Alyn's declaration of gratitude.

"There are not enough words, not even in the five languages my wife speaks," he said, teasing Kella, "to thank you, each of you, for making this day so wonderful. May you all be blessed as you've blessed us." His words carried well, like those of a bard.

Until he ran out of them. Something Alyn O'Byrne rarely did. If possible, the flush of his face deepened, and the strands of his muscle supporting Kella tensed even more as he sought out the senior priest for help.

"Bishop Martin?"

The old man waved from his seat at the Gowrys board and rose, though it took a while with his arthritic joints. "Ah, yes," he said, clearing his throat. He made the sign of the cross over the one on the front of his white dress robe and bowed his head, arms spread as though to embrace them all. "Great Father in heaven, go with this man and this woman as they start their life together as man and wife. Bless their table with bounty, their union with children, and their home with love. Amen."

To the echo of *amens*, Martin raised his voice even more, so that even those who were deep in conversation round the hearth stopped speaking. "Now go in peace, Alyn and Kella O'Byrne, and may the rest of us be mindful of Egan's memory," he said, sweeping the room with a challenge. "For *if* he were here, that big red-haired giant would plant himself in the door to stop any mischief that might follow these two into the night. Do I make myself clear, good friends?"

Disjointed murmurs of agreement and complaint followed Kella and Alyn out into the keep yard. The fresh air helped clear the dizziness that had nearly made Kella swoon inside.

"I … I think I can walk now," she told him as he struck out for the training grounds. "But 'twas so warm in there, I lost my breath."

His indignant snort shook her. "And I thought it was my kiss."

Though his ribs surely plagued him, Alyn did not put her down. Even when he fumbled with the latch on the door of Egan's house and nearly dropped her.

With a nervous laugh, Kella pushed his hand away. "Allow me, Sir Mule-head." She lifted the latch and pushed.

"Mule-head, is it?" he bellowed. "Why—" He broke off as the door swung wide. "*Merciful Father!*"

CHAPTER SIXTEEN

Kella could no more believe her eyes than Alyn. Without the impos-
ing weaponry hanging from every peg, Kella wondered if they were
in the wrong abode. An inviting lamp-lit room with a fire glowing
near the foot of a newly polished box bed welcomed them. More
garlands of fresh flowers had been strung along the beams overhead,
lending their fragrance and color, while the mattress had been stuffed
with new heather till it rose almost as high as the bench at the foot.

Against the wall, the customary month's supply of honey mead
was stacked next to the small table where her father used to dine when
he wanted privacy. On it was a platter of loaves, fruit jams, and cheeses.
Right there under that window, she used to sit and listen to tales of
his wondrous adventures or how he'd courted and adored her mother.

More than ever, Kella knew this was right.

"I can't wait to see Da's face when he learns we've wed," she said
as Alyn carried her through the door and put her on her feet.

"'Twould be a sight." Alyn went straight to the honey mead and
took out a bottle to fill one of the matching goblets set out on the table.

It was hard to tell what he really thought about her father's
survival. Fear kept Kella from pressing it. Lorne's death had been

witnessed beyond doubt. But no one had seen what had happened to her father. He'd simply vanished.

"Should I go outside while you dress?" He glanced at her night-dress, which had been hung on a peg over the few belongings she'd brought from Carmelide. The peg on his side of the bed, where his things were stored, held nothing.

That *nothing* fanned fire to her face. "You're my *husband*," Kella replied. 'Twas his right to remain. Though she'd never disrobed before any man, not even Lorne. Theirs was an intimacy stolen one night in the queen's own garden … in the shadows of the very trellis where Alyn had taken that kiss.

Begone, Lorne, begone! You've no place here now.

"Were I a *proper* husband—"

Like your prince. Alyn didn't say it, but Kella heard the insecurity between his words.

"—you'd have a servant to help you."

And this would not do.

"Just turn your head," Kella instructed. "I'll not have you ridiculed for your gallant consideration." Which would surely happen, should someone see the groom waiting outside. "Or listen to you ridicule yourself." She sniffed. "*Proper* indeed! You are more than proper, Alyn. You are *God-sent*."

Kella meant it. Aye, she still grieved. But because of Alyn's godly assurance and noble sacrifice, she was not without hope. God had provided for her and her child through a man she held dear.

While Alyn helped himself to the mead and squatted by the fire, Kella hastily worked at the laces of her gown. Try as she

might to loosen them, they would not cooperate with her fumbling fingers. She felt for the troublesome knot until her arms
ached.

"Husband." She bowed her head in hot-cheeked surrender. "I
need your help."

"Are you certain?"

Kella huffed with impatience. "It's either that or go fetch toothless Annie."

"Heaven forbid!" Alyn shot to his feet in mock alarm and hurried to her. "Let me have a look."

Kella determined not to shrink from Alyn's fingers as they
worked at the knot. Two women warred within her one skin—one
demanding she withdraw into a cocoon of grief lest she betray Lorne,
while the other would have her repay this man for rescuing her body,
baby, and soul from her shame. *Both* were right.

"There you go," Alyn announced, his expression perfectly rakish.
"Glad to oblige."

"You'd think you'd done that before, *Father*," she teased. At least
he had in his youth with a certain milkmaid. Though why Kella
should think of it now was beyond her. Besides, at sixteen, what laddie wouldn't naturally choose the company of an experienced—and
willing—milkmaid over a petulant fourteen-year-old?

Perhaps they *both* played a game of nerves. But he'd started it.

"I've untied many a knot since I was a wee laddie," he replied,
refusing to rise to her bait.

And hadn't she had a right to be nervous? This was her first
time. At least, as a bride filled with shyness and insecurity. With
Lorne—faith, 'twas so quick and done, there was no time for the

sweetness of getting to know each other. Nor was there a long-established bond to play upon like that between her and Alyn.

Kella pulled her linen nightgown over her head and shed her dress and undershift, so that when they dropped, the other covered her. Plain with ruffles about the neckline and cuffs, it wasn't her best, but she'd not packed for a wedding night. After some hasty adjustments, she slid beneath the covers.

"Your turn." She gave him mischief for mischief. "Should I cover my head?"

"Oh, that won't be necessary for *my* part."

Undaunted, at least on the surface, Alyn rose from his haunches by the fire and unfastened his belt, which he laid across the table. Leveling a smirk at Kella that flushed her face, he lifted his tunic over his head.

His bindings were gone, though a nasty bruise remained where the brigand had struck him. But it was the cabled rippling of his torso that caught Kella's eye. Her fingers remembered that surprising strength from the other night, the kind that gave him the grace and agility of a cat in fight or dance.

Lorne had been a strapping bull of a warrior.

Oh, *why* could he not stay away tonight? How could Kella give herself to one man while haunted by another? Alyn dropped to the edge of the bed and unlaced his boots. His stockings came off with them, landing on the floor where they may.

She closed her eyes, inhaling the sweet scent of the flowers permeating the room. But when her husband pulled the covers back, her eyes flew open, and she flinched as if expecting a lash. She couldn't help herself.

This is my husband. I will give myself to him because he is good and it is right, no matter how wrong it feels. Lorne is gone. God, help me lay him to rest in my heart.

Grinning as if he knew something she did not, he nudged her hips with the back of his hand. "Move over, you *two*."

Only then did Kella realize he still wore his trousers. "B-but—"

Alyn slid beneath the covers and propped himself up on one elbow. "My dearest Kella," he said, tugging the blankets up to their chests, "you are a beautiful, desirable woman. I've thought of none other since the kiss we shared in the garden."

Kella remembered most heartily the shock, the forbidden discovery.

"But your heart belongs to another, and I know you do not love me in the same way that I have come to love you. So, until that day"—he cleared the huskiness from his throat—"I shall wear these braccae to bed and beg your indulgence if the wool is uncomfortable."

God be thanked! If ever there was a more considerate man on this earth, Kella knew him not. Alyn not only spared her now but offered time to bury Lorne's memory.

"Oh, Alyn, I *do* love you!" Overcome with gratitude and relief, she drew his face down to hers and kissed him, a short but wholehearted effort. "And I pray, *husband*, that I will be worthy of your untold patience and generosity."

"You already are, wife." A shaft of pain grazed his smile as he rolled away and turned his back to her.

"Your ribs are hurting," she surmised. How could they not after the foolrede of carrying her here from the hall? "Should I fetch the liniment from your bag?"

"My ribs are fine."

"You should have kept the bindings on."

"Kella," he snapped, all semblance of patience gone, "for the sake of all three of us, I pray you, *please*, just go to sleep."

Sun bathed the barnyard where Glenarden servants packed Alyn's and Kella's belongings into a cart hitched to a small but sturdy highland pony. While horses would be faster, the cart lent credibility to their charade as a priest of the Celtic Church and his wife bound for Fortingall at Queen Heilyn's bidding. Not that Alyn wore his unbleached robe of the church, which always drew attention and, hence, could slow them down. Instead, he counted on the common dress allowing them to blend in with the traveling mercers on their way to various local fairs now taking place.

Though a quarter of their honey mead had been consumed, their first week as husband and wife had not been one of idle days of holding hands and long impassioned nights, but one of preparation for the journey north and exhausted sleep. They would sorely miss Daniel's company, guidance, and strong arm, but there was a mission to be accomplished. Two, for Alyn had told Kella about Arthur's strange fit and his asking Alyn to get a feel for the political inclinations of the villages they passed. Serving the Dux Bellorum and his queen appealed to Kella's adventurous side, making life as the wife of a priest far more interesting.

But then, she'd learned her husband was no ordinary priest, but a man of many facets. While he devoted time to God, leaving their bed before daybreak and retiring long after she'd fallen asleep at night, he'd also spent time skillfully fashioning a false bottom in the cart with equally aged wood to hide the sacred volumes entrusted into his care. Kella dutifully saw that their travel clothing was washed and mended and personally reinforced the hidden pockets sewn into his travel cloak.

"In case we need a little magic," he'd explained.

It was amazing, the things Alyn had learned to do with what looked to be little more than different sorts of dirt, although when she'd encouraged him to show everyone how he'd started a fire without flint and steel, he'd refused.

He revered the study of God's creation yet seemed to fear it at the same time. Even now, Alyn carefully rolled up his alchemy box into the pallet that Brenna had made them for Kella's comfort. Between that, the wagon, and a tarred cloth covering large enough to protect the wagon from inclement weather, they could endure nights when hospitality wasn't available or offered.

Considering they would travel alone and without protection, both Alyn and Kella devoted their afternoons to weaponry practice with the sword, knife, lancea, and staff. So between that and the fact that they retreated to their love nest as soon as the children were put to bed, snickers and speculation as to the nature and future of their marriage abounded. If only the good folk knew that when her father's door closed at night, naught went on behind it save sweet, exhausted sleep.

Magnus, the captain that her father had trained and left in charge of Glenarden's guard, was as merciless with them as Egan. The exercises were rigorous and his combat fierce. Kella's staff practice and swordplay were confined to a pell, which could not strike her back. Nonetheless, several hours' combat with a wooden stave padded the thickness and height of a man had made her realize how inadequate her few hours a week spent in swordplay with Gwenhyfar had been.

Alyn had fared better against Magnus. The masters at the School of Wisdom included wrestling and combat games in the schooling, for the development of the body as well as for the mind and spirit. His lightness of foot made up for his slighter mass against the more powerful Magnus, but if Alyn misstepped, his trainer would have had the killing blow if not for skilled restraint and Alyn's mail shirt.

Kella's short sword was also hidden beneath the wagon seat. Alyn's staff lay within easy reach. As did a small sewing bag containing tiny pattern pieces that Kella and Brenna had cut from remnants of linen. Since only Ronan, Daniel, and Brenna were aware of Kella's condition, they'd worked each morning in the privacy of Egan's hut. Not only would the bairn's forthcoming wardrobe be a distraction on the journey, it would hone the skill of someone more accustomed to the pen than the needle and provide for the baby.

And now that the time had come to leave, Kella was almost dizzy with anticipation. She was renewed, strong as Maeve of legend and ready to ride into battle with a child as hearty as she. "Just rest when you need to, nourish yourself and the babe," Brenna had advised, "and remember that your father wouldna' have you risk yourself or the child for his sake."

Kella asked the healer if she'd any hint of Egan's welfare or harm, but alas, the answer was nay. "Sometimes we must go with faith," Brenna told her. "It is good that you can search for Egan while serving the Dux Bellorum and his queen, but keep in mind that God has a plan for you, Alyn, and the babe. You must accept that Egan may have already fulfilled God's plan."

"But I don't feel his loss in my heart. Could it be God's way of telling me not to give up?" Kella argued.

"All things are possible, Kella. Just be alert for God's nudges and follow them."

How Kella adored her sister-by-law for not shattering her hope. And for the teas and concoctions to ease the travel and protect the pregnancy. If only Brenna could explain how to recognize if the nudges be of God or of her own stubborn will.

God, I am so grateful that I have seen Your presence in my life again, Kella prayed as Alyn checked and double-checked the cart and contents. As much as lay upon his shoulders, he strove most to see to her and the babe's comfort. Like a promise from tomorrow, a laughing Conall and Joanna raced about the yard with the dogs and Fatin, who, after much wheedling on their part, was being left in their care. Ronan approached the wagon from the keep, laden with a huge basket, most likely foodstuffs, his wife beside him.

"There," Alyn announced. Still standing in the cart, he jumped and tested the ropes till he was satisfied his precious box could not possibly be jostled or slide loose from the sideboard to which it was tied.

"I still don't know why we don't leave that here," Kella told him. "We aren't going north to start a laboratorium."

"Or maybe we will. We will need a place to live."

His grin gave Kella second thought. Surely he wasn't proposing accepting an appointment in the north among those tattooed savages who'd murdered Lorne and—she was loath to think it—possibly her father. He was nearly three weeks gone now. Besides, they had the land Alyn had given her as a bridal gift. It would provide modest support.

"Or maybe we'll need medicine or …" Alyn's voice trailed off at the blast of a horn announcing the arrival of someone. Judging by the coded blast of the trumpet, it was more than one rider. A rain last eve allowed no dust to rise beyond the stockade walls from the hooves of their steeds, but Kella could hear them now, like a distant thunder.

Da!

Kella tried to shove her hope down as she waited for the identification process to take place. But upon hearing the guard's "From Strighlagh" shout down to Ronan, who handed over the food basket to Alyn, Kella started running for the gate.

God had sent Alyn. Was it too much to hope—

The gate opened, admitting seven weary riders, each clad in the white tunics with the red dragon emblem and scarlet capes of Arthur's guard. The horses had been ridden hard, their coats shining almost black with perspiration, and froth gathered round the bits they chewed.

Kella reached them first, addressing the man she assumed to be their leader. "Have you news of Egan O'Toole?"

She knew from his bewildered look that he did not.

"I'm here to seek Queen Gwenhyfar, milady, though I did not see her banner flying with Glenarden's."

Gwenhyfar? Kella mind reeled with confusion. The queen should have been in Strighlagh well before now.

"That is because our cousin is not here, sir," Ronan told him. "Was she expected to stop at Glenarden?" The question was not unreasonable. Gwenhyfar often visited her cousin's family en route to or from Strighlagh.

The man's face blanched. "Then 'tis better if we speak in private, milord."

chapter seventeen

Gwenhyfar was missing.

The news was an ominous start for Alyn and Kella's journey to Fortingall, though they got underway as soon as they heard the news. But the vision of the raven, eagle, and dove, and the roar of the bear that had visited Alyn at Merlin's feast of honor haunted him. Had he *seen* Gwenhyfar's abduction? he wondered as their horse strained to pull the cart over the high and narrow stone bridge across the River Allan. This was not *sciencia*. This was utter fantasy, and yet …

Unable to hold his secret any longer, he hesitantly told Kella about the vision of the scavengers and the eagle making off with the dove. "It sounds absurd, though the symbols do apply," he reasoned aloud as they passed a small cluster of huts.

Those inhabitants who were outside, working the ground cleared from the thick forest lining both sides of the river, stared at Alyn and Kella as they passed. The men grasped their farm tools like weapons while women and children made a rush for their huts.

Aye, the aftermath of the Miathi raid and skirmish with Arthur's troops still hung over the land like a black cloud, despite the sunny spring day. Alyn waved but kept his focus mostly on the road ahead. He'd been here before, and under ordinary circumstances, it was a friendly village that eagerly offered to sell or trade any of their excess produce with passing traffic. Today, even the dogs stayed in the yards, barking until Alyn could no longer hear them.

"Urien bears the raven as his standard," he reminded Kella, when woods thickened about the rough road again. "Modred the eagle, and our Gwen, the dove." He showed Kella his onyx ring with the mother-of-pearl dove.

"This smacks of Merlin's prophecies," Kella observed, sitting almost as tall as he on her cushion next to him. Since their cart did not insulate the body from a bone-jarring ride as the springlike legs of a horse did, he'd insisted she use the padding in consideration of the bairn, if not herself.

"Have you had such dreams before?" she asked.

"Not in the midday or about birds."

Intrigued, she cocked her head at him. "What then?"

Alyn hesitated. "The night at Lockwoodie, I dreamt I was the priest who conducted your wedding. But that wasn't exactly how it happened, as you well know."

Astounded into silence, Kella looked ahead at the rhythmic swish of the horse's tail.

"Besides, I cannot believe Modred would be foolish enough to abduct Arthur's queen," Alyn argued on. "That same young Arthur slew Modred's father, Cennalath, for his alliance with the Picts against Gododdin. It is by Arthur's grace that Modred rules there now." That, and Modred's mother was Arthur's aunt.

"What did you see of our wedding?"

"Besides," Alyn thought aloud, absorbed with the mystery, "if the queen *has* been abducted, where did it happen? Where were the bodies of the Guardians of the Dove?" Unlike Arthur's war-red dragon on white, Gwenhyfar's personal troops wore the symbol of the white dove on peaceful blue. All men pledged to the Grail Church, they'd have died rather than give up their lady. There would have been evidence.

"Is *that* why you proposed marriage?" Kella persisted. "Because you dreamed it?"

"She must be safe somewhere between Carmelide and Strighlagh. An illness along the way … or a delay."

"Alyn!"

Alyn drew up the horse, startled from his musing by Kella's high-pitched shriek. "I proposed to you because I loved you," he snapped, "not because of some untenable dream caused by indigest—"

Kella's stricken eyes were fixed not at him but beyond the pony, where the road split to the right ahead. It led to the Ochill Hills and Dumyat, the Miathi capital.

And it was lined with pikes, each bearing a severed head—most likely those of the border guard who did not return to Strighlagh.

Like Egan and Lorne.

God's mercy! Alyn drew Kella's face against his chest. "Don't look, *ma chroi,*" he said, smothering her moan. "I will drive past it and stop, so that you won't have to see. But I will examine each one, just in case …"

He didn't have to finish. *Lord, how much more must she endure?*

Such fences had been used since time began to warn off prospective invaders or lawbreakers. Rome hung the whole bodies of its enemies on crosses lining the roads to and from its cities. Had Joseph of Arimathea not had the favor of Pontius Pilate—and God a perfect plan—Christ Himself would have been one of them.

Before Christianity came to Albion, such fences were considered cursed by druidic priests so that ill befell any who crossed those lines. Though some pagan wizards still existed, Alyn did not think twice as he left Kella in the wagon and approached the gruesome sight. At least not of superstitious curses—or even demonic ones. Romans 8 echoed in his mind as he approached the shells of the men they had been.

"What shall we then say to these things? If God be for us, who can be against us?"

Ravens had pecked away most of the identifying flesh. Still, Alyn stopped before each one, looking past the dried blood-mangled hair and beards for a sign of Egan's red bush of hair or the cornsilk likeness that Kella attributed to Lorne. As if a human could have cornsilk-like hair!

But for her, he looked, and despite his continued prayer for help, Alyn could not discern either of the men who meant so much to Kella.

Nor could he bring himself to leave any so exposed.

"We have to go back," he told Kella upon reaching the wagon. He hated the idea of delaying the journey. But that was the least of his concerns.

"What?" Alarm razed her tearstained face.

"Neither your father nor your betrothed is among them, as far as I can tell," Alyn assured her. "But each one is *someone's* father, beloved, or son. I will fetch a shovel from the village we just passed and bury them, ere this day is done."

Kella gathered breath for objection, but Alyn headed it off.

"No doubt you would want someone to do the same if it were your Lorne or Egan. And who knows?" He shrugged. "Perhaps 'twill loosen some tongues that may help us expedite our mission."

Tongues, he prayed. *Not tempers.*

Once Alyn convinced the man that he truly was a priest of the Celtic Church, a local farmer at the bridge-side village was more than willing to part with a shovel for a piece of the Gaulish triens Alyn offered. The silver cross Alyn wore was not enough to convince the man, however. While Kella was glad Alyn declined to shave his hairline high in the Celtic tonsure, her new husband had to explain one of the symbols on his carved staff as well as the story behind it. To her astonishment, as he spoke of Jonah and the whale, man after man after woman after child gathered to hear the most marvelous words.

Was it because Alyn was her husband that he held even her spellbound, or was this his true calling? The words of so many priests seemed dry and old, but from Alyn's lips, they were alive and moving. Perhaps she'd been wrong in thinking Alyn's ambition to serve God was a waste. Heaven knew, she'd been wrong about God's not caring about her. He'd sent Alyn to save her—and more important, the babe—from her foolish heart.

For another bit of the gold coin, farmer Lugh agreed to help with the task. "'Twas so moonie comin' croos th' bridge, I tought 'twould surely fall doon b'neath 'em. Me 'n' the wife hid in the wood till the next day after the heads were hangit," the farmer told them from the back of the cart as they returned to bury the unfortunates' remains.

He and his neighbors had heard and seen the skirmish from where they'd sought refuge in the forest. The Dumyat army outnumbered the border guard at least two to one, though Lugh's estimation of a thousand men locked in a battle for their lives stretched the man's credibility, at least with numbers.

Kella waited with the horse and cart in the shadow of the tree line, while Lugh and Alyn set to work digging. She tried sewing to pass the time but found herself studying the landscape, trying to imagine what her father would have done. Sorely outnumbered, he'd have fought until none of his was left standing or perhaps would have helped the wounded into the trees. Dragged himself there if wounded. They'd have laid low till nightfall at the least. He wouldn't have gone near the roads. Not in his right mind, that is.

But if he'd done all that, why wasn't he home by now? 'Twas no more than a day's travel. And Strighlagh had sent forces to collect the dead. Why hadn't he—

She couldn't think about it.

So she watched from a distance as Alyn gathered the remains, using rags the farmer's wife had scrounged for them as gloves. After a short prayer for each departed soul, he placed the head gently as an infant into the mass grave. She should have known that, if her husband insisted on burying a man who'd tried to rob and kill him, he would feel more obliged to bury Arthur's and the Angus's men.

When he put it to her as he did—what if those heads belonged to someone *she* loved?—Kella could only admire his compassion and

sense of duty to his neighbor. Although, how, with his weak stomach, he stood the pungency of decay that occasionally wafted Kella's
way on the whim of a breeze, she couldn't imagine. Yet gore, like the
gaping gash on Daniel's leg, didn't seem to bother him. To say Alyn
O'Byrne was complex was an understatement.

Once the last grisly skull was interred, Lugh began to cover the
lot with dirt, while Alyn fashioned a cross. Longing to do something
for the lost men that would not fill her dreams with ghastly visions,
Kella gathered wildflowers—white, purple, pink, and yellow blossoms that grew in the clearing along the forest's edge—to place on
the grave.

Just when she'd picked all she could carry, she heard the distant
thunder of horses. Straightening in alarm, she saw a force of Miathi
warriors bearing down upon them. Over a dozen, she guessed, as
she dropped the flowers and rushed to the cart to coax the horse far
enough into the woods that they wouldn't be seen.

And then what?

God be with us. God be with us. The prayer was all her panicked
brain could muster as the horse reluctantly gave up its grazing spot
and followed her into the cover of the trees.

The weapons. She'd ready the weapons.

By now the party on horseback had surrounded Alyn. But the
traitorous Lugh walked through the unfriendly circle and pointed
directly to the spot where Kella hid. Two horsemen broke away,
riding straight for her. Kella's hand found one of the lances hidden
among their belongings, but something checked her.

She wasn't at war. She was the wife of a priest. One who'd felt
duty bound to bury the dead he'd found along the roadside. Lifting

her chin proudly, Kella stepped out of the cover of the wood and began gathering up the flowers she'd dropped.

One of the riders charged straight at her, pulling up his horse just short of running her over. Kella held her ground as the horse reared in protest and came down, circling full round until the rider faced her again.

"Good day for a spirited ride, sir," she said, proud that she'd not cringed as he'd expected.

Ignoring the chuckle of his comrade, the intimidator, a large man with a leather tunic trimmed in fur, growled at her. "What are you about, woman?"

Kella held up the flowers, brandishing a smile. "Isn't it obvious?"

"She's too pretty to be a priest's wife," the other rider observed.

"And you, sir," Kella addressed him, "are most gallant. But alas, Father Alyn is my new husband. We were on our way to Fortingall to King Drust's court when we spied the remains of those poor souls. No Christian, no man or woman, in good conscience could pass by such a sight and not give them a decent burial."

With an expression of utter disgust, the leader motioned toward his men. "Get down there with your husband. Athol, you get yon cart."

So these were the savages who killed Lorne. Possibly her father, too. Kella wanted to turn on the horse breathing down her neck and whip its face with the flowers to unseat its rider. 'Twould only take a moment to spring upon him like a cat and bury the dining dagger sheathed at her waist in his heart. But for Alyn's sake, she played obedient.

The circle of warriors opened to allow Kella to join her husband, but she made them and the two official-looking men speaking with Alyn wait until she'd spread her flowers over the freshly turned earth. Aware that every eye was upon her, Kella approached Alyn and hugged him.

"I would have found more, but my escort was impatient." With that, she met the fierce glare of the chieftain. It was as sin-dark as his hair and beard, reminding Kella of the bear whose claw adorned the chieftain's hat. With all the authority of the queen herself, Kella held her head high. "To whom do I have the pleasure of speaking?"

Her boldness took the chieftain aback. He glanced aside at the tall, gangly old man, whose gray hair shot wildly from a druidic tonsure like Alyn once wore. The druid gave him a barely perceptible nod, for the wizard could not take his narrowed eyes from Alyn. Kella wondered if his vision were clouded by age.

"I am Garnait, prince of Dumyat," the chieftain announced. "And this is Dumyat's chief druid, Idwyr."

"Prince Garnait, Lord Idwyr," Alyn replied, "as I was telling you before my wife joined us, we saw the remains of our fellow man by the wayside and, though we could not save their lives as the Good Samaritan did the victim found helpless and wounded upon the side of the road, we could spare their remains further desecration by the scavengers and send them back to the dust from which they were made."

But did that loony old man even know the story from the Scripture? Kella wondered. These were pagans, by their look.

"We sought not to insult you or your kinsmen," Alyn continued, "but to follow the Word of our God who loves all His children, those who believe and those who have yet to learn of His power and glory. The story I speak of—"

"How did you do it?" Idwyr interrupted. A picture of bewilderment, he stepped forward and felt Alyn's smooth-shaven face, then the wrinkles of his own. His eyes glistened in wonder. "What youth magic do you practice, *Merlin Emrys*?"

chapter eighteen

Merlin Emrys?

Kella could have sworn even the horses held their breath at the mention of that name. But surely this old wizard didn't think that Alyn was—

Understanding dawned on Alyn's face. "Good friend," he laughed, clasping the thin tattooed arm of the wizard and pulling him into an embrace. Undoubtedly the two exchanged a secret handshake, though the signal was not visible to Kella's untrained eye. Druids, priests, or druidic Christian priests—they all were a secret order of knowledge with respect of one another. Knowledge was so valued that it was taboo to kill any of them, punishable by death. That was not to say it wasn't done, which was why Kella was so concerned about Alyn. It simply wasn't lawful.

"I assure you," Alyn said, "that my youth is no disguise, though our late friend Merlin was ingenious at such. Still, I serve Emrys's God and knew the great man so well that he passed the belt you've been eyeing so closely on to me, that I might attempt to carry on his legacy."

Idwyr turned to his prince. "*That* is how they breached my spell," he exclaimed, as though someone had lit the wick in his brain.

"My spell of creation's forces are strong, but this man's power comes from the Great Creator. The Creator's magic cannot be outdone by earthly means—either seen or unseen. The man who wears Emrys's belt speaks for the old church, not this new one Arthur tries to force upon us."

The Grail Church. Like its successor, the Celtic Church, it held the respect of the pagans because it respected their right to worship as they saw fit. 'Twas the church's example and witness that won them over, not political enforcement.

Kella breathed a sigh of relief. If Idwyr only knew that the church's very records lay hidden in their cart. They were all that stood proof of Albion's equal authority to worship closer to the Hebrew-Christian ways established by Jesus and John. Rome claimed and insisted on Peter and Paul's authority for its more formal mode of service and worship.

Yet, for all Idwyr's regard for the Grail Church, Alyn and Kella dared not let anyone know of their quest. Certainly not this fanatic.

"Sadly, my friend, the old church has failed," Alyn told the old druid. "It is removed to the Holy Land for safety with all its relics. We are but its remains in Columba's fold."

"You mean Arthur of Dalraida has failed the old church," Idwyr said with disdain. "That Scot is no kin to us. Naught but a bull to get us a true heir by Gwenhyfar, and he's even failed at that!" Idwyr made a vulgar gesture that caused snickers to erupt about them. "Even yer Columba says Arthur will fail." Idwyr seized Alyn's hand, holding it up so that Garnait saw the dove. "This is a fair man. A free man of God who sides with Modred's church."

The color rose to Alyn's cheeks, and Kella held her breath, for she knew he would disagree. It was his nature to stand by the truth, not this convoluted version of it.

"I serve God alone, Lord Idwyr," Alyn averred. "Not Modred, nor Arthur, nor any other man. My druid is Christ Jesus. With Him as my teacher and guide, I am on a mission to protect the integrity of the Grail Church."

"A mission!" Idwyr cackled in delight and danced in a little circle. "And Christ Jesus supports Modred! I told you that we will win. Let them be on their way, Garnait. They serve a God of tolerance and justice, not the one whose priests come clad in Rome's scarlet with the muscle of the empire hidden beneath it. Those men serve a dictator. A dictator, I tell you!" Idwyr slammed his oak staff into the ground, narrowly missing Garnait's foot.

"Better yet"—the wizard sniffed the air as though it held information for him—"escort them to Crief. These woods and hills are full of brigands, and I'd have no harm come to this man or his pretty bride." He poked his staff at Alyn, brightening. "And you can tell me all about your Jesus and them story carvin's on yer staff while we ride."

Alyn invited Idwyr to join them. Riding a mule alongside the wagon, the old man listened intently to each story represented on Alyn's staff. Though Kella had heard them before, her husband brought the stories to life as though he'd been there himself. All within earshot rode close to the cart, exclaiming in wonder. The remainder of the day passed so quickly that it seemed no time before they camped overnight in Dunblane.

After an uneventful but companionable evening, the stories continued through the next day's ride to Crief. The endless string of trees and meadows, villages and farms, and burns and hills steepened as the day progressed, so that when the Knock of Crief rose before them, Kella was relieved. She was tired and looked forward to a hot meal instead of the cold bread, cheese, honey, and bannocks that had sustained them on their journey.

It wasn't yet dark on the heather-dashed hill where the dun presided. Townfolk wandered down along River Earn, where a caravan of merchants bound for the fair in Fortingall were camped near some trees. There, selling and bartering took place as if it were the weekly market day. Alyn pulled their cart to the edge of the encampment.

Across the river, cattle dotted the hilltops where men guarded them. 'Twas to Crief that the highlanders brought down their cattle in the fall to sell at the tryst and trade with their lowland neighbors. According to Idwyr, the hills were black with livestock and rife with blackguards and thieves, men who followed the money, which, in the case of Crief, was in beef.

"I've a keen nose for trouble," the wizard told Kella as he dismounted with his men. His dark eyes intensified, as though he were immediately gathering information.

At the start of their journey, Kella had thought him a bit crazy, but given his discussions with Alyn throughout the afternoon, she'd discovered Idwyr was surprisingly learned.

"Well," Idwyr announced with a sniff, "trouble is always about. I advise you to ride with these merchants the rest of the way. There's safety in numbers. *Merlin*," he said, addressing Alyn, "I thank you kindly for an entertaining journey."

"I am *not* Emrys," Alyn objected, "but to be compared to him is a compliment. Thank you."

"I *know*," Idwyr snapped. "I'm not the fool I look."

"Or act," Alyn said with a grin.

Idwyr responded, sheepish and snaggletoothed. "I'm saying that you might do more for your faith as a merlin than a priest." He offered his hand. "If our people dealt with the likes of you—or Emrys—instead of Arthur, much bloodshed could be avoided."

Alyn shook his head. "Nay, I loathe politics of government. As Jesus said, give Caesar his due, but my life belongs to Christ." Alyn helped Kella down from the wagon seat.

Faith, she was weary and stiff as a hag. Surely the plump mattress Brenna had sent with them would be welcome this night.

"Ah," Idwyr protested, "but if Caesar were surrounded by men like yourself, this world would be a better place."

Kella had to agree. She'd seen so many self-serving wolves at court who pretended to be Arthur's sheep. She could count the true champions for Alba and Alba alone on her fingers.

"You honor me again." Alyn extended his hand. "Now allow me to buy you and your good men drink to wash down the dust of the road. Surely you'll not ride back this night."

But wait. These were the men who'd killed Lorne and, at the least, wounded her father. How could Kella forget that? How could Alyn? Yesterday, she'd expected them to hang her head on a pike. A bit of talk about Jesus, and suddenly they were hearth companions?

Idwyr glanced over at the leader of the small escort. "I'm bone weary. What say we spend the night here and make our way home on the morrow?" It was a courtesy, for there was little question of who was in charge. "Always trouble on the road at night," he added, as if the men needed encouragement. Their relief was written on their faces.

But visions of a good night's rest vanished with Kella's heavier-than-necessary sigh. The men had talked half last eve with no drink stronger than honey mead. Tonight, with taverns close at hand—

Alyn heard her unspoken opinion loud and clear. "I can check at the inn to see if they've more comfortable accommodations. Perhaps you might retire early."

An inn crowded with folk headed to Fortingall's spring fair? Kella shook her head. "Unless the weather bodes ill, I'd as soon sleep here on this fresh, clean mattress. Does it look clear?"

Her husband was obsessed with weather signs. Kella could never keep them straight.

"Clear tonight, indubitably," Alyn and Idwyr said at the same time.

Old and young, wizard and priest—Kella couldn't help but giggle at the similarity in the unlikely pair. Those who were educated were few and far between. When one found another, they thrilled in sharing and comparing knowledge. Idwyr, like Emrys on occasion, apparently played the wizard to appease his superstitious followers, or the fool, at least at first, to loosen Alyn's tongue—each role to suit his purpose.

"Thank you, kind sirs. Now off with you," she ordered. "I can unroll the mattress and bed down, but if I hear you two talking into the wee hours, I shall rise screaming like a banshee. Understood?"

The two agreed as quickly as two boys caught with their fingers in the pie. While Kella climbed into the back of the cart to prepare it for the night, the men quickly saw to the horses. By the time the bed was made up and her lance and sword hidden but close at hand, the horses were fed, watered, and tethered, tack-free, for the night. Two guards stayed behind for the steeds' and the lady's safekeeping. Idwyr was certain someone with questionable character lurked, waiting for a good man to become careless.

Kella shared some of the honeyed mead with the guards until some of their mates came back with food and drink from the tavern. Over ribs, salmon pies, bread, and cakes from the tavern and honey from Kella's stores, she learned about the guards' families and how they felt betrayed by Arthur. That she spoke their native Pict, like their beloved Queen Gwenhyfar, made her one of them. They said that rumor had it Arthur was becoming paranoid, trusting no one but his priest. Aye, Kella had heard it—*seen* it. That Arthur had chosen a Rome-favored Briton over his queen's own people—over his own cousin, as his second-in-command and successor—affirmed it. She understood their concern, felt it, but knew war was not the way to solve it.

"What concerns me," she told them, "is that, if the Picts and Scots kill off each other, who will remain to fight the Saxons?"

"The highlands," one of the men replied. "Urien and the lowlanders canna hold their footin' in our land any more than the Saxons. We can gnaw them away a bit at a time, like a spreadin' canker on their buttocks. Beggin' yer pardon, milady," the man added hastily.

The other guard's wife had just had a baby. To see the man so giddy with excitement raised mixed feelings within Kella.

Lorne would never know that joy.

Yet Alyn would. Alyn, a man among few who would take another's child as his own and love it, because, he said, it was hers. But if he'd loved her, why hadn't he said so before now? Why had he always treated her like the little sister and scolded her for her fanciful dreams of becoming the wife of a gallant prince or nobleman? He'd never approved of any of her suitors.

Because they were not him.

Despite the late hour, *that* was a thought that kept Kella pondering as she wandered along a makeshift row of stalls to see what the merchants had to sell. Food and the bit of activity had renewed her, at least long enough to satisfy her curiosity. While most villages were self-sufficient, these mercers were importers of luxuries—spices, Mediterranean wine, beautiful silks, and other fabrics, carpets, glass, and jewels. Even if she had no intention of buying, Kella loved to examine items from places she'd only read about.

"I tell you, the lord of this village is a thief!" a plump vendor with a heavy accent and a black patch of beard on his chin complained to his companion. "I will be blessed if I am to sell enough to pay the toll for moving through his lands."

Upon seeing Kella slow at the board he'd set up on trestles to display his laces, his demeanor changed. "Good day, milady. May I show you the most beautiful and well-crafted laces in the world?"

"They're lovely," she agreed, fingering the small purse she'd tied securely to her waist in case she changed her mind.

There was one roll of tiny width that would look precious on the little gown she was sewing, if the baby were a girl. If a boy, perhaps she might put the lace aside for a later child … Alyn's. Just the thought sent rills of embarrassment through her, for she certainly did not know her new husband in that way. *Yet.*

But she had grown accustomed to the warmth of his body, the protective way he held her, the tender brushes of his lips across the top of her head and the occasional stolen kiss on the cheek. He made her feel as if she was the most important thing in his life, next to God. Something about his godliness filled her with peace, even joy. How foolish she'd been to scorn him when they were younger for choosing such a boring future. It was his love, not his station, that would make life good for her and the babe—

Kella caught sight of a big bush of red hair at the far end of the row of camped vendors. Whoever it belonged to was nearly a head taller than most of the crowd.

"No, no, milady, where do you go?" the vendor called after her as she dropped the lace and hurried away. "I will give you good bargain."

Kella moved steadily through the crowd toward the man's head. Her pace increased to a run when she saw him turn from a stall selling leather goods and start away. She'd only caught a glimpse of the man's face. Though shaved of Da's thick beard and wide mustache, it looked so much like him.

"Da!" Kella didn't mind the faces that turned her way, startled by her loud cry. Her heart beat to the rhythm of her racing feet. She had to stop the man. "Da!"

The big man paused at the corner of the last tent and turned to stare. The cluster of trees next to it cast a shadow over his face, but Kella was certain it was her father.

"Da, it's me, Kella!" It had to be him. "Wait!" she cried out, but in her blind haste, she tripped over an uneven rise in the terrain and fell facedown. Her skirts tangled with her feet as she scrambled to get up. Each time she rose, they or her undershift would hold her back.

Finally, instead of staring at her as if she were part of a gleeman's act, a tall man in an indistinct cloak of brown and green helped her up. "Here now, miss, take your time. If your da's got ears, he's heard you for sure."

Kella stared hard though mist-filled eyes at the tent where her father had been, but alas, no one stood there waiting. With a scant breath of "Thank you, sir," she hastened toward the spot, but upon reaching it, there was naught but a scatter of cottages with gardens at the rear, edged by a thin green wood. A couple of children and dogs milled close to the doors, and chickens were penned for the night, but there was no sign of the giant redheaded man.

"He … he's gone." But Kella knew it was Da.

She spoke to no one in particular, so she was astonished when the same man who'd helped her to her feet replied.

"I'm thinking he went through the woods there, milady." He pointed to a barely distinguishable pathway. "I'll go with you, if you wish." The words were an offer, but the hard clasp on Kella's arm made her wary. "If we hurry, we can catch him."

Kella wanted desperately to chase her father down the narrow path, if he'd indeed gone that way, but not with this stranger. Swarthy of complexion and clad in common tunic and braes that met worn boots at the knee, he had no problem taking possession of her arm. And from the way he looked at her, more, if she gave him the chance.

"No, thank you. I … I must have been mistaken."

"Come along now, miss," he cajoled, ignoring her resistance. "If we hurry, we can catch—"

Kella wrung her arm out of his grasp the way her father had taught her. "I'm not going anywhere with you." She was fully prepared to shriek for help from those at the edge of the campsite who watched.

Or brandish her dining dagger. His gaze shifted from their audience to the hand she tightened about its hilt.

Suddenly, he held up both hands as if in surrender and backed away. Kella noted that he favored one leg, a weak point, should she need it.

"No need for hysterics, milady. I only meant to help." Though if looks could kill, Kella stood no chance. The man must be crazed.

"And I thank you for it," she replied, hoping not to antagonize whatever she saw in his eyes. "I'm clearly overtired. I thought I'd seen my missing father," she explained, both to the man and the gathering who'd noticed them. "Da—he's not been well, and he wandered off. A giant of a red-haired man." She held up her hands as high as she could. "With a great thatch of hair and beard and a wide mustache that he waxed to make it look as if he always were smiling."

A merchant's wife smiled before Kella's misting eyes blurred out the sympathy. How Kella hated tears, yet they seemed in endless of supply of late. "I'll raise no whinybairns," Da used to warn her. But Kella was too tired to hope, much less fight anymore.

"I a-apologize for the fuss. I simply thought I'd seen him and … and I miss him so much."

Run.

Kella followed the urge, weaving her way half blind through the waning crowd toward the safe haven of her cart and the Miathi guards. The irony that she could be safe with possibly the very men who'd slain Lorne almost made her laugh.

She no longer knew how she fit in this world. Except at Alyn's side. There was a rock-solid refuge in her husband that put things back in order. Oh, for his faith instead of this wretched anxiety!

God, please don't let him try to save souls half the night. Tonight I, too, need saving.

Chapter Nineteen

Alyn could hardly believe his ears when Kella told him that she'd seen her father. Because of her condition and stubbornness, he'd humored her on the journey by agreeing to search for Egan. Accepting one loss at a time might be easier. As for his own thoughts, he was torn between faith and logic. He didn't *want* to blindly accept his old friend's loss, but he, Daniel, and Ronan had all agreed that it wasn't logical that Egan had survived and not been able to return home.

But with God all things were possible, despite logic.

Alyn promised to ask around about Egan the following morning. Then he held Kella as she drifted off to sleep, a smile on her lips that tortured him beyond measure. When he'd resolved to wait until she came to him to claim his husbandly rights, he'd had no idea how difficult it would be with the curves of her body fitted against his. Or how many silently recited psalms and prayers it took before fatigue overcame raw desire.

Kella rose fresh as a morning glory before sunrise to prepare bannocks on the fire, while Alyn fed and watered their cart horse. He learned that the leader of the merchant caravan had decided to stay on another day. The interest shown in the mercers' hastily displayed wares yesterday upon their late-afternoon arrival gave them hope of recouping more than the hefty toll that Crief's chieftain charged them for passing through.

Idwyr, who'd drunk more than a good share of the tavern's fine beer, ambled over to Alyn's hearth fire and joined them. Given his uncommon silence, the wizard's tongue was likely thick and dry from too much drink the night before. Though the reason for Alyn's groggy silence differed, both men stared dully at the fire, while Kella chattered enough for the two of them. She was determined to go door to door in the village scattered atop the hill until she found the whereabouts of the redheaded giant she'd seen.

Alyn didn't see the scrawny, wiry man approaching them until feet appeared in the line of Alyn's vision. After introducing himself as Goll, the shoemaker, the man waved hands bearing the calluses of his trade as if they powered his speech. There was, he said, indeed a large, red-haired stranger in town.

"I seen your lady chasin' after him last eve and heard she was lookin' for her da. But t'be honest"—Goll turned a bit sheepish—"I wasn't keen on lockin' horns with that tall 'un followin' her about. He looked like the kine to know his way wit' weapons."

Alyn straightened with alarm. Kella had told him about seeing her father but said nothing about someone threatening her. "*What* tall one?"

"Aha! I knew I smelt trouble." Idwyr pulled his curved shoulders back as far as they'd go and rolled his eyes up until they almost disappeared beneath their wrinkled lids. "Aye, there's *somethin'* amiss."

The old druid had fallen back into his crazed wizard role for the benefit of his audience. Sure enough, the shoemaker put a good two strides between them and would not look at Idwyr's face: Fearing the evil eye, most likely, Alyn guessed.

"About the tall one," Alyn reminded the shoemaker. "Is he a stranger also?"

"Aye. But not as strange as 'im." Goll nodded toward the swaying, blank-eyed Idwyr but riveted his focus to Alyn.

"Yep, I'm thinkin' I just might tag along with ye to Forty-gal," Idwyr chanted in a singsong tone.

With an exasperated cut of a glance at the not-so-crazy wizard, Alyn pressed the townsman. "What about the stranger?"

"He offered to help me catch Da," Kella put in. She inadvertently rubbed her arm and winced. Alyn suspected it was bruised beneath the sleeve. "But he was so insistent that I go with him into the wood that I refused."

Alyn fisted his hands at the very idea that someone might intend Kella harm. "Have you seen him today, Goll?" As bonnie as his wife was, Alyn didn't have to guess the villain's intentions.

"Nay," the shoemaker replied. "Never seen him come nor go. Just seen him with the lady near dark. Didn't look right to me."

Kella tapped her dagger. "But I *was* armed."

Armed and trained by Egan with a knife, but still the weaker. And she was with child. *God have mercy!* Alyn was almost as angry at her for thinking she was invincible as a champion's daughter as he was at her would-be assailant.

"Them types is always about," Idwyr claimed.

"Do you know where the redheaded man is? Is he still here?" Alyn asked the shoemaker.

"If word wasn't out that you was a priest, I'd say nary a word to nane. But them who bless God get blessed." Goll stood on tiptoe, staring at Alyn's forehead. "Though ye don't have the look of a priest. A mite young, too."

"The big redheaded stranger," Alyn prompted.

"Aye, he's been here nigh two weeks," Goll said. "Rode in on a farm wagon from Dunblane, out of his head. Found the giant playin' with the children by the river, lettin' 'em climb on 'im like he was a mountain and slide off his back. Had a nasty clot o' blood on his head, like as not from that skirmish t'the south we heard about, though I can't say what side he took."

"It *is* Da! I knew it! He loves children. Such a gentle heart," Kella declared, giddy with elation. "I just knew it in my heart. I felt his heartbeat with mine."

She'd said the same about Lorne's as she'd cried in Alyn's arms the first night out of Carmelide, but Alyn could say nothing now. At least about Egan. It was feasible for the champion to head north if he was confused. *Possible.*

"So where is this giant?" Alyn asked.

"We took him to the healin' woman in the glen, and he's lived with her since. Taken a real strong likin' to her, if you get my meanin'."

Kella gasped, puffing like a wet hen with outrage. "My father would not 'take a real strong likin' to' any woman after my mother, but especially to some old hag living in a … a cave."

"*I* might," Idwyr offered. "Has she any teeth left?"

Alyn checked his amusement. 'Twould be more than could be said for the wizard.

Instead of answering, Goll turned to the river. "Just follow the burn upstream about an hour's distance. Brisen will show herself, if she is receiving visitors."

"Receiving visitors?" Alyn echoed. "You make her sound as if she's royalty."

"To those she's saved, she is," the shoemaker told him.

Kella was ready to walk to the glen by the time Alyn thanked Goll for his information with a coin and sent him off with a blessing to assure him that Idwyr had in no way put a spell on him.

Convincing Idwyr that his services were not needed was more difficult. "Jesus 'n' me will help ye divine where to find yer one lost sheep," the wizard offered.

Alyn groaned. He'd done too well in convincing Idwyr of biblical truths. The man was like a sponge, soaking up every word, weighing each one, then bobbing with enthusiastic agreement. But the druid added his own twist to the truth, which didn't necessarily make it true.

It was agreed at last that Idwyr and company would wait until Alyn and Kella returned before heading home for Dumyat. And that was only after Alyn and Kella promised to wait another day to travel with the merchant caravan for protection. Alyn was certain the wizard would be tempted to search the wagon to satisfy his infinite curiosity, but there was little choice.

Still, Alyn began his morning prayers with one for God's protection over the wagon and its contents as they started the uphill journey to the healer's glen. Since his return, his prayer discipline had been sorely compromised, perhaps when he needed it most. Certainly, there could be no more beautiful reminder of God being with them than their surroundings.

To one side of the pass was a thick rise of spring-greening oak, beech, lime, and sweet chestnut trees. On the other, the land sloped down to the carseland between water and higher ground. There, all manner of birds and wildlife cavorted in and among the waving river grasses. Herons and kingfishers searched the sun-glazed surface for the fat salmon and trout swimming beneath the surface, while fishermen in small cobles tried their hand to bring the fish in with nets.

Kella returned the wave of one young man drifting in a boat closest to the rushes. Alyn could hardly blame the smitten fisherman for flirting with the golden-haired lassie bounding up the hill like a wild child. Like this, she reminded Alyn of the little girl who'd tagged along with him in the days of their youth spent in Glenarden. Except she was a full-grown woman, rounded in all the right—

Heavenly Father! Alyn renewed his prayers. One to distract him from this innocent kindled longing. Another that her soaring spirit would not be shot down if Egan was not the man she'd seen; she'd suffered so much heartache of late that he wondered if her pain was felt by the baby. Another that the man who'd stalked her had gone back to wherever he'd come from. And another that his teachings to Idwyr might take root and grow true. He even prayed that he would not run out of things to pray for.

Eventually, the trail curved away from the river and uphill through the woods into a sun-dappled glen where honeysuckle perfumed the air. It boasted a small garden, well tended, with all manner of herbs, roots, and vegetables planted in neat rows and patches.

A vine-covered archway to the east led to yet another open space. Upon closer examination, it revealed a chalybeate spring warmed by the earth, judging from the Eden-worthy plant growth around it. On a shaded, grassy bank sat a crudely made table with benches. The furniture was worn smooth and bleached almost white by the weather, but no cottage or shelter was to be seen.

"There's no one here," Kella said. "Nothing but wild vines and undergrowth and this bit of a clearing." Her struggle to hide her disappointment was futile. "But Da *has* to be here. Do you think we left the river path too soon?"

"It ended in the marsh," Alyn replied, kneeling to sample the water. Warm and tasting of iron salts. "But this is a healing well." A place that once belonged to the druids of old and, for the super-stitious, the fairies. He cupped his hands to his mouth. "Hallo! Is anyone here?"

There was no reply save the patter of the water springing from a rocky rise into the gathering pond, and the hush of the birds, whose song he'd interrupted.

Then a rustle of leaves, as if someone was dragging branches across the ground, attracted Alyn's attention to an ivy-infested thicket deep in the trees. A door opening appeared, not much taller than a child, as what Alyn thought to be a cluster of dead branches was swept aside. A woman climbed out from what had to be a partially sunken dwelling—at least four feet below ground level, Alyn guessed.

The lady was nearly as tall as Alyn with waist-length, ink-black hair shot silver with age. Her oval face had been etched by a light heart at the corners of her lips and eyes. A long, faded blue dress skimmed her slender body as she approached, gliding barefoot toward Alyn and Kella with a regal grace that had escaped the stiffness of arthritic joints.

Like Gwenhyfar, age had been kind to her, though Alyn knew better than to guess the number of her years.

"*You're* Brisen?"

Her dark eyes danced as she closed his slack jaw with a tapered finger. "That I am, young priest." Curious, she examined his belt, reducing Alyn to a hot-faced stammer.

"I ... I apologize, it's just that—"

"You're certainly not what we expected," Kella finished for him. At least one of them had kept a cool head. "I believe your name is a derivative of the Welsh word for *queen*, if I'm not mistaken."

"You are not, milady." Brisen turned her appraisal to Kella. "But I am not Welsh."

"You are a Pict ... Cruithne," Kella replied in the Pictish tongue of Gwenhyfar and Alyn's own mother.

That surprised Brisen. Two fine tapered brows—the kind women used charcoal or plucked to imitate—arched over the woman's gaze. "Yes, I am. And I am queen of *this* kingdom." She opened her arms to encompass their surroundings. "Do take a seat at yon table by the spring. I've put water on for tea, but it will be a while. Rest yourselves in the shade, my dears. It's the perfect spot—"

"We're here to see the red-haired stranger you've been healing."

Brisen smiled, unruffled by Kella's directness. "Finn will be along shortly." A pretty pink colored her cheeks, making her almost seem girlish. "He's a roguish influence on me. I'm usually up, breakfasted, and working in my garden by now."

"*Finn?*" Alarm grazed Kella's face. "Did he *say* his name was Finn?"

"Nay, 'twas the name I gave the *brawny*"—Brisen turned the word into a low purr—"man."

The spring and sway in the lady's return to the thicket dwelling from which she'd emerged left Alyn staring in her wake. If they had indeed found Egan, they'd no doubt find the old dog grinning ear to ear to have such a remarkable woman so taken with him.

"You can close your mouth again." Kella planted her hands on her hips, less than enchanted with Brisen *and* him.

"But she's stunning! Never in my wildest … did you expect Brisen would look like *that?*" he whispered.

Kella ignored his question and his offered arm. Instead she marched through the archway of flowering vines as if ready to do battle, not have tea at the table and benches. "She's an educated woman … not the hag I expected."

Alyn agreed but held to silence until he could fathom what was going on behind his wife's snapping eyes. He'd have thought she'd be thrilled. It was very likely they had found Egan. Giant, red hair …

"And Egan *is* certainly brawny," Alyn deduced aloud.

"He is not!"

"Kella, your da is a big, brawny man. You can't deny that."

"Not brawny the way *she* said it," she hissed through her teeth.

Alyn tapped his fingers on the table, processing this bad turn of humor until Kella's earlier peeve with Goll came to him.

"*My father would not 'take a real strong likin' to' any woman after my mother.*"

Aha!

"Kella, my love." Alyn covered her hand with his. "If this *is* your da, and he doesn't know who he is, how can he remember his love for your mother?"

She pursed her lips, thoughtful.

Kissable.

Alyn rushed past the thought. "And if it *is* Egan, and he found someone who makes him happy, someone to love him like you've found to love you and your baby, would it be so bad?"

"Alyn, they are not mar—" Kella's face reddened.

Alyn could almost see the guilt that cut her off and continued to batter her. "*We* are," he told her, wiping away with his thumb the single tear that trickled down her cheek. *Well, mostly.*

"Oh, Alyn, I-I'm such a hy"—she hiccupped against his chest—"hypocrite."

"But you're a *forgiven* hypocrite," he consoled. "No," he added when she tensed. "I meant, you're forgiven because you feared for your father's soul, not because you judged him."

Why was it that he could guide even an old pagan's soul-searching, but when it came to Kella, his words tumbled out in a jumble?

"Let your father get well first," Alyn advised. "We must take one step at a time and pray for God's direction. He will take care of the rest," he whispered against her ear. The whisper became a kiss. Just a little one, though he yearned to show her just how much he loved her.

"Excuse us—have we come at an inopportune time?"

CHAPTER TWENTY

Alyn jerked away to see Brisen standing in the archway, an inlaid tray with a fine Romanware teapot and four cups in her hand. Behind her, for there was no room for the two side by side, stood Egan O'Toole. At least the man resembled Egan. He wore a kilt of Glenarden's red, black, and gray, and a black leather vest with no shirt to cover the red-bristle spread across his broad chest. A leather thong filled with gold and silver trophy rings glistened there. But this man was clean-shaven, with his hair pulled into a thick copper braid in the back, instead of loose and wild as Scotch broom.

Thawing from the same shock that bound Alyn, Kella tore away from him and flung herself at her father. Brisen sidestepped, lest the young woman knock the tea and her aside in her eagerness.

"Da, it *is* you!" Kella cried. "It *is* you!"

Alyn could see right off that Egan didn't know Kella. Glancing at Brisen as if for a cue as to what to do, the big man humored Kella, allowing her to hug him and babble about how much she'd worried, how she'd known he wasn't dead, how she'd felt it in her heart.

Father God, help us. Help Kella.

Alyn stood behind Kella at the ready when she finally realized that Egan was not responding to her declarations of love and joy. When the moment came, he caught her as she shrank away, supported her as she looked up into her father's familiar face in wounded disbelief.

"You … you really don't know me?" Her voice was little more than a squeak. She leaned against Alyn's reinforcement. "I am your only daughter … Kella. Mam died when I was born. You said you could never love another but your colleen."

The pleas evoked naught but pity from the brown eyes staring down at her.

"My dear child," Brisen said softly to Kella, "come, sit down. Give the man time to think. To speak with you and your companion."

Alyn ushered Kella over to a bench and sat beside her.

"Come along, Finn," Brisen encouraged Egan. "Let us talk with our guests. Maybe they can help us determine what happened to you."

Joining them, Egan sat arrow straight, hands that, when fisted, were big as hams folded before him. Alyn had seen Glenarden's champion knock more than one man off his feet with a single blow. His bare tattooed arms bore the scarred badges of his courage in battle. A few were fresh. Yet here he was, reserved and polite, sipping tea from a cup instead of reveling, boisterous and jolly, with a mug to his lips. 'Twas like seeing another man in Egan's skin.

"Ye're a bonnie young lassie," Egan said, breaking his silence as he put down his tea. "Any man would be proud to call ye his daughter, but I swear, I dinna ken ye … or yer laddie, for a' that."

Her father didn't know her.

It didn't matter that Kella told him about her mother, at least the stories he'd shared with her, for Wynn had died at Kella's birth. Kella searched the warm brown eyes she adored for any flicker of recognition as she relayed memory after memory, but there was nothing. Nor was there any sign of joy when she told him that she'd married the young man he'd favored for her husband and that they would soon make Egan a grandfather. His gaze was not merely empty, but resistant to the recollections she tried to reestablish.

"I'm happy for ye, lassie, what with the bairn and yer laddie. But nothin' ye say sounds familiar to me ear," he apologized as they sat alone on a wooded bank overlooking the river.

Brisen had suggested they go for a walk to give them privacy to talk, while Alyn remained behind to discuss Egan's injuries and possible treatments.

"I'm wishin' it did," her father told Kella, "for ye both would make a fine family for any man."

"At least come with us," Kella pled with him. "We're on our way to Fortingall to deliver a package for Queen Gwenhyfar. Perhaps time in our company will nudge your memory. We have a good life at Glenarden, Da. People love you there. *I* love you and want you to enjoy your grandchild."

A thoughtful smile pulled at the corner of her father's lips. He looked so strange without the kilt of his mustache to accentuate it. "I canna think my life could be better than it is now with Brisen."

The twinkle in his eye tore at Kella's heart. She'd only seen it light so when he mentioned her mother, Wynn. Her father loved the healing woman. Or at least he thought he did.

"Mine musta been a lonely life before *this*." He pointed to a long row of careful stitches that closed up a gash behind his ear. Brisen had shaved enough hair away to secure and treat the wound, but the spot was barely noticeable on that full bush of Egan's hair unless one knew where to look.

It never occurred to Kella that Da had been lonely. He seemed to relish filling his days with weapons and training and his nights about the fire with his hearth companions. He was born to fight and make merry, he'd say.

"I canna explain the pure joy that woman has given me."

His dreamy expression was no more familiar than the rest of him. Had the warrior turned lovestruck poet? Was it possible that his bluster about battle had done what ambition had done for Kella— isolated them from a chance at love?

"I'm by Brisen like yer young man is by you."

"*What?*" The shift in the conversation took Kella by surprise.

Egan snorted. "Ye're married and carryin' his bairn, lassie. Surely ye know he worships the verra ground ye walk upon."

Kella couldn't help feeling guilty for misleading her father. As for Alyn, the only one Alyn worshipped was God. Next came *sciencia*. Though he had been more than tender since he returned, and more than once he'd said he loved her.

"He's a kind man," she allowed. "And generous."

Were Alyn's declarations of love *real*—not the product of pity and generosity of heart? Or of a dutiful spirit? Aye, he said he'd always loved her, but she'd always loved him, too. In a brotherly sense. Yes, once, when she was barely grown, love for him had even been a romantic fancy. Now Alyn had changed, become more manly.

"He's a good man. Smart, too. Smart as you." Egan shook his head. "I dunno how the likes of me could get a child as bonnie and keen-witted as you, lassie. Ye're like a princess."

Egan used to call her his princess. "Da …" Kella caressed the night's growth of stubble on her father's cheek. "You're one of the smartest men I know. Born with a keener wit than half the students schooled with me. You're a champion and have always been my hero."

"Maybe so," Egan admitted, "but yer man's a champion too. 'E's got heart bigger'n me to travel about armed with n'more than a stick."

"You taught him how to use that *stick*," Kella teased. Her smile faded as Egan studied her. She resisted the urge to squirm, for when Da gave her that look, she swore he could read her thoughts.

"Beggin' yer pardon, if I overstep me bounds, lassie, but …" He frowned.

"No," Kella encouraged. Maybe his memory was warming. "Go on."

"If the two of ye are wed as ye say …"

"We *are*," she averred strongly. That much she could admit.

"Well, ye act like *acquaintances*." Egan tended to draw out big words he rarely used. "Not like lovers."

Indignation stirred her embarrassment. How dare this man— who was her father—question her as if …

He was her father?

"I … I don't know what you mean, Da." Whether he'd lost his memory or nay, he'd not lost his knack for spotting curdles in the cream.

"Ye sit apart as if to touch one anither is a crime. I don't even know the man, but it's easy to see as this big nose on me face. He loves ye with his heart and eyes, but I'd wager not with his—"

"Da!"

The mischievous wink Egan gave her was so much like him. "I wasna goin' to speak untoward now," he chided. "But the way ye act together—it makes no sense to me. Ye don't *know* each other like a man and his wife should."

"I'm with child, for heaven's sake." Kella had never been a good liar. At the moment, she surely glowed like a firefly at midnight.

"Just because there's a bairn on the way is no reason to limit the bed to sleepin' alone." Egan leaned forward, folding his arms across his knees. "I'd bet the poor laddie finds every reason in the world not to go to bed at night."

Like staying up and talking half the night with his family. Then with Idwyr. Kella glanced away from the probing arch of her father's brow. The brow of a man who claimed he didn't know her but spoke to her as if she were his own.

"I canna keep from touchin' Brisen, just to be sure she's real," he confessed. "Do ye feel that way about yer man?"

Her man was dead.

Even so, Kella had not felt that way with Lorne … had she? They'd not shown their affection for each other aside from that stolen moment. Stolen and gone.

Father God, tell me it was real and not some flight of fancy craved by a lonely heart.

His image, even Lorne's words of love, was hardly more than smoke in the wind. 'Twas Alyn filling Kella's mind of late.

"Alyn is a fine man," she conceded, as much to herself as to her father. And brave. When he'd been surrounded a few nights ago, she'd been frantic to save him. The way he'd coddled Fatin, pretending he didn't care for the wee monkey, was heart melting. And the way he brushed the top of her head, her cheeks, her lips with his own. The way he held her at night, laid his hand over her belly as if to protect her child. The way he tried to anticipate her every need, dry her every tear. Always thinking of her comfort and well-being.

Thoughts of Alyn warmed Kella through and through, where thoughts of Lorne … were becoming as lifeless as he.

"Return his love, child. Life is too short to let even a day slip away," her father advised.

The inevitable conclusion taking shape in her mind left her stunned. Alyn *did* love her. And hard as it was to accept, perhaps she'd never stopped loving him as more than a friend. She'd merely given up hope when he'd declared his intention to become a priest.

As for Lorne …

He no longer existed.

Alyn had filled Lorne's place, given more than he had, though it was by no fault of Lorne's own. Alyn would raise his child and love it with as close a love to his heavenly Father as could be found in This World. She'd been so caught up in her grief and shame, she hadn't seen what was before her very eyes or heard what Alyn really said.

"I've been a fool, haven't I, Da?"

Egan reached around her, giving Kella a quick hug with his long arm. "We fill the world, bonnie Kella. We fill the world."

CHAPTER TWENTY-ONE

Perhaps God had led Egan to this garden spot, where his head and heart would be healed. Regardless, Alyn gave Him the praise as he and Brisen conferred about the man's memory loss and what might be done to help, though Egan didn't seem to mind his infirmity. As for the hermit healer, she looked like a woman in love. Each glance at the big Irishman had been a caress, each mention a fondness. A more unlikely match, given this woman's formal learning and Egan's lack of it, was hard to imagine.

"All things are possible."

That truth continued to become clearer and clearer. Although God was the master of logic and order, He also could bend both to His will. That was a facet of faith Alyn needed to work on. For today, he chose to enjoy God's blessing, rather than reason it through.

While waiting for Egan and Kella to return, Alyn used a piece of Brisen's precious parchment and some ink to pen a note to Glenarden, announcing that Egan had been found alive and mostly well. Hopefully, Idwyr would take it back to Bridge of Allan and send it by messenger on to Ronan and Brenna.

Egan and Kella could be heard coming up the path by the time he'd finished the missive and sealed it. Though Brisen withheld her opinion, Egan was insistent that he would not leave the healer. Not for Kella. Not for the grandchild who was to come.

"If I be yer father as ye say, then leave me happy where I am," he told Kella. "But the two of ye are welcome to visit and bring the babe if ye're of a mind."

"I would be delighted to have you visit," Brisen chimed in. "I so love to coddle little ones."

Alyn expected Kella to become obstinate, but for some reason, she accepted her father's unwavering decision without rebellion or tears. Alyn counted that another blessing, though Brisen had explained that some women were more prone to hysteria when carrying a child than otherwise. She'd also assured him that, unless Kella had shown signs of a troubled pregnancy, there was no reason for her not to do anything a healthy young woman could do.

Alyn doubted that included fighting off brigands in the night. He wondered if Kella might consider staying with Egan and Brisen, now that her father had been found. Brisen was surprisingly pleased with his idea of her getting to know more about the man she cared for and his family.

"I've a small room I keep for the visiting sick that Kella is welcome to use."

The healer and Egan accompanied Kella and Alyn back to the riverside. Brisen was anxious to see what exotic imports the mercers had to offer, and where his lady went, Egan followed. She was an enigma to Alyn. Her tableware had demonstrated a taste for finer things that were uncommon to a hermit. It was easy to see how Egan—or any man—might find Brisen enchanting.

Along the way downhill, Brisen brought the idea up of Kella remaining with her and Egan while Alyn carried out his mission for Queen Gwenhyfar. "It might help Egan's memory return to spend time together," the lady said. "And I would love to get to know you better, Kella."

"It would be good for you to rest awhile as well, Kella," Alyn pitched in. "You and the baby."

Kella slowed as though considering her words carefully. "But I am as much in the queen's service as you. I made the copies of her majesty's documents."

"You're a scribe?" It was Brisen's turn to be impressed. "Where were you educated?"

"At her aunt's convent in Ireland," Alyn informed her. "Kella is fluent in five languages. One wasn't enough to satisfy her chattering tongue."

Kella gave Alyn a sharp elbow jab. "I grow so weary of that jest."

"I'll say not another word, if you'll remain with Brisen and your father while I go on to Fortingall."

"My place," Kella said, circling his waist with her arm and pressing the curves of her body into his, "is beside you, my *husband*."

What little objection Alyn harbored to his wife's words vanished at the suggestive tone she used.

It was all for show, Alyn reasoned. Kella probably didn't even realize how tantalizing her nearness, the intimation of her words was. He shook his head to clear it of fanciful notions. The "husband," the hug, meant nothing, Alyn reasoned. Nothing but a hopelessly smitten priest's hope.

God, forgive me for all the times I've felt disdain at the confessions of love-befuddled fools, for now I know their torment.

"A queen's scribe and a priest," Brisen marveled behind them. "You have quite a family, Fi—*Egan* O'Toole." She blushed. "I'll have to get used to your real name."

"Ye can call me anything ye want, milady."

Egan lifted Brisen's hand to his lips while Kella, like her father, continued as though nothing mind shattering had taken place.

"I appreciate your generous offer to make room for me, Lady Brisen ... oh!" Kella put her hand to her mouth.

"Just Brisen, dear."

"I meant no insult," Kella apologized. "You comport yourself like royalty."

"Because she's me queen," Egan put in. "Or she will be, if she'll have me."

Brisen stopped short. "Is that a proposal of marriage when I've only just learned your name, sir?"

Egan scratched his head. "I guess it is. After all, we got us a priest."

Alyn began to demur, not because he objected to the idea, but he anticipated Kella's objection. "I'm not, that is to say—"

A thunder of horses' hooves caused the ground beneath their feet to shake. From below where the road ran past, a cacophony of voices rose from the caravan campsite.

Brisen frowned. "That does not bode well."

Alyn agreed. Something was clearly amiss downhill, although by the time the foursome reached the riverside, nothing remained of the troops who had passed by except a cloud of dust on the horizon.

The merchants and villagers were abuzz with the news the soldiers had left in their wake. King Arthur's warband had invaded Lothian. Modred was not there, but Arthur had found and arrested Queen Gwenhyfar, who had sought refuge there in Modred's Din Edyn fortress, for treason.

The vision of the birds played through Alyn's mind. The eagle had not seized the dove. Gwen had evidently gone willingly to Modred. And the bear's roar was vicious. Arthur had declared that Gwenhyfar was to be dismembered by horses at the month's end, unless Modred surrendered himself to save his lover.

"I don't believe it," Kella claimed as they made their way to their campsite. "Gwenhyfar corresponds much with Modred as archbishop of the Grail Church, but they are not lovers. I'd have known."

Alyn agreed because he was convinced of his cousin's morality. He could believe in Gwenhyfar's preference of Modred as Arthur's successor and as the last archbishop of the Grail Church. But he could not believe that Gwenhyfar had conspired against Arthur or had consorted with Lothian's king, any more than he could accept that Arthur believed it.

Although there was the High King's unprovoked rage that morning at the tavern over even the hint of someone committing treason. Arthur had been adamant that, man or woman, the culprit would face the same fate—death. Had he suspected Gwenhyfar of betrayal then? Was that the source of the High King's pain, that blackness Alyn had summoned the Holy Spirit against?

"Mayhap she went as an emissary to smooth Modred's ruffled feathers," Kella suggested. "As both queen and high priestess."

"Why not tell Arthur then?" Alyn countered.

Kella had one word for him. "Cassian."

Ice formed along Alyn's spine. Had Arthur fallen into that dark pit of madness and paranoia again? Or had he been pushed into it by Cassian, who had no use for Gwenhyfar or her church?

While Alyn yet wrestled with that grim possibility, the news grew worse. After Arthur pronounced Gwenhyfar's fate, the men of Errol rebelled. Led by Elkmar, they abducted the Roman priest Cassian from under the High King's nose, stalemating Arthur on Modred and the queen's behalf. The men were now on their way to where Modred met with King Drust and the Pictish chieftains to garner their support for Lothian.

"Drust mustn't ally with either Modred or Arthur!" Brisen echoed Alyn's very thoughts.

"Aye," he agreed. "A battle of champions at the most is appropriate. The Cymri and Pictish leaders must allow Modred and Arthur to settle their personal dispute without the blood of others. And while I don't condone treason or kidnapping, Cassian's abduction gains my cousin time that cooler heads might work to resolve this by diplomacy."

Brisen's brow lifted. "Queen Gwenhyfar is your cousin?"

"Aye, my mother's first cousin, actually."

Kella crossed her arms, indignant. "I'm glad the Perthshiremen abducted that conniving Cassian."

Alyn wanted to put a finger to his wife's lips, but it was too late. "Say no more, for ears are everywhere," he warned. "Let us take neither side but God's, good wife," he said in a louder voice. "These acts of war must be unraveled before the pattern is set."

Alyn rubbed his temples where his head had begun to ache. Not another vision, he prayed in silence. No bewildering birds. They'd told him nothing until after the fact.

"You are right, young priest." Brisen took Egan by the arm. "I must go to Fortingall with these young people, beloved. I'll be here at daybreak," she informed Alyn.

What could a reclusive healer possibly …

Brisen read the question before Alyn could voice it. "I have Drust's ear," she said. "I have tended his household for years."

"Ye'll not be goin' anywhere without me," Egan declared with characteristic belligerence.

Brisen caressed his broad jaw. "I'd hoped you'd say that."

The giant's indignation melted into an oafish grin that remained through their good-byes and even as he followed Brisen toward the hill path.

"*For My thoughts are not your thoughts, neither are your ways My ways.*"

No, Lord, they are not, Alyn mused. The words of Isaiah faded as he watched the mismatched pair disappear up the wooded rise. Sometimes he wondered why he even tried to understand God. At the moment he felt like a babe, thrust into a role meant for wise men.

Do those two even have transport?

That was, Alyn realized even as he thought it, the least of his concerns.

So, too, was the fact that Idwyr and his Miathi escort had also departed. A merchant from Frisia whose tent was set up near Alyn and Kella's wagon said the wizard and his Miathi left when they'd heard news that Modred's troops were mustering at Gododdin's borders.

"But he put a spell round dere," the merchant said. "A funny leetle dance and den de bones, dere on de vagon seat."

"He is a witan, no?" the man's wife, a plump Frau with thick braided hair, asked.

"Very like the Saxon wizards, yes," Alyn replied. Except the Celtic druids were allowed to ride stallions and fight in battle.

Idwyr had left a human finger bone, likely from his necklace. Another of undetermined origin had been laid out on the wagon bench atop it in the form of a cross. The crazy old man probably called on Jesus as well. And meant it, Alyn had no doubt. Idwyr's heart was leaning toward Jesus, but there was a lot more understanding that had to go with it to make it right.

Alyn couldn't blame the Miathi for leaving. While the merchants planned on getting on the road at dawn, hoping to move north before fighting broke out in the borderlands as clans took sides, Idwyr's men rode home *for* the battle. This was what their people had been waiting for. A chance to invade and take back lands lost more than a generation ago.

The false bottom of the wagon containing the genealogies had not been disturbed, nor had his locked alchemy box been forced open. But it had been moved, perhaps in a curious attempt to see what it contained.

Alyn made rounds about the caravan and spent the rest of the afternoon in the village while Kella, under the watchful eye of their Frisian neighbors, set about preparing a fresh hot meal over the fire. Her father's daughter when it came to living in the wild, she roasted a salmon purchased from one of the local fishermen who'd profited from the unusually large gathering of customers encamped at the foot of the knock.

As darkness cloaked the land that evening and Alyn and Kella shared the delicious fish and a loaf of bread Alyn bought from the village baker, only nature remained unaffected by the grim news. The usual sound of merry camaraderie in the riverside encampment was suppressed, but the stars sparkled like jewels in the midnight velvet canvas of the sky. Night birds and insects chorused in a soothing lullaby as if to reassure Alyn that God was still in charge. He even suggested good weather on the morrow.

"Do you think the Angus had a hand in Cassian's kidnapping?" Kella asked.

The question startled Alyn from his focus on all that was still well in the world and plunged his mind into yet another quagmire of conflicting loyalties. The Angus was sworn protector of the queen *and* pledged militarily to Arthur.

"Nay," he replied. He wondered more about Lorne's loyalties, but let that dead dog lie. "Only Perthshire men have abandoned Arthur, thus far. But I do not envy his position. Nor ours, for that matter," he reflected aloud. "My brothers' and mine."

"Oh!" Kella hadn't thought that far ahead. As Gwen's kin, yet oathsworn to the High King, the O'Byrnes would be forced to choose whom they would serve as well.

But was ever there a more perfect rose than the worried purse of Kella's lips? 'Twas enough to take a man's mind off the world gone mad and think of other things. Like the way she'd been acting. Warmer. Implying an intimacy not there.

"My place is beside you … my husband."

Had he not known she still harbored feelings for Lorne, Alyn would have sworn the sentiment behind the word had been real.

"Caden's in the worst position," she observed later over the delicious meal. Her brow furrowed beneath renegade wisps of hair that spiraled about it. "What if he is forced to fight oathsworn for King Modred, while Ronan—"

"Let us pray it doesn't come to that."

Alyn intended to pray. With all his fervor. All night. For the sake of *all* Alba, not one side or the other. For words to disarm outrage and restore reason. And for relief from this relentless longing.

chapter twenty-two

After seeing to the best-fed and groomed cart horse in Crief, Alyn returned to the wagon where Kella was readying for the night.

"What on earth is this?" she exclaimed, tossing out a stick that she found inside the bedroll. "How did that get in here?"

Alyn picked it up and grinned. "Idwyr," he told her. "It's in one language you can't speak."

"I don't want anything he leaves behind in my bed," Kella said with a shudder from beneath the tarp they put up each night to keep the dampness away.

Holding the stick closer to the firelight, Alyn made out the symbols of the druidic ogham carved on it. Had Kella not missed the fire when she tossed it out of the wagon bed, Alyn wouldn't have seen it. Though it had been a while since he'd studied the old writing form, he made out enough to bring a smile to his worry-thinned lips.

Safe … friend … true … Word. His signature *I* was the only Roman letter the old wizard had used.

"If all heads were as cool as that crazy old fox, there is hope for us after all," Alyn murmured to himself. He feared the next time they met, it would be on opposite sides of the conflict.

Father, forbid I take either side but Yours.

Each had valid grievances against the other. Perhaps God would enable him to point out the planks in the eyes of Modred and Arthur without losing his own head in the process.

True … Word.

Aye, Idwyr had the key. Stay true and use the Word to diffuse the situation. Both leaders claimed to uphold it. Though that seemed as impossible as …

As finding Egan alive?

Modred wouldn't act right away. He had Cassian, Alyn reasoned, so Gwenhyfar was safe for now. Arthur made no decision without his Roman bishop, nor would he risk sending his warband this far into Pictish territory until he knew who stood with him. Each leader would line up his enemies, perhaps wait until after the summer harvest, so that they went to war fully supplied with men and food. So there was time for heads to cool, unless skirmishes escalated into battles, and battles into—

"Alyn," Kella called from the cart, "aren't you coming to bed?"

The silky siren song from the wagon splintered his thoughts, scattering them in every direction. Summer, battle, skirmishes were lost like smoke in the wind. But his senses could light signal fires on every hill in Alba.

"I'll be along in a while," he promised. "I thought I might go down to the river to pray, what with war bearing down upon us."

The war and another night of torment.

"But …" Her head bobbed up from beneath the tarp Alyn had tied over the wagon to keep the night dampness at bay. "Why not pray *here*, husband? I fear being alone this night."

Their Miathi guards had gone. Alyn had forgotten that. And the Frisian couple had long since bedded down by their cart.

"Aye," he said, checking a heavy sigh. "I'll stay close, then."

Though woe to the man who set foot in that wagon bed uninvited. The champion's daughter slept with sword, dagger, and lance at hand. The notion made Alyn smile. That was his bonnie—

"Alyn!" Kella's sharp exasperation cut through his musings. She motioned him over to the wagon. "Get in here *now*."

"What is the rush?" Alyn couldn't help his impatience. Kella had no idea how impossible it was to rest when—

"Please." There was that pout again. But it was more than that. There was an urgency in her eyes, grazed with apprehension, as though she needed reassurance. And who wouldn't this night?

Heavenly Father. There was no need for Alyn to pray further. God knew the wagon-bed prayers by heart now.

"And you needn't wear your braccae."

Misjudging the height of the wagon floor, Alyn cracked his knee soundly against the edge of an unforgiving oak plank. Through the pain and the stars shining overhead, he was certain he'd not heard right. But after what he *thought* he'd heard, there was no climbing into that bed without embarrassing them both.

"Wh-*what* do you need?" he asked as if he'd swallowed a fist of gravel. More annoying, confusing, she'd disappeared beneath the tarp. "Where *are* you?"

When Kella's head popped out from under the tarp at the end of the wagon where he stood, he stepped back. Her undershift slid off an alabaster shoulder as she rose to her knees. "I *need*," she said, reaching across the distance between them, "my husband …"

She fisted the material of his shirt and drew him closer. "In my bed …"

Like one of the dreams that made his sleep as unbearable as wakefulness.

"*Now*." Kella closed his slack jaw with the tip of her finger. Still, it wasn't until her lips met his and her fingers crept into the hair at the back of his neck that Alyn finally *heard* her.

He heard her until his heart threatened to explode, and his breath and hers had become one. He heard the music of the spheres rotating in the heavens, their song of praise ringing in his ears. Yet, when Kella finally drew away with a smile that curled even his toes, he had to ask.

Even if this dream came crashing down about him. "Why *now?*"

The gaze that met his was bright with an emotion far from the grief that had dominated it so long. "Because life is too short to let love slip through our fingers one more night."

Kella awoke before dawn, her head resting in the curve of her husband's arm. Not even the birds stirred. All she heard was Alyn's soft snoring and the slow, steady beat of his heart. Such a beautiful heart, she thought as memories of the night before slipped into her mind. Not only had he married her, saving her and her child from shame, but he actually loved her. His life pledge to her had not been out of some priestly sense of duty or protection as she'd believed.

Her night with Alyn had been nothing like that stolen moment with Lorne. Lorne's words of love had not been reflected in his rough haste to satisfy himself. He'd left her in the garden, feeling unfulfilled and clinging desperately to the fading sweetness of his vows.

Alyn turned his words of love into gifts of tenderness and worship that had made Kella all but swoon. And here, in the morning's aftermath, she felt nothing but a joy and completeness the likes of which she'd never imagined. In all the five languages she knew, there were not enough words to describe how she felt at this moment.

Easing out of the bed so as not to disturb Alyn, Kella tucked her pillow against him. Hopefully he'd sleep a little longer, giving her time to bathe with the lavender soap she saved for special occasions. She might even have time to rinse out her dress and shift before they had to leave. As they traveled north, she could spread it on the wagon tarp to dry in the sun.

Kella intended to be suitably attired when she accompanied her husband to Drust's court. If Heilyn became his benefactress, he and his family would be well provided for. Though Kella would follow him to the windswept and desolate likes of Iona, as long as she could be at his side.

Who'd have thought a few weeks ago that she could know such happiness? Much less that it would be with a priest and scholar.

Father, Your forgiveness and mercy have overwhelmed me.

Kella gathered the sack of belongings she stowed under the wagon at night to make room for the bed and picked up a bucket for her bath. The river water was way too cold for a swim. Beneath the cloak she drew over her shoulders against the remaining night chill, her knife was tied at the waist of her shift.

Not even the dogs stirred as she made her way to the river. The moon still afforded light on the silver stretch of the Earn as Kella drew water with her bucket and retreated a short distance into the shadow of some trees for privacy. Maybe she'd have time to fix her husband a warm breakfast. There were apples left and—

A large hand clamped over her mouth, nearly sealing off the air to her nose as well. "I've got ye this time, missy."

The man with the limp?

Kella tried to think, but body and mind froze at the press of a cold blade to her neck. Its promise of death was so certain that time slowed. Memories filled her mind. She saw her sleeping husband, mourned the time they'd lost, cherished the night they had shared. And she cursed herself for choosing vanity over Alyn's warning not to leave the campsite alone.

"'Tis your head, or the cap'n'll have mi—"

The bucket of water slipped from her hand.

Her assailant grunted.

Cold river water drenched Kella's feet, shocking her out of the calm acceptance of her fate. As the blade jerked away from her flesh, she bit the loosened fingers over her mouth, kicked backward with all her might. The man erupted in a stream of curses as she spun out of his grasp. When she faced the tall, dark, shadowy figure again, she'd tossed aside her cloak, her knife at the ready.

"Alyn!" The lavender-bent bride in her shrieked, but it was the champion's daughter who hurled the blade as her assailant charged her.

It didn't stop the big man. He barreled into her, dragging her to the ground. Her head hit hard. A tree root? A stone? Regardless, the umbrella of the trees, dark against the paling sky, turned a bright white. Her assailant's weight atop her crushed the remaining breath from her lungs.

Torn between a world of pain and numbing light, Kella shoved the man to the side as she dragged in fresh air, fodder to fight. Fight for the life within her and the one that lay ahead. Now that she knew what love was, she was not about to let it slip away. If only her head would stay in one world or the other.

"Come, milady. You're safe now."

A friendly voice. Not Alyn's. Kella tried to focus on the apparition before her. One ... *two* heads against the moon-dappled branches overhead? A wave of nausea rose at the back of Kella's throat as they separated. Two men tried to help her up.

If they did, surely her head would explode. "N-no ..."

"We mean you no harm," one of them said, though the words echoed as if in a duet.

Good. "Call my ..." *Husband* became thought only.

"We must move her quickly, brother."

"Get her feet. We'll move her into the boat."

Were her feet elsewhere from her body? Kella couldn't tell. Couldn't make out who her rescuers were. And why move her to a boat?

"Wh ..." The question wouldn't form on her tongue. It floated somewhere in her mind as the men picked her up and carried her through the rushes. Kella felt the cut of the sharp blades on her arms. "No ..." The jostling alone was going to make her sick.

"I swear it," she shouted at them. That is, she meant to.

"Mary, mother of God!" one of the men hissed in surprise. "The coble's sunk!"

"What?" The man holding her under the arms nearly dropped her. Agony jarred her head till the confusion went white.

Yet not even that remote place was immune to the ungodly howl that erupted nearby, as if a demon from Hades had come up out of the water after them all. Frigid, moving river water suddenly swallowed her. River, rushes, pounding drums of pain, and shouts for God's help—Kella scrambled through them all in an attempt to return to Alyn. The two men who'd dropped her unceremoniously into the water slogged through the mud to escape the scrawny, gnarled demon dancing on the shore.

"Ha, ha, hee, hee, I *knew* I smelt trouble!"

Kella knew it. Or, rather, him.

She flailed about in the water in an attempt to get up, striking her hand on the edge of the sunken boat. Using it for leverage, she gained her footing on the river bottom. The dawn's cool air penetrated her soaked shift and skin to her very bones. There was no sense to be made of the mad commotion several feet beyond her on the banks. Men. Struggling with other men.

But the wasplike figure waded in toward her. "Ye're a headstrong 'un, little wife, but ye got spirit."

"Idwyr." The name was relief upon Kella's lips.

Like his gnarled staff, Idwyr was surprisingly strong as he lent his support to wade out of the shallows. "Too much for yer own good."

Once ashore, the old man fetched her cloak. She stepped into its woolen warmth, grateful for it and the friend who delivered it. "Thank you, dear friend."

"Kella!"

Alyn. She knew her husband, though she could not see the face of the man coming at them in a hard run.

"Slow down, priest, or all of us'll have ta dry out," Idwyr warned.

Alyn stopped short, seizing her by the shoulders. "Kella, what happened?"

Truly, she wasn't certain. There was the man with the knife at her throat, then the other men with their sunken boat … and dear little Idwyr. What Kella did know was that she'd nearly died because she'd ignored her husband's caution.

"I bumped my head," she mumbled, her knees buckling with relief. It was over.

Whatever *it* was.

"I only wanted to look and smell beautiful for you." Kella buried her face against the bare-skinned warmth of Alyn's chest where nothing could harm her. Where only love lived.

CHAPTER TWENTY-THREE

"I warned you, *don't leave the campsite alone!*"

Alyn paced back and forth along the side of the wagon bed where Brisen tended Kella. He was furious at Kella for leaving without bothering to wake him. Furious at himself for not even noticing his wife was gone until he'd heard her scream his name. He'd barely collected his wits enough to wrap his plaid about his naked body before bounding from the wagon, only to realize he had no idea where her call had come from. He still could feel the sickening panic that had run him through as he searched the dark for any sign of movement.

"You are *not* invincible! I don't care if you did put a dagger in the blackguard's heart."

"I know," Kella replied. Her uncharacteristic meekness caused Alyn even more concern than the nasty lump on the back of her head that Brisen gently examined.

'Twas Idwyr's banshee howl that drew Alyn to the river as fast as his bare feet would carry him. And woke up everyone, including the dead in the mound on the yon side of the river.

"From now on, *you*," he stopped pacing and jabbed his finger at her, "go nowhere without me. *Nowhere!*"

The faint cut of an assassin's blade on her shoulder showed just how close he'd come to losing her. Faith, Alyn still shook. So did she, even though she'd donned her old hunting shirt and trousers after the abrupt dunking in the river shallows.

"I won't."

Unassuaged, Alyn turned his vent on Idwyr, who stood next to Egan, awaiting Brisen's verdict as to whether Kella should travel. "And where were *you* when he nearly cut her throat?"

"Follerin' them two." The wizard nodded to where the remainder of his Miathi escort guarded the men who'd tried to abduct Kella until Crief's own guard arrived. The knaves were priests, of all things, and poorly disguised once their caps were removed to reveal the Roman tonsure. "I seen 'em pokin' about the wagon after my men left for Dumyat. Me 'n' them," he said, nodding at his two Miathi companions, "is all that stayed."

"Why didn't you go with the rest of your men?" Alyn asked more gently.

Idwyr cackled. "I told ye, I smelt trouble. Caught these two snoopin' 'round yer things soon as me men rode off. Fell right into me trap, they did. We tailed 'em till they come back this mornin'. But the scoundrel who tried to cut her throat took us all by surprise. Not even Jesus saw 'im!"

God, forgive him. Idwyr at least recognized the presence of the Holy Spirit. Maybe God *had* used a half-crazed wizard to spare Kella. Maybe all this madness was part of some master plan, but all Alyn could fathom right now was that he'd almost lost her.

Yet he hadn't. Because the Lord *was* watching over her.

"Jesus saw the villain, Idwyr," Alyn told the old man. "He sees everything, even the tiniest sparrow when it falls." The Word added to the peace Alyn gathered from the Spirit. "And He gave Kella the presence of mind to fight sensibly."

"A bird?" The way Idwyr's wrinkles gathered spelled doubt, at least about the sparrow.

"You did the rest, my friend." Alyn extended his hand. "For that I thank you, Idwyr. And I thank God for blessing you with that nose for trouble."

Idwyr's snaggletoothed grin scattered the skepticism. "Always your friend, *Merlin*. Ye know that."

Alyn held his tongue, not about to get into that discussion now.

"I think someone's head will be sore for a bit," Brisen announced, "but some oak bark tea will see her fit for travel. Though I can't vouch for how safe she'll be."

Egan stepped up, patting the sword at his waist. "She'll be safe. Don't ye worry yer pretty head aboot that."

"I shan't," Brisen promised with a wink. She patted Kella's hand. "You rest, dearie. The tea should be ready by now."

Alyn moved to the edge of the wagon bed, taking a seat next to his wife. His best weapon here was a calm, clear head to find the facts. "Did you know the man who tried to kill you?"

"I wasn't thinking, Alyn. I'd forgotten about him—the man who'd tried to force me into the wood the other night. All I could think of was you and—" She glanced to where Egan and Idwyr listened, her head dipping with blushing shyness. "You know."

Aye, he did. Now he began to see the merit in celibacy, for when she smiled like that, even the most pious of minds became a muddle. 'Twas no wonder the ancient Levites practiced abstinence from their marriage bed when they actively taught and served at the temple. Certainly Alyn's wits wouldn't have been dulled to a sleep so deep that his wife had left him without his knowledge. Before last night, he could have heard a gnat sneeze from the next campsite.

"All I could think about was using my special soap against the dirt and stench of the road, so that when I sat next to you, I'd remind you of a field of lavender in bloom."

"I'd rather you smell like a pig than lose you."

Alyn didn't need Egan's outright snort or Idwyr's tutting noise to know he'd misspoken. The fire beneath his collar was sufficient.

But instead of taking offense, Kella leaned in and kissed him on the cheek. "You *do* have a way with words."

Alyn strove to recover his chain of thought. "So your villain was the same—"

Kella's expression lit up. "He said it was my head or his." She pondered a moment. "Something about the captain having his head if he failed."

At her shudder, Alyn sheltered her beneath his arm. "He's dead, Kella."

She grew silent, her face troubled, as though she relived the struggle again. "It was him or me," she concluded simply. "Just like the men who attacked us on the way to Glenarden. Had we not killed them, they surely would have killed us."

"Someone tried to kill ye before?" Egan queried.

"There's somethin' worryin' someone about reachin' Fortygall," Idwyr chanted at the sky. "Somethin' in that wagon, or someone." He shifted sharp eyes from Alyn to Kella, his bush of a brow lifting. "Am I right?"

"Aye, most likely. We just need to find out which." Alyn slid off the edge of the wagon. "Let's see if our prisoners are ready for confession." If Egan and Idwyr were committed to protecting Alyn and his wife, he might as well find out why this had happened.

"Alyn," Kella called after him.

"Aye?"

She hopped to the ground and caught up with him. "Let's see if our dead man has a wound in his thigh."

Kella braced herself to view the body of the man she'd killed. The man who would have killed her, she reminded herself. Alyn cut away the dead man's trouser leg to reveal what Kella suspected might be there. A barely healed wound from the lance that had saved Alyn's life and sent the villain running away, yelping and limping like a three-legged hound. Now she knew what she saw in his eyes when he'd tried to force her away from the crowd. Vengeance.

So this man—Kella tried to study his face, but death had frozen a sinister snarl on his lips that still chilled her—*so this man* had been working for someone with military rank? A ship's captain?

It made no sense. Who would want to kill her, for undoubtedly that was what the blackguard had on his mind?

At least the motive of the Brothers Ennis and Laol was more transparent. Once Kella looked past the new growth of their beards and the shabby peasant garb they wore, she recognized them as part of the black-robed flock that followed Cassian around.

The two were tight-lipped about their reason for the abduction attempt until Alyn pointed out that, unless he spoke to the authorities on their behalf, the fine hospitality of the dungeon at Crief awaited them. This was, after all, Pictish territory, where Rome had never been welcome as friend or foe. And given yesterday's turn of events, it was more dangerous than ever to outsiders.

"We were supposed to make certain that you traveled for the reasons you stated, not for Gwenhyfar," Laol informed them. "Cassian suspected the queen of having more than one copy of the books."

"But you were guarded at every turn," Ennis complained. "First in the keep at Glenarden. Then by this Satan's spawn."

"The books belong in the Archbasilica in Rome," Laol stated with as much indignation as the plump little man could muster, trussed as he was like a fowl bound for the cook's pot. "With the pope … not with these *pagans*."

Idwyr shook his necklace of bones at them. The poor priests blanched as white as the clouds spotting the blue morning sky. "Books, ye say. All this about *books*?" He turned to Alyn. "The Books of the Word?"

Alyn shook his head, fixing his attention on his Roman brethren. An attention that grew increasingly dark. "And you two expected to accomplish what by abducting my wife?"

"'Twas his idea," Ennis said, jerking his head toward Brother Laol.

"My body was sore from all that riding and riding and riding," his companion responded in defense. "And as our Cymri brother had pointed out, 'tis more risky than ever going deeper into this godforsaken land."

"*He*," Ennis said, "thought that if we took the lady, you might consider handing over the books."

"Though we never meant her any harm," Laol added hastily. "We didn't know what to do when we came upon that cur."

"We'd been watching for a chance to catch the lady alone and thought at first rise would present the best opportunity, but just as we were about to come out of hiding—"

"The villain stalked by us, quiet as a ghost, and grabbed her," Laol finished for his partner.

Kella kept her eyes on the confessors rather than face the accusing glance she felt burning into her skin. Her husband was right to be angry.

Father, help me to be a more obedient wife. The kind to support such a good man as my—

Alyn exploded with a bellow. "Did it occur to you to *help* my wife?"

Kella gasped, clutching her hand to her chest. Even Idwyr jumped back a step.

"Are you men or *mice* of God? Are you even *of* God?" he challenged. Kella could see the veins at his temples bulging, as if about to burst.

"We are unaccustomed to violence," Ennis said in a timid voice. Laol nodded.

"Mice carrying crosses," Alyn muttered in disgust. "We are supposed to be on the same side, not Arthur's, not Modred's, not Cassian's. *God's!*" He ran his hands over his temples as if in pain and stormed away.

"Brother Alyn!" Ennis called after him.

He pivoted with an abrupt "What?"

Never had Kella see Alyn like this. As if some beast had been loosed. One he struggled to control.

"We've told you everything we know," the bolder of the two ventured. "Will you speak for us with the lord of Crief?"

For a moment, Alyn looked as if he might return and strike the man.

"In the name of Jesus, sir," Laol added faintly.

'Twas Jesus's name that made the beast in Alyn flinch. Alyn fingered the cross that hung about his neck, his lips moving faintly. Kella didn't realize she held her breath until he spoke.

"Aye. Even mice can carry messages."

Relieved, not only for the priests but for her husband, Kella hurried to catch up with him as he strode over to the fire where Brisen poured the medicinal tea.

"I've need of that tea, if you've any to spare, milady," he told her. "Perhaps it will silence the devils gnawing on my mind."

Devils? The word worried Kella as much as what she'd just witnessed.

CHAPTER TWENTY-FOUR

It was a perfect day for travel. Fair, warm … and without any further sign of trouble.

Alyn drove the cart past peaceful fields freshly turned and planted. Newborn calves followed their mothers about, nuzzling them for milk. Bees hovered near every blossom that colored the roadside.

But it was just a facade. Like a tapestry, it captured only the moment, only what the eye could see. Not all that transpired before or behind it.

Arthur, the golden champion of God, had apparently gone mad. Gwenhyfar, the queen of the holiest line of priests and priestesses, and Modred, the archbishop of the Celtic Church, conspired against the High King, at the least. They were adulterers—or worse—at the most.

Alyn had thought this mission, saving the Grail records that established the British church's direct connection to God's ordained kings and priests, might be a second chance at righting himself with God. Instead, he'd gone from feeling unworthy of serving the church to feeling the church was not worthy of serving.

"We've only a few miles to go," Kella said, climbing onto the wagon bench from the back as he slowed the cart.

"Aye." And if he were to remain a good husband, he'd take his wife away from this madness, not into it.

Ahead, a line of humanity waited to cross at the Bridge of Tay. It was definitely fair time. There were nobles and their ladies, warriors and clansmen in bright colors, some afoot or with wagons and carts. Alyn believed that the merchant caravan from Crief was the one now inching over the stone crossing that marked the divide between the river and the loch of the same name.

"Why so glum?" Next to him, Kella used her fingers to pull her mouth into an exaggerated frown.

"I could go on and on, but let's settle for just today's events. Someone is trying to kill the woman I love."

Kella snuggled close, her arm going about his waist as she laid her head upon his shoulder. "He's dead."

Simple as that.

"His captain isn't," Alyn replied, giving up the unending trail of thought.

"Now, *husband*," she cajoled, not without effect. "Jesus knows where the villain is. Like you told Idwyr, He sees all," she reminded him with childlike conviction. "He may have already punished him."

"Verily I say unto you, Whosoever shall not receive the kingdom of God as a little child, he shall not enter therein."

God, I do thank You for saving her, Alyn apologized. *I praise You for her renewed faith … but it nearly got her killed.*

Alyn wanted to take Kella away from all this backstabbing to some remote glen like Brisen's and just live and love. Once he made certain this *captain* would never threaten her again.

Vengeance—

I know vengeance is Yours, Lord, he argued against the teachings ingrained in his mind. *But I want to send this man to the Other Side.*

"Will we make it to the holy mount by dark?" Kella asked. Her face had turned a little pink while sleeping in the sun.

"If we're not held up long here at the bridge."

Though, with murder on his mind, Alyn shouldn't go near the place. If it *was* sacred. Little else he'd believed sacred was.

At the sound of horses approaching behind them, Alyn guided the cart to the side of the road to allow the mounted group to pass. Yet, while mounted parties might move ahead of cart and foot traffic on the road, they, too, would have to wait for the merchants to clear the bridge to pass.

"Make way for the king of Errol!"

With a gasp, Kella pivoted in her seat to watch as a herald rode by at the head of a color guard bearing banners marked with the emblem of a black falcon surrounded by an ornate border of blues and black.

Alyn grimaced. *That* ghost was all he needed. All *she* needed.

The king followed, head high, a tall, towering man with hawk-like nose and deep-set eyes. Time and the elements had etched character on his face. Alyn guessed him to be well past his thirtieth year, though a young queen rode behind him with her lady-in-waiting. Both were bedecked in finery with gold rings and torques that cast off the sunlight as though it were not good enough.

But what held Alyn's attention most was the Errol lord's long fair hair. 'Twas almost as white as the bleached horsetails streaming from the helmets of his warriors. His thin lips curled as his companion, perhaps a son or cousin given the likeness, leaned in and made an observation.

"Lorne!" Kella breathed the name as though a knife lodged in her heart.

Alyn gathered her tightly in his arms as she slumped against him. "'Tis his king … and kin," he assured her. "And you were right." Would that the kiss he planted atop her head wash away the memory forever. "His hair *is* the color of cornsilk."

"Nay, nay …" She fisted her hands about the hem of her shirt as row after row of armed soldiers passed, riding two by two. "Do you think I don't know the man who fathered this child?" She pulled away from him, her eyes flashing like a summer storm. "'Tis Lorne of Errol, and curse his soul, he's *not* dead."

Impossible. "Kella," Alyn began, "Elkmar witnessed—" Elkmar, who abducted Cassian, turning traitor against Arthur. *Captain* Elkmar? The implication was staggering.

"He lied!" Kella rolled off the wagon bench and into the back onto the mattress where she'd napped earlier. Frantic, she dug through their stowed belongings.

"What's happened?" Egan O'Toole drew close to the wagon astride one of the fine steeds delivered to Brisen that morning from the fortress stables.

Alyn handed the cart reins over to the Irishman at the sound of metal scraping from the bottom of the pile. A sword. Realizing the fury he'd seen in Kella's eyes was about to be unleashed, Alyn swung over the bench in time to wrestle the short sword away his incensed wife.

"I'll kill that—" she began.

Alyn kissed her. He could think of no other way to stop her from turning the entire Errol procession on them.

The brunt of scorn's fire turned upon him. The sweet lips that had returned his affections only hours ago now cursed him in five languages, while her fist pummeled away at him. Just as he finally pinned her wrists, Kella jerked up her knee and nearly rendered him useless as a man. Alyn rolled away, inhaling her name with a gasp.

"I'll kill the lying—ow!" she cried as he kicked the sword from her hand. The wounded look she gave Alyn ran him through.

"I'm sorry!" Did she even *see* him?

"I want his head on a stake!" Kella lunged for the weapon again.

Aware that they drew an audience, Alyn shouted, "'Tis a fit!"

And fell upon his wife again, from a safer angle. Faith, he'd rather wrestle Egan … anyone who wasn't the woman he loved and with child.

"The *child*!" he muttered through clenched teeth as she pulled one hand free and scratched at his face. He caught her hand, forcing it to the mattress … or what was left of it. Her feet flailed the heather stuffings everywhere. "Think of the baby."

A hint of understanding flickered in Kella's wild eyes as they settled upon his face.

"The *baby*," he repeated hoarsely. "We must protect the baby."

"Alyn." Kella spoke as if she just now recognized him.

"I'm here, my love. For you and our child."

The fight went out of Kella as fast as it had come.…

And into Egan O'Toole. "Never ye mind, lassie," the big Irishman said, grim as death. "I'll kill the traitor for ye meself."

Fortunately, Egan's anger built more slowly than his daughter's. The sight of Errol's troops had cracked the dam that had held back the memory of his identity.

The troops from Errol had crossed the bridge and were well on their way to Fortingall's fairground by the time Egan revealed how Lorne of Errol had led Strighlagh's border guard in chase of the raiders into a narrow, wooded pass against Egan's advice. There, the blue, black, and white of Errol's small contingent melted into the wood, and all the Miathi in the world came out of it, swarming behind the Strighlagh guard to prevent its retreat, while its prey turned back on them as predator.

Egan recalled being struck down. But how he came to Brisen, he attributed to God. "Sent me to an angel, He did."

By then Alyn and his motley assembly were on the other side of the Tay, and Errol's contingent was nowhere in sight. The group stopped the wagon long enough to purchase fresh bread and cheese at the village. There the last piece of the puzzle fell into place. The young woman who followed the king and prince of Errol was not the queen of Errol, but Lorne's new bride, Morgana. Daughter of Modred.

Though Alyn already suspected it, Kella was the first to say it.

"The captain who sent assassins after me *is* Elkmar."

After all, Kella wasn't the type of woman to take a lover's lies lightly and accept the lot he left her. The champion's daughter would fight for the truth.

That made two men Alyn truly wanted to kill. Unless Egan got to them first.

Lorne of Errol, the man she'd loved—or believed she'd loved—was married to a princess. Kella had not given herself to love, but to a lie. And, though God forgave her, Kella could not forgive the man who had willfully done this to her. It was so clear now. Lorne always looked for a chance to spend time with her *and* Gwenhyfar. The queen's well-being and thoughts were utmost on his mind … or, rather, his benefactor Modred's.

Kella wanted the father of her child dead, his poisonous influence ended. Perhaps then this madness Lorne had infected her with would end. The venom that surged through her at the sight of Lorne, healthy and happy—after all she'd been through for his sake—had made her snap. Turn against the one man she really loved—Alyn. Not because he set her fancy free beneath the moonlight, though he was most capable of that. But because he'd shown her what unconditional love was. Loved her when she was not lovable. When she'd scratched his face and screamed her rage at him.

Now she was adamant. Her baby, girl or boy, would never know anyone but the noble, generous, forgiving father God had sent.

The sight of Mons Seion rising gently beyond the glenside village of Llanarch at sunset not only robbed Kella of her breath, but of the vicious revenge weaving through her thoughts, as though dark thoughts were not allowed in such a holy place. An ethereal mantle of pink and blue clouds tucked about the ancient, timeworn mountain, so that where they ended and the soft rock grays and verdant greens of Seion itself started was hard to tell.

Even the village seemed otherworldly, as if untouched by the woes that had plagued the weary travelers on their journey. Though not a monastery, it was a holy community where people gathered at night around a great yew, said to be the offspring of the Giant's tree in Fortingall. An inn called the Upper Room offered a welcome quote from Jesus painted on its tall gable: "*Come unto Me, all ye that labour and are heavy laden, and I will give you rest.*"

Kella and her traveling companions waited there while a servant went to fetch Mairead, abbess of the sisters of Mons Seion. Soon the genealogies would be safe among other secrets of the ages.

God was no stranger here. Tradition said that the Holy Mother's grandparents had been born here, while the Arimathean family established a metals trade in the islands, long before Jesus's birth. Some said Pontius Pilate was born or educated in these hills when his father, a Roman general, served in Fortingall.

Then there were stories the innkeeper was more fond of. Those of the ancient ones called Giants, who first discovered the healing properties of the holy mount and its springs. Those folks burrowed underground, becoming the fairies of Schiehallion, when the first Jews arrived prior to Christ.

While the men favored ale, Kella washed down the dust of the road with a lovely blend of tea that seemed to seek out and soothe every muscle and joint stiff from the hours of riding. And even though she'd had bread and cheese from the Bridge of Tay, the sticky honey cakes the innkeeper put out for them were so tempting that she ate two.

The innkeeper's wife kept a wary eye on Idwyr and his two war-riors, while the innkeeper himself held his audience captive by passing along tales about the mountain. "Some call it Schiehallion, fairy hill of the Caledonians," he said in a melodic voice that reminded Kella of a bard ... or priest.

She sought the hand of her own beloved priest and felt it wrap about hers.

"Once home o' the gods," the innkeeper continued. "Not that we've seen a god or fairy in all our years here." He chuckled.

"Nay, but they been here." Idwyr moved a lamp over a plaster wall, squinting at tiny specks that caught the light and held it.

"'Tis a special blend of ground glass mixed in the daub," the man informed the wizard. "A secret passed down by the God cult who mined the mountain."

"God cult?" Alyn repeated. "You mean the Culdees. They were Jews akin to John the Baptist, hermits who baptized with water and prepared the way before Christ Himself appeared."

Idwyr perked up. "*Jesus?*"

"Now what would the likes of you know about Jesus?" the innkeeper's wife asked. There was no condemnation in demeanor. Simply a wary curiosity.

"We see eye ta eye, Jesus 'n' me. Like that." The wizard held up two fingers pressed together.

With no idea what to make of Idwyr, the goodwife fetched a bucket and began to scrub the tables, though they were already rubbed smooth and clean.

At that moment, the door of the inn opened. The servant who'd left earlier returned leading a cloaked and hooded female. The room went silent. Even Brisen and Kella's father, who were engaged in an intense conversation in the corner, quieted. Not even Mons Seion had calmed the storm of revenge brewing in Egan's chest.

"Blessed be, it is good to see that you finally arrived," Mairead said. "I welcome all the friends of Gwenhyfar."

It wasn't until Kella spied the rod in her hand, too thin for a staff, that she realized the priestess was blind. That shock had barely registered when Mairead threw back her hood to reveal a full head of wild flaxen hair that hadn't seen a brush in … Kella couldn't imagine how long. Gwenhyfar had told her that the brush and mirror—any items of vanity—were left behind when a priestess served in the temple. But it was this woman's face that left Kella speechless. It couldn't be.

Alyn leapt to his feet in disbelief, for there before them stood the first wife of his brother Caden. But that witch was dead. *Twice* dead. Still, there before them, clad in evergreen shift of a Grail priestess stood the image of—

"Rhianon!" Alyn exclaimed.

CHAPTER TWENTY-FIVE

"Nay, sir, I am Mairead, one of the few Grail priestesses left in all of Albion. This sacred mountain is our abbey."

Alyn instinctively brandished his staff as if to protect himself and the others. Mairead never flinched, but the innkeeper and his servant hastened to put themselves between him and their friend.

Instantly, Alyn felt foolish. One didn't fight the likes of Rhianon with a staff.

"She fools you," he charged. "This is the witch who nearly destroyed my brother and my family. My father's death was by the manipulation of her hand."

"Father Alyn, I swear it isn't so," the innkeeper replied. "I have known this woman since she was brought to the sisters of Seion as an infant. She has never left this mountain."

"Her family abandoned the wee bairn to nature's teeth," his wife put in. "From the valley of the Solway as I recall, though I canna say for sure."

"Tell me about this witch you speak of." Mairead tapped her way to a bench a distance away from Alyn and sat. Her demeanor exuded naught but an infectious calm. "Fiona?"

"Aye, milady," the goodwife answered her from behind the tavern grate. "I'll fetch your tea anon."

The priestess's answering smile was a light unto the room itself. Innocence looked out from beautiful blue eyes, much like Kella's. Still, Alyn had been taken in by them, had a boyish infatuation with the conniving woman who was a master at manipulating men.

"Rhianon was … is …" At this point he didn't know. "My brother's wife, from Gwynedd. She practiced witchcraft along with her nurse."

The beautiful smile faded. "'Twas as I feared, though I'd no cause for despair until now. I have lived in seclusion for so long, but God has been good to me."

Could it be she told the truth? The likeness was incredible. Alyn handed the staff over to the innkeeper. Women like Rhianon were fought with faith, not weapons. Yet, as he joined the lady at the table, he suspected—before she spoke—the story she'd tell.

For no reason other than ignorance, otherwise good Christians killed the second-born of twins, fearing it had been spawned by the Devil. It was especially prevalent in noble families, where inheritance could be in question. But rather than soiling their own hands with blood, they abandoned the newborn to the wild.

In this case, Mairead's parents had discarded the wrong twin. And the priestesses of the Grail had taken her in and sent her to where it was unlikely the two would ever meet—Mons Seion.

Darkness had finally claimed the sky outside when Mairead, Alyn, and Kella left the others, including Egan, to the inn's exceptional hospitality. The mission begun in Carmelide was almost complete. Still coming to grips with the events of the last several weeks, Kella's father agreed not to rush off vengeance-bound ... at least until he had "further words" with Alyn.

Further words. Alyn knew that phrase too well. There was no doubt in his mind that Egan had put together that Alyn and Kella had been wed only a week or two, yet they expected their first child. A fool could discern the timing was all wrong, and Egan was no fool. The Irishman's blue gaze had sharpened all the more since his daughter's exceedingly passionate reaction to Lorne.

Ahead, Kella tripped over a thick vine growing across the almost-hidden path but caught herself before falling or dropping the box containing the volume of genealogies she carried. "How can you possibly go so fast?" she exclaimed to Mairead. The priestess seemed to glide without effort up the mountainside.

"I know this path by heart," Mairead replied. "An infection took my eyesight when I was an infant, so I've memorized all the passages in and around the mountain."

The lantern the priestess carried for their sake intrigued Alyn as much as she, for it produced the light of four candles from its one. Had it a unique element like the plaster at the inn—one that magnified the light? Alyn did his best to catch glimpses of it as he lugged the other two boxed volumes at the end of the procession.

As curiosity piqued, his earlier skepticism about the reverence for Seion waned. If the Culdees had been here, like their Essene counterparts in the Holy Land, they'd preserved all manner of knowledge, both holy and the *sciencia* of God's creation. Still, he couldn't help the astonished drop of his jaw when Mairead placed her hand upon a stone that would take a horse to move, and it rolled away as if of its own accord. As he passed over the threshold into a cave, he spied the track on which it moved.

"Amazing."

As was the room they entered. It reminded Alyn of the cave in which his sister-in-law Brenna had once lived. Furnished for comfort, with a hearth carved into a wall that vented somehow, for there was no smoke in the room to indicate otherwise.

"You will stay here tonight," Mairead said, indicating a bed with a thick, suspended mattress near the hearth. "There is water for tea by the fire. Cheese and fruit bread on the table—and heather ale."

By the time she finished speaking, a tapestry slid aside on the far wall, revealing a narrow entrance into a lighted passage from which three women emerged. Like Mairead, they were clad in simple shifts dyed green, though some were more faded than others.

"My sisters will take the Grail records from here," she told them. "They will be safe here from Rome and those who would use them for their own purposes."

Like Arthur ... or Modred? Alyn kept his thoughts to himself as he handed over the boxes he and Kella had protected with their lives. "The church should rest easier." His cryptic tone revealed a heart jaded by disillusionment.

Mairead stared at him—except that was impossible. "This is the chamber of music. Our gift to those who have journeyed long to serve the church."

"Chamber of music?" Kella asked, peeking out from behind the tapestry. Unlike Alyn, she'd boldly followed the other priestesses to see how it worked.

"Following God isn't always easy," Mairead told them. "I sense from Father Alyn that it has been a difficult task. Sometimes we wonder if our sacrifices are worth it. Sometimes we question the very nature of a God who sees the sparrow fall and does not catch the helpless bird. Sometimes we question *ourselves*." Again, she looked at Alyn. "Are we up to the tasks that God has prepared us for?"

Hair pricked at the back of Alyn's neck. It was as if this blind woman looked into his mind. "And this chamber puts all those anxieties to rest, does it?" Did she see the murder in his heart as well?

Mairead shook her head. "Nay, weary traveler. Only God can do that."

"*God* lives here, as well as the fairies and other gods?" he quipped wryly. A gifted people had been here, to be sure. Those with the most knowledge had always been thought of as gods.

"Father Alyn." Mairead's disappointment carried the same sting that his mother's had, reducing Alyn to a chastened child. "You of all men should know God lives everywhere … *wherever* His children are."

That much, Alyn believed.

Father, he prayed as Mairead bade them good night. *I do not doubt You. Only the claims people make in Your name.*

The priestess left by the same passage as her sisters.

"Did you see the exquisite embroidery and knotwork on her dress?" Kella asked as a wooden door closed behind Mairead and the tapestry covered it once more. "'Twas so simply made, yet the skill … Are you listening?"

Lost in the churn of mind and soul, Alyn picked up the lamp Mairead left behind. There was nothing remarkable or visible to the naked eye that would multiply the light shining through it, yet—

"Alyn!"

"How I would love to explore this place. Chamber by chamber." He strode over to the entrance, where an intricate series of pulleys and gears moved the stone along a well-greased track. Just the touch of a hand—

Nothing happened when he touched the stone. It remained in place. He felt the wall and frame around it, searching in vain for the trigger. Sweat broke out on Alyn's brow upon the realization that he was sealed in. Not that he minded the stone in place. Only that he couldn't control it.

"Alyn, what is it?"

"Wait."

Alyn hurried to the tapestry. The wooden door behind it was also fixed in place, refusing to move aside as it had for the priestesses. He could perhaps breach that if he had to. He glanced at the hearth where an iron poker rested, but compared to the thick oak planking, it was paltry. And his sword, even his staff, was in the wagon stored in the barn behind the inn.

"We're not guests, Kella. We're *prisoners*."

But this was a spacious room, he consoled himself. Filled with amenities for their comfort. And there was light. It wasn't at all like the chest that had nearly suffocated him as a child.

His pounding heart didn't seem to care.

"Nonsense," Kella argued. "Mairead said if we needed anything, to pull the cord by the bed."

Kella poured a cup of heather ale from the jug on the table. "Drink this, and calm yourself. Enjoy the comforts—"

A thin strain of harp music drifted into the chamber as if through invisible cracks. Perhaps like the one that vented the fire. Harmonious chords, sweet notes that plucked at the heart. Then a voice, like that of an angel, joined in. *With a psalm*, he thought.

"If we are trapped, husband, 'tis in the luxury of kings...." Kella handed him the cup. "Our heads are sore with all that has happened this day, and I know not what to think or feel." She wrapped her arms about his waist in a hug. "But I know in my heart and soul that God sent you to me to show me what love truly is. Now," she said, pulling away, "you may sit and stew or join me in that delicious bed. I prefer the latter."

The quirk of her lips, the saucy dip of her lashes, her white shoulders ...

Sweet Solomon! If Alyn were to be trapped, let it be in Kella's arms. Alyn's voice grew husky with a more potent intoxication. "We need no ale this night." He poured it out. All of it, for he still did not know what to make of Mairead.

"What—"

"*Let her kiss me with the kisses of her mouth: for her love is better than wine.*" He murmured the words from Solomon's song.

Even if the wine was the best the world had to offer, Alyn meant every word.

CHAPTER TWENTY-SIX

Alyn was missing from the comfortable rope-slung bed when Kella awoke the following morning.

Yet only last night he'd spoken as if their mission was over. He talked about returning to Glenarden, perhaps opening a school in conjunction with Bishop Martin's monastery.

"Let them kill each other if they must." He'd been very disillusioned by Arthur, Modred, and the church as they talked about his and Kella's future into the wee hours of the morning. "You and the baby are all I care about now."

So where had Alyn gone? Had his insuppressible sense of obligation caused him to change his mind?

Kella hastened to dress. Alyn was not going to Fortingall without her. Though she couldn't blame him if he did, after she'd nearly called down Lorne's soldiers on them.

To her astonishment, her traveling clothes had been removed, replaced by her dress and shift. Someone had taken pains to smooth it with a slickstone. The heated stone had even formed pleats so the gussets didn't bunch her skirts around her hips.

Though this was a cave in a remote mountainside, Kella could easily grow accustomed to such luxury. The music alone had helped her sleep without waking during the night, as she had done since leaving Carmelide. Well, the music, and Alyn's husbandly attentions had also helped. How beautiful was love fulfilled as God intended. No shame. Glory, 'twas pure joy.

Almost the moment Kella tied the gussets of her dress, Mairead knocked on the door of the chamber and entered at Kella's invitation.

"Your husband was most eager to leave us this morning," she said. At Kella's gasp of dismay, she added, "He waits for you at the inn. I came to show you the way."

Every bird in Scotland seemed to sing them down the mountainside. Branches of all manner of trees covering the path quivered with life. Nature danced, Kella mused. Danced to its own music, like that of the cave still echoing in her mind.

"I am most impressed that Father Alyn discovered the release for the stone without help," Mairead remarked. "The masters who engineered such a wonder are long gone."

"He is a man of *sciencia*. Mysteries intrigue him."

"He is a troubled man as well. The sisters and I prayed through the night that God would put his concerns to rest, that he might fulfill the purpose for which he is sent."

Kella stepped over a vine, likely the one that had almost tripped her the night before. "And what might that be?" Aside from saving her and her child and showing her what love is.

"Your husband is a merlin, a man capable of building a bridge from creation to Creator, and a peaceweaver who can speak with kings," Mairead responded. "He will need your support to fulfill God's role for him."

Kella scowled. "I thought women were peaceweavers, like Queen Heilyn. Born for arranged marriages to ensure peace."

"And to bring forth the church as Grail princesses. 'Tis why she sent for a priest. Drust is pagan. But *your* husband," Mairead explained, "is gifted with the voice of reason, a heart for love, and a soul for the Word."

A bridge between believer and nonbeliever. Idwyr and Brisen came to Kella's mind. But Merlin Emrys bridged even more. He found common ground for enemies. Made peace treaties. Advised kings.

"*Blessed are the peacemakers: for they shall be called the children of God.*"

"Is he going to Fortingall?" Kella asked. It would be dangerous enough with Lorne and Elkmar there, but if Alyn tried to speak against Modred and for Cassian …

Mairead didn't answer.

But Kella knew. Knew before she saw her husband dressed in priestly attire. Glenarden's princely red, black, and gray had been put aside for an unbleached robe that fell from broad, straight shoulders and was belted at a waist devoid of excess flesh with the worn belt that once belonged to Merlin Emrys.

When he turned on sandaled feet from where he spoke privately to Egan O'Toole under a nearby tree, a simple silver cross glimmered upon his chest and—

Kella breathed a sigh of relief.

He had *not* shaved his forehead in the Celtic tonsure. If God had given him such a thick mane of raven-hued hair, 'twould be a sacrilege to shave it. *Father* Alyn was as beautiful as … as an angel. One who smiled as she hurried to him.

Heart quickening, she went into his extended arms and, oh, the sweetness of his kiss. Was it wrong to lust after a priest if he was her husband?

"Good morning, wife," he said almost smugly as he delved into her gaze with the blue fire of his own.

He knew, the devil. "Everyone is ready," he told her, "so I hope you won't mind breaking the fast while on the way."

"Nobody's goin' anywhere till I've congratulated ye both properly, now that me mind is back," Egan exclaimed.

Before Kella realized what her da was about, the Irishman gathered her *and* Alyn into a bear hug, lifting them off the ground. "'Tis the answer to me prayers all these years."

Kella tensed until her father put her down gently and gave her a wink twinkling with love. "And a grandchild on the way already. Miracles never cease."

Da knew, and he loved her anyway.

Confound it, she was going to cry … *again*.

But her eyes were dry by the time Mairead, the innkeeper, and his wife waved good-bye as the odd mix of companions set off on the narrow road leading downhill toward Fortingall. Idwyr and his Miathi took the lead, while Brisen and Egan chatted privately behind the wagon.

Kella finished off her breakfast of fresh-baked scones and honey and licked the sticky residue off her fingers while the wagon lurched this way and that, depending on the disbursement of the rocks along the way.

"So what made you change your mind?" she asked. "About leaving for Glenarden today?"

Such a lovely life they'd planned the night before. Not riding into Alba's conflicts. Not that Kella was against this mission. She realized that, even in Glenarden, those conflicts would eventually catch them.

"I can't explain it, Kella, though I would if I could." The set of her husband's shaved jaw underscored his reluctance to talk. "Suffice it to say that God spoke to me last night, and now I know what I must do."

"In a dream?" For she'd heard naught but the harp and women singing like angels.

"Yes …" He frowned. "I think. 'Twas no hallucination, for I poured out the ale in case Mairead had altered its integrity in any way."

Had this come from someone other than Alyn, Kella would be skeptical. But one thing Alyn was not given to was fancy. He took no word at its value save God's Word. "What did God tell you?"

"I must try to resolve these conflicts. They are not so different from those God's prophets addressed in the past," he observed. "I must speak to Drust and the Pictish kings against going to war with the Britons or sitting by idly while the Saxons defeat their island brethren. And I must convince Modred and Cassian of the error of their ways and bring Cassian back to Strighlagh."

But hadn't Alyn once said that not even Jesus could reason with Albion's kings? And Kella knew what had been done to Jesus for telling the truth to the powers that be.

God be with us. The prayer was all the anxiety icing her spine would allow. Alyn had the fierce determination of a man with a quest, his thoughts consumed with it as he looked ahead, yet without really seeing.

Kella was tucking the extra food from her breakfast into the bag behind the wagon seat when she noticed a worn leather satchel stuffed with something, given its thickness.

"What's in that?" Such bags were common among teachers, priests, and scholars. "Did Mairead give you a manuscript from the archives hidden in the mountain?" Perhaps something that would help Alyn.

"Nay!" he said, so sharply that she jumped. "And let no one touch it, save me. No one, not even you." He pinned her with an intense look. Unlike the warm one that met her earlier, this one was absolute, unwavering as stone … cold stone.

"What's in it?"

Alyn closed his eyes. "Something I pray I will not have to use."

"How?"

Without warning, Alyn pulled the cart horse up short. Kella toppled forward, caught by his arm. Behind them, Egan made an exclamation of surprise as he and Brisen struggled to soothe their startled mounts.

Alyn threw up his hand, signaling silence.

Ahead, on hearing the creak of the wagon stop, Idwyr turned his horse back. "Ye smell 'em too?" he whispered.

"What?" Kella mouthed. She neither smelled, heard, nor saw a thing out of the ordinary.

Except that the birds had gone silent in the trees on both sides of them.

Alyn's soft reply chilled her. "We're being watched."

Someone *had* been watching them, and Alyn thought he knew who. Idwyr's men investigated and found a scrap of blue-and-black cloth hung on a blackthorn bush. Errol blue and black, most likely, which meant they had been noticed yesterday during Kella's fit. And Prince Lorne did not want Kella jeopardizing his marital bliss with the Princess Morgana.

Horse tracks farther along indicated at least a dozen men. Enough to accomplish Lorne's objective. Twelve warriors against a wizard, an unarmed priest, and two women. Even with Egan, Alyn's small group had been in grave peril. Yet, for some reason, their enemy abandoned their plans and rode off.

"What do ye think happened?" Idwyr scratched his balding head, bemused.

"*Because thou hast made the* Lord, *which is my refuge, thy habitation,*" Alyn repeated from the psalm he'd heard sung throughout the night, "*there shall no evil befall thee.*"

There was no other reasonable explanation. Like there was none for his sacred visitation. It had begun as a dream. A nightmare Alyn had relived many a night. He was on his way out to a lecture. While Abdul-Alim heated a newly mixed concoction over a small flame, he turned to search the shelves where Alyn arranged various ingredients in meticulous order so that the blind alchemist might not select the wrong one.

But this time, the dream revealed a new detail. Something fell as Alyn opened the door and stepped through it. His teacher had inadvertently knocked a package that Alyn had prepared for a local apothecary off a shelf.

Alyn started back into the workshop to fetch it when the teacher inadvertently stepped on the leather-bound parcel. There was a crunch of a breaking jar. Then a flash of light and fire that consumed all until Alyn awoke in agony days later.

"*It wasn't your fault.*"

The voice of Merlin Emrys woke Alyn. Soaked in perspiration, he blinked in disbelief at the apparition of the old priest before him. In spite of the relief that washed over Alyn, that he'd not caused his teacher's death, new alarm edged it out.

Alyn would welcome his old friend, but this could not be Merlin. "Begone in the name of Christ, demon, for I'll have naught to do with necromancy. The earthly Merlin is dead, absent from his rotting body and present with the Lord."

Alyn grasped his cross, useless silver without the faith he clutched even more.

To his amazement, Merlin dissolved into a pure light form that stood in starbursts of even more light, forcing Alyn to shade his eyes. "Well discerned, prophet. But I come with a message from God."

"*Prophet?*"

Suddenly the form expanded with unfolding wings, singing. "Glory be to God the Father, God the Son in Jesus Christ, and the Holy Spirit." The deafening praise sounded as if all the angels of heaven chorused with him.

Now Alyn doubted his sanity. Somehow he found himself out of the bed and on his knees, trembling in awe. He couldn't speak. Couldn't take his eyes off the light form.

"You must speak the Word of God to kings and priests alike."

But what shall I say? Alyn thought. His tongue was like a stone, yet he was heard.

The being reached out to Alyn and touched his lips. *"Behold, I have put My words in thy mouth."*

Spirit, fire, comfort, peace, love—a myriad of sensations swept through Alyn, over him, and around him, yet only one word could define them all.

Jesus.

Later, when he'd awakened, lying prostrate on the rug covering the stone floor next to the bed, he'd wondered how Kella could have slept through it all, if it had been real.

Who was he to receive such a visitation?

Yet, his conviction would not let Alyn dismiss it or the voice that had haunted him since he'd arrived in Carmelide.

"Glorify Me."

CHAPTER TWENTY-SEVEN

Spread over a sloping landscape up to the knoll where the Fortingall fair took place was an explosion of colorful tents and banners. The scent of roasting meats and baking breads beckoned like invisible fingers, drawing Kella's small party ever closer until they reached the gate that had been fashioned to take tolls for King Drust from fair-bound folk.

"Fortingall's folk dinna work for free to keep the roads clear of rock and the grounds fit for walkin', Father," a guard said to Alyn as he paid the fee. "We need to work for our livin', same as you."

Not that her husband offered complaint. Every clan was responsible for the maintenance of the roads through their property, and in the event of a fair, even more care was expected to keep the land cleared and dry. Alyn was more preoccupied with the armed soldiers watching them with interest as they moved forward. Far keener scrutiny than that given to the travelers ahead of them. Alyn blessed the guardsmen as the wagon passed them by.

Although he had shared the incredible vision that relieved him of guilt on the one hand and charged him with a grim responsibility on the other, Kella's anxiety grew all the more with the soldiers' marked lack of response.

"What do you think is wrong?" She moved even closer to Alyn, desiring both his warmth and his strength.

"The enemy is expecting us." He patted her knee. "But God has given His angels charge over us. Trust Him." The fierce passion of his commitment was hardly that of the man who was ready to leave all this behind last night.

Kella believed that he believed—though his staff lay within easy reach and the shoulder on which she rested her head was coiled for action. *I believe too, Lord. But help Thou my unbelief.*

Unlike at Strighlagh's fair, where Glenarden held a place of honor among other nobles and near the king's dun, Alyn and Kella left the wagon in a spot among the camps of the visiting lesser clans. Once arrangements were made for the care and safety of the horses and their belongings, the group began their ascent toward a giant yew holding court over the fair as it had for centuries. Next to Kella, Alyn shouldered the satchel from the back of the wagon, protecting it like a mother would her child against anyone who might bump into it.

And no wonder, if it contained the kind of package she suspected.

He had shared with her what had been revealed to him—how Abdul-Alim had dropped a package put together for a local merchant and then blindly stepped on it. The burst of fire had come from the crushed package, not from a mistake Alyn had made in putting away the teacher's chemicals. That had to be the *bundle* discerned by Brenna's gift of second sight, yet understood by no one.

And Kella's poor husband had carried that guilt for naught. Though when she'd questioned him as to the wisdom of having such a similar danger in their midst, he simply repeated his earlier words.

"God has given His angels charge over us."

Kella comforted herself by envisioning a score of angels perched in the giant tree standing over the meeting ground. Below it was a surround of noble campsites and a skirt of vendors at the foot of the knoll. Judging from the colorful banners circling the open arena of the court, it was a hearing day for kings and chieftains, not the general populace.

So it was no surprise when yet another company of guards, one that formed a human barrier around the court assembly, stopped them. A swarthy man with a paunch that betrayed an affinity for excess food and drink stepped forward to greet them. "What kingdom do ye represent?"

"The kingdom of God," Alyn replied calmly.

The man smirked. "Only kings and princes from This Side are to be admitted, Father."

"I am Father Alyn O'Byrne, servant of the King of Kings, prince of Glenarden in Strighlagh, and cousin to the High Queen Gwenhyfar." Alyn held out his hand that the man might see his ring bearing the Grail emblem—the dove.

"King Modred is archbishop of the same church," observed one of the other soldiers who'd closed in around them. "He'll speak for you."

"I was sent for by Queen Heilyn."

"Then see her when she is receiving visitors at Dun Gael on the morrow." The first man jerked his head toward a whitewashed fortress watching over the fairground nearby.

Kella wondered if Alyn noticed that more and more guards were moving their way. And then she saw why. Captain Elkmar and some men from Errol stood a distance away, as if directing them. Elkmar, the *captain* who would have her and her child dead. If Elkmar had sway with the guards, at the least he could have them arrested.

Angels, stand ready. Because, aside from dining knives, all other weapons had been checked with the horses and their belongings. No swords were allowed within the fairgrounds, though Fortingall's guards were armed to keep order.

"I must speak to Drust," Alyn insisted. "It is a matter of life and death."

"Excuse me, Commander." Brisen moved up to Alyn's other side and shoved back her hood, revealing a shining display of silver-shot black hair, braided and wrapped in a crown about her head.

Immediately the commander's countenance changed from indifference to awe, perhaps even fear. "Queen Brisen!"

"Queen?" Alyn's astonishment echoed Kella's own. The healer in the glen was assuredly an educated lady, but a queen?

"I speak for myself *and* my son, Drust," Brisen declared with all the authority due a queen mother. "These people are guests of Dun Gael. Unless you would deny a daughter of Bridei entrance as well."

Bridei—overking of the Pictish nation? Stunned failed to come close to what Kella felt. God had provided a way before they needed it … with an earth angel.

"Nay, milady," the guard swore. "Never!"

He started to bow, but Brisen caught him. "Captain, I would have no one but you know that I am here. There are some who would cause my guests harm."

The guardsman gave her a puzzled look. "Aye, Queen Brisen."

"I shoulda known she was too good for me," Egan muttered under his breath.

The hurt in her father's voice made Kella's heart ache.

But Brisen would not have it. "Love falls where it will, and mine has fallen upon you, Egan O'Toole." She offered Da her arm. "Will you continue to be my champion, or will you break the heart you hold in those big, callused hands of yours?"

Discovering Brisen's identity and seeing the marvel and joy upon Da's face was almost enough to make Kella forget Elkmar. When she did seek him out again, the captain and his men had fallen away, melting into the crowd. No matter. The unseen angels in the tree would keep an eye on him. Perhaps even the one who looked like the glowing Merlin Emrys her husband had seen in his vision was among them.

"Now, sir," Brisen said to the waiting guardsman, "here is what I want you to do."

Alyn stood confident, staff in one hand and his bag over his shoulder as a herald approached the dais accommodating King Drust and his royal company. God used the imperfect, including a young, disillusioned priest and a pagan healer. Surely only the Lord could have placed such a benefactress in the right place at the right time. Brisen had fulfilled her role. Now it was time for Alyn to fulfill his.

"Father Alyn O'Byrne," the herald announced. "Servant of the Grail Church, cousin to our beloved High Queen, Gwenhyfar, and prince of Glenarden."

Alyn strode into the open grassy area in front of the dais to a ripple of astonishment in the sea of onlookers—all of noble families, mostly Picts. Perhaps some of his mother's kin were here, but this was not a homecoming. Far from it. His impertinence for insisting on an immediate audience had piqued the curiosity and irritation of everyone, including the king and his honored guests upon the dais.

Only one among them looked relieved. Archbishop Cassian sat at the foot of the dais under guard. A more miserable soul Alyn had never seen, though the priest was unfettered and, if the ruby glass goblet in his hand was any indication, he'd been treated well, as was custom.

"What business have you this day that cannot wait its turn, Father?" Drust demanded. He had his mother's intelligent gaze, as well as the same dark hair and proud facial structure, though his was more pronounced. Brisen's grace and patience, however, were sadly lacking.

"I was sent to Mons Seion on behalf of our High Queen and then on to Fortingall at Queen Heilyn's request to speak to her about building a church here at Fortingall. But, as Your Majesty knows, much has happened since my departure from Carmelide—"

"That is a lie, King Drust." Lorne of Errol stepped forward, his face beetled with rage. "My own captain tells me that this man has led a legion of well-armed warriors down from Schiehallion. They hide in the forests about Fortingall ready for his signal to attack."

Had the prince lost his wits?

Modred, who sat on Drust's left, leaned forward on his polished rowan staff and peered at his new son-in-law as if so. Even Alba's littlest children knew that only fairies, the mountain's priestesses, and their small village inhabited the place.

"My lord," Alyn protested, "I did indeed lead a group down from the village of Llanarch, but not of warriors. Unless last night's drink led the prince's captain to hallucinate. Or mayhap the fairies played tricks upon him?"

Amusement trickled from an uncertain audience. Even Drust's lips curled slightly.

As Alyn jested, the truth came to him, a vision that raised hair upon his arms. 'Twas all he could do to keep from dropping to his knees, humbled that a legion of heavenly warriors—similar to those who had once protected Elisha—had appeared to Elkmar.

Alyn beckoned Kella, Brisen, Egan, and his Miathi companions to join him. "Indeed, here is my *legion*."

The blood rage drained from Lorne's face as Kella marched forward unscathed, head held high in the confidence of God's forgiveness.

"I present Queen Gwenhyfar's scribe, master of five languages, and my *wife*"—Alyn shot the man who'd so cruelly deceived her an accusatory glare—"Lady Kella of Glenarden."

Yesterday Alyn wanted to slay him for threatening Kella. But if he was to make his case today, he had to live by the same counsel he'd given his wife and father-in-law earlier. Vengeance belonged to God, not man.

"This, my lord Drust, is my Miathi friend Idwyr, druid of Dumyat's court," Alyn informed the audience, "and his good men."

Besides, the astonishment on Lorne's face at seeing one of the Miathi with whom he'd conspired was most rewarding.

"Welcome, Idwyr. I am glad that someone from Dumyat is able to attend," Drust told the little man.

As a chief ovate and equal to a king, Idwyr nodded rather than bowed. "The only thing close to a legion we seen, yer majesty, was a handful o' outlaws waitin' to ambush us."

Quite the showman, the old wizard walked in a circle around Alyn, Kella, and his men, drawing every eye in the crowd. Then, almost out of thin air, he produced the scrap of material one of his men had found in the forest brush. Surprise echoed all around.

"They was wearin' these colors and skedaddlin' like they seen ghosts." Idwyr lined the cloth in his squinty view with Lorne and his companions. "Well, lookee that!" The old man leapt back as though shocked by what he'd seen. "Looks jus' like yor'n, pretty man!"

"If that scrap belongs to one of my men, I'll have his head before the day's out," Lorne replied stiffly.

"And lastly," Alyn continued before Idwyr started having too much fun, "Milady Brisen of Crief, whom I believe Your Majesty knows well, and her guardian, Egan O'Toole, my father-by-law."

Lorne looked fit to faint. Modred, curious. Cassian, appalled, as if he'd abandoned all hope for Alyn and himself, given Alyn's heathen company.

But Drust leapt eagerly from his chair and came down from the dais. "Mother!" The king greeted Brisen with a great hug. "Do join us in the shade. I'll have a seat fetched for you."

"Son, I have been in the saddle these last two days," she confessed to him. "Besides, you have a queen at your side now." She blew a kiss to the fair-haired young woman sitting arrow-straight on the right of Drust's throne seat.

Queen Heilyn returned the gesture with a polite wave, leaving Alyn to wonder if there was love lost between the two women. Perhaps over Heilyn's faith … or Brisen's. "We will talk later," the healer queen promised. "But do hear this man out, for I believe he holds the ear of at least one god."

Drust returned to his throne, casting a droll look at Lorne of Errol. "Hardly a legion, sir. I would find myself a new captain." A louder round of guffaws erupted at Prince Lorne's expense.

It was not shared by the king of Lothian. Modred appeared stymied by his brethren's purpose. He and Alyn not only served the same church but were both descended from the Grail lineages.

"My lord archbishop," Alyn addressed him, "I was privileged to spend last night in Mons Seion at the invitation of the abbess Mairead."

Modred nodded, a quickening in his dark eyes revealing he understood more than what Alyn said. Certainly if he and Gwenhyfar had been in constant contact, he would know about the fate of the genealogies.

"While completing the queen's request at Mons Seion, God revealed a message for this assemblage—for all who ponder war and bloodshed—a message I must deliver for the unity of His church and all the peoples of Alba, believers and nonbelievers alike."

"Accomplish this, Priest," Brisen said next to him above the mixed response of the multitude, "and even this high priestess of Cailleach, our mother of creation, would hear more of your God."

"It will be my honor," Alyn replied.

Before Alyn's very eyes, Modred's expression turned to stone. Alyn steeled himself against the same uncertainties that must have assailed the likes of the old prophets. He would either open the cold eyes boring into him to the light … or make a deadly foe.

To God be the glory.

CHAPTER TWENTY-EIGHT

"God has seen all your deeds and revealed them to me that your darkness may see light." Alyn encompassed the dais with a sweep of his
arm. "Conspirators all, not for God's glory, but for your own gain."

Modred shot up from his seat. "I will not hear such blasphemy
against an archbishop of the Grail Church, not from some wet-eared
pup of a priest!"

"But these good people would." Cassian, it seemed, had found
some backbone and an unbecoming dose of smugness. "Especially if
you lead them into war for your own gain."

"As you push Arthur to establish Rome's authority over the
British church?" Modred challenged back.

At the edge of tolerance, Drust held up his hand. A tall, distin-
guished adviser who stood behind the throne seat leaned over and
whispered something in his ear. Drust nodded. "Gentlemen, both
my druid Beathan and I feel that this is a matter for your God, not
us," he exclaimed. "It is the border conflict that concerns the Pictish
people."

But Cassian and Modred turned upon each other like two
vipers tossed into the same basket, inflaming the onlookers beyond

Drust's control. Controversy spread like wildfire clan to clan around the arena. Fortingall's guards rallied to diffuse the arguments that became physical here and there—believers and nonbelievers, warmongers and those who craved peace.

"My lords," Alyn shouted in a vain attempt to regain control of the proceedings.

The cacophony was deafening, enough to drive a man away from the lot, leaving them to their own end.

"*Glorify Me.*"

Alyn knew what had to be done.

"All of you," he warned his companions, "get as far away from me as you can at the edge of the area and remain there, no matter what happens."

"But Alyn—" Kella glanced fearfully at his satchel.

Alyn kissed away her objection. "Angels," he reassured her. "Egan …"

The champion nodded. Only Kella suspected what Alyn was about. But Egan and the others trusted him enough to follow his command and would see that she did as well. If something went awry, only Alyn would suffer.

Consumed with purpose, he moved to the center of the arena. Carefully, he eased the package he'd made that morning out of his satchel. It was bound tightly in leather, like the one prepared in Abdul-Alim's workshop for the apothecary. But protruding from it was an innocuous length of coiled string.

He dug a small hole in the dirt with the end of his staff and fixed the package firmly in it, then stood upright and assessed the circle of humanity about him. Nearly double the longest dimension of Abdul-Alim's workshop. More than adequate room for safety.

He hoped.

Borrowing from Idwyr's flair for drama, Alyn paced sunwise around the circumference of the clearing. At the easternmost point, where Kella and his friends waited, he winked. There and at the southernmost, westernmost, and northernmost extremities, he tapped the earth with his staff, as if marking it in some ritual and prayed that, by God's grace, all were beyond harm, including him. Yet, at the same time, he prayed for a spectacle that would gain him the ear of pagan and believer alike.

Quadrant by quadrant fell silent in his wake. By the time he returned to the package and picked up the end of the attached string, even the leaders upon the dais gave him their undivided attention. Alyn could almost see Merlin Emrys smiling down at him from some heavenly loft. His old friend loved drama and *sciencia* almost as much as the Word.

"What *is* this?" Drust demanded. By now he was more than annoyed. He'd not only lost control of the proceedings, but an upstart priest had seized it.

"I beg you, my lord, order your guards to keep everyone outside the circle I marked, for anyone inside risks a terrible death."

Uncertainty darkened Drust's face. In his world, an unseen God's displeasure was no threat, but Alyn's druidic drama set all the pagan king's earthly senses on edge. He nodded to the guardsmen awaiting his orders. "Do as the man says."

Alyn brandished his staff, swinging it full circle simply to see for himself that the king was understood, but to many who observed, the supernatural was at work. Alyn prayed it was. *God forbid anyone be injured.*

Next to Drust, Modred and Lorne conversed quietly, their attention fixed, like everyone else's, upon Alyn. He turned his back to the conspirators. Not even they would risk harming him in front of so many onlookers. Backing away from the package slowly, Alyn uncoiled loop after carefully wound loop.

Attached at the other end of the string, which ran through a pin-sized hole in the outer wrapping, was a plug to a vial of the same plant extract that Alyn had packed along with his master's black salts for Abdul-Alim's customer. Alyn now knew what had caused the explosion. At least he *thought* he knew.

The glass vial of the oil had broken when his teacher stepped on it, cutting and leaking through the wrapping around the black salts. Separate, each was harmless, used in salves for skin afflictions. Even when mixed, as Alyn had done the night spent in the Roman fortress, they produced the smallest flame. Never would he have guessed them capable of the blast that destroyed the workshop.

It had to be the binding that made the difference. Alyn prayed he was right, because in that hole was the last of his teacher's preparation of the substances. This was Alyn's only chance to use it—this time for good.

The string reached its full length. One sharp tug ...

Alyn hesitated, shuddering as the vision of the death-dealing disaster flashed in his head. Faith, it branded him even now, for his scar screamed in anguish. So much that his senses retreated from it, making him feather light.

Nay! Alyn grappled for them with a will beyond his own.

"To God be the glory!" he shouted.

And yanked the cord as hard as he could.

The arena came into focus. His feet bore the weight of his returning consciousness. He watched the hole, breath held.

Nothing.

Alyn replayed the vision in his mind. How long had it taken for the mix to—

A roar from the far end of the field yanked his focus from recollection to where a man broke through the guard's line, shouting madly, "He deceives you all with wizardry and makes me the fool!"

Elkmar! The captain seized a sword from one of the Fortingall guards and charged across the arena, his course set straight for Alyn and the package between them.

"No!" Alyn motioned Elkmar away ... and the disarmed peacekeeper in his pursuit. "Guard, go back! Go back or die!"

The guard heeded Alyn, but Elkmar charged on, deaf to all but the feral lust for blood on his contorted face.

It was the last call the captain heard on This Side.

A thundering monster of fire and smoke burst out of the ground, consuming Elkmar as he passed the pit. The very ground trembled under Alyn's feet. Dirt scattered, stinging the flesh of those closest to the barrier. The onlookers fell away, some to the ground, others at a run. Some screamed. Others cursed.

Soon the black smoke of the beast's form began to dissipate in the spring breeze, but there was nothing left of Errol's captain. Nothing but unrecognizable bits of charred flesh ...

And a sword lying on the blackened ground near the hole that Alyn had dug. Except the small hole was now a crater at least two lance lengths in diameter.

God's mercy! Numbed by icy revulsion, Alyn bowed his head and made the sign of the cross. Elkmar's maniacal charge had left him no chance of repentance, no chance for God's grace. Given that yesterday Alyn was ready to help Elkmar *and* his lord Lorne to the Other Side, the irony of this regret was not lost upon him as he turned to face the white-faced men, frozen where they stood, or crouched, upon the dais.

"Thus saith the Lord!" he bellowed, arms raised to the heavens. "Will you hear me now, kings and priests?"

Alyn cast his eye upon Modred and Cassian—the two most despicable of the lot, for they were avowed men of God. His throat was dry and raw from the smoke as he repeated his demand.

"Will you hear God's word for you now, sirs?"

A born merlin. Just as Mairead had said that morning. Never had Kella been more frightened for Alyn or proud of him. Her husband had won the attention of every eye and ear that had not fled and feared to return. She could only imagine the courage and faith it had taken for him to loose the fiery monster that had haunted him beyond the healing of his flesh. 'Twas worse than she imagined, though she did not mourn Elkmar's loss.

Kella followed Queen Brisen, at the lady's request, around the crater and its blackened skirt of grass to where the gentle Heilyn had fainted in her throne seat. Heilyn's ladies-in-waiting had been among the many who fled in hysterics. While those closest to the spectacle brushed debris off their fair finery, some of the soldiers found backbone enough to leave their posts and stamp out patches of grass still burning on the ground.

"There was once a kingdom blessed by God that turned on itself, dividing into two kingdoms. Israel was threatened by foreigners, and Judah was content to let Israel fight the enemy alone. God sent a prophet to warn their leaders—" Alyn looked first to Cassian, then to Modred. "But the leaders wouldn't listen. They had their own motives to satisfy, motives that had naught to do with following their God.

"Just like these men before you today. You two abuse the name of the Christ with your misdeeds, one as vile as the other," Alyn railed against Modred and Cassian. "You do not have the interest of God's church in mind, Archbishop Modred, not when you seek to turn God's children against each other. It matters not if they believe in the Father or nay, He cares for them," he added for the sake of those unfamiliar with God.

"Your God didn't care for *that* man." Drust glanced, fear-struck, at the crater where what remained of Elkmar's blackened torso steamed like a roast fresh from the pit.

"You care for your children, my lord," Alyn explained gently. "Yet they must at some time face the consequences of their actions, do they not?"

Nodding, Drust covered his queen's hand. The gesture warmed Kella's heart. He loved the mother of his children. Such love would open a heart for Alyn's petition for the Word.

"Modred," Alyn addressed the Lothian king, "God has shown me the white dragon that you hide beneath your robes. Aethelfrith Flamebearer," Alyn commanded, "show your face if you dare!"

Kella's gasp of astonishment was one of many. With her gaze, she searched the company of Lothian, many priests of the Celtic Church. But who among them would even recognize Bernicia's brutal High King if he were in their midst? Not her.

When no one stepped forward, Alyn was unfazed. "Have you not learned from Vortigern's example?" He turned to the onlookers. "These good people know the curse Vortigern brought upon us!"

Nods and shouts of assent answered him. Every Albion-born child had been told how, after Vortigern allied with the Saxons against his own kind, the Germanic savages slew his son and drove the British warlord into Wales. From the resulting enemy foothold in the south, British kingdom after kingdom along the coast fell—and were still falling—to them.

"I am not Vortigern." Frost coated each word Modred spoke. "I seek to unite my Pictish neighbors against yon Roman eagle disguised as a church."

"Hah!" Alyn mocked. "You, Modred of Lothian, seek vengeance for your father's death at Arthur's hand. Worse, you seek to betray Arthur as your father—and Vortigern—did, by allying with the Saxon wolves. And there's the vengeance you crave to satisfy your wounded pride," Alyn derided before Modred would weave another lie. "How dare Arthur choose Urien as his successor, when the role was promised to you!"

"I am the natural choice. My father is Pictish. My mother is Arthur's own British aunt. *And I know a trick or two also, so tread softly, boy,*" he threatened lowly, though his thin-lipped mouth barely moved.

"The evil eye," Heilyn whispered, covering her face as if the hard onyx gaze Modred leveled upon Kella's beloved was truly a spell.

Modred knew how to stare a man down in the old way, reduce him to a shivering mass, and put the fear of more than God into him as Alyn had done the crowd with his *sciencia*. Believing themselves cursed, many had died from such intimidation.

But the archbishop had not met the likes of Alyn O'Byrne.

"*Vengeance is mine; I will repay, saith the Lord,*" Alyn quoted to him. "You know well this is God's Word. Revenge is *God's* right, not yours."

Lorne growled like an angry dog on a leash from the seat next to Modred's empty one. "My lord, let me deal with this madman."

His father-by-law ignored the offer. Had Alyn penetrated the king's hardened heart with this truth?

"It is not too late to make right your intentions, my lord archbishop," Alyn reminded Modred, brother to brother. "Follow not your father's example, nor Vortigern's. Allow your hostage Cassian to return to Strighlagh with me ... to speak on the queen's behalf to—"

At the mention of Cassian, Modred's brittle disposition snapped.

"*He* is the enemy, not me." The Celtic archbishop thrust an accusing finger at the Roman one. "*He* seeks to establish Rome's authority over our British church. Ask your wife how he manipulates Arthur to that end. If you've eyes to see and ears to hear, see and hear how your own cousin's reputation has been defiled by him because she is a priestess of our church."

"You speak the truth," Alyn conceded, "for God has revealed that also."

Cassian's indignant gasp surely pulled at the leaves of the yew overhead. "Nonsense, utter nonsense!"

"Do you think God has not seen your sin as well, Cassian?" Alyn challenged. "We are none without it," he reminded the archbishop.

"I have done nothing but serve God and His church." Despite his huff of righteousness, Cassian's guilt gleamed damp and rosy upon his face and the bald circular tonsure on the crown of his head.

"You, sir, have fostered distrust between my cousin and her husband."

"*Gwenhyfar* sought to betray the church," Cassian blustered. "*She* ran to the bed of her husband's enemy. I did not send her there."

The insult to the queen cracked Modred's cold, dark armor, when naught else would. "By God's wrath, you slander us *both*, you little weasel of a man! I will have your blasphemous tongue and feed it to the dogs!"

Modred lunged at Cassian, but Drust's guards stepped between them and confiscated Lothian's jeweled dagger from his belt. After being escorted firmly to his seat, Modred offered a stilted defense of the lady.

"Gwenhyfar came to me to speak for Arthur and resolve our differences," he said. "Sadly, I was not at Din Edyn, or I'd have fought to the death to defend her and her honor."

"And why did she remain?" Cassian replied, smug behind his guards.

"Because she feared the husband you turned against her with your lies about our church," Modred replied.

That was true. Gwenhyfar had shared information about Arthur's irrational outbreaks with Kella, made more frequent by his closeness with Cassian. Foolishly, Kella had shared them with Lorne—a traitor and deceiver of the worst sort.

"You, Cassian," Alyn charged, "promised the Dux Bellorum that *your* church had the authority to spare Arthur from Columba's curse—the prophecy that the Dux Bellorum would not live to inherit his birthright as king of the Scots. Not God's church. *Yours!*"

"*That* is a lie!" Cassian declared.

"Cassian," Alyn reprised gently, "God knows."

"He believes that Rome has authority over the church founded by our Lord's family and followers ... perhaps even *before* the one in Rome took root," Modred fumed.

"Modred, Cassian, listen to your own words," Alyn pleaded, lest pandemonium ensue again. "This debate is for a church synod. Drust cares naught about these matters. How can we win favor for God's love when we do not demonstrate it *even among ourselves?*"

Folding his arms across a broad chest, Modred resumed his icy simmer.

"Come now, brethren." Alyn held out his arms as if to embrace the two enemies. "*And let us reason together, saith the LORD.*" He chanted the poetic words again, this time lifting them with music like a bard that the crowd might hear.

Since there was never a Celt not drawn to music, the discontent among the onlookers hushed.

"Hear the good news, people!" he sang, that his message might fall like soothing rain upon a parched earth. "*Though your sins be as scarlet, they shall be as white as snow; though they be red like crimson, they shall be as wool. If ye be willing and obedient, ye shall eat the good of the land.*"

"But ..." Alyn brought his staff down hard upon the dais, giving those closest to him a start.

"*But if ye refuse and rebel ...*" Lyrical turned thunderous when he spun to warn the archbishops. "You, Modred, and you, Cassian," he said, pointing first to one, then the other, "*ye shall be devoured with the sword: for the mouth of the LORD hath spoken it.*"

Truly those housed in the white dun fort a knoll away heard the pronouncement. It settled in the minds of the listeners, leaving a sober countenance and midnight stillness in its wake.

"Good king, good people ..." Alyn took on the manner of a father to his children with one of Kella's favorite Scriptures. "God challenges us not to judge one another as these two judge not only each other, but those who do not believe. This is the type of judgment that causes men to stumble and fall, into dispute ... and into war. God calls us to treat one another as we would have them treat us. Would you have war waged against you by friend while your foe nips at your heel?"

Drust considered the question. "What happened to these lands you spoke of?"

"They are no more, milord," Alyn replied solemnly.

"But there are times we must fight," Drust objected. "To defend our land and liberty."

"But not for another man's vengeance," Alyn replied. "Modred's princes are rebellious and companions of thieves—"

Lorne started at the accusing hand Alyn thrust his way.

Kella grew cold inside. Surely her husband would not expose her to shame.

"They are assassins and deceivers."

"You dare speak to me, Priest?" Lorne rose.

Nearly two hands taller than most men, Errol's prince towered upon the dais over Alyn. Chin jutted upward, Alyn met the prince's ice-blue gaze, as unyielding as he'd been with Modred.

"If you feel the sting," her husband replied, "the glove has rightly struck."

CHAPTER TWENTY-NINE

Lorne shook off the restraining hand placed upon his arm by his dark-haired bride and strutted up to the edge of the platform. "You seek to trick us all with your wizardry, but Lorne of Errol does not fear you."

Modred and his prince were certainly up to something.

"Not wizardry," Alyn denied. "What you saw, sir, was a display of *sciencia*, knowledge of God's creation. As Archbishop Modred will agree, the more one learns about creation, the closer one is to understanding the mind of the Creator." Because Modred was a student of nature magic, or *sciencia*, the Lothian lord and his Celtic brethren might be the only ones who did understand.

"So you say," Lorne mocked. "*I* say it's black magic." Lorne glanced back at Modred, even to Cassian. "What say you, sirs? You who are archbishops of the same God?"

A chill ran up Alyn's spine. Wizardry … magic. The first wasn't illegal, but black magic was punishable by death.

"Magic," Modred pronounced, stone-faced.

Alyn's estimation of Modred as a scholar plummeted to the same level as that of his church leadership. The man was blinded by his own designs.

Cassian hesitated. "I … I have never seen such a spectacle among our learned men of God."

It was a fairer opinion than Alyn expected. What Rome did not discover on its own and understand was feared. And if it was feared or distrusted, it was heresy.

Alyn would gladly show all that no special power was needed to mix the plant oil and black salts, but there was no more. Nor was he certain exactly how Abdul-Alim had made the compounds, even if he *wanted* to duplicate them.

Discouragement assailed him. If Lorne and Modred pressed for another demonstration, Alyn's credibility with this audience was lost. If only he had depended completely upon God to impress the multitude rather than relying on his own limited efforts. Hadn't God purposely directed Moses to put the Israelites back to the Red Sea, that He could show His supernatural power to the Egyptians?

But God, why did I see the package—

"I challenge you, Priest," Lorne announced. The thump of his arm slamming against his chest surely reached the far side of the arena. "I *seize*"—he grabbed dramatically at the air with his other hand—"the gauntlet of words you have thrown in the face of my lord Modred and myself."

Alyn shot an incredulous look at Kella. How could she have fallen in love with this preening peafowl?

Lorne shrugged off his bright-blue mantle and tossed it to his wife. "I do not challenge the truth of God's Word," he declared with a modesty sorely lacking in substance. "I challenge that God Himself instructed you to speak so to us this day. If this priest wins the combat," the prince told the crowd, "he speaks truth."

Combat? Alyn's spirit leapt. That he would welcome. Lorne was big and muscular, but Alyn had bested even Egan on occasion in the past. He had speed and agility on his side. Except—

"I cannot accept." Like deeply rooted teeth, his words came out with painful difficulty.

A smug smile spread upon Lorne's lips like a banner declaring Alyn a godless coward.

"The Word of God is the sword of a priest, and righteousness is my armor," Alyn informed the court. "As all can see …" He held out his arms and turned full circle. "I carry no weapon save a dining knife."

"You carry yon staff," Lorne taunted him. "I"—he made a grand show of a bow—"will arm myself likewise."

Beyond Lorne, Alyn saw Kella shaking her head at him in warning. He knew her thoughts. Lorne was a seasoned warrior. Alyn had not trained seriously for combat since he left for his studies at Llantwit. But for the recent attack on the way to Glenarden, he'd never done battle for his life.

God …?

"*Glorify Me.*"

Alyn knew what he must do. Validate God's Word in the eyes of the excited clansmen and their king. Defeat Lorne … and spare him, no matter how much Alyn wanted to beat that cocky smirk off his face.

"I will not kill you."

The words spilled out before Alyn could process all that flooded his mind. A few in the crowd snorted outright at the temerity of his statement.

Lorne reached down and fingered the strap of his satchel. "Put your magic bag of tricks aside, Priest, and I *will* kill you." He opened his arms to the crowd. "For the people of the Pictish nation!"

The plethora of huzzahs erupting around them faded as Egan O'Toole walked over two guards, easy as stepping over a log, toward Alyn.

"Don't worry, laddie," Egan roared over the dying din. "I'll kill the pretty buffoon for you *and* God."

"Ah, the father-by-law," Lorne scoffed as soldiers formed a shield wall in front of him.

Egan grinned, but something terrible glowered in his gaze. "Ye don't mind me, do ye, ye filthy, lyin' son of a sow?"

"Why would I bother remembering, *old* man?"

"Because I saw you lead men who trusted you into a trap. I held off yer Miathi allies till what was left of our men could cross the river to safety."

Recognition overtook Lorne's scrutiny. "*That* O'Toole." The prince shrugged. "I followed my orders; you followed yours. This is war, Champion."

"'Twas an unprovoked raid and a cowardly betrayal."

Alyn rushed in before Egan charged the wall of men barehanded.

"Egan." Alyn felt the rage heaving against the restraining hand he placed on his father-by-law's chest.

"I'll fight as your second," Egan said. "'Tis no dishonor in that, laddie."

"Trust me. I'll be fine," Alyn assured him. "I was taught by the best."

"Many years ago, laddie."

"God has given angels charge over me." Alyn meant it. "Mind you, Elkmar saw their legions. Brisen got us past the guards. The explosion won the court's attention."

Egan's red hedge of a brow lifted, studying Alyn from head to toe with the same sharp-eyed assessment he gave on the practice field. "Then it better be some big 'uns." He leaned in closer. "Watch 'im when he drops to his knee like he's fought out. He'll spring up like a cat and skewer ye … if ye fought with blades. With the staff …" Egan hesitated, stymied. "Don't think I ever seen 'im with one."

Alyn clapped his friend on the back. "Thanks for the warning."

Did no one think he had a chance? he wondered, watching Egan return grudgingly to the sideline, the shield wall following.

"Your majesties, if I may," Kella spoke up. She curtsied before Drust and Queen Heilyn. There was naught for Alyn to do but admire her beauty and poise, for he knew there would be no stopping her from having her say.

"It's forbidden to kill priest or druid," she reminded them. She turned a pointed look to where Lorne shed his gold rings, chains, pendants, and armbands to prepare for the combat, adding, "By penalty of death."

"As if these heathens care," Cassian denounced. "Look at them. They thirst more for combat than for God's Word."

"What's wrong, Roman?" Modred taunted. "Do you fear your champion will fail?"

When would they learn? Alyn dropped his head to his chest, breathing deeply to calm his kindled fury at the futility of it all. But he could not. He raised his staff high over his head to garner attention.

"I champion no one but my Lord and Savior, Jesus Christ!" Alyn shouted at the top of his lungs. "Certainly not either one of these pretenders. I spit on them both!" He slung the leather bag toward the pit and addressed Drust. "No death. The first to have both shoulders pinned to the ground for a three count wins. Agreed?"

The king looked to Lorne, who nodded, his lips in a cryptic twist.

"Agreed," Drust said.

A herald was summoned to announce to the onlookers the terms of combat, while guards moved the clustered clansmen back off the field.

"Alyn, this is crazy. You have every right to refuse," Kella told him, meeting him at the edge of the dais.

He handed his adornment to her. A silver cross pendant and his dove ring.

"In the eyes of man, yes," Alyn admitted. "But I have set my love and faith upon the Father, not my own power, Kella. He has never abandoned me."

He stripped down to short black trousers hanging loose above the laces of his sandals. The queens Heilyn and Brisen caught their breath upon seeing the angry red scar on his chest. It had shocked him the first time he saw it in a mirror. As Alyn rolled his clothing into a ball, Kella embraced him.

"What did you tell me about vengeance? Is *that* what this is?" Her lips trembled against his ear. "Because I don't need you to be my dead hero. I need a husband and father for my baby. He will kill you without second thought."

"But will my words have steel in these people's eyes if I hide behind these robes, rather than God's promise?" Alyn shook his head. "Nay, I fight for the Word of God." He caressed her cheek with his hand, wishing he could dry the tears welling in her eyes. "I give you my solemn vow, *ma chroi*," he whispered. "This is not about vengeance." *God make it so.* He squeezed her tight, not really wanting to let go of her or the future they'd planned together.

That alone gave him second thought. There had been no combat in his vision. Only Scripture, words revealed to him to speak to the kings as in the case of the prophets of old.

And God had protected them from much more than a pompous warrior with *cornsilk* hair.

Kella watched the cabled interplay of Alyn's torso as he walked casually out in the arena, his staff slung over one shoulder as if on a day's jaunt. She'd seen him fight and fight well. But his ribs had barely healed and—

A rattle of bones drew her attention to the edge of the area. Idwyr had stepped up to champion Alyn, though whether his support would help or hinder her husband, Kella wasn't sure. The wizard danced at the edge of the crowd, drawing such attention that the guards soon allowed him just inside so that all might see his antics. He leapt side to side, front to back, moving in circles and singing.

Kella caught the words about a great warrior riding off to war to face a giant. Appropriate, she mused. Naught but a boy, Idwyr's hero armed himself with a staff and three pebbles. Listening closer, she began to recognize the druid's improvised version of the story of David and Goliath that Alyn had told him on the road to Crief. Except in this version Jesus sent David and a spirit to help the boy.

Though the facts were questionable, that canny old wizard knew how to grab an audience. At least they'd stopped smirking at Alyn. Mayhap she sensed some support. Or perhaps those who had not heard the story believed the hero to be Alyn. Regardless, hardly anyone noticed when Lorne stepped off the dais.

His tattooed torso and arms had been oiled, Kella realized with distaste. How could she have been swayed by such a vain man as this?

The prince of Errol strode toward Alyn, who waited calmly as if for a friend instead of a man intent on killing him. Lorne tossed a dark, polished rowan staff—Modred's—from ringed hand to ringed hand. His men had replaced his gold adornment with iron. Though these trophies of battle were borrowed, Kella had seen Lorne bedecked in an ample share of his own, the result of his spending hours on the practice field or the battlefield. When not seducing foolish maids …

Who were forgiven, blessed be.

Kella focused on the combatants. If time could be measured by brawn, Lorne would outlast Alyn, even though her husband had the advantage of speed and agility. His armbands and bracelets made his biceps look even larger. A reassuring arm went around Kella's shoulders. Brisen's. The lady smiled as if all would be well. At the same time, Alyn winked across the distance, implying the same.

And then Lorne broke into a roaring charge.

Alyn blocked staff with staff, digging one end into the ground for additional leverage, but the bullish impact bowled him to the side and onto the ground, where he continued to roll, dragging his sturdy weapon with him. As Lorne lumbered forward off balance, Alyn sprang to his feet like a sprite and struck the larger man on the side of his head, exacting a roar … and first blood.

Chapter Thirty

Lorne touched the blood on his temple in disbelief and growled at those who dared cheer the smaller man's speed and agility. Or worse, laugh outright as Egan O'Toole did.

Lesson one: brute strength alone is not enough. Though Alyn realized it was a short victory in what could be a long ordeal.

He assumed the on-guard position, staff at ready as Lorne did the same. This time the prince measured his step, lips fixed in a snarl as he approached … and calculated. He'd learned fast.

Watching for a tell in his opponent's gaze, Alyn circled until Lorne struck right for his head. Alyn blocked, and again the crack of wood split the air. But as Lorne sought to use his other shoulder to knock Alyn off balance, Alyn freed his stick and danced away. But not so far that he didn't catch the prince's elbow with the tip of …

He hadn't named his staff.

Lorne yelped as a thousand needles pricked along the length of his forearm. At least that was the case if Alyn had struck the sensitive spot where the forearm met the upper. And he had, rendering his opponent's forearm, wrist, and grip numb enough that, but for help from his good arm, Lorne would have dropped the rowan rod completely.

Sting? Nay, that wouldn't do for a priest's staff.

"What magic is in that staff?" Lorne demanded as he rubbed feeling back into the affected elbow and arm.

"Magic? Tell me, laddie, this is not the first time you've struck your elbow and tingled to your fingers," Alyn taunted for all to hear.

A few in the crowd affirmed Alyn's reply with sympathetic *huzzahs* and *ayes*. And if he was any judge, their sentiments favored him, not the offended prince. Mayhap Lorne was offensive and arrogant to more than an upstart priest … with knowledge of the human body and its weak points, thanks to medical scholars from the East. The trick was to strike them accurately. So far, God's grace was with him.

"But if you fear my staff has an advantage, I will gladly trade weapons with you," Alyn suggested.

Grásta! Grace was the perfect name for the staff. 'Twould surely be by *grace* if he survived this trial.

Suspicion vied with anger in Lorne's gaze. "Nay, I trust it no more than you, Priest." He paced like an angry cat beyond Alyn's reach, waiting for his grip to return.

Alyn raised the staff over his head, aware that Lorne still suspected the length of oak carved by the hands of Iona's holy men. "Father, I dedicate to Thee *Grásta*, symbol of Your *grace* and protection."

Alyn returned to his defensive stance as Lorne assumed his. "Concede now, and I will offer you God's grace, rather than this humiliation, Lorne. Repent. Seek peace, and God will forgive your vile sin, but—"

Lorne rushed him. Oak and rowan, neither forgiving, attacking again and again. Thrust, strike, parry to the outside, inside, middle. Alyn defended himself, waiting, watching until his opponent tired of using brawn to beat him, rather than leverage. And when the opening presented itself, Alyn brought the butt end of his staff down hard upon the prince's instep.

No banshee howled so loud. No crowd guffawed so hard. Alyn's was no trick of magic, but a fighting maneuver taught to peach-faced laddies by their fathers. And while the prince struggled to regain himself, Alyn smacked his kidney area hard. Another battle tactic. Not lethal, but a man might wish it were.

Lorne went to his knees, nostrils flaring, his oiled body shedding perspiration. He used the rowan for support. Still, the man had wits enough to turn that brawn against Alyn in hand-to-hand conflict. That's what it would take to pin those wide shoulders to the ground. Grásta had to render that sweat-matted cornsilk head of his senseless.

"Concede. Receive God's grace."

Lorne swore an oath of rejection and brought one knee up. Before he could bring up the other, Alyn went in. Lorne blocked his strike and came up under it, catching his staff and wrenching it from Alyn's grasp. Grásta flew a short distance away. Alyn dodged Lorne's follow-up blow … almost.

Pain ripped and raged along his barely healed rib cage as he lunged for Grásta and rolled away. The hand he clenched to his side came away bloody, confirming what his flesh already screamed. The rowan had a blade in one end. Maybe both.

Intriguing. No wonder Lorne wouldn't trade weapons.

Lorne gave him a demonic grin. "We're even, mite."

Given his earlier cockiness, 'twas no more than Alyn deserved. *Humiliation accepted, Father.*

"Yer doin' fine, laddie," Egan called to him. "Keep your head. Don't let him rile ye."

"Shut your trap, old man, and see to that trollop of a daughter you have," Lorne shouted.

The prince dared not speak further. Not with his bride listening. But Alyn's blood boiled as he assessed his tormentor. Lorne's hand wasn't right yet. His foot throbbed by his limp. He'd fight on his strong right. Shield his left to buy time.

"You didn't think I'd forget her, did you?" Lorne jeered, his words aimed at Alyn. "Aye, she was a bit cold at first, but I got her—"

Lorne's goading was a tried-and-true tactic. Alyn charged like a mad bull. The prince responded with a mighty downward thrust, exactly as Alyn hoped. He nimbly dodged past the thrust, bringing Grásta around, catching the prince behind the head with a hearty smack that dropped the mighty warrior to his knees. Rather than crow about staffs and grace, he struck Lorne's temple with Grásta's other end.

Dropping the rowan, Lorne keeled over to the side. Alyn was upon him quick as a cat, shoving Grásta against his throat. His knees pinned the stunned prince's broad shoulders to the ground.

Someone began the count.

"One!"

Silence him now. Alyn clenched his teeth until they hurt in his struggle to hold the powerful Lorne down. The villain shook his head from side to side, but his faculties were too scattered for him to do more than flail for relief.

"Two!" The crowd joined in.

Forever.

A fist struck Alyn's ribs, unleashing demons of pain that threatened to tear flesh from bone with their teeth. Oh, how they screamed.

"Three!"

No more pain. No more betrayal. No more threat to Kella and the babe.

The crowd thundered. Or was it the black storm raging in Alyn's mind? It steeled Alyn so that nothing his arrogant, treacherous foe did could dislodge the death hold he so deserved. A dark satisfaction swept through Alyn, numbing him to all but the sight of Lorne's bulging eyes rolling up in his head ... robbed of breath by Grásta.

Grace. The very thought burst into brightness, driving the sinister cloud from his mind with light ... pure light.

Grace to give as well as receive was in his hands.

"*Glorify Me.*"

Alyn gave. Lifting Grásta from Lorne's neck, he backed off and used the staff instead to climb to his feet. The prince convulsed with a huge gasp and looked up, unfocused, at the sky. His senses were still caught in that limbo between This World and the Other Side, where Alyn had nearly sent him.

Alyn waited until the man's senses returned and offered Lorne a hand up. Still dazed, the prince accepted. Beyond them, the crowd was wild with enthusiasm.

"God spared you today," he told Lorne, "when I would not. Do not take His gift of a second chance lightly."

"Well done, Priest!" Drust called out to Alyn as he, with Kella and Brisen at his flank, approached the two combatants. "I have not seen such a display of staff combat since Merlin Emrys appeared at my grandfather's court to arrange Arthur's marriage to Gwenhyfar. 'Twas a harmless contest, of course."

"I know'd he was Merlin!" Idwyr chortled. "Know'd it, know'd it, know'd it."

"Alyn!" It was Kella that Alyn heard over the tumult. She burst past the king and into Alyn's arms.

He winced as she returned his embrace, but such sweet pain he would endure just to have her near. Of all God's angels, Alyn thanked Him most for the one he kissed. No matter that they were surrounded by others. At that moment, his world contained only him and Kella.

"Alyn, behind you!" Queen Brisen's warning broke the heavenly illusion.

Alarm, or something else, seized Alyn, taking over his body before his mind could catch up. Suddenly he was watching the scene before him unfold from some unknown perch. To his horror, he thrust Kella away, sending the woman he loved sprawling upon the charred ground. In the next instant, he'd turned as though to face an invisible enemy, one Alyn himself was oblivious to. As he—or whoever had overtaken his body—hefted Grásta into a blocking position, Alyn watched, bewildered, as he batted at thin air …

And struck metal.

A *flying* sword?

The weapon careened to the side and buried itself in the ground beyond him. Dumbstruck, Alyn stared at it as his mind melded once again with his body. Whatever had possessed him left his senses

tingling with uncommon awareness in its wake. Behind him a scuffle
ensued. Men shouted. Kella cried. Alyn wanted to go to her, but all
he could focus upon was that sword.

He heard it quivering upright in the dirt a few yards away,
yet it felt as if it were buried in Alyn's brain. He blinked as blood
formed on its brimstone-blackened blade and slid down its length
to soak the ground, spreading and spreading … while the world
whirred around it.

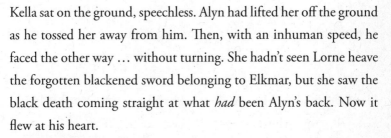

Kella sat on the ground, speechless. Alyn had lifted her off the ground
as he tossed her away from him. Then, with an inhuman speed, he
faced the other way … without turning. She hadn't seen Lorne heave
the forgotten blackened sword belonging to Elkmar, but she saw the
black death coming straight at what *had* been Alyn's back. Now it
flew at his heart.

The staff moved faster than the eye, batting the blade to the
side as one might a fly. The dull clang of metal against the wood
of Alyn's staff still echoed in her ear as she stared at the quivering
blade buried in the dirt not far from him. Pandemonium broke
out around Alyn. As guards seized the vile coward who had nearly
killed him, Alyn stumbled blindly toward that sword and drew it.

He let out a cry as if he'd felt the anguish of the world.

Kella scurried to her feet and started toward him, but he waved
her and anyone else who tried to help him away. Giving him wide
berth, Drust, Brisen, and the others hastened back to their guests on
the dais. Guards resumed their positions. But every eye and ear was

fixed upon the sweat-soaked, bloodied merlin—warrior and speaker for the Creator God.

"Let Modred fight Arthur man to man." Alyn weaved upon his feet as though drunk—or in some sort of trance—yet he did not fall. Instead he pointed to Cassian. "And let this excuse for God's servant serve as Arthur's second."

Alyn buried the sword before the dais of officials, then knelt before it. Head back, black hair trailing down his back, he stared wild-eyed at the clear sky overhead. As if what he actually saw was far more menacing than the white puffs of cloud against the blue mantle. His face contorted with mortification.

Words wrenched from his throat. "So much needless bloodshed in the name of our Christ." He clutched at the scar on his chest. "It soaks the ground of Alba and colors her waters crimson."

Dear God in heaven. Not only did the raw crucifix on his chest bleed red, but even the sweat upon Alyn's brow had turned to blood.

"The eagle clutches, and the bear roars." Tears of blood fell unashamed down Alyn's cheeks. "But the raven and the wolves wait."

Kella had seen enough. But as she started for her tortured husband, he stopped her again with upheld hand. "Hear me, woman!"

After all she'd witnessed, Kella froze. She was not alone. Like figures in a painted scene, the onlookers waited, collective breath held, that they might hear the rest of the young merlin's prophecy.

"The raven and the wolves will pick the flesh of the dead, while the dove takes its last breath."

'Twas like listening to Merlin Emrys.

Of course. Arthur the Bear of Britain, Modred the Eagle of Lothian, Urien the Raven, the Saxon wolves, the Grail dove ...

Kella realized her role and raced to fulfill it. "Write it down," she ordered the scribes assembled to record the king's court decisions. But the men were as dumbstruck as the other witnesses. Kella yanked one of the scribes off his stool by his robe and took up his quill.

"Bold men astride swift steeds with flying manes; high spirits fueled by the songs of minstrels, mead aplenty and prospects of gold; kings and princes long in pride, short on life; arrays of bright-colored pendants, dark armor, and shining coats of mail thrusting through armies with spear points and swords sharpened; lions roar from Kintyre, Sassenach; wolves howl; the blood of friend and foe mingle on the crimson field, their flesh food for the carrion; the bear and the eagle carried off on their shields and the angels cry, oh hideous harvest of misled souls, all to be lost in the mists of time...."

Kella looked up from her frantic scratching when Alyn paused. Slowly he got up and, with his foot, trampled the sword flat upon the dirt. His head and shoulders dropped in despair. The merlin—*her* merlin—finished, heartbroken and weary.

"And God bows His head at the senselessness of it all."

Kella didn't write the words down. This was something that neither she, nor anyone who witnessed this day, would ever forget.

epilogue

Fortingall
Early seventh century AD

While Mons Seion still slumbered in the mist-shrouded mountains of the north, to the south a rising sun made Dun Gael's fortress glow white against a spring-blue sky. On the knoll next to it, the ancient yew seemed to yawn and stretch its green wings out like a mother hen over the banners, tents, and stalls of the fairgrounds below. 'Twas spring again.

Standing on the tower ramparts of her new home, Kella took a sip of steaming tea sweetened with honey gathered by the brethren of Heilyn's church. Since the structures shared the same flat-headed hill, she'd awakened at the sound of its bell summoning the Brothers to morning prayers. Not that she minded. The church bells helped her keep precise track of her busy days as a master of language at the fledgling school she and Alyn had founded with King Drust's support.

In exchange, Alyn promised to advise Drust as a merlin, working in concert with his secular adviser Beathan regarding court decisions and justice. It was an effective effort born of mutual respect with Beathan's expertise in the old Brehon laws and Alyn's in God's law. And when Idwyr, who'd studied Scripture since the school opened, joined them over a cup of ale at the day's end in Drust's hall, Kella knew God's mysteries would keep all three, and some of the court, awake until the wee hours.

Kella looked out with wonder over the spread of huts that housed students and masters. Had it been four years since she and her husband had come to Fortingall on their desperate mission? In some ways they'd achieved more than they ever dreamed, but in others they'd failed.

Aye, the genealogies were safe, hidden in the bowels of the holy mountain, but the Grail Church had given way to Iona's dominion. Heilyn established her church, and Alyn's intervention at Drust's court prevented Arthur and Modred's feud from erupting into an all-out war of the Scots and British kingdoms against all the Pictish nations. Many lives had been lost at the battle of Camboganna, including Arthur's, Modred's, and the cowardly Lorne's, but many more had been spared.

Cassian vouched for the queen's innocence upon his return to Strighlagh with Alyn, but the gauntlet between Arthur's Scots and Cymri and Modred's Miathi and Saxons had been cast and picked up. Neither priest could stop it. While a grieving Gwenhyfar saw to the transport of her husband's body back to Carmelide, Cassian and Alyn walked together as equals on the bloody fields in the aftermath of the fighting to pray for the dead and dying.

The archbishop had been so distraught at his hand in the senseless bloodfest that he'd resigned from his post and gone into seclusion … at Iona. He didn't question his Roman doctrine, but he wanted to learn more about his Celtic brethren. 'Twas Cassian who carved the sign over the Seion School of Wisdom's great hall door where students and masters met for food, fellowship, and learning: *Proverbs 1:7. "The fear of the LORD is the beginning of knowledge."*

The creak of the new oak door to the inner stairwell of the tower startled Kella out of reverie. She turned to see Alyn emerge, preceded by a black shot of energy in the new red jacket she'd made. Fatin scampered up on the wall and over to his favorite corner, where he promptly relieved himself. Thanks to his stay with Brenna and the recovering Daniel, he'd been broken of urinating on the cookfires. At least *inside* fires.

"I thought I'd find you here." Alyn came up behind her and wrapped his arms about her waist.

They followed Fatin's progress to the highest point on the wall, where he tried catching the fluttering white banner. Embroidered on it was a shield divided by an ornate cross. David's harp, a quill and inkwell, a mathematical sign, and the sun occupied the quadrants.

Kella held her breath as she always did when that dear little imp frolicked so close to the brink of falling. "One of these days he's …" She warded off thoughts of the unthinkable and leaned against her husband, drawing on his warmth, strength, and endless supply of love.

"He's escaping the barbarian hoards who have taken over our hall below," Alyn whispered into her ear. *There* was her kiss, warm upon her cheek. He always had one just for her. "The cousins are corrupting our daughter, much to Nona's dismay."

Their daughter, Aeda, had been born healthy and with a lusty set of lungs just before the harvest. Queen Heilyn sent the nurse Nona to help care for the babe, a godsend that enabled Kella to teach once recovered from the childbed. Brenna and Brisen arrived at Fortingall early to act as midwives and for Brisen and Egan's wedding. After hearing more of Alyn's teachings, Brisen had accepted Christ, and Egan's proposal. The couple had barely finished their vows when little Aeda decided to join the party.

Both Brenna and Brisen declared Aeda's was an easy delivery. Kella did not hold the same view. Still, that little towheaded angel had been worth the agony just to see the utter wonder and adoration on Alyn's face when Brisen handed him his new daughter.

"'Tis like looking at her mother," he'd said.

From what Kella had seen of the wrinkled little mite at that point, she forgave her husband's misty-eyed babble. But wrinkled or nay, it was love at first sight for each of them.

"Aeda needs no help when it comes to mischief," Kella reminded Alyn with a wry chuckle. She wasn't such a doting mother that she failed to see when their child's angelic qualities turned toward the impish. "Are our guests awake?"

Alyn's brothers and their wives had traveled to the Fortingall fair to visit and to enroll their eldest children in Alyn's school.

Even though Caden and Sorcha's land of Trebold was now under Saxon rule, borders were blurred enough that the families still saw each other. Thanks to Sorcha's Saxon upbringing and Trebold's hospitality, the transition for her and the many Saxon refugees working the land had been tolerable, if not welcome. And for her sake and God's, Caden had put aside his sword for a barrel tap. "Caden and I have learned to play the tune God gives us," Sorcha had written after the invasion occurred.

"Are they awake?" Alyn snorted. "How could anyone sleep through that? Our kinsmen help Nona keep order while breaking the fast in the hall."

Ronan and Brenna's Conall would join the younger students, though he didn't understand why he needed more than physical training to be a warrior king. On the other hand, Caden and Sorcha's adopted son, Ebyn, couldn't wait to study poetry and song with the older boys under the tutorship of Eadric, Sorcha's cousin and master bard. Sorcha and her dwarf friend, Gemma, had already taught Ebyn to play the harp and pipe.

Then there was Conall's younger sister, Joanna, who was vexed that she wasn't old enough to study healing at the school, when the child lived with the best healer in all Albion—her mother, Brenna. The willful girl and Caden's lively six-year-old daughter, Aelwyn, contented themselves to treat Aelwyn's twin brothers, Rory and Lachlan, as their patients. The toddlings of three wore their splints and bandages like badges of honor.

As images of the chaos below gathered in her mind, guilt jarred Kella. Here was the mistress of the manor lost in the solitude of the morning instead of seeing to her guests!

"Oh, Alyn, I must get down there," she fretted. "I am the worst hostess—"

"Our steward has reinforcements both for the meal and maintaining order," Alyn assured her. "When I left, Daniel and Papa Egan had summoned the lot for a race. Though how the two men move about with children hanging on every limb is beyond me."

"Da is too old for that." Not that Kella would try to dissuade her bullheaded father. "Still, I should at least—"

Alyn grabbed her in midretreat and nipped at her ear in playful warning. "So stop casting aspersions against my good wife, for whom I thank God every day."

Once upon a time, Kella had thought this kind of love did not exist this side of heaven … a love that her considerable imperfections could not faze. Then again, she hadn't believed in angels, either. Now she knew better.

"Give way, Babel-Lips." He turned her in the circle of his arms.

Kella surrendered willingly to her husband's descending lips. How many sweet words they told her, declarations of love and devotion, worship and need.

Aye, there were still wars and rumors of wars, but here and now love prevailed.

God be thanked for this little bit of heaven here on earth.

... a little more ...

When a delightful concert comes to an end,

the orchestra might offer an encore.

When a fine meal comes to an end,

it's always nice to savor a bit of dessert.

When a great story comes to an end,

we think you may want to linger.

And so, we offer ...

AfterWords—just a little something more after you

have finished a David C Cook novel.

We invite you to stay awhile in the story.

Thanks for reading!

Turn the page for ...

- **Historical Aftermath**
  - **Glossary**
- **Arthurian Characters**
  - **The Grail Place**
  - **Bibliography**
- **Scripture References**
  - **About the Author**

hISTORICAL AFTERMATh

The Battle of Camboganna unfolded just as Alyn described. Having mortally wounded each other, Arthur and Modred were carried from the fields on their shields, fulfilling Columba's historical prediction that Arthur would not succeed his father, Aedan. Grass and water turned crimson with the blood of hundreds of Scots, Britons, Picts, and Saxons. The Pictish Gwenhyfar returned to her childhood home in Meikle, where she shed her alleged Grail name for Anora. Her grave can be seen there today. Urien of Rheged rose as leader of the Britons, who never did unite with the Picts, though the Picts and Scots eventually united to form today's Scotland.

Urien's Men of the North alliance almost succeeded in driving the Saxons out of Albion … until Urien was assassinated by an envious ally. The last stand of the Britons was immortalized by Aneirin in *Y Gododdin*, about the battle of Catraeth, led by Urien's son Owain and Hering, the Saxon son of Hussa. (In my previous novel *Thief*, the historical Prince Hering took shelter with the Scots after his cousin Aethelfrith seized his rightful throne in Bernicia.) Merlin's prophecy that the Saxon White Dragon would prevail over the Britons' Red came to pass, and the Saxons thus won control of most of Albion.

In the seventh century, the victorious Saxons chose the Roman Church authority over the proto-Protestant Celtic Church, a decision that held until Henry the Eighth's rule. Only the highlands of Scotland, the far west of Wales, and Ireland resisted Rome's influence for a while longer. The pursuit of *sciencia*, confused with and abused as magic, was driven underground until the Renaissance.

As for the Grail Church, some scholars believe there is a thread of truth to its existence, a thread that has been carried on in some form through later secret societies such as the Knights Templar and Masons. It's closely linked to Arthurian legend, which also is considered to have some historical basis. Whether its records—if they existed—were destroyed by the Roman Church to establish authority as some scholars claim, no one knows. The whole truth belongs to the ages to intrigue readers, as it has for centuries.

In *Rebel*, we've seen the same human conflicts rehashed over and over in the history of the world—Christian churches who would dictate rather than shepherd, insisting their authority/doctrine is the only authority/doctrine; church and political leaders using and abusing the name of Christ for power and prestige, rather than advancing peace and the care of the needy; and lastly, the still ongoing battle between church and science.

AUTHOR'S NOTE: It is important to understand that, like our churches today, neither the Celtic nor the Roman Churches were without blemish. *Though much evil has been done in the name of Christianity, both believers and nonbelievers must take care not to throw Jesus and all He stood for out with the dirty church water.* We must remember that good works, such as the many done in His name, rarely make the headlines of past or present.

GLOSSARY

Alba—Scotland

Albion—the Isle of Britain

Alcut/Alclyd—Dumbarton on Firth of Clyde

anmchara—soulmate

arthur—title passed down from Stone Age Britain, meaning "the bear," or "protector," connected with the constellation of the Big Dipper; equivalent of Dux Bellorum and Pendragon; the given name of Arthur, prince of Dalraida

a stór—darling

behoved—beholden

braccae—Latin for woolen drawstring trousers or pants, either knee- or ankle-length

bretwalda—leader/king of Saxon warlords or thanes

cariad—dearest

Carmelide—Carlisle

Cennalath—*ken'-nah-lot*; Pictish king of the Orkneys killed by Arthur for treachery

colleen—an Irish girl

Cruithne—Pict

Cumbric—language of western Celtic peoples of Britain, close to today's Welsh

Cymri—brotherhood of the Romano-Britons and Welsh

Cymric—language of the Romano-Britons and Welsh

druid—an educated professional—doctors, judges, poets, teachers, and protoscientists, as well as priests. *Druid* meant "teacher, rabbi, magi, or master," not the dark, hooded stereotype assumed by many today. Those who were earnest sought light, truth, and the way. Others abused their knowledge, which was power.

Dux Bellorum—Roman reference to Arthur, meaning duke of war; in Briton and Irish, *High King*; and in Welsh, *Pendragon* or *Head Dragon*

Eboracorum—York

earthways—to death/burial

fell—rocky hill

foolrede—foolishness

gleemen—entertainers for the common people akin to circus performers, as well as singers and dancers

Grásta—pronounced *graws-tah,* meaning "grace"; name of Alyn's staff

Gwenhyfar—*Guinevere*; considered by some scholars to have been a title like *arthur* and *merlin,* as well as a given name. Some scholars believe the Pictish Gwenhyfar was called Anora.

haegtesse—witch

haws—medieval term for a house in a town/borough that is part of a larger country estate; a house on a small lot in a borough

heremon—an ancient Irish name and a title meaning "High King"

highlander—someone from the highlands of Alba

hillfort—an enclosed fortress/village on a hill, usually with earthenwork and/or wood stockade about its perimeter

Joseph, the—the high priest of the Grail Palace on the Sacred Isle

Leafbud—spring

Leaf Fall—fall

Long Dark—winter

mathair—mother

merlin—title for the adviser to the king, often a prophet or seer; sometimes druidic Christian as in Merlin Emrys, or not, as in Merlin Sylvester

Merlin Emrys (Ambrosius)—the prophet/seer/Celtic Christian priest descended from the Pendragon Ambrosius Aurelius; thought to be Arthur's merlin; suggested to be buried on Bardsley Island

mind—remember or recall

mo chroi—my heart

Pendragon—Cymri (Welsh-Briton) for "Head Dragon" or High King, dragon being a symbol of knowledge/power; see *arthur, Dux Bellorum*

rath—walled keep and/or village

sciencia—Latin for the study of science

scop—Saxon bard or entertainer

Strighlagh—*strī'-lăk;* Stirling

Sun Season—summer

sunwise—clockwise

thane—a high-ranking chief, noble, or warlord of the Saxon bretwalda/king; the king's sword-friend (comrade in arms) and hearth friend, who usually led his own warband and received his own lands in reward

toll—interest on a loan

tuath—*tŭth;* kingdom; clan land

widdershins—counterclockwise

ARThURiAN ChARACTERS

Most scholars agree that Arthur, Guinevere, and Merlin were titles shared by various personas throughout the late fifth and sixth centuries. The ones in this book are the late sixth-century characters. Because of inconsistent dating, multiple persons sharing the same titles and/or names, and place names as well as texts recorded in at least six languages, I quote Nennius: "I've made a heap of all I could find."

* historically documented individuals

* Arthur—Prince of Dalraida, Dux Bellorum (Latin "Duke of War") or Pendragon (Welsh) / High King (Scot) of Britain, although he held no land of his own. He is a king of landed kings, their battle leader. A Pendragon at this time can have no kingdom of his own to avoid conflict of interest. Hence, Gwenhyfar is rightful queen of her lands, Prince Arthur's through marriage. Arthur is the historic son of Aedan of Dalraida/Scotland, descended from royal Irish of the Davidic bloodline preserved by the marriage of Zedekiah's daughter Tamar to the Milesian king of Ireland Heremon Eoghan in 587 BC. Ironically the Milesians are descended from the bloodline of Zarah, the "Red Hand" twin of Pharez (David and Jesus's ancestor) in the book of Genesis. Thus the breach of Judah prophesied in Isaiah was mended by this marriage of very distant cousins, and the line of David continued to rule through the royal Irish after Jerusalem fell.

* Aedan of Dalraida—Arthur's father, Aedan, was Pendragon of Britain for a short time and prince of Manau Gododdin by his mother's Pictish blood (just as Arthur was prince of Dalraida because of his marriage to Gwenhyfar). When Aedan's father, the king of Dalraida, died, Aedan became king of the more powerful kingdom, and he abandoned Manau Gododdin. For that abandonment, he is oft referred to as Uther Pendragon, *uther* meaning "the terrible." He sent his son Arthur to take his place as Pendragon and Manau's protector.

Angus—the Lance of Lothian. Although this Dalraida Arthur had no Lancelot as his predecessor did, Angus is the appointed lesser king of Stirlingshire/Strighlagh and protector of his Pictish queen, Gwenhyfar, and her land. As with his ancestral namesake Lancelot, Angus's land of Berwick in Lothian now belongs to Cennalath, who is ultimately defeated by Arthur. (See *Cennalath* and *Brude*.) Angus is Arthur's head of artillery. It is thought he was raised at the Grail Castle and was about ten or so years younger than his lady Gwenhyfar.

Scholar/researcher Norma Lorre Goodrich suggests he may have been a fraternal twin to Modred or Metcault. That would explain Lance not knowing who he really was until he came of age, as women who bore twins were usually executed. The second child was thought to be spawn of the Devil. Naturally Morgause would have hidden the twins' birth by casting one out, only to have him rescued by her sister, the Lady of the Lake, or Vivianne del Acqs. This scenario happened as well in the lives of many of the saints, such as St. Kentigern. Their mothers were condemned to death for consorting with the Devil and begetting a child or a twin. Yet, miraculously, these women lived and the cast-off child became a saint.

* **Brude/Bridei**—see *Cennalot/Cennalath/Lot of Lothian*.

* **Cennalath/Cennalot/Lot of Lothian**—Arthur's uncle by marriage to Morgause. This king of eastern Pictland and the Orkneys was all that stood between Brude reigning over the whole of Pictland. Was it coincidence that Arthur, whose younger brother, Gairtnat, married Brude's daughter and became king of the Picts at Brude's death, decided to take out this Cennalath while Brude looked the other way? Add that to the fact that Cennalath was rubbing elbows with the Saxons and looking greedily at Manau Gododdin, and it was just a matter of time before either Brude or Arthur got rid of him.

* **Dupric, bishop of Llandalf**—a historical bishop who *may* also be Merlin Emrys per Norma Goodrich.

* **Gwenhyfar/Guinevere**—High Queen of Britain. This particular Gwen's Pictish name is Anora. She is descended from the apostolic line and is a high priestess in the Celtic Church. She is buried in Fife. Her marriage brought under Arthur the lands of Stirlingshire, or Strighlagh. Her offspring are its heirs, as the Pictish rule is inherited from the mother's side. There were two abductions of the Gwenhyfars. In one she was rescued. In the other she *slept*, meaning she died (allegedly from snakebite), precipitating the fairytale of *Sleeping Beauty*. In both Gwenhyfar's abduction and that of Sleeping Beauty, thorns surrounded the castle, thorns being as common a defense in those days as moats were. Also note the similarities of names, even if the definitions are different—Anora (grace), Aurora (dawn).

* **Merlin Emrys of Powys**—a Christian druidic-educated bishop of the Celtic Church, protoscientist, adviser to the king, prophet after the Old Testament prophets, and possibly a Grail king or Joseph. Emrys is of the Irish-Davidic and Romano-British bloodlines as son

of Ambrosius Aurelius and uncle to Aedan, Arthur's father. Merlin Emrys retired as adviser during Arthur's later reign, perhaps to pursue his beloved science or perhaps as the Grail King. In either case, he would not have condoned Arthur's leaning toward the Roman Church's agenda. Later the Roman Church and Irish Celtic Church priests would convert the Saxons to Christianity, but the British Celtic Church suffered too much at pagan hands to offer the Good News to their pagan invaders. (See *Dupric* and *Ninian*.)

Modred—king of the Orkneys and Lothian, also a high priest or abbott in the Celtic Church; Arthur's cousin and son of late Cennalath and Morgause.

* **Morcant**—king of Byrneich, now mostly occupied on the coast by the Saxons and called Northumbria. The capital was Traprain Law.

* **Ninian**—Merlin's protégé, priestess in the Celtic Church.

* **Vivianne del Acqs**—sister to Ygerna, Arthur's mother, and Morgause of Lothian. She is known as the Lady of the Lake. Vivianne is a high priestess and tutor at the Grail Castle. It's thought that she raised both Gwenhyfar and Angus/Lance of Lothian, all direct descendants of the Arimathean priestly lines.

* **Ygerna**—Arthur's mother and a direct descendant of Joseph of Arimathea, was matched as a widow of a British duke and High Queen of the Celtic Church to Aedan of Dalraida by Merlin Emrys to produce an heir with both royal and priestly bloodlines. It is thought her castle was at Caerlaverock.

The Grail Palace

Norma Lorre Goodrich suggests that the Grail Palace was on the Isle of St. Patrick, and recent archaeology has exposed sixth-century ruins of a church/palace there. But what was it, or the Grail itself, exactly? Goodrich uses the vast works of other scholars, adding her expertise in the linguistics field to extract information from Arthurian texts in several languages. Weeding out as much fancy as possible, the Grail Palace was the church or place where the holy treasures of Christianity were kept (not to be confused with the treasures of Solomon's Temple, which Jeremiah and Zedekiah's daughter Tamar allegedly took to Ireland in 587 BC, or the Templars found during the Crusades). The Grail treasures consist of items relating to Jesus: a gold chalice and a silver platter (or silver knives) from the Last Supper, the spear that pierced Christ's side, the sword (or broken sword) that beheaded John the Baptist, gold candelabra with at least ten candles each, and a secret book, or gospel, attributed directly to either Jesus Himself, John the Beloved, Solomon, John the Baptist, or John of the Apocalypse.

Or was this book the genealogies of the bloodlines, whose copies were supposedly destroyed by the Roman Church?

If the house of the Last Supper was that of the wealthy Joseph of Arimathea, is it possible that Jesus used these rich items and that Joseph brought them to Britain in the first century as tradition holds? The high priest of the Grail Castle tradition was called the Joseph. Of all the knights who vied for the Grail or the high priest position as teacher and protector of the bloodlines and treasures, only Percival and Galahad succeeded. Did they take the place of Merlin Emrys when he passed on?

The purpose of the Grail Palace, beyond holding the treasures, was one of protecting and perpetuating the apostolic and royal bloodlines … hence the first-century Christianity brought to Britain by Christ's family and followers. It was believed that an heir of both lines stood a chance of becoming another messiah-like figure. Such breeding of bloodlines was intended to keep the British church free of Roman corruption and close to its Hebrew origins. Nennius, who was pro-Roman to the core, accused the Celtic Church of *clinging to the shadows of the Jews*—the first-century Jews of Jesus's family and friends.

But by the time the last Arthur fell, the hope of keeping the line of priests and Davidic kings, as had been done in Israel prior to Zedekiah's fall, was lost. With the triumph of the Roman Church authority, political appointment from Rome trumped the inheritance of the priestly and kingly rights divinely appointed in the Old Testament. Celibacy became the order of the day to keep the power and money in Rome.

Goodrich suggests that there were three Grail brotherhoods: Christ and His Twelve Disciples, Joseph of Arimathea and his twelve companions, and Arthur and the Twelve Knights of the Round Table. After Arthur's death, the order of the Grail with its decidedly Jewish roots gave way to Columba at Iona and the Roman Church. The Grail treasure—which had been brought from the Holy Land by Joseph of Arimathea, first to Glastonbury and later, after Saxons came too close for comfort, to the Isle of Patrick off of Man—had to be moved again. Percival and Galahad returned it to the Holy Land.

And it is there, centuries later, that the Knights Templar allegedly entered into the mystery, perhaps with privileged information kept and passed down among the sacred few remnants of the bloodlines that shaped early Christian Scotland, England, and Ireland.

Étienne Gilson said that the Grail veneration started in Jerusalem with Arimathea and Jesus's family and friends and that it stood for grace. God's grace. Christ's grace by sacrifice.

Or is it that only those truly baptized by Pentecostal fire are fit to care for the Grail treasures, just as only the high priest Aaron was allowed into the Holy of Holies in ancient Israel? And is finding the Grail a metaphor for the Holy Spirit embodied in the apostles, or entering into the presence of God? Lancelot only dreamed of it, while Percival and Galahad actually achieved it as evidenced by the fires on their tunics.

The truth has been veiled by time, muddied, or intentionally destroyed by later anti-Semitic factions in the church, and turned into a fantasy by later medieval writers who vilified most of the women, romanticized the men, and changed the now-lost original accounts to suit the tastes of their benefactors. Yet still this quest haunts the imagination and the soul—to be like, and hence in the presence of, Christ.

bibLiOGRApђy

For Readers Who Want More:

There are *over* seventy-five books from which I've garnered information and inspiration for this novel. However, I am listing those of the most influence for the reader who wants to delve into the history and tradition behind this work of fiction.

David F. Carroll makes a case for the historically documented Prince Arthur of Dalraida as *the* Arthur. This documentation is why I chose Arthur's story as the background for this series, while incorporating many of Norma Lorre Goodrich's observations as well. Her scholarly analysis of Arthurian history suggests that there is more than one Arthur, Guinevere, and Merlin. This, and the fact that there was no standard for dating, explains Arthur and company having to have lived for nearly a hundred years, as well as the many dating discrepancies in historical manuscripts. She, among others listed, uses geographical description and her knowledge of linguistics to place Arthur mostly in the lowlands of today's Scotland. Shortly after she suggested the location of Arthur's Grail Palace on an island near Man, the ruins of a Dark Age Christian church were discovered there.

Isabel Elder's *Celt, Druid and Culdee* provides a wonderful insight into the origins of the early church in Britain and how the similarities of these three groups made them ready to make Christ their Druid or teacher/master. A must-read to understand the New

Age philosophy of today. Andrew Gray's *The Origin and Early History of Christianity in Britain—From Its Dawn to the Death of Augustine* is fascinating and impacts *Rebel* as it lends some credence to some of Goodrich's observations on Arthur and the church.

The oral traditions about Joseph of Arimathea and Avalon/ Glastonbury are underscored by ancient place names and Roman, British, Irish, and church histories in books by Gray, Joyce, McNaught, and Taylor. They also provide a compelling case for the British church's establishment in the first century by Jesus's family and apostles. Books regarding the Davidic bloodlines preserved through Irish nobility that married into the major royal houses of western Europe, Britain in particular, include those of Allen, Capt, and Collins.

To separate magic from science from miracle, I found Charles Singer's book one of the best I've read for clarification throughout history. Kieckhefer's is also an excellent historical resource for medieval customs, superstitions, and medicine and their darker side as well.

I do not advocate the practices featured in Buckland's book on witchcraft, although reading it has helped me develop a clearer understanding of where much New Age thought comes from, that I might more effectively witness to the similarities and differences in the future in my case for Christ. After reading the above and more on my magic/miracle/science research, I found the scriptural perspective in Rory Roybal's *Miracles or Magic? Discerning the Works of God in Today's World* reassuring and spiritually grounding. And, of course, enough can't be said of the King James Bible referred to throughout *Rebel.*

Arthurian Works

Barber, Richard. *The Figure of Arthur.* New York: Dorset Press, 1972.

Blake, Steve, and Scott Lloyd. *Pendragon: The Definitive Account of the Origins of Arthur.* Guilford, CT: The Lyons Press, 2002.

Carroll, David F. *Arturius: A Quest for Camelot.* Goxhill, Lincolnshire, UK: D. F. Carroll, 1996.

De Boron, Robert. *Merlin and the Grail: Joseph of Arimathea, Merlin, Perceval.* Translated by Nigel Bryant. Rochester, NY: D. S. Brewer, 2005.

Goodrich, Norma Lorre. *Guinevere.* New York: HarperCollins, 1991.

_____. *The Holy Grail.* New York: HarperCollins, 1993.

_____. *King Arthur.* New York: Harper and Row, 1986.

_____. *Merlin.* New York: Harper and Row, 1988.

Holmes, Michael. *King Arthur: A Military History.* New York: Blandford Press, 1998.

Reno, Frank. *Historic Figures of the Arthurian Era.* Jefferson, NC: McFarland & Company, 2000.

Skene, W. F. Edited by Derek Bryce *Arthur and the Britons in Wales and Scotland.* Dyfed, UK: Llanerch Enterprises, 1988.

Church History

Allen, J. H. *Judah's Sceptre and Joseph's Birthright.* Merrimac, MA: Destiny Publishers, 1902.

Capt, E. Raymond. *The Traditions of Glastonbury.* Thousand Oaks, CA: Artisan Press, 1983.

_____. *Missing Links Discovered in Assyrian Tablets: Study of the Assyrian Tables of Israel.* Thousand Oaks, CA: Artisan Sales, 1983.

Collins, Stephen. *The "Lost" Ten Tribes of Israel ... Found!* Boring, OR: CPA Books, 1995.

Elder, Isabel Hill. *Celt, Druid and Culdee.* London: Covenant Publishing Company, 1973.

Gardner, Laurence. *Bloodline of the Holy Grail: The Hidden Lineage of Jesus Revealed.* New York: Thorsons/Element, 1996. (Used for tracing Jesus's family members/apostles, not His sometimes alleged direct bloodline.)

Gray, Andrew. *The Origin and Early History of Christianity in Britain—From Its Dawn to the Death of Augustine.* New York: James Pott & Co., 1897.

Joyce, Timothy. *Celtic Christianity: A Sacred Tradition, a Vision of Hope.* New York: Orbis Books, 1998.

Larson, Rick. "The Star of Bethlehem." Accessed January 1, 2008. www.BethlehemStar.com.

MacNaught, J. C. *The Celtic Church and the See of Peter.* Oxford: Basil Blackwell, 1927.

Taylor, Gladys. *Our Neglected Heritage: The Early Church.* London: The Covenant Publishing Company, 1969.

General History

Adamnan of Iona. *Life of St. Columba.* Translated by Richard Sharpe. New York: Penguin Books, 1995.

Alcock, Leslie. *Arthur's Britain.* New York: Penguin Books, 1971.

_____. *Kings and Warriors, Craftsmen and Priests in Northern Britain AD 550–850.* Edinburgh: Society of Antiquaries of Scotland, 2003.

Armit, Ian. *Celtic Scotland.* London: B. T. Batsford, Ltd., 2005.

Ashe, Geoffrey. *A Guidebook to Arthurian Britain.* London: Aquarian Press, 1983.

Cummins, W. A. *The Age of the Picts.* USA: Barnes and Noble Books, 1995.

Ellis, Peter Berresford. *Celt and Saxon: The Struggle for Britain, AD 410–937.* London: Constable, 1993.

Evans, Stephen. *The Lords of Battle.* Rochester, NY: Boydell Press, 1997. (Excellent resource for the life of a warlord and his men.)

Fraser, James. *From Caledonia to Pictland: Scotland to 795.* Edinburgh: Edinburgh University Press, 2009.

Hartley, Dorothy. *Lost Country Life.* New York: Random House, 1979. (A wonderful look at rural life in Britain by the season.)

Hodgkin, R. H. *A History of the Anglo-Saxons.* Vol. 1. Oxford: Clarendon Press, 1935.

Hughes, David. *The British Chronicles, Book One.* Westminster, MD: Heritage Books, 2007.

Johnson, Stephen. *Later Roman Britain: Britain before the Conquest.* New York: Charles Scribner & Sons, 1980.

Laing, Lloyd and Jenny. *The Picts and the Scots.* Stroud, UK: Alan Sutton Publishing Ltd., 1993.

Lowe, Chris. *Angels, Fools, and Tyrants—Britons and Anglo-Saxons in Southern Scotland, AD 450-750.* Edinburgh: Cannongate Press, 1999. (Excellent illustrations.)

Marsden, John. *Alba of the Ravens: In Search of the Celtic Kingdom of the Scots.* London: Constable and Co. Ltd., 1988.

Marsh, Henry. *Dark Age Britain: Some Sources of History.* New York: Dorset Press, 1987.

Martin-Clarke, D. Elizabeth. *Culture in Early Anglo-Saxon England.* Baltimore: Johns Hopkins Press, 1947.

McHardy, Stuart. *A New History of the Picts.* Cornwall: MPG Books Ltd., 2010.

Palgrave, Sir Francis. *History of the Anglo-Saxons.* New York: Dorset Press, 1989.

Skene, W. F. *Chronicles of the Picts, Chronicles of the Scots, and Other Early Memorials of Scottish History.* Edinburgh: H. M. General Register House, 1867.

Snyder, Christopher. *The Britons.* Malden, MA: Blackwell Publishing, 2003.

Smyth, Alfred P. *Warlords and Holy Men: Scotland, AD 80–1000.* Edinburgh: Edinburgh University Press, 1989.

Magic, Miracle, and Science of the Dark Ages

Buckland, Raymond. *Scottish Witchcraft: The History and Magick of the Picts.* Woodbury, MN: Llewellyn Publications, 1991.

Kieckhefer, Richard. *Magic in the Middle Ages.* Cambridge, UK: Cambridge University Press, 1989.

Roybal, Rory. *Miracles or Magic? Discerning the Works of God in Today's World.* Longwood, FL: Xulon Press, 2005.

Singer, Charles. *From Magic to Science: Essays on the Scientific Twilight.* New York: Dover Publications, 1958.

SCRIPTURE REFERENCES

Chapter Five

For after that in the wisdom of God the world by wisdom knew not God.—1 Corinthians 1:21

Chapter Seven

Father, forgive them; for they know not what they do.—Luke 23:34

For God hath not given us the spirit of fear; but of power, and of love, and of a sound mind.—2 Timothy 1:7

Chapter Eight

For I am persuaded, that neither death, nor life, nor angels, nor principalities, nor powers, nor things present, nor things to come, nor height, nor depth, nor any other creature, shall be able to separate us from the love of God, which is in Christ Jesus our Lord.—Romans 8:38–39

Chapter Twelve

All they that take the sword shall perish with the sword.—Matthew 26:52

Chapter Seventeen

What shall we then say to these things? If God be for us, who can be against us?—Romans 8:31

A certain man went down from Jerusalem to Jericho, and fell among thieves, which stripped him of his raiment, and wounded him, and departed, leaving him half dead. And by chance there came down a certain priest that way: and when he saw him, he passed by on the other side.... But a certain Samaritan, as he journeyed, came where he was: and when he saw him, he had compassion on him, and went to him, and bound up his wounds, pouring in oil and wine, and set him on his own beast, and brought him to an inn, and took care of him.—Luke 10:30–34

Chapter Twenty-one

All things are possible to him that believeth.—Mark 9:23

For my thoughts are not your thoughts, neither are your ways my ways, saith the LORD.—Isaiah 55:8

Chapter Twenty-four

Verily I say unto you, Whosoever shall not receive the kingdom of God as a little child, he shall not enter therein.—Mark 10:15

It is written, Vengeance is mine; I will repay, saith the Lord.—Romans 12:19

Come unto me, all ye that labour and are heavy laden, and I will give you rest.—Matthew 11:28

Chapter Twenty-five

Let [her] kiss me with the kisses of [her] mouth: for [her] love is better than wine.—Song of Solomon 1:2

Chapter Twenty-six

Blessed are the peacemakers: for they shall be called the children of God.—Matthew 5:9

Because thou hast made the LORD, which is my refuge, ... thy habitation, ... there shall no evil befall thee.—Psalm 91:9–10

Behold, I have put my words in thy mouth.—Jeremiah 1:9

Chapter Twenty-seven

For he shall give his angels charge over thee, to keep thee in all thy ways.—Psalm 91:11

Lord, I believe; help thou my unbelief.—Mark 9:24

And Elisha prayed, and said, LORD, I pray thee, open his eyes, that he may see. And the LORD opened the eyes of the young man; and he saw: and, behold, the mountain was full of horses and chariots of fire round about Elisha.—2 Kings 6:17

Chapter Twenty-eight

It is written, Vengeance is mine; I will repay, saith the Lord.—Romans 12:19

And let us reason together, saith the LORD: though your sins be as scarlet, they shall be as white as snow; though they be red like crimson, they shall be as wool. If ye be willing and obedient, ye shall eat the good of the land: But if ye refuse and rebel, ye shall be devoured with the sword: for the mouth of the LORD hath spoken it.—Isaiah 1:18–20

Let us not therefore judge one another any more: but judge this rather, that no man put a stumblingblock or an occasion to fall in his brother's way.—Romans 14:13

Chapter Twenty-nine

Because he hath set his love upon me, therefore will I deliver him: I will set him on high, because he hath known my name.—Psalm 91:14

Epilogue

The fear of the Lord is the beginning of knowledge.—Proverbs 1:7

ABOUT THE AUTHOR

With an estimated million books in print, **Linda Windsor** is an award-winning author of seventeen secular historical and contemporary romances and fourteen romantic comedies and historical fiction for the inspirational market. Her switch to inspirational fiction in 1999 was more like Jonah going to Nineveh than a flash of enlightenment. Linda claims God pushed her, kicking and screaming all the way. In retrospect, the author can see how God prepared her for His writing in her early publishing years and then claimed not just her music but also her writing when she was ready. At that point He brushed away all her reservations regarding inspirational fiction, and she took the leap of faith. Linda has never looked back.

While all of Linda's inspirational novels have been recognized with awards and rave reviews in both the ABA and CBA markets, she is most blessed by the 2002 Christy finalist award for *Riona* and the numerous National Readers Choice Awards for Best Inspirational that her historicals and contemporaries have won. *Riona* actually astonished everyone when it won against the worldly competition in the RWA Laurel Wreath's Best Foreign Historical category.

To Linda's delight, *Maire,* Book One of the Fires of Gleannmara Irish Celtic series, was rereleased by WaterBrook Multnomah

Publishers with a gorgeous new warrior-queen cover in 2009. Christy finalist *Riona* and its sequel, *Deirdre*, are now available with print on demand through standard and Internet booksellers.

Another of her novels, *For Pete's Sake*, Book Two in the Piper Cove Chronicles, is the winner of the Golden Quill; finalist in the Gayle Wilson Award of Excellence, Colorado RWA 2009 Award of Excellence, and Holt Medallion Avon Inspire in 2008; and winner of the Best Book of 2008 Award—Inspirational (Long & Short Reviews). It also won the 2009 National Reader's Choice Award—Best Inspirational and Best Book of the Year—Inspirational (*Romance Reviews Today*).

Linda's research for the early Celtic Fires of Gleannmara series resulted in a personal mission dear to her heart: to provide Christians with an effective witness to reach their New Age and unbelieving family and friends. Her goal continues with the Brides of Alba series, which reveals early church history, much of which has been lost or neglected due to intentional and/or inadvertent error by its chroniclers. This knowledge of early church history enabled Linda to reach her daughter, who became involved in Wicca after being stalked and assaulted in college and blamed the God of her childhood faith—a witness that continues to others at medieval fair signings or wherever these books take Linda.

Linda is convinced that, had her daughter known the struggle and witness of the early Christians beyond the apostles' time and before Christianity earned a black name in the Crusades and Inquisition, she could not have been swayed. Nor would Linda herself have been lured away from her faith in Christ in college by a liberal agenda.

Linda's testimony that Christ is her Druid (Master/Teacher) opens wary hearts wounded by harsh Christian condemnation. Admitted Wiccans and pagans have become intrigued by the tidbits of history and tradition pointing to how and why druids accepted Him. She not only sells these nonbelievers copies of her books, but she also outsells the occult titles surrounding her inspirational ones.

When Linda isn't writing in the late eighteenth-century home that she and her late husband restored, she's busy speaking and/or playing music for writing workshops, faith seminars, libraries, and civic and church groups. She and her husband were professional musicians and singers in their country and old rock-and-roll band, Homespun. She also plays organ for her little country church in the wildwood. Presently, she's trying to work in some painting, wallpapering, and other house projects that are begging to be done. That is, when she's not Red-Hatting or, better yet, playing mom-mom to her grandchildren—her favorite role in life.

Visit Linda Windsor at her website:

www.LindaWindsor.com